VANISHED

Tim Weaver is the international bestselling author of the David Raker mystery series. He has been longlisted for the prestigious Dagger in the Library Award from the Crime Writers' Association and his work has been nominated for a National Book Award in the UK. He is also the host of the award-winning podcast *Missing*, about why people disappear and how investigators track them down. A former journalist and magazine editor, he now writes fiction full time and lives with his wife and daughter in Bath, England.

ALSO BY TIM WEAVER

TIM WEAVER

Vanished

PENGUIN BOOKS

PENGUIN BOOKS
An imprint of Penguin Random House LLC
375 Hudson Street
New York, New York 10014
penguin.com

First published in Penguin Books (UK) 2012
Published in Penguin Books (USA) 2016

LIBRARY OF CONGRESS CATALOGING IN PUBLICATION DATA
Names: Weaver, Tim, 1977– author.
Title: Vanished / Tim Weaver.
Description: New York, New York : Penguin Books, 2016. | Series: A David Raker mystery ; 3
Identifiers: LCCN 2016028181 (print) | LCCN 2016035375 (ebook) |
ISBN 9780143129639 (softcover) | ISBN 9781101993347 (ebook)
Subjects: LCSH: Missing persons—Investigation—Fiction. |
Private investigators—Fiction. | GSAFD: Suspense fiction. | Mystery fiction.
Classification: LCC PR6123.E2245 V36 2016 (print) | LCC PR6123.E2245 (ebook) |
DDC 823/.92—dc23
LC record available at https://lccn.loc.gov/2016028181

Printed in the United States of America
1   3   5   7   9   10   8   6   4   2

Set in Garamond MT Std Regular
Designed by Eve Kirch

For Lucy

"The fathers shall not be put to death for the children, neither shall the children be put to death for the fathers: every man shall be put to death for his own sin."

DEUTERONOMY 24:16

Author's Note

For the purposes of the story, I've taken some small liberties with the layout and working practices of the London Underground. My hope is that it's done subtly enough not to grate, and remains true to the amazing history of the city's railway lines. Those schooled in the Tube will see echoes of Whitechapel's past in my version of Westminster station, will note I've altered Gloucester Road ever so slightly and I hope will forgive my reinterpretation of night-time hours on the network. Residents of north London will no doubt also recognize Fell Wood as being based closely on Haringey's Parkland Walk.

Vanished

Healy looked down at the temperature readout as he pulled up outside the estate. Almost twenty degrees. It felt hotter than that. He'd had the air conditioning on all the way from the station but, on the journey over, nothing had cooled. His sleeves were rolled up, his top button undone, but the car was still stifling. Even in the middle of the night, under cover of darkness, the heat continued to cling on.

He paused, looking out through the windows of the Mercedes to the maze of broken homes beyond. The most dangerous housing estate in London had gone into hibernation. There were no lights on in the flats, no kids in the alleys, no gangs crossing the walkways between buildings. But then, as more marked cars arrived, lightbars painting the ten-story slabs of concrete, he could make out shapes in the night, watching him from darkened windows and doorways.

He got out. Away to his left, the media were encamped behind a strip of police tape, in shirts and summer dresses, faces slick with sweat. It was mayhem. Journalists jostled for the best position. Feet slid on grass banks. Noise. Lights. Voices screaming his name. In another life, he might have enjoyed the celebrity. Some cops did. But when he looked at the entrance to the building, ominous and dark, like a mouth about to swallow him up, he realized it was all a trick. This wasn't celebrity. This was standing on a precipice in a hurricane. They were behind him now; with him on that precipice. But if it went on any longer, if it got any worse, if the police still hadn't found the man responsible by the time the media were camped out at the next crime scene, all they'd be trying to do would be to feed him to the darkness beyond.

He moved across the concrete courtyard to the entrance and looked inside. Everything was broken or cracking, like the whole place was about to collapse under its own weight. The floor was slick with water, leaking from somewhere, and along the corridor a broken door, leading into the first set of flats, was hanging off its hinges. Litter was everywhere. Some people would go their whole lives without seeing the insides of a place like this: a two-hundred-apartment cry for help. The sort of place where even the night at its darkest wasn't black enough to hide all the bruises.

A uniformed officer with a clipboard was standing at the bottom of a stairwell to Healy's right. He looked up as Healy approached, shining a flashlight in his direction. "Evening, sir."

"Evening."

"The elevator doesn't work."

Healy glanced at the lift. Across its doors was a council notice telling people it was unsafe to use. On the damp, blistered wall next to it, someone had spray-painted an arrow and the words "express elevator to hell."

After showing the officer his warrant card, Healy headed up three flights of stairs, most of it barely lit. Everything smelled like a toilet. Glass crunched under his shoes where lightbulbs had been deliberately smashed and never cleared away. At the third-floor landing, people started to emerge—other cops, forensics—a line snaking out from Flat 312. A crime-scene tech broke off from dusting down a door frame to hand Healy a white paper boiler suit and a pair of gloves. "You'd better wear this," she said. "Not that you're going to be disturbing much evidence."

Healy took the suit.

Inside the flat, a series of stand-alone lights had been erected, their glare washing into the corridor. Apart from the buzz of a generator, the apartment was pretty much silent. The occasional click of a camera. A mumble from one of the forensic team. Brief noises from other flats. Otherwise, nothing.

After zipping up the boiler suit and pulling up the hood, Healy moved into the flat. It was just like the ones the other victims had lived in. Rundown. Squalid. Damp. In the kitchen, which led off from the living room, a big brown watermark had formed on the linoleum. Healy spotted DCI Melanie Craw looking around inside. There was a door off the living room, opening on to a bedroom. Chief Superintendent Ian Bartholomew stood in the doorway, the bed in front of him. He looked back at Healy, a pissed-off expression on his face, then to Craw, who'd arrived from the kitchen.

"Melanie," he said. "What the bloody hell am I supposed to tell the media?"

Bartholomew backed out of the bedroom and let Healy take it in. The crime scene. A small bedroom with a tiny walk-in closet, a dresser, and a television on a chair in the corner of the room. The carpet was worn, the wallpaper peeling. On the pillow, placed in a neat pile, was the victim's hair. He'd shaved it all off, just like all the others, and left it there. The mattress was where the body should have been.

But that was just the problem.

He never left the bodies.

PART ONE

1

Her office was on the top floor of a red-brick four-story building just off Shaftesbury Avenue. The other floors belonged to an advertising agency and a big international media company. Two code-locked glass doors protected sharp-suited executives from the outside world, while a security guard the size of a wrestler watched from inside. Everything else in the street was either dead or dying. Two empty stores, one a shoe shop, one an antiques dealer, had long since gone. Adjacent to that was a boarded-up Italian restaurant with a huge NOW CLOSED sign in the window. The last man standing was a video rental store that looked like it was on its way out: two men were arguing in an empty room with only a single DVD rack and some faded film posters for company.

It was a warm June evening. The sun had been out all day, although somewhere out of sight it felt like rain might be lying in wait. I'd brought a jacket, just in case, but for the moment I was in a black button-up shirt, denims and a pair of black leather shoes I'd bought in Italy. They were the genuine article, from the Galleria Vittorio Emanuele in Milan, but I didn't wear them much; mostly their purpose in life was to cut my feet to shreds. Yet they were a sacrifice worth making for the woman I was meeting.

Liz emerged from one of the elevators in the foyer about fifteen minutes later. People had been filing out of the building steadily since five, but the office she worked in was also the office she ran, so she tended to be the last one out. She spotted me immediately, standing in the doorway of the now-defunct antiques shop, and I was struck by how beautiful she looked: dark eyes flashing as she smiled, long, chocolate hair pulled back from a face full of natural angles. Elizabeth Feeny, solicitor advocate, had thrived in a city packed with dominant males: she'd gone up against bigger fish and won; she'd taken their clients and retained them; she'd brought together a team of formidable lawyers under the umbrella of Feeny & Company and she'd fronted a number of high-profile cases that had secured her growing reputation. It would have been difficult not to be impressed by her, even if I hadn't been seeing her for eight months and living next door to her for a

lot longer. She completely looked the part, moving across the road toward
me in a white blouse and black pencil skirt that traced the gentle curves of
her body. But her biggest asset was that when she smiled, she made you feel
like the only person in the room. That was a useful skill when you were
pacing the floor of a court.

"Mr. Raker," she said, and kissed me.

"Elizabeth."

She gave me a gentle slap—she hated being called Elizabeth—and I
brought her into me and kissed her on the top of the head. "How was
your day?" I asked.

"Full of meetings."

We stayed like that for a moment. This was new for both of us. It had
been two and a half years since my wife Derryn had died of breast cancer, and almost sixteen since we'd first met. Liz was married at twenty-
one, pregnant six months later and divorced shortly after that. She spent
two years bringing up her daughter Katie, before returning to the law
degree she'd started and completing her training as a solicitor. She hadn't
dated seriously since before she'd married her husband.

"Where are we eating?" she asked.

"There's an Italian place I know." I shifted us—still together—around
to face the closed restaurant just down from where we were standing.

She squeezed me. "You're a funny man, Raker."

"I booked us a table at a South African place just off Covent Garden.
We can get drunk on Castle Lager."

"South African?"

"Ever had babotie?"

"Can't say I have."

We started walking slowly. "Well, tonight's your lucky night."

The restaurant was in a narrow cellar in a side street between Covent
Garden market and the Strand. The stone walls had holes carved in
them, framed photographs of South Africa sitting inside. In the one
closest to us, the Ferris wheel at Gold Reef City was caught in black and
white, frozen for a moment against a markless sky. I'd spent a lot of time
in and around Johannesburg in my previous life as a journalist, and been
stationed there for a year in the run-up to the elections in 1994. It had
been a different place back then, more like a war zone than a city, its people massaged by hatred and fear.

Liz let me choose, so I ordered two bottles of Castle, peri-peri chicken to start and babotie—spiced mincemeat, baked with egg—for the main course. While we waited for the food to arrive, she talked about her day and I told her a little of mine. I'd just put a case to bed a couple of days before: a seventeen-year-old runaway who'd been hiding out close to Blackfriars Bridge. His parents, a couple from a sprawling council estate in Hackney, had told me that they only had enough money to cover my search for three days. It took me five to find him, the job complicated by the fact that he had no friends, talked to pretty much no one, and, when he'd left, had literally taken only the clothes on his back. No phone. No cards. No money. Nothing even remotely traceable. I'd been to see his mum and dad and told them to pay me for the three days, and then return when they felt they could afford to square up the extra two. They were good people, but I wouldn't see them again. I wasn't normally in the business of charity, but I found it even more difficult to leave things unfinished.

After the babotie arrived, conversation moved on from work to Liz's daughter and the university course she was doing. She was finishing the final year of an economics degree. I hadn't had the chance to meet her yet, but from the way Liz had described her, and the photos I'd seen, she appeared to be almost a mirror image of her mother.

I ordered two more bottles of Castle and, as Liz continued talking, caught sight of a woman watching me from across the restaurant. As soon as we made eye contact she looked down at her food. I watched for a moment, waiting for her eyes to drift up to me a second time, but she just continued staring at her plate, picking apart a steak. I turned back to Liz. Ten seconds later, the woman was looking at me again.

She was in her late twenties, red hair curling as it hit her shoulders, freckles scattered across her cheeks and nose. She had a kind of understated beauty, as if she didn't realize it, or she did but wasn't bothered enough to do anything about it. The thin fingers of her right hand grasped a fork; those on her left were wrapped around the neck of a wine glass. She was wearing a wedding ring.

"You okay?"

The woman was looking away again now, and Liz had noticed me staring at her. "The woman in the corner there—do you know her?"

Liz looked back over her shoulder. "I don't think so."

"She keeps looking this way."

"Can't say I blame her," Liz said, smiling. "You're a good-looking man, Raker. Not that I want to inflate your ego or anything."

We carried on eating. A couple of times I glanced in the woman's direction, but didn't catch her eye again. Then, about thirty minutes later, she suddenly wasn't there any more. Where she'd been sitting was empty; just a half-finished steak and a full glass of wine. Money sat on a white tray on the edge of the table, the bill underneath it.

She was gone.

2

Just before we left, Liz got a call from a client. She rolled her eyes at me and found a quiet spot in an alcove. I gestured to her that I'd meet her upstairs when she was done.

The rain that had been in the air earlier had now arrived. I pulled my jacket on and found shelter a couple of doors down from the restaurant. Across the street people emerged from Covent Garden Tube station, a few armed with umbrellas and coats, but most dressed in short sleeves or T-shirts, blouses or summer skirts. After about five minutes I spotted a figure approaching me from my left, moving in the shadows on the opposite side of the street. When she got close, the light from a nearby pub illuminated her, freeze-framing her face, and I realized who it was.

The woman from the restaurant.

She crossed the street and stopped about six feet away.

"Mr. Raker?"

I immediately recognized the look in her eyes. I'd seen it before, constantly, repeated over and over in the faces of the families I helped: she'd either lost someone, or felt she was about to. Her face was young, but her eyes were old, wearing every ounce of her pain. It gave her a strange look, as if she was caught somewhere in between, neither young nor old, not beautiful or ugly. Just a woman who had lost.

"I'm really sorry I had to come up to you like this," she said, and pushed her hair behind her ears. She seemed nervous, her voice soft but taut. "My name's Julia. Julia Wren."

"What is it you want, Julia?"

"I, uh . . ." She paused. A bag strap passed diagonally across her chest. She reached behind her and pulled it around, opening up the front flap. She took out her purse and removed a piece of paper from it. As she unfolded it, I could immediately see what it was: a printout. "I read about you," she said. "On the Internet."

It was a BBC story, a photograph showing me being led out of a police station, flanked by a detective, two uniforms and my legal counsel, Liz. Three days before the picture had been taken, I'd gone right into a nest of killers and almost lost my life. Eighteen months had passed since then, but my body was still marked by the scars.

There had been other stories on the same case. Many other stories. I'd given no interviews, even to the people I'd once worked with, who'd called begging for comment. But it had gone big. For a week it had played out in the nationals until, like all news stories, it eventually burned itself out. For everyone else, it was consigned to history.

But not for this woman.

"Have you been following me for long, Julia?"

She shook her head. "No."

I believed her: I'd spotted her straight away in the restaurant, and seen her the second she started to approach me. If she'd been following me for any length of time, it wouldn't have gone unnoticed. Tailing was an art. If you followed someone, you had to stay invisible at the same time.

"I've read about you," she continued, nodding at the printout. "I mean, you can see that. I read about what you did when you found that place up north. How they tried to hurt you. What . . ." She stopped, glancing at my body, as if searching for the scars my clothing hid. "What they did to you. Then I saw another story about you in the papers last year. To do with that man the police found. The one who took those women. When I saw those stories, I thought, 'That's a man who can help me.'"

"Help you?"

"Do you believe in fate?"

I shook my head. "No, I don't."

That seemed to stop her in her tracks. But then she found her feet again. "I saw you and your . . ." Her eyes drifted to the restaurant. "Your friend. I saw you walk past me. The man I'd read about on the Internet. So when you passed me I couldn't help but see it as fate. And I suppose I lied a little. I did follow you—but only after I saw you tonight. I followed you to the restaurant because I wanted to be sure it was you. And when I saw that it was, I realized I needed to speak to you."

"What do you want, Julia?"

"I want you to find my husband," she said, pausing and kneading her hands together. For a moment she seemed to shrink into the shadows: head bowed, shoulders hunched, protecting herself in case I turned her away. "Six months ago he got on to the Tube at Gloucester Road. And he never got off again."

3

Twenty minutes later, we were sitting in a café on Long Acre. Liz had taken my car and gone home, doing a good job of disguising her curiosity. She'd seen enough in the eight months we'd been dating to know this wasn't how it normally worked. I liked some sort of plan in place before I met the families; liked to know who they were, and where they were coming from. But, with Julia Wren, there was no plan. She was a blank.

We ordered coffees and sat at the window, neon signs smeared in the drizzle, the sky black and swollen. She laid the printout on the table, manicured hand across it as if scared it might blow away. Often, they were caught halfway between expectation and fear: expectation that this might be the moment their loved ones came home; fear that it would be in a body bag.

She glanced at me, tucking a cord of red hair behind her ear. I couldn't tell yet if she was naturally timid or just nervous. "I read that you used to be a journalist."

"In a past life."

"Did you enjoy it?"

"It definitely had its moments."

"You got to travel, I expect."

"I got to see a lot of the world, but it was more like a busman's holiday." I smiled. "With added warzones."

"Where did you go?"

"The States on and off for five years. South Africa before and after the elections. Israel and Gaza, Iraq, Afghanistan."

"You must have seen some things."

An image formed in my head: running for my life through a South African township, bullets ripping holes through the air, bodies scattered across the road, blood in the gutters, dust and debris and screams of pain. "Let's just say you gain an appreciation of what people are capable of."

She paused. Rocked her head from side to side as if sizing up her next question. I knew what was coming. "Did you give it up because of your wife?"

"Yes." I didn't offer anything more. "Why don't you tell me about your husband?"

She nodded and produced a photograph from her bag. "This is Sam."

He was in his late twenties, had bright blue eyes, fair hair and a nose that seemed too big for his face. He was unusual-looking, but not unattractive. In the picture he was dressed in a black suit and red tie, and standing in the front room of a house. At a guess, he looked about five-nine, but a little underweight. The suit didn't fit, and there were minor hollows in his cheeks where his skin seemed like it was pulled too tight. I made a note to ask her about that later: people were underweight either because they were ill, weren't eating enough—or had something to worry about.

"When was this taken?"

"Six months ago. Tenth of December."

I pulled the photograph in closer. There was a Christmas tree reflected in one of the windows. "How long after this did he disappear?"

"He was gone six days later." She paused. "The sixteenth."

About two hundred and fifty thousand people went missing every year in the UK, and while two-thirds of them were kids under eighteen, the next commonest group was men between the ages of twenty-four and thirty. Sam Wren was a perfect fit for the statistics. The reasons why adult men went missing were often predictable—relationships, financial issues, alcoholism, mental illness—but the resolutions normally weren't. Many were reported missing long after they'd disappeared, when it was impossible to pick up the trail. And even if that wasn't the case, even if they were reported missing within a day or two, they had often planned their escapes in advance, given thought to their route out, and had a fair idea of how to cover their tracks. Sam had been gone six months and, as I looked at the photograph, I imagined—at the moment it was taken— he'd already firmed up his exit strategy.

I gestured toward the picture. "Tell me about the day he disappeared."

She nodded but then paused. This is where it started, where it began to unravel, where the road split, and eventually she was either lying next to him in bed again or standing over him in a morgue.

"He left a little earlier than normal," she said, starting quietly. "Usually he was gone by about 7:20, 7:30. That day, it was 7, 7:10."

"Any reason why?"

"He just said he had a lot of work on. That wasn't unusual. He'd often head off at that time on the days he knew were going to be busy."

"What did he do?"

"He worked for an investment bank in Canary Wharf. He advised people on where to put their money—stock, shares, that kind of thing."

"Which company was that for?"

"It's called Investment International. I2 for short. It was set up a few years back by a guy Sam worked with at J. P. Morgan. They'd been to university together. Sam had originally gone into the graduate program at HSBC but never really liked it, so his friend helped him make the move to JPM, and then got him involved at I2 as soon as it got off the ground."

"Was the company doing okay?"

She rocked her head from side to side. "Not great. They're a relatively small company, so the recession hit them pretty hard. Sam's wages were frozen at the end of 2010, and so were his bonuses."

"Did he still like his job, despite that?"

"It was a bit stressful, but I'd say he liked it about as much as any of us like our jobs. He'd come home sometimes and tell me he'd had enough of it, but the next day—if things went well—he'd be completely different. I didn't really look harder than that, to be honest. We all have ups and down, bad days and good days."

I glanced at the photo of Sam again: the gaunt, thin features, the suit hanging off him, a faint look of disquiet in his face. *Maybe there were more bad days than good.*

"So, he didn't seem any different the day he disappeared?"

"No. And, if he was, it was so subtle I missed it."

"You two were getting on okay?"

"Fine," she said, eyes flicking to the window and then back to me. She didn't elaborate. Instead she just sat there, looking for me to pick up the conversation and move it forward, the muscle tone changing at the side of her face; tighter and more rigid, like she was clenching her teeth.

Did you just lie to me?

I let it go for the moment, and decided to come back to it when I had a better feel for who she was and why she might sidestep the question.

"Where do you live?"

"Half a mile from Gloucester Road Tube station," she said. "We bought a place in a little mews about five years back. This was when Sam used to get bonuses."

"Are you still there?"

"Yes." But there was a forlorn expression on her face now, like she didn't want to be living alone in a house they'd bought as a couple. "I used to be the manager at a deli in Covent Garden, so most days, as long as he wasn't too swamped with work, we'd walk to the Tube together."

"You don't work at the deli any more?"

"I was made redundant in March last year." She paused; and then her cheeks started to color, as if she thought she'd second-guessed me. "Don't worry: I'll have enough to pay you. I've got another job now, at a restaurant in Bayswater. I've got some savings; money we kept for a rainy day. I figure this is the day we were talking about."

"I wasn't worried about the money," I said.

But she just nodded.

"How long were you unemployed?"

"Almost eleven months."

"So you started working again early this year—January time?"

"January the sixteenth."

Thirty-one days after her husband disappeared. I wondered, for a moment, how that must have felt: starting a new career, a new part of your life, while the biggest part of your old one had vanished into thin air.

"How did you both cope financially during the time you were out of work?"

She shrugged. "Sam's bonus helped buy that place, but we'd still been lumbered with a massive mortgage, even by London standards. Suddenly we were in a situation where his wages had been frozen, he wasn't bringing home anything extra and I wasn't bringing home anything at all. You can cut out the restaurants and the clothes and the weekends away, but you can't do without your home. Defaulting on our mortgage was the thing that worried us the most."

"What about now?"

She frowned. "What do you mean?"

"Can you pay the mortgage on your own?"

"Sam didn't take any money with him the day he disappeared, and he hasn't taken any out since. So my rainy-day fund will last me another three or four months."

"And after that?"

A humorless smile. "Well, I guess I've just got to hope you find him."

If she thought finding her husband would solve all their problems, she was going to be disappointed. If he'd gone for a reason, he'd purposefully removed himself from his marriage, his job and his life. There was no instant fix. If I found him, if he was even alive, things would never be the same as they were before.

I changed direction. "So, his commute was Gloucester Road to Westminster and then change to the Jubilee? Or did he get the DLR from Tower Hill?"

"He changed at Westminster."

"The Circle or District?"

"Circle."

"He never got the District?"

"Rarely."

"Why?"

"One of the reasons he left HSBC was because he didn't really like the guys he was working with there. It wasn't any massive conflict of interest, more that Sam just couldn't take to them, and the way they worked. You know how you meet some people in life who, from minute one, you just know you aren't going to see eye to eye with?"

I nodded.

"That's why he started looking for a way out of there, and that's why he ended up moving to JPM to work with his friend from university." She looked at me, and could see the question in my face: *Yeah, but why did he never get the District line?* "Three of them lived in Wimbledon," she said.

"So they used to get the District line."

"Right."

"But the chances of them bumping into each other must have been minimal."

She shrugged. "Sam got into a routine with the Circle."

"Do you think these guys had anything to do with Sam's disappearance?"

She shook her head: absolute certainty. "No. It wasn't anything serious. They just rubbed each other up the wrong way and it started making Sam unhappy."

I noted that down. "When did you report him missing?"

"The evening of 16 December. He never came home, I couldn't get him on his mobile, and his boss had left a message on our answerphone wondering where he was."

"He hadn't turned up for work at all?"

"No."

"You went to the police?"

"Yes. They were pretty thorough: wanted to know about his friends, relatives, his medical history, his financial details. They came to look around the house too, and even took away his toothbrush to get a DNA sample. When I told them that he hadn't turned up to work, the officer said he'd check the CCTV footage from the stations too."

"But he didn't find anything?"

"No. He called and said they were in the process of requisitioning the CCTV footage from the Tube. A couple of weeks passed and I heard nothing. So, I chased him up and he returned my call a few days later. He said they hadn't found anything."

"At all?"

"He said Sam didn't get off the train again."

"And that didn't bother him?"

There was a bleakness in her face. "I don't know."

"What was the guy's name?"

"PC Westerley. Brian Westerley."

They weren't exactly bringing out the big guns for Sam's disappearance, but then he wouldn't have raised many flags at the Met: a man in his late twenties, good job, solid marriage, just about in the black, no history of mental illness. There wasn't an obvious reason for him to go missing, which meant more manpower and more resources would be needed to find him. I'd seen the full force of the police emerge in the aftermath of a disappearance on another case, when a seventeen-year-old girl vanished into the ether. But she'd ticked three big boxes: white, female and a minor. Sam was different, his circumstances different. There was no media pressure and no headlines. The Met had palmed off his case on a PC, and it had been allowed to drift.

Despite that, there was still one massive question mark over this whole thing: how exactly *did* a man get on to a train and never get back off again? It might not have bothered Westerley enough to pursue it to its conclusion, but it bothered me.

"I'll call Westerley and see what he says."

"I hope he's helpful."

I doubt he will be. The last thing the police wanted was an outsider sniffing around trying to solve one of their cases, even if it was a low-priority one like Sam Wren. A detective I used a lot during my days as a journalist used to have a shelf in his filing system marked "DGAS"; as in "Don't Give a Shit." That was where the low-priority missing people, the drug addicts and the repeat offenders got stashed and forgotten about. But I'd never met a cop who didn't start giving a shit the minute an outsider stepped into view.

"Does Sam have any family?"

"A brother. Robert."

"Is he here in London?"

"He works here. But he lives in Reading."

"I'll need his address," I said.

She reached into the handbag and brought out a diary. She'd prepared for this day; prepared for the questions I was going to ask. She leafed through it, found the page she was looking for and then ripped it out of the book. She set it down in front of me. It was a list of names—numbered 1 to 15—of the most important people in Sam's life. Each name had full contact details.

"That's everybody I could think of," she said.

Each name had an entry after it, headed "Relationship to Sam." His brother was top, followed by friends and work colleagues. "This'll work," I said, smiling.

"If I think of anyone else, I'll let you know."

I folded the piece of paper up. "I'll need to have a look around the house."

She nodded. "Whenever you need to."

"Tomorrow?"

"I'm working the morning shift. I'll be home about two."

"I'll be there for three." She gave me the address and I noted it down. "Can I take this?" I asked her, and touched a finger to the photograph of her husband.

"Of course."

I nodded my thanks and pulled it toward me. Part of the reason for going to the house—apart from the fact that it was one of my routines; a way to understand the person better—was to find out if there were any older photographs of him. I wanted to see how he looked; if he had always been as thin as he was at the end.

My watch beeped gently. Eleven o'clock.

"One last thing before I go," I said. Outside the rain had stopped and with it had come a strange kind of silence. No drizzle drifting against the window any more, no people passing in the street. She studied me expectantly. "If I start looking into this, there can't be any secrets between us."

Her eyes flicked to her coffee cup and up again. "Secrets?"

"Any secrets, any conflicts that existed between the two of you, any problems Sam might have been having, I need to know about them. I'm not here to make a judgment on you. I'm here to find Sam."

I let that sit there for a moment.

But she didn't take the bait.

If she was lying to me, the lie would surface eventually. They always did. Usually families lied out of some misguided belief that it might affect how I did my job; as if my performance was based on how picture-perfect their life was. But the truth was, no life was perfect. Everyone had secrets.

It's just some were buried deeper than others.

4

I walked Julia Wren back down Long Acre and then watched her disappear into the Tube station at Covent Garden. The streets were starting to empty now, the noise drifting away, a different, softer city emerging from the shadows. I took out my phone and thumbed through the address book until I got to the name I wanted: Ewan Tasker.

"Task" was in his early sixties, retired for a couple of years but still employed in an advisory role at the Met. Before that, he worked for the National Criminal Intelligence Service, the precursor to the Serious Organized Crime Agency. Our relationship had started off slowly: he'd come to me with a story he wanted to break about Kosovan organized crime, hoping to force one of its leaders out into the open; I used it as a bargaining chip, and a way to secure him as a long-term source. We sparred for a while but eventually, over time, became good friends. These days, I wasn't able to offer him column inches in return for his help, so he made me turn up to a charity golf day once a year on his birthday. For me, it was eighteen holes of misery. For him, it was hilarious.

"Raker!" he shouted down the phone. "What time do you call this?"

It was late, but I knew he'd be awake. Task enjoyed his golf, but he wasn't built for retirement: he'd spent the first six months driving his wife up the wall, and the next six on bended knee begging any agency he could find to give him something to do.

"How you doing, old man?"

"I'm good. Up to my arse in work, but otherwise good."

"I'm not sure lifting beer cans to your mouth counts as work, Task."

He laughed. "I didn't even have time for a pint at the clubhouse this morning, and you know I always make time for a pint or ten."

"I thought you were just advising the Met part-time?"

"I am. Normally it's more sedate: meetings once a week at Scotland Yard, the rest of the time here at home reading up on cases and offering my devastating insight."

"But not this week?"

"There's a few things going on," he said, "but nothing exciting. Not yet, anyway. You been following this Snatcher stuff?"

"Not closely."

"You're losing your touch, Raker."

I smiled. "If I ever had it. I only know what I've read in the papers: he gets inside their houses and takes them from their beds."

"Yeah," Tasker said. "He's got some balls, I'll give him that."

"You're not working that case, are you?"

"No. Definitely not my area. But it's the watercooler case at the Met: everyone's talking about it, everyone's got an opinion. The press are all over it like flies on shit."

"Can't blame them. It's the biggest story of the year."

"Spoken like a true hack." He laughed. "So what can I do for you?"

I needed to get hold of the CCTV footage from the day Sam disappeared on the Tube, but I didn't have any sources at Transport for London, or at the Transport Police. Task's contacts at SOCA—soon to become the National Crime Agency—were a decent alternative: they'd be policing organized crime, people trafficking, e-crime and fraud at the London Olympics, which meant securing CCTV footage through them wouldn't raise any flags and probably wouldn't require a lot of paperwork. They'd be watching the Tube for suspicious activity anyway, and as a way to identify potential suspects, so it was natural they'd be analyzing footage as prep in the months leading up to the Games. I told Task what I needed.

"What do you want the footage for?"

"A guy I'm trying to find—he disappeared somewhere on the Circle line."

"Disappeared how?"

"Just disappeared. Got on the train and never got off again."

"You serious?"

"You know me, Task: I don't have a sense of humor."

Another laugh. "That's true."

"His wife came to me tonight and asked me to find out where he went. The Met opened a missing persons file on him and had one of their uniforms look into it."

"Sounds like they pulled out all the stops to find him."

I smiled ruefully. "PC Plod doesn't seem that bothered."

"You gonna call him?"

"Yeah. I'm sure I can look forward to my usual warm welcome from the Met."

"I can ask around if it's easier."

"No, it's fine," I said. "I'll give you a shout if I need a hand."

"Okay, well, I'll put in a request now, but it won't get picked up until the morning. I can probably cash in a favor and get it prioritized, so I might be able to get you something for mid-morning. You going to be home?"

"Yeah. You coming past?"

"I've got a golf tournament up in Ruislip. I can't promise anything, but if I've got something, I'll drop it in. Probably be around about 10, 10:30."

"Perfect. Thanks, old man."

"Don't thank me yet. You owe me a round of golf."

Fifteen minutes later, the Piccadilly line train pulled into Gloucester Road Tube station. It was 11:35 and the platform was deserted. Somewhere above me, where the Circle and District lines ran parallel to one another, Sam Wren had stepped on to a carriage and never got off again.

As the doors wheezed open, I leaned out and took in the length of the station. The morning of 16 December 2011 wouldn't have looked like this. Sam had got on at another line, on another platform, and was headed in a different direction. He would have been surrounded by commuters too. But, at its heart, the mystery remained the same: how did a man disappear from the inside of a train? If he'd ridden the Tube to the end of the line, he would still have had to get off, because every journey terminated somewhere. And if he had got off at one of the other stations on the Circle line, rather than at Westminster, his exit would have been recorded on CCTV.

Maybe Julia honestly believed neither had happened. Maybe the PC who opened Sam's missing persons file, who sat down and watched the footage, didn't care enough to take more than a cursory glance and find out. But the reality, however well concealed, was that Sam must have got off at some point.

Because there weren't any genuine magic tricks.

Only illusions.

5

Liz left early the next morning. She didn't need a lot of sleep, which was probably one of the other reasons she was so good at what she did. Less sleep meant more prep time, and more prep time meant she was better in court. Often I'd stumble through and find her hunched over a laptop in the front room, having been up for hours. But not today.

I got dressed and headed next door—to my real home. It was chilly inside. My house faced north, so only got sun in the mornings and evenings, on either side of the property. But that was okay. The summer was good, but I preferred a cooler home.

Moving around, I started getting things together for the drive over to Julia Wren's later. Once I'd had an office, a place that separated work and home. But it became clear pretty quickly that the two always merged, however much I tried to avoid it, so when the lease ran out on the office, I shifted everything back home: files, pictures, memories.

I sat down at the desk in the spare room, and while my Mac hummed into life, took in my surroundings. Folders. Files. Notepads. Pens. Opposite, pinned to the wall, was a corkboard I'd had in my office. It was full of photos given to me by the families: missing people, some barely even in their teens, freeze-framed in a different life.

I was good at finding them. Liz once said I had a kind of gravitational pull, an ability to drag the lost back into the light—and although she had only been joking, I did feel a connection to them. Sometimes it felt like more than that. Sometimes it felt like a responsibility; an unwritten contract. And maybe that was the reason I was drawn so quickly into their world—and why, at times, I'd been prepared to go as far as I had.

Ewan Tasker very rarely let me down, and at just gone 10:30 he pulled into the driveway in his dark-blue Porsche 911 Turbo. It sounded better than it was. He'd had it for years, but while he loved it like his daughter, hardly a month went by without something falling off it.

He got out, locked it and made his way up to the open porch. His frame filled the doorway: six-three, sixteen stone, wide and strong even if his muscle definition had started to fade. His black hair was being reclaimed, gray streaks passing above his ears, but it was one of his few concessions to age.

I made coffee and we headed through to the back garden. There was a small patio area immediately outside, with a table and a couple of chairs. Task eased into a seat with a theatrical sigh, playing on the fact that he was sixty-two and already in semi-retirement—but he wasn't just physically imposing: he was quick-witted and sharp too.

"You're not convincing anyone with your OAP act," I said.

"I like to lure people into a false sense of security." As he leaned forward to sip his coffee, I saw a USB stick in the breast pocket of his shirt. He took it out and handed it to me. "That's everything I could get for you in the time I had available to me this morning. It's a pretty fast turnaround, even for a man of my skills. Luckily for you I know a guy who knows a guy who knows a geek." He pointed to the USB stick. "One thing: you asked for footage from inside every eastbound Circle line carriage between 7:30 and 8. That's a problem. The District, Jubilee, Northern, Waterloo and City lines all have onboard CCTV already, but the Circle and Hammersmith lines are late to the party. My guy tells me that they're in the process of refurbishing all those trains and that a lot of them are in service now—but, going back six months, to when your man disappeared, they didn't have cameras."

"So it's just the station cams on here?"

"Right. Sorry."

"No—this is great. I really appreciate it, Task."

But the truth was, it wasn't great: having onboard footage would have helped narrow down Sam's route in and out easily, and given me a much closer view of his movements. Now I'd have to rely on picking him out from a platform camera positioned about twenty feet up, and tracking him through a London rush hour.

I looked down at the USB and turned it with my finger. Task had got me footage from every Circle line station for the day Sam Wren disappeared. That was 36 stations, which meant about 19 hours of CCTV for each station, and roughly 680 hours of video total. Sam got on to the Tube at approximately 7:30 on the morning of 16 December, which made things easier. But if—as expected—it wasn't obvious when he got off, it was going to make for a hell of a morning.

6

After Task left for his golf tournament, I ran the footage from Gloucester Road. Sun poured through the window of the spare room, the air
still, the heat prickling against my skin. I felt the familiar buzz that came
at the start of a case. The lack of onboard footage was a problem, but not
an insurmountable one. I'd just have to work around it.

Onscreen, there was a time clock in the bottom left, with the date
adjacent to that. It was 5:30 a.m. In the video, there was no one in shot.
Off to the left, the District line platform was visible; on the right were
two Circle line tracks, one for westbound trains, one for eastbound. At
5:38, a woman entered the shot, walked to the middle of the platform
and stood there checking her phone. Three minutes later, more people
joined her. Then more. By 6 a.m., the station was starting to get busy.

I grabbed the timeline on the video window and dragged it right,
stopping at 6:50. By now, the station was in full flow, people filing off the
trains, but mostly filing on. The camera above the entrance to the platform gave a good view. If the Wrens' house was half a mile from the
Tube station, and he was averaging two miles per hour, Sam would enter
at about 7:20, and be in shot by 7:30.

He took a little longer.

At 7:45 a.m., he emerged on to the eastbound platform, moving in a
mass of bodies. It was incredibly busy, even for a weekday morning. At
one stage, he got stuck behind an old couple—tourists—who looked
shell-shocked by the carnage unfolding around them, but eventually he
found a space on the platform, about two lines back from the edge. He
was holding a takeaway coffee in his left hand, which was why he must
have taken longer to get to the station, and a briefcase in his right. The
coffee was interesting. It suggested a routine; as if this day wasn't that different from any other and he hadn't been expecting any surprises. And
yet, in the washed-out colors of the CCTV footage, he looked even worse
than in the photo Julia had given me: paler, thinner, his eyes dark smudges
against his face. He just stood there the whole time, staring into space.
Did you have a plan? I thought. *Or did you only decide to take off once you were on
the Tube?*

The train emerged from the edge of the shot, its doors opening, and the scramble began. You could tell the regular commuters: they barged their way on to the train, eyes fixed on the doors, everyone around them expendable. Sam was the same. When someone tried to move in front of him, he shuffled into their line of sight.

Then he was on the train.

The doors closed.

And the train was gone from shot.

I got up, poured myself a glass of water, returned and loaded up the second video—South Kensington—and fast-forwarded it. Sam's train had left Gloucester Road at 7:51; two minutes later it was pulling into South Kensington. I leaned in, trying to get a handle on the chaos. Like Gloucester Road, the platform was packed: shoulder to shoulder, men and women stood on its edges, jostling as the train doors opened.

A second's lull, and then people started pouring out. I shifted even closer to the screen and pressed Pause. This time, I edged it on manually using the cursor keys. The camera was about three-quarters of the way down the platform, and was taking in about 80 percent of the train. At Gloucester Road, Sam had boarded the second carriage from the front, so—unless he'd spent the two-minute journey sprinting from one end of the train to the other, barging commuters out of the way—he would be visible if he got off.

But he didn't get off.

The whole place was jammed. I played it and replayed it a couple of times just to be sure, but there was still no sign of him.

It was the same story at Sloane Square.

At Victoria, it was going to be even harder to pick him out. It doubled up as a mainline station, so the platform was just a sea of heads. Then I saw something else: a group of men and women, all dressed in the same red T-shirts, all holding placards.

A demonstration.

I downsized the video file and googled "16 December protest." The top hit was a report from the *Guardian* about a march on Parliament by opponents of the government's spending cuts. I remembered it. Authorities had asked that protesters use the Circle line, and commuters, tourists and everyone else use the District. The warning looked to have been heeded by some, but not all. And certainly not by Sam. If he'd planned his escape beforehand, he couldn't have picked a better day.

I checked Victoria's footage, without any sign of him, then moved on to the next stop, St. James's Park. More protesters. More commuters. The same thing: train arrived, no sign of Sam, train departed. Next I loaded up Westminster. Zipping forward to just after 8 a.m., I hit Play. Sam's train wouldn't be arriving for another five minutes, but I wanted to get a sense of how it was before his arrival.

Westminster was a battlefield: a sea of faces, a mass of bodies. Basically the perfect place to instigate an escape plan. The doors opened. I watched closely, every head, every face, while my mind continued to turn things over.

The station had been set up to funnel people off and away from the trains as fast as possible. In the middle, one of the exits had a sign on the wall next to it that said: PROTESTERS EXIT HERE. At the far end of the station, I could just about make out another sign above another exit: NON-PROTESTERS EXIT HERE. The attempt to smooth traffic flow hadn't worked: the platform was jammed with people not moving at all.

As Sam's train emerged into the station, I hit Pause and inched it on again with the right cursor. When the doors opened it was like a dam breaking: people poured out—almost fell out—a mix of suited executives, tourists looking lost, and legions of red shirts, all heading for the march. The wave of movement had been too fast, and scattered in too many directions, to keep track of properly, so I stopped the video before it got any further, dragged the slider back sixty seconds and started again.

This time I went even more slowly. I knew which carriage Sam had been in, so kept my attention fixed on it as the doors slid open. A ton of people spilled out—but not Sam. Once or twice, I thought I spotted him—fair hair, black suit, blue tie—but then a face would turn in my direction and it was someone else. I rewound the footage a third time and concentrated on the protesters. If I was assuming he might use the demonstration as cover, I had to consider the possibility he might pull on a red T-shirt too. I slowed the action down to a crawl and searched the sea of faces. Anyone who looked like him. Anyone with a T-shirt over a suit, or over a shirt and tie. Anyone carrying a jacket, a briefcase or both. There was nothing. On the fourth and final run-through, I kept my eyes on the carriage itself. As it emptied, I hoped to glimpse Sam still inside the train. But, once again, there was no sign of him.

Then, further down the platform, a fight broke out.

At first, there was a swell of movement, like the eye of a whirlpool, and then it spread out, crowds pushing back in all directions, trying to avoid being caught up. Pretty soon it became obvious what was going on: two men, one in the red of the protest march, another in a white T-shirt with a Union Jack on the back, were throwing punches at each other.

Six Underground staff, stationed at equal distances along the back wall of the platform, descended on them immediately, but not before people had stopped to watch and the whole station had come to a halt. From the carriages of the train, people peered out, trying to see what was going on. Some even stepped on to what space they could find on the platform to take a look. From the bottom of the shot, another member of London Underground emerged, waving his hands, presumably telling people to move up the platform and create space. But it was complete chaos: people seemed to be ignoring him, unable to hear him or see him, or more interested by what was going on further up. Within ten seconds, the Tube staff had created a kind of makeshift wall, three of them in a semicircle around the fight, the other three trying to break it up and move everyone on. It took another twenty seconds for them to put an end to it, and then the two men were taken off through the exit at the middle of the platform, and the remaining staff got things moving again. As the man in the white T-shirt got closer to the camera, I could see what was printed on the front: CUT NOW, STRONGER LATER.

But, throughout it all, there was still no sign of Sam.

Not even a close call.

I replayed the entire thing again, from the moment his train entered the station to the moment it left. I went back to the possibility that he had moved between carriages, but it just seemed improbable: there was barely room to breathe inside the trains, let alone maneuver yourself from one carriage to another. It seemed much more likely that he'd got on and remained inside the same carriage between Gloucester Road and Westminster. There'd been no face like his, no one dressed exactly like him, no one with the same build or holding the same briefcase. Despite the crowds, I would have spotted him.

Which meant he was still on the train.

And there were thirty more stations to check.

Three hours later the train terminated at Hammersmith. I paused the footage and edged it on. About twenty people filed off, a couple in clumps, but most out on their own and easy to identify. None of them was Sam Wren. I'd followed his train all around the Circle line, even— in something approaching desperation—retreating back from Glouces- ter Road to Edgware Road in the ten minutes before he got on, and hadn't spotted him once. Not leaving the train, not even moving around inside it.

The camera at Hammersmith was angled lower than some of the other stations, giving a better view of the carriages, and there was no one left inside. I let the video run anyway and, a few minutes later, two Tube staff, both in bright-orange high-visibility waistcoats, emerged from the bottom of the shot and started walking the length of the platform, checking each carriage. A couple of minutes later, the doors closed, they had a quick word with the driver, then the train pulled off and melted into the tunnel.

So where the hell is he?

I'd have to go through the whole thing again.

Every second of video. Every station. Every face.

Every moment in Sam Wren's vanishing act.

7

Healy entered the office, the traces of old Christmas decorations still hanging limply from whiteboards and computer monitors, and headed for his desk at the back of the room. In the two months he'd been off, it had been used as a dumping ground: printouts, files, random stationery and magazines made up a landslide of discarded items. Cups from the machine had been stacked up in towers as well, one after the other along the edge of the desk. In places, they'd obviously been knocked over and the coffee never cleared up: sticky residue formed in pools, and there were marks on the carpet where it had run off.

The only thing that hadn't been touched were his photos, pinned to the wall on the left of his desk. There were five: individual shots of his wife and three kids, and then a picture of all of them, in happier times, on a holiday in Majorca. He sat down at the desk and wheeled in closer to the photos, his eyes falling on Leanne. Something tremored in his throat, like a bassline coming up from his chest, and he turned away from her before the emotion could take hold.

He started to clean up, sweeping everything on his desk off into a bin, and then grabbed a dishcloth from the kitchen area and rubbed off the coffee stains. About ten minutes later, at just gone 6 a.m., he looked up to see two men enter the office, laughing at something one of them had said. When their eyes locked on Healy, they briefly stopped—frozen for a moment—and then they tried to disguise the movement by continuing their conversation. They all knew each other—the two men were Richter and Sallows—but the division inside CID would be something he'd have to live with: some of them understood why he'd done what he did, the road he'd walked and the laws he'd broken; others only saw him as reckless. A man that couldn't be trusted.

About twenty minutes later, his desk clean and his computer on, he saw someone coming toward him out of the corner of his eye. The office was busy now. He'd had a short conversation with a couple of detectives— a guy called Frey who had joined in the time he'd been off, and who told him he was sorry about Leanne; the other a cop called Sampson who he'd known professionally since they'd first got their uniforms—but mostly it had been nods of the head, or just a complete blank. People hadn't been openly hostile so far, but as he turned to see who was approaching, he knew that was about to change.

"Watch out," a voice said, "it's the Return of the Living Dead."

There were a couple of titters from elsewhere in the room. Healy looked out and saw Richter and Sallows smiling as Eddie Davidson stepped in closer.

"How you doing, Eddie?" Healy asked. He didn't make eye contact, just fiddled around with the things on his desk: straightening, adjusting, tidying, trying to defuse the situation. Davidson was a DS in his early fifties, podgy and aggressive, with small dark eyes, thick black hair and an unruly beard. He had always been the worst-dressed detective on the force, and Healy noted that he hadn't disappointed today: too-tight jeans, a red T-shirt with some kind of road-sign motif on it, and a leather jacket which he'd zipped up as far as it would go, which wasn't very far— his belly was a big round mass.

Davidson was a decent cop: not the best, not the worst, but good enough. What he definitely was, though, was a zealous believer in the religion of the police force, which was why he hated Healy. Healy had gone against the religion and moved against his own. There was some added bad blood too: in a moment of desperation, as he'd searched hopelessly in the shadows for the man who'd taken his daughter, Healy had pulled a gun on Davidson.

"How's it feel to be back?" Davidson asked.

"It feels good."

"Yeah?"

The whole office stopped, some covertly eyeing the two of them, some fully turned around in their seats. Healy looked up. "Yeah, it feels good."

"You screwed up yet?"

Healy felt the first pulse of anger rise in his throat, and then pushed it back down again. Movement registered with Davidson—the tightness in Healy's neck, the tension in his muscles—and he realized he'd got to Healy; picked at a wound and made it bleed. He looked out to the rest of the office, like he was working the crowd, and then shuffled in even closer. Healy glanced at him. "Was there something else, Eddie?"

Davidson smirked. "Is that a fucking *joke*? You walk in here after two months and ask me that? Do you even remember what you did?"

Healy looked at him again. "I remember."

"You remember waving a gun in my face?"

They stared at each other. Healy didn't reply this time, but suddenly it felt like the office was closing in. Other detectives stepped closer, the whole room squeezing shut around him. He laid a hand flat to the desk and leaned back in his chair, keeping his eyes fixed on Davidson, but gaining some room to breathe. Davidson noticed, pulled an empty chair in from behind him and wheeled in close to Healy again, so the two of them were almost touching knees.

"Let me be clear on something," he said quietly, "just so there's no gray areas here: no one wants you back, Healy."

"I'll keep that in mind, Eddie."

"You do that. Because you can play by the rules, you can pretend nothing ever happened, but the truth is you're not a cop any more. You're not one of us, and you never will be. You're just a snide, backstabbing piece of shit."

It took everything he had not to reach across and grab Davidson by the throat. But then, through his peripheral vision, he saw someone else enter the office, pausing in the doorway. A few people noticed, returning to their work.

"Have we got a problem here?"

They all looked around at DCI Melanie Craw, a tall, slim woman in her forties. She was leaning against the door frame, arms crossed, a resigned expression on her face.

"No problem, ma'am," Davidson said, immediately backing away.

"What about you, Healy?"

He glanced at her, and then back to Davidson. Davidson, his face out of sight of Craw, was half smiling. "No," Healy said eventually. "There's no problem."

That night, as Healy made his way outside to his car, sleet sweeping across the car park, he noticed something wedged in place beneath one of the wipers. He reached forward and removed it, brushing off the moisture.

It was a toy knife.

He looked back at the station and, at one of the windows, he saw movement: there and then gone again. But he got the message. *A snide, backstabbing piece of shit.*

8

Before heading out to Julia's, I made a couple of quick calls. The first was to Spike, an old newspaper contact of mine. He was a twenty-something Russian hacker, here on an expired student visa. During my days as a journalist, he'd been an incredible source of information. He could get beyond any firewall without leaving a trace of himself, bagging names, numbers, e-mail addresses, even credit histories and contracts while he was there. As long as I forgot about the fact that he was basically a criminal, and that I was his accessory, he was an unbeatable information source.

"Pizza parlor."

I smiled. "Spike, it's David Raker."

"David!"

He had been here so long now, he hardly had an accent at all; just a slight twang, refined and smoothed by hours of watching English-language TV.

"How's things at the pizza parlor?"

He laughed. "Good, man. It's been a while."

"Yeah, a few months. Did you miss me?"

"I missed your money. So, what can I do you for?"

"I'm hoping it's pretty simple. I need a financial check done on someone. Bank accounts, credit cards, mortgage, investments, pensions—basically anything you can lay your hands on. I need the whole thing, A to Z."

"Who's the victim?"

I gave him Sam Wren's name, address and personal details, as well as a mobile number Julia had passed on to me. "I'll need his phone records as well."

"What dates are we looking at?"

"The last eighteen months, from today back to January of last year. I'll be on my mobile, or I can pick up e-mails on the move. Just let me know when you get something."

"You got it. I'll give you details of my bank too."

Spike's "bank" was a locker at his local sports center. For obvious reasons, he was a cash-only man, and he used the locker as a drop-off, changing the combination every time someone deposited his fee there.

Next, I dialed Sam's brother Robert at work, and immediately got his voicemail. He was out of the country on business until Friday. That was another forty-eight hours away. I left a message, telling him who I was and what I was doing, and gave him my number.

Finally, referring back to Julia's list of names, I cold-called PC Brian Westerley, the cop who'd filed Sam's missing persons report. He answered after three rings, sounding pretty chirpy. By the time I'd told him who I was and why I was calling, the mood had changed. Pretty quickly I realized, if I was going to get anything from him, I'd have to work for it—or back him into a corner. Often, uniforms were the most difficult cops to deal with; their relative lack of power meant they took the first chance they could to lord it over someone.

"I can't release any kind of information to you," he said. He sounded in his late fifties and originally from somewhere in the northeast. "If Mrs. Wren wants to come and see me again, she can."

"She already came to see you."

He paused, uncertainly. I'd just lied to him but, even from our short conversation, it was obvious he was having trouble remembering the details of the case. He probably recalled the train part—because how many missing persons enquiries started like Sam's?—but not much else. The truth was that Julia had called him a couple of weeks after she filed the missing persons report to chase up the contents of the CCTV footage, rather than actually gone to see him. But it didn't really matter. If she'd turned up and perched herself on his lap, he probably wouldn't have been able to tell me who she was.

"I'm not sure Mrs. Wren came to—"

"You completely forgot to follow up her husband's case," I continued, laying it on thick. "It was devastating for her. She's still waiting for you to call her back."

I felt bad about playing him, but the alternative was telling him the truth and getting a brick wall in return. I didn't say anything else; just left the rest of the conversation there, unspoken. He worked it out pretty quickly: if she was pissed off, she was willing to do something about it; and if she was willing to do something about it, she was willing to file an official complaint.

"What is it you want?" he said eventually.

"I'd like you to pull the file."

"I clock off at four and then I'm not back in until Friday."

Same as Robert Wren. I hated having to wait. "Can you pull it now?"

"No. I'm not in front of a computer and I need to get some more pressing things completed before I go. If that's not good enough, then do what you have to do."

He'd called my bluff, but I remained silent for a moment so he knew I wasn't backing down lightly. I could have called my contacts at the Met and got them to grab the file for me, got the thing printed out and delivered, but by taking a chance on Westerley I'd alerted him to my interest in Sam Wren; and if he logged on to the database and found another cop had been snooping around in Sam's file, my source would be compromised.

"Okay," I said, giving him my mobile number. "Call me back Friday."

9

The Wrens lived on a narrow street, permit parking on one side, houses on the other. Every home was identical but attractive: bricked on the ground floor, plastered and painted cream on the first. Doors sat at the bottom of two downward steps, and the windows housed rectangular flower baskets, the trays full of pink geraniums. As I drove up to Julia's place, the door opened and she came up the steps holding a key fob, a remote control attached. I bumped up on to the pavement and buzzed down my window.

"Here." She handed me the remote. "There's underground parking just around the corner at the end of the road. Head left and you're there."

When I returned to the house, the door was ajar. I stepped through and pushed it shut behind me. Immediately inside was a long hallway, floored in laminate. The kitchen was directly in front and Julia was standing at one of the counters, pouring water into a kettle. Tucked into an alcove next to the kitchen was a corkscrew staircase.

As I moved toward the kitchen, I eyed the other rooms off the hallway: a bathroom, a bedroom doubling up as a graveyard for cardboard boxes, and a living room. In the living room were hundreds of books in a bookcase, surround sound, a TV, an expensive Blu-ray player, a Sky decoder, and a big leather sofa. A coffee table sat in the center, loaded with art books as big as slabs of concrete, and a bowl of fresh fruit. I could see photos of Sam too, squared into a pile.

"Tea or coffee, David?"

She brought out a tin of instant. I preferred my coffee through a percolator, but I didn't want to offend her on the first day. "Coffee, thanks. Black, no sugar."

We moved through to the living room and sat on either end of the sofa. She had made herself some kind of fruit tea; it smelled tangy and sweet. She placed it down next to the photos, and pushed them across the coffee table toward me. "That's the last five years of Sam's life," she said, eyes fixed on the top picture, where her husband was standing, wine glass raised, black suit buttoned up, in a hospitality suite at the Emirates Stadium. Immediately I could see a physical difference in him: bigger around the face, better-color skin.

"When was this taken?" I said.

She ripped her eyes away. "March last year."

We talked for a while about Sam, about the kind of person he was, the things he liked doing, the places they'd been together. She'd told me about a time, when they first got together, that he'd been sent on a business trip to Barcelona and—on the quiet—had paid for her to come too. "He was very spontaneous like that," she said, and then the smile slipped away, as if she realized how prescient that was. After all, there was nothing more spontaneous than getting up one day and not bothering to tell your wife you were leaving.

I listened some more as she continued building a picture of their marriage. They both got on. They liked the same things. They'd talked excitedly about having kids. But the whole time she was holding back. There was a reservation to her; moments where she stopped herself before she wandered into territory she couldn't back out of. The previous night I'd wondered if she was timid or just nervous, but as she'd started to warm up, I realized it wasn't timidity—and it might not have been nerves either. There was a secret sitting between us, and we both knew it.

"Let me ask you something," I said, placing down the photograph I'd taken from her the night before. "Is there a reason Sam lost a ton of weight before he disappeared?"

She studied me, surprise in her face. "What do you mean?"

"You must have noticed that between March and December last year he'd lost a lot of weight."

Her eyes flicked between the pictures. "I never . . ." She paused again. She was about to say she'd never realized. But it would have been a lie. She *had* realized. She'd noted the changes in his face; the changes in his body. She'd seen everything. "Financially, we were stretched," she said eventually.

"That's why he lost weight?"

She looked up from the pictures. "This house cost us £850,000, and our mortgage was £3,000 a month. That was more than my entire wage packet, every month. Sam was on £78,000 a year basic, which meant he was bringing home just over £4,000 a month. Maybe that sounds like a lot, but once you start chipping away at it with the mortgage, council tax, gas, electricity, water, insurance policies for both of us, food for both of us, phone bills, even things like Oyster cards for both of us, it starts to disappear fast. And it only got worse after I lost my job."

In her face I could see the financial burden had weighed heavily on them both, but I expected the bitterness she felt at him leaving her on her own weighed even heavier. I saw the logic in everything she was saying; knew how a big mortgage and big bills could grind you down and spit you out, especially if you were down to one wage and that wage couldn't cover everything you needed it to. But I had become good at reading people and, when I looked at Julia Wren, it was obvious there was more to it than that.

I decided to play hardball. "What aren't you telling me?"

"What do you mean?"

"You know what I mean."

She stared at me, eyes locked on mine, but I knew I was right. If I'd been wrong, she would have been indignant; instead there seemed a kind of sad resignation to her, as if she felt I'd outwitted her.

"I'm sorry," she said quietly. "I wanted to tell you last night but I just . . ." Another pause. She looked up. "I feel responsible. Guilty."

"About him losing weight or leaving?"

"Both."

"Why?"

She shrugged. Another long silence. This time I could see her trying to put it all into words. "Our marriage was good. *Great*. That part wasn't a lie. We'd been together seven years, married for four, and I can honestly count on the fingers of one hand the amount of serious fights we had. One, maybe two. And usually they resolved themselves pretty quickly. We just seemed to be on the same wavelength." She paused and laced her fingers together. "But in those last months, it became different. We started fighting. Niggly stuff at first, and always about his work. He just seemed to have become consumed by his job. I think he felt, because I wasn't bringing anything in, and because his wages had been frozen and his bonuses phased out, he had to single-handedly find a replacement for the money we were missing out on."

"And how was he going to do that?"

"Sam was one of those people who always felt like he needed to be doing more. He was his own harshest critic. If he wasn't improving, going further, earning more, he saw it as some kind of failure. He hated standing still. So, the longer he went without the bonuses, the longer his wages remained frozen, the more it started to frustrate him, and the more hours he was clocking up while trying to put it right. That was when the niggly stuff started: I'd ask him what the point was of working long hours if he knew there wasn't going to be a reward at the end of it."

"And what did he say?"

"Nothing, really."

"He didn't tell you why he was still working so hard?"

She shook her head. "I was living the life of a single woman, feeling him slip into bed at eleven, and back out again at six. Some weeks we probably weren't saying more than a couple of words to each other. It wasn't a marriage any more."

"And it was never like that before?"

"No. I mean, he always worked hard. He did his fair share of late nights. But there was always a compromise. We'd get away at weekends, or he'd come home early one day to make up for working late on the others. But not in those last six months."

"He never talked to you about it? The exact reasons why he was working so late all the time, who his clients were, that kind of thing?"

"No." She brought her tea toward her and held it below her chin. "He'd always talked to me before. I knew his clients by name, I knew who they worked for and what he thought of them, because he always came home and opened up. He'd laugh about them, talk about the jokes they'd shared, the things they'd discussed, the places they'd been for dinner. He'd share his day with me. But, at the end, when I asked about why he was working so hard all the time, he'd just fob me off."

"By saying what?"

"He didn't want to bring his work home." She looked at me. "That's all he kept saying to me: 'Leave work at work.' So, I tried to come at him from a different angle. I tried to bring it up at weekends, casually, when we had a little time together; when the office wasn't open. But he just refused to discuss it."

"But he wasn't bringing any more money home."

"No."

"So, do you think he was working harder and longer hours because it was just the type of person he was—the type you just described him as being—or because he had some other venture on the side?"

"Oh, I'd say the first."

"Why?"

"We had a joint account which I checked regularly when things began to change. There was no extra money coming in."

None he let you know about, I thought. I took down some notes, and then realized there was no easy way to phrase the next question, even though it was an obvious place to head. "Did you think he might have been seeing someone else?"

For a moment she was taken aback, her eyes widening, her cheeks flushing, but she must have asked herself the same question. "Because he was working so many hours?"

"Right."

"I really don't think so."

"You never had any reason to suspect him?"

"No."

"You didn't entertain the possibility?"

"I thought about it a lot at the start. I checked his e-mail, checked his phone, but Sam just . . ." She stopped, shook her head, then glanced up at me. Her cheeks colored a little. "For a man, he didn't have much of a sex drive. I mean, most men, it's all they ever think about, right? The men I was with before Sam, they were always angling for it. But Sam was never like that, right from before we were even married. We used to have sex a couple of times a week to start with, but then it dropped off after that. By the end, we weren't doing it at all."

I nodded and let her compose herself in the silence.

"So why is it you felt responsible for him leaving?"

She shrugged. "We fought."

"Everybody fights."

"But these weren't *just* fights. These were screaming matches. I wanted to know what was going on; why he was working so hard when he knew there was no chance of earning any more money. So I kept chipping away at him, but the more I tried to find out what was happening, the more angry he got, and the more we fought."

I nodded, as if her reasoning were sound, but the reality was he wouldn't have left because they were fighting. If you fought with your partner, you separated or moved on. You didn't engineer your disappearance.

"What about when you didn't discuss his long hours?"

"That was the weird thing: as long as we didn't talk about it, as long as I didn't try to find out what was going on, we got on brilliantly."

"How was he with friends and family?"

"Exactly the same."

"No problems?"

"Speak to Rob, his brother. See if he says anything different. Sam may have said something to him—you know, brother to brother—but somehow I doubt it."

I changed tack. "He didn't ever complain about feeling unwell?"

"In what sense?"

"In any sense." I nodded toward the last picture she'd taken of him, thin and pale. "I just want to be sure I'm not missing anything."

She shook her head. "Sam didn't get ill much. And when he did, he rarely let it affect him. He even went into work when he had shingles."

"Any favorite places you guys used to go to?"

She thought about it, but not for long. "Not really. At least, not the kind of place he might disappear to. We liked to holiday, but that all stopped after I lost my job."

"Did he owe any cash to anyone?"

"No."

"Any problems with alcohol or drugs?"

"Definitely not."

"Anyone he fell out with in those last six months?"

Again, she shook her head.

I'd been through the list of names she'd given me, and the two best angles seemed to be his brother and his work. Julia had painted a picture of a reliable, decent man, one not prone to big mood swings or changes in character. Yet something had altered. In his work, in how he dealt with his wife, he changed completely in the half-year before he vanished. He got secretive. Stressed. Lost weight. And, ultimately, whatever had been eating away at him was enough for him to leave one morning in the middle of December and never come home again.

10

At the top of the stairs, there were three doors. The first opened up into a small, smartly decorated bathroom, all black slate tiles and chrome fixtures. Adjacent to that was a spare room that probably looked the same the day the two of them moved in: plain cream walls, curtain poles without any curtains attached, no furniture except for a desk and a leather chair, and a PC. The third was their bedroom. It was small but unusual: the ceiling was slightly slanted, dropping down the closer to the window it got, and a series of shelves had been built into a V-shaped alcove on the far wall. The room looked out over angled red roofs to a residents-only park, gated and locked, and dominated by huge oak trees. It was hot and stuffy: the window was closed, and sunlight was streaming in across the bed.

All of Sam's clothes were still in his wardrobe, but everything he'd once owned was a mess: shoes were piled up at the bottom, clothes were half on hangers. Julia had left it exactly as it was; all she'd done was close the doors and seal it off from the world. I turned to his bedside table. Inside one of the drawers were four different novels by four different authors, each with a bookmark about halfway in. In the next drawer down was a shoebox full of gimmicky boy toys: corkscrews, alarm clocks, beer mats, battery-powered lumps of plastic that looked like they'd come from an expensive Christmas cracker. She'd called him spontaneous—but, in missing persons, spontaneity meant you didn't place a lot of importance on routine. It meant you were impulsive, moved around, started things but didn't finish them. Four half-finished books also suggested he was finding it difficult to concentrate.

Sam wasn't a creature of habit, and that would immediately make him harder to find. People who thrived on routine left a footprint: the same route in and out, the same stop-offs along the way. It seemed likely he'd thought about disappearing in advance, because you didn't just walk away from a marriage, a home and a job on a whim. But I doubted he'd made the decision to actually follow through with it until he got up on the morning of 16 December. There were big question marks, though: why didn't he take any money with him? Why was he working so late for no obvious reward? And how did he exit a train without being caught on film?

Underneath the bed were some empty suitcases, a box of dusty LPs and a pile of photo albums. I pulled the albums out and started to go through them. They were the trips abroad Julia had mentioned: New York, San Francisco, Vancouver, Berlin, Paris, Rome, Prague. Not a beach in sight. City breaks would have suited Sam's working life as they'd mean less time out of the office. They probably also suited the type of person he was. Seven days on a sunlounger would have driven him insane.

Sliding the albums back under the bed, I did a last circuit—going over everything again—and then made my way across the landing to the spare room. Thankfully, it was cooler. Sam's PC was Alienware, built for gaming, and on top of the hard drive were a pile of games. I sat down and booted it up.

On the desktop was a folder, created three months before, where Julia had placed all of Sam's files. Word docs, spreadsheets, gaming software and a couple of illegally downloaded films. I fired up the Web browser and started going through the history. Most of the recent pages shared a similar theme: my cases. A tabloid account of one I'd had the October before showed a picture of me emerging from my house:

He's a private investigator who doesn't waste his time trying to trap cheating spouses and get to the bottom of insurance scams. Instead, publicity-shy Raker is an action man who has been labeled "Mindhunter" for his ability to track down some of the country's most vicious criminals.

It was a complete lie. No one had ever called me that or was ever likely to, but I understood why Julia Wren needed to believe it.

As I continued to move through the Internet history, there was a jump of three months, presumably between the first time Julia had started searching for someone to help find Sam, and the last time Sam had used the computer. He'd custom-set his Internet history so that it remembered the last 350 pages, regardless of how far back they were logged. The date of Sam's last session was 11:12 p.m. on 15 December— the night before he vanished—and the last site he'd been to was an Arsenal fan forum. Not exactly indicative of a man contemplating his disappearance—if he was even contemplating it in the first place. There was always, in the background, the possibility that something else had happened to him. An accident. A desperate decision. Something worse than both. No evidence supported those theories, and nothing so far backed them up. But, as I scanned the rest of the links in his Internet history, the idea didn't entirely fade.

Once I was back home, I returned to the CCTV footage. This time, rather than watch it in QuickTime, I opened the Gloucester Road video in a custom-built film-editing suite Spike had passed on to me during one of my first cases. In that one I'd been trying to spot a woman entering her place of work in some footage I'd shot, but she'd been so far away all I could see was a vague blur. The software, built by Spike, allowed me to select a portion of the video and zoom in for a closer look. The quality of the recording didn't become better—in fact, it became much worse, which was the reason I didn't use it a lot—but, once you'd pinpointed the person you wanted to track, it allowed you to follow them more easily, even if all they were at that kind of magnification was a blur of pixels.

I selected the area around Sam and then used the zoom function, stopping about 50 percent of the way in. The quality of the recording deteriorated, and his features became less defined, but by cutting out the noise around him—the other people, the detail of the Tube station—I was able to follow him on to the train before he disappeared from view. This was the point at which I'd lost him the first time. Now, though, the zoom function allowed me to identify a thin red tag on his briefcase— little more than eight or nine pixels in length—and a couple of seconds after vanishing, the briefcase, along with the red tag, reappeared: Sam was standing midway inside the carriage, hidden behind a sea of legs.

But he was there.

The briefcase and his legs were all that was visible, which was why I'd missed it the first time: his trousers were the same color as 95 percent of those around him, and without the red tag it would have been impossible to tell which briefcase belonged to him. I inched the video on a frame and the doors started to close. At the very last minute another commuter made a dive for the doors and managed to sneak on, and after that Sam finally *did* disappear from view: his legs, his briefcase, any indication of where he was in the carriage. My impressions from the first watch were right: there was no way he could have moved from where he was. There were too many people around him, too much traffic either side to transfer between carriages, which meant, when he moved between stations on the Circle line, he would be in the same place. And I'd have the red tag.

At South Kensington and Sloane Square I struggled to make him out, but when the train pulled into Victoria I picked up the briefcase again. He'd shifted position, closer to the doors. He was half turned, luckily with the red tag facing out toward the camera, but he was definitely still on the train, standing still as people got off and on around him.

I moved on to St. James's Park.

And that was when he disappeared.

The carriage was still packed, so—again—it was unlikely he could have swapped to the ones either side of his, but I couldn't see the tag, or anything recognizable as Sam. I moved to Westminster: played it and replayed it, magnifying the open doors of the carriage further with the zoom function. Nothing. At Westminster there was more going on—a bigger crowd, Tube staff funneling protesters, then the fight—and, at one point, Sam's carriage even emptied a little as people stepped out to see what was going on further up the platform. That was the point at which he should have been visible, even without the zoom on.

But I couldn't see him anywhere.

I paused it and moved between passengers: those at the doors of the carriage looking out at the fight, and then the clumps of protesters stepping around them. Beyond that, a few remained inside. A man in a suit, his face buried in a book. Another demonstrator in a red shirt with checked sleeves, reaching down to pick up a protest sign. A woman with headphones on, blissfully unaware of everything. Through the scratched, reflective glass of the carriage, it was difficult to make out their faces, but I knew instantly neither of the men left behind were Sam. Both of them were taller, weightier and older, dressed differently with different color hair. And as the footage moved on, the second man—the protester— left the carriage anyway, sign hoisted up, moving quickly to catch up with the others.

Somewhere, somehow, I'd managed to lose Sam.

As I got to Hammersmith for the second time with no further sign of Sam, the house was starting to get dark. I glanced at the clock: 9:30. I was fried. I closed the footage and shut down the Mac, then showered. As the cool water ran down my face, my mind rolled back once again to what I'd seen, and then over everything Julia Wren had said earlier. I didn't need to have seen him on the footage to move things on: I already had Sam's work, his brother and the obvious loss of weight. The case was already shifting, and would do so with or without the recording. But the video was a useful starting point and, in an odd way, a symbolic one; a means of zeroing in on Sam's physical location that day, and—in the moment he exited the train, wherever that might have been—a way to get inside his head.

By choosing a station to leave at, he would have given me a compass bearing for that area of the city, and while it might not have led me to him, it would have given me an advantage. But most of all it would have helped erase the impossible: that a man really *could* step on to a train and then—three stops later—disappear into thin air.

12

As I entered Liz's house there was the smell of coffee and perfume and the buzz of the electric shower along the hallway. Her living room was understated but stylish: an open fireplace, two black leather sofas, a TV, a huge bookcase; and then a potted palm, big and out of control, which looked like it belonged on a Caribbean island.

I went to the kitchen, got two mugs from the cupboard and poured some coffee, then padded through to the bedroom. She'd finished showering and was drying herself off, steam pouring off her, condensation on every surface. I announced my arrival by singing the *Psycho* shower-scene music.

She smiled. "Very funny."

"It's like a volcano in here."

Rolling her eyes, she hung her towel on the door, and started hunting around in her drawers for underwear.

"How was your day?" I asked.

"I was defending that hit-and-run driver."

She looked at me, her opinion on him clear to see. Even outside of the courtroom, in the privacy of her own home, she maintained a kind of dignified silence. It wasn't that she didn't want to discuss her cases with me, more that she preferred not to judge people, even if sometimes—like tonight—it was hard not to. I liked that quality in her.

"And yours?"

"It was okay."

She looked at me. "Just okay?"

I put her coffee down and sat on the edge of the bed. "So this guy I'm trying to find gets on at Gloucester Road and then disappears. Just . . ." I looked at her. It sounded strange saying it out loud. "Vanishes."

"How do you vanish from the inside of a train?"

I shrugged. "That's just the point. You don't. You *can't*. He must have got off at some point—but I can't see where. I've been over the footage twice today."

"No sign of him?"

"Nothing after Victoria."

"He'll turn up." She sat down on the bed and squeezed me, then shifted slightly, as if she'd suddenly remembered something. "Oh, I bumped into an old friend of yours today."

"I didn't realize I had any left."

Another smile formed on her face. "He was giving evidence in one of the other courtrooms."

"Who was the friend?"

"Colm Healy."

His name made me pause.

The last time I'd seen Healy was at the funeral of his daughter the previous November. He'd been in a bad way at the time: emotionally damaged, physically broken, estranged from his wife and suspended from his job at the Met. In the weeks before he buried his girl, we'd formed an uneasy alliance, one built not on trust, but on necessity, as we both came to realize we were hunting the same man.

"Did you say hello?"

"Yes. He passed on his best."

"Is he back on the force?"

"Since 9 January. He said he'd had to suck up a demotion."

"But he seemed okay otherwise?"

Liz looked up at me. "He seemed better."

He couldn't have been much worse. Healy had gone against all the rules of his profession to find his daughter. In the interviews afterward, police had accused me of feeling a kinship for him, using it as a stick to beat me with, a way of cornering me. But they'd failed to understand the relationship. We'd caught a monster—a murderer who'd eluded police for years—and, in order to do that, in order to go as far as we had, there had to be something deeper tethering us to each other. The police thought it was that I felt sorry for him.

But it was more than that.

Until you'd buried the most important person in your life, it was difficult to understand how grief forged a connection between people. Yet, ultimately, that was what had happened with Healy and me. I didn't trust him, in many ways didn't even really like him, but we each saw our reflection in the other, and—as we tried to stop a killer who had preyed on us both—that had been enough.

13

The grass around the front of the building was still covered in frost and, in the sky above, unmarked by cloud, a pair of seagulls squawked, drifting beyond the walls of the prison. There was a faint breeze in the air, carried in from the Thames, but otherwise it was still.

Healy passed through the front entrance and waited in line at security. Ahead of him, a man in his seventies was being patted down, a prison officer's hands passing along both legs. The old man's coat, jacket, belt and shoes were already sitting in a tray on the other side of an X-ray machine, and—once he was done being searched—he had a door-shaped metal detector to contend with. A second prison officer lay in wait beyond that, looking like he'd come off the same production line as the one doing the rub-down: shaved head, mustache, semi-aggressive.

The old man was still putting on his shoes by the time Healy was done. In the corridor ahead were a series of lockers where visitors were asked to store all personal possessions. Healy made a show of switching off his phone, and opened one of the locker doors. But he didn't put anything inside.

He wasn't planning on staying.

A couple of minutes later, as he pretended to check his phone, he saw her emerge through a security door. She was wearing a visitor's badge on her front and holding a slip case. As he watched her, he felt a prickle of anger form at the bottom of his throat, but then she seemed to sense she was being watched and looked vaguely in his direction. He stepped in front of the open locker door and disappeared from view.

A few seconds later, he leaned back out and saw that she was chatting with one of the prison guards. There was a smile on her face that pissed Healy off, as if nothing was on her mind. As if she'd forgotten where she'd just come from and who she'd been talking to. He'd missed her the week before because she'd been finished by the time he'd fought his way through London traffic—but he hadn't missed her this week. He'd made sure of that.

Now he needed to get to know her.

He needed to get a fix on her routines, her habits, her quirks, her route into and out of this place.

And when he knew all that, when he was sure, then he'd move in for the kill.

An hour later, Healy pulled his Vauxhall up outside the station. He killed the engine and glanced at himself in the rearview mirror. He'd hardly slept the night before, knowing he was due at the prison early, and it showed in his eyes and in his face. He'd told Craw that he was going to the doctor, and maybe she'd believe that for a while. But she was smart. She'd see it in him. And, after a while, she'd realize it wasn't a lack of sleep that was getting to him. It was the anger and resentment.

It was the need for revenge.

His eyes flicked back to his reflection. *Get yourself straight. Don't let them see any weakness.* He took a deep breath, the heat from the car fading as winter started to creep back in. Then he reached for the door, opened it and headed inside.

13 February

Healy looked up to see he was the only one in the office. It was 10 p.m. For a second, twenty-three years of instinct kicked in and he reached for his jacket, his first thought of Gemma and what she would say when he got home. But then reality hit: Gemma had left him, their marriage was over and the only home he had to go to was a dark, pokey flat in King's Cross he was renting from a friend at Scotland Yard.

He leaned back in his chair and fixed his eyes on the clock at the far end of the room. Below it was a map of central London and two photographs of two different men. Their names were Steven Wilky and Marc Evans. The map had pins, Post-it notes, pieces of paper and marker pen all over it. Healy glanced at his in-tray: burglaries, violent domestics, dealers. He'd been given a second chance at the Met, survived the disciplinary procedure and come out the other end, but he hadn't done it unscathed. He'd taken a demotion, from detective sergeant down to detective constable, and now he was working the sort of cases he'd left behind a decade ago. They were his ticket back in, the way to win Craw's favor, but he hated them; hated the satisfaction it gave people like Eddie Davidson to see him working shitty cases that were plainly beneath him.

What he wanted was something bigger.

What he wanted was Wilky and Evans.

Voices in the corridor. He looked over the top of his monitor and saw Davidson, Richter and Sallows approaching the office, laughing at something one of them had said. He thought about grabbing his jacket and heading out the other door, but it was too late to make a swift exit without being noticed. He'd have to ride this one out.

Davidson entered first, saw movement out of the corner of his eye and zeroed in on Healy. The other two followed suit, the pack mimicking their leader. A smile spread across Davidson's face, his small dark eyes flicking from one side of the room to the other, making sure no one else was around. Then they all started to approach.

"I didn't think you'd need to clock overtime working domestics, Colm," Davidson said by way of a greeting. The other two smiled. Davidson came right up to Healy, into his personal space, and then backed away slightly, perching himself on a desk opposite. "Or maybe you're finding them tough to crack."

The other two laughed. Healy looked at Davidson, then at Richter and Sallows, and felt the muscles in his jaw tighten. *Don't let them get to you.* There was a flash of disappointment in Davidson's eyes when Healy didn't rise to the bait.

"Seriously, Colm, what are you doing here?"

"What does it look like, Eddie?"

Davidson's eyes flicked to Healy's desk and then back again. "It looks like you're still here at ten o'clock and all you've got in your tray are piece-of-shit cases."

"Even piece-of-shit cases need closing."

Davidson frowned, like Healy had said something stupid. Then he looked him up and down, his desk, his work space. "What *is* this?"

"What's what?"

"This," he said, waving an arm in Healy's direction. "You were away—what?—ten weeks, and suddenly you're the fucking Zen master?"

"I don't follow."

"You don't follow?" He shuffled off the edge of the desk, running a hand through his beard, and stepped in closer. "The old Healy was a prick, but at least you knew where you were with him. You said something he didn't like, and he flipped out. Screamed in your face, did everything in his power to fuck things up for you and everyone around him. But this new one . . ." He stopped, looked Healy up and down like he was pond life. "You're just a shell. You're fried. You've got nothing left in the tank."

"I guess we'll see."

"What the fuck's that supposed to mean?" Sallows this time. He was in his early fifties, just like Davidson, but unlike Davidson he was tall and skinny. The two of them had been together for years. Before things went wrong, before Leanne went missing, Healy used to joke that they were an old married couple. But not any more. There were no jokes now. Those days were gone.

Healy glanced at Sallows. "What do you think it means, Kevin?"

"I think it means you're done," Sallows said.

Healy looked between the three of them. He'd known Richter for the least amount of time and, judging on his performance tonight, he wasn't going to be much to worry about. But Davidson and Sallows were different. They'd keep chipping away at him until the first cracks appeared, and then they'd get into the cracks and prize them as far open as they'd go.

Davidson leaned forward, into Healy's personal space again. "Look at you—you're pathetic. You can't even get it together for a fight any more."

For a second, Healy imagined reaching up, grabbing Davidson by the neck and smashing his face through the table; felt the tremor in his hands, the fire in his chest, the need to react and hit out. But then he remembered standing in a darkened courtyard the October before, waving a gun in Davidson's face, and telling him that he would kill him if he got in the way of finding Leanne. Healy had meant it too; never been so sure about anything in his entire life. But it had cost him—his position, his marriage— and now he needed to maintain control in order to claw his way back out of the hole and get his teeth into something better. He looked beyond Davidson, to the photographs on the far wall.

He wanted a piece of that.

He wanted to help find those two men.

He wanted to hunt the Snatcher.

PART TWO

14

At 1 a.m., I was still awake. Through the open window, I could hear the soft drone of cars from Gunnersbury Avenue and the gentle whine of a plane overhead, but otherwise the streets of Ealing were still. No breeze, no animals rummaging around, no people passing.

The first day of a new case it was always difficult to sleep. Everything was new—the people, their world—and every question you asked at the beginning only led to more questions. Those that remained unanswered were like holes; little punctures in the case that you had to find a way to repair before the whole thing collapsed.

And there were already big holes in Sam Wren's life.

When the clock hit 1:30, I finally accepted I wasn't going to sleep, flipped back the covers and sat up. Grabbing my trousers, I padded through to the living room where Liz's MacBook was still set up. I cleared the screensaver and plugged in the USB stick Task had got for me, saving the contents on to the desktop. Then I opened the videos again and watched them through. A shiver of electricity passed along my spine as I saw Sam for the last time, his legs and briefcase disappearing as the train doors slid shut. And then the train jerked forward and headed into the black of the tunnel.

Gone.

Behind me, I heard footsteps in the hallway and looked back to see Liz emerge from the darkness. She moved through to the kitchen, filled a glass with water and returned to where I was sitting.

"Can't you sleep?"

"No. I've got first-night insomnia."

She nodded. Her eyes fell on the laptop. I'd rewound the footage to the seconds before the train doors closed. "Is this your guy?"

"That's his train."

"Where's he?"

I pointed to his legs. "There."

"All you've got are his legs?"

"In Victoria, yes."

"What about after?"

"This is the last time you get to see him."

She leaned in even closer and tabbed the footage on. Doors sliding shut. Train taking off. Disappearing into the tunnel. "That's a bit . . . *creepy*, isn't it?"

"In what way?"

"Well, he just disappears."

"People disappear all the time."

"Yeah, but they don't just *disappear*, do they?" She tabbed the footage back and looked at me. "When people disappear, they wander off somewhere, hide, try not to resurface. Or they die: they commit suicide, someone kills them, *something*. Their body goes *somewhere*. But you've been through the footage and you can't see the join. You can't see where he went. To me . . ." She faded out. "To me that's a bit creepy."

I didn't say anything, but in the silence I realized Liz might be right: there *was* something disquieting about Sam Wren's journey that morning, more so now I'd seen the CCTV video. I still knew, in the rational part of me, the part I built cases on, that Sam *had* to have left the train—but without being able to see him do it, without the physical act of stepping on to the platform, something troubling remained.

"I'll see you in bed," she said quietly.

I watched her go and then turned back to the footage. There were twelve thousand CCTV cameras in and around the London Underground. The ticket halls. The platforms. The walkways. The trains. Sam couldn't have avoided them all.

I had to widen the search.

I woke with a start. Outside I could hear people talking, a car idling, and—even more distantly—the sound of a dog barking. Disorientated and half asleep, I sat up in bed, feeling the sheet fall away, a faint breeze reaching across from the window and clawing at my skin. Seconds later, my phone began buzzing.

I grabbed it. "David Raker."

"David, it's Spike. You okay?"

"Yeah. Late night. What time is it?"

"7:15. Do you want me to call back?"

"No." I got to my feet, grabbed one of Liz's least feminine dressing gowns and put it on. I made my way through to the living room, set the phone down and switched to speaker. "What have you got for me, Spike?"

"Sorry it's taken me so long."

"Not a problem."

"So, you asked for a complete financial picture, as well as his phone records. I'll send them through as a PDF, so you can grab them on the move."

"Great. Anything I need to know?"

"Nah, it's all pretty self-explanatory. The financial stuff runs to about twenty-five pages. The phone records I'm doing a bit of work on: for each of the incoming and outgoing numbers I'll get you a name and address."

"Great work—are those coming over today?"

"Yeah. Not until a bit later on, though. Getting these names and addresses for you will take longer, but it'll save you a load of time."

"You're the man, Spike."

I thanked him and killed the call.

Now it was time to brave the Tube at rush hour.

15

Gloucester Road Tube station sits on the corner of Gloucester Road and Courtfield Road. Its two-tone facade—all glazed terra-cotta tiles and sandy brick—harks back to the grand old days of the Underground; to a time when the Tube wasn't just a vessel to get people to their destination, but an experience, a day out. In truth, it was hard to imagine those times on the hot, cramped District line, moving through the bowels of the earth where there was no air, and eventually no daylight.

Heading out of the Tube, I walked the half-mile to the Wrens' street, then did a 180 and retraced the same route, just as Sam would have done the day he went missing. Fifteen minutes later I was at the main entrance, passing through the three thin arches that would lead me back into the earth.

I took the stairs down to the Circle line platform. The crowds had thinned out in the time I'd been outside. The westbound train was already in the station, but I wanted to go eastbound, so I took a seat on one of the gray metal benches and watched the other passengers. People had always fascinated me: what made them different, how they lied and covered up, how they emoted and broke down. I hadn't missed the crush of the commute in the years since I'd given up journalism, but I missed the opportunity to watch and learn from the crowds. All the books on kinesics, on the language of the body and the psychology of interviews, helped fill in the blanks. But I'd never learned more than on weekday mornings when I'd been surrounded by a sea of commuters.

Once I was on the eastbound train, I got out at every Circle line station, took the escalators or the stairs up to street level and then made my way back down again. At Westminster—the station that would have been the best and most obvious escape route on the day Sam vanished—I spent a couple of minutes moving between the Circle and Jubilee lines. On a regular work day, Sam would have made the switch in order to go east to Canary Wharf.

Then, about two hours in, I started the journey in reverse—and for the first time a part of me wondered what I was hoping to achieve. In any investigation, you had to feel like you were moving forward; every place you went to, every person you spoke to, had to push the case on.

Riding the Tube was a way of understanding Sam better, of getting a feel for his routine. His life. But I'd found nothing of him. No trace of him here, and no trace of him on the footage.

I pushed the doubts down and carried on.

At 11:30, I got back to the gateline at Gloucester Road and noticed a couple of Tube employees. One was standing in a booth watching people pass through; the other was talking to a group of Japanese tourists and pointing to a map. The one in the booth looked up as I approached. He was small, wiry, his eyes dark, his face pale. Close in, his skin seemed too thin, as if it were tracing paper that was about to tear.

"Morning."

He nodded in reply. Nothing else.

I ignored the lack of response and pressed on, introducing myself and telling him about Sam. When I was done, I got out a photograph and showed it to him. It was a long shot given the number of people who must have passed through the station every day, but it was a question that needed to be asked. Sometimes, even when you built cases on precision and reason, you had to throw a little mud at the wall and see what stuck.

"Don't recognize him," he said, his eyes straying across the photo and then away again. He shifted back on the stool he was on, and his thin summer jacket opened a little. Underneath I could see a badge pinned to his shirt: DUNCAN PELL. I assumed, given he was at the gateline, that he was a regular customer-service assistant. It was hard to see him as anything more, as a station supervisor or duty station manager.

"Are you here permanently?" I asked.

His eyes came back to me. "What?"

"Do you always work out of this station?"

"Yeah," he said, a frown forming across his brow, as if I was suddenly speaking in a language he didn't understand. All the time his eyes continued darting left and right; to the gateline, then to the entrance, then back again. Basically anywhere but me.

"My guy used to pass through here every day."

Pell snorted. "So do a lot of people."

"You don't recognize any of the faces that pass through here?"

"Some."

"But not this one?"

I held up the photograph in front of him again. He glanced at it and away, off to where a group of girls in their late teens were entering the station. Then he shrugged. "It's busy," was all he offered, still watching the girls rather than me. I nodded, put the picture away, but didn't move. The momentary pause seemed to make him uncomfortable. His eyes switched to me, away, then back and there was something in them.

A flash of fear.

"Right, I'd better be off, Dunc." The other member of staff was back at the booth. He looked at me, looked at Pell, then must have assumed he'd interrupted a conversation, and held up both hands in apology. "Oh, sorry—didn't mean to jump in."

"It's fine," I said. "I think we're done."

Pell glanced at me sideways and then shifted away, further back into the booth. The other guy reached down and grabbed a portable ticket machine off the floor, slinging it over his shoulder. He was an RCI; a ticket inspector. When he came up, he looked between us again and must have sensed something was going on.

"Is everything okay?"

Pell didn't say anything, so I stepped forward and introduced myself. I held up the picture of Sam again. "Do you recognize him?"

The RCI patted the breast pockets of his jacket and then reached into the left one and removed a pair of half-moon glasses. He looked older than Pell—forty-three or forty-four—but was taller, broader and in better condition. His nose was uneven—angled slightly left—like it might once have been broken and not properly reset, and I wondered if he'd grown up in and around boxing clubs. He had the build of a middleweight. "Did he use this station?" he asked, eyes still studying the photograph.

"Every day."

But he'd already started shaking his head. He looked up, lips pursed, face telling me everything I needed to know. "I'm sorry. We get so many people through here."

I took the picture and thanked him.

"Did you recognize him, Dunc?" the man asked.

Pell's face dissolved into panic again as he was drawn back into the conversation. He ran a hand across his face, stubble crackling against his hands, and I saw he was wearing a silver ring with an old rune symbol imprinted on it. Then he looked down at the floor. He brushed an imaginary hair from the thigh of his trouser leg, cleared his throat, reached down further to his boots—black steel toe caps with red stitching in them—and scratched something else unseen from them. He didn't want to answer.

"Dunc?" the RCI asked again.

"No," Pell finally said, then quietly added, "No, I didn't."

The RCI started frowning, as if he didn't understand what was going on with Pell, then turned to me and shrugged. "I can ask around if you like."

"No, it's fine. It was a long shot."

"Okay, well, I'd better be off."

I nodded. "Thanks for your help."

He smiled and headed through the gateline. When I turned back to Pell, he was out of the booth and standing next to the ticket machines about thirty feet away—like he was trying to put some distance between us.

But it didn't matter.

Distance or not, I'd remember Duncan Pell.

16

Spike texted to tell me he'd e-mailed through Sam's financial history and phone records, so, back home, I made myself a sandwich, then sat down and booted up the computer. There were two PDFs waiting for me.

The first one took in everything he'd ever paid into or set up: bank accounts, credit cards, mortgages, ISAs, health care, insurance policies, pensions and student loans. A man's adult life reduced to twenty-five pages. There weren't many surprises, but there was a more detailed breakdown of the couple's life and health insurance, and a year's worth of statements from both bank accounts.

Sudden, unexplained changes in insurance policies are one of the warning signs in the moments before a person goes missing, but the Wrens' policies seemed pretty standard, and the premium had remained consistent for the last three years. The biggest concern, as Julia had outlined the day before, was their mortgage: they had just shy of £600,000 to pay back; massive by any standard.

I moved on to the bank statements.

The first set was for the Wrens' joint account. Before June 2011, they'd never been in the red. Then Julia's redundancy caught up with them. Suddenly they were struggling to make ends meet every month. The patterns of their life which had marked out the first three months of 2011—the restaurants they ate in, the cinemas they went to, the places they went on weekends—began to dry up, and soon the only constant was the lack of those things. By autumn 2011, they hardly seemed to go out at all.

The second set of bank statements was for Sam's own personal account, which had little activity, and none after the day he disappeared until it was closed on 3 April 2012. I flipped back through my notes to the discussion I'd had with Julia about their finances. Halfway down I'd written, "Julia had account closed and money transferred to joint account on 3 April this year." It must have been painful for her: the moment she finally accepted he was gone.

Sam's mobile was registered to Investment International but doubled up as a personal phone. In the second PDF, Spike had secured names and addresses for every incoming and outgoing number. During the week, most of the calls were to other businesses, or to clients, although there was at least one call a day made to Julia, a text or a call to his brother Robert, and more irregular calls to friends of his. The one he called most often was a guy called Iain Penny, but there were other repeats—David Werr, Abigail Camara, Esther Wilson, Ursula Gray—and when I cross-checked them with the list Julia had given me, I saw they were Investment International employees. On weekends, business-related calls were stripped out, leaving Julia, Robert Wren, Iain Penny—who, judging by the number of texts that had passed between them, was a good friend as well as a work colleague—and a few others: a cousin in Edinburgh, an aunt and uncle in Kent, a few to his boss, a man called Ross McGregor.

The document was split into two sections: twelve months of records for the period beginning 1 January 2011 and running through to the day Sam went missing on 16 December; then, secondly, the six months to 1 June this year. After 16 December there wasn't a single call made from the phone by Sam, but a lot of people had tried to call him: Julia, his brother, Ross McGregor, friends. There was a call from a number at the Met too, which was presumably PC Brian Westerley, who had opened the file on Sam.

Then I noticed something.

Cross-checking the phone records with Julia's list for a second time, I realized I'd made a small oversight: Ursula Gray. Her calls came during the same periods of time as the other people Sam worked with—between 9 a.m. and 7 p.m. on weekdays—but while Ross McGregor, David Werr, Abigail Camara, Esther Wilson and Iain Penny were all down on Julia's list of names as work colleagues of Sam, Ursula Gray wasn't.

She wasn't on the list at all.

Which meant Julia didn't know anything about her.

In the period between 7 January and 2 September 2011, Sam and Ursula Gray had had 97 telephone conversations with each other, and sent 186 texts. After 2 September, contact dropped off dramatically: 4 calls and 10 texts in September, half that in October and none at all in November and December.

Straight away, my thoughts turned back to the conversation I'd had with Julia the day before.

Did you think he might have been seeing someone else?

Because he was working so many hours?

Right.

I really don't think so.

You never had any reason to suspect him?

No.

You didn't entertain the possibility?

I thought about it a lot at the start. I checked his e-mail, checked his phone, but Sam just . . . For a man, he didn't have much of a sex drive.

I wrote down Ursula Gray's name and address.

Julia seemed unconvinced by the idea of Sam cheating on her, though I wondered how much was belief and how much was denial. In reality, nothing in the phone records backed her up. And, sooner or later, it seemed likely she'd have to face the truth about her husband: that he'd lied to her—and, worse, that the man she thought she knew, she didn't really know at all.

17

Investment International was on the thirty-seventh floor of One Canada Square, right at the heart of Canary Wharf. Around it, vast buildings climbed their way into the cloudless sky, its color an unending blue like the surface of a glacial lake. The size of the towers seemed only to amplify the heat, as if there were no space for it to escape, and One Canada Square was the biggest of them all: fifty stories high, a mountain of steel and glass, its windows blinking in the sun like thousands of eyes.

I'd called ahead to check with the receptionist that Sam's boss and friend Ross McGregor was in, but only that. I didn't speak to him, or anyone else. The more time you gave people to prepare, the easier it was for them to bury their secrets. That was assuming McGregor—or anyone else at Investment International—had any secrets to bury.

I entered the building, crossed the foyer and rode the elevator up.

Ten seconds later, the doors opened out on to a smart reception area with brushed glass panels running the length of the room on my left, a curved front desk in front of that, and black leather sofas in a line on the right. Beyond the sofas were floor-to-ceiling windows with fantastic views toward South Quay.

"Can I help you, sir?"

The receptionist looked like she'd left school about five minutes ago: she couldn't have even been nineteen, her blond hair scraped back into a ponytail, her skin flawless. She had the traces of a south London accent, but was obviously trying to put the brakes on it now she was working out of a Canary Wharf office block.

"I'm here to see Ross McGregor."

"Do you have an appointment?"

"I don't, no."

She blinked. "Uh, okay."

"My name's David Raker. I'm sure he'll be able to spare the time to see me." I gave her my best smile. "I'll wait over here."

I went and sat by the window and looked at the view. The receptionist made a call, but I couldn't hear exactly what was being said; her voice was lost behind the drone of a plane close by, dropping out of the sky toward London City Airport. After a couple of minutes she came over and told me McGregor wouldn't be long, and then offered me something to drink. I thanked her and asked for a glass of water.

Ross McGregor emerged a quarter of an hour later and was immediately on the defensive, a scowl on his face, suspicion in his eyes as he zeroed in on me. He was a tall man in his thirties, with thick black hair—glistening slightly—swept back from his face, blue eyes and pockmarked skin. As I stood and waited for him to come over, I saw he was wearing a blue and white pinstripe shirt, a terrible maroon tie and thick black braces. *Wall Street* was obviously a film that didn't come out of his DVD player much.

"Mr. McGregor, my name's David Raker."

I held out my hand and he took it gingerly. "Ross McGregor," he said, eyes still narrowed. "What is it I can do for you?"

"I'm here about Sam Wren."

His expression immediately softened. "Oh. Right."

"Julia said you wouldn't mind if I came over."

It wasn't strictly true, but already the dynamic had changed. McGregor had known Sam since university, had headhunted him for the company. I was playing on their friendship, using it as a way in.

"Do you have a few minutes, Mr. McGregor?"

It looked like the wind had been taken out of his sails. He'd puffed himself up at the thought of coming out here to see me, readied himself for a fight. I wasn't sure who he'd expected—because I wasn't sure who would drop by an investment firm, thirty-seven floors up, on the off-chance of a meeting with the MD—but he hadn't expected me and he hadn't expected to hear the name Sam Wren.

"Mr. McGregor?"

He seemed to start, as if he'd drifted away. "Let's go through," he said, gesturing toward a door at the far end of the glass panels.

We passed the front desk, where he told his receptionist to bring us some coffee, and then moved through the door. On the other side of the panels was a room about the same length as the reception area with sixteen desks in it, all of them filled. Some of his employees were on the phone, some were staring into their monitors.

McGregor veered left toward an L-shaped kink in the room. Off to the right was his office. It was entirely encased in glass, standing on its own like a transparent mausoleum. There were no windows on this part of the floor, but any potential darkness was offset by a series of bright halogen lamps running across the ceiling. Inside was his desk, a big leather chair, filing cabinets lined up behind him and a second table with six chairs around it, which I assumed he used for meetings. His screensaver was an extreme close-up of the side of a pound coin, shot in black and white. We sat down at the second table and he pushed the door shut.

"I didn't know Julia was trying to find him," McGregor said as he shuffled in at the table. "When did this start?"

"Tuesday."

He nodded. "You had any joy?"

"Not yet." I got out my notepad, laid it on the table, and then removed a business card and pushed it across the desk toward him. "I find people," I said, "but not for the police or any other agency. Just so we're clear."

"You work for yourself?"

"Yes."

He leaned back in his chair. "Do you get many jobs?"

"Well, I'm not on the breadline." But I could see in his face what he really wanted to ask: how much money did I make? "Can you tell me how you first got to know Sam, and how he ended up here?"

"Sure." He paused. He looked much more composed now. "We both did Banking and Finance at London Met. I was a mature student. Arsed around for a couple of years after school, did some traveling, that kind of thing. Then came back, signed up for the course, and that was how I got to know Sam. I only really became friendly with him in the second year, but we hit it off straight away. After finishing, he went into the graduate program at HSBC and I got a job at J. P. Morgan. He didn't really like the people at HSBC so he jumped at the chance to move across to JPM with me."

"Working with you, or for you?"

"For me," he said, picking a hair off his cuff.

"And then you left J. P. Morgan?"

"Yeah." He shrugged. "I got the hump with a couple of the bosses there, and just fancied trying something myself. So I set up this place."

"What do you do here?"

"We make people lots of money," he said, like it was the dumbest question he'd heard all day. "That's the bottom line. We specialize in emerging markets: Russia, Latin America, the Middle East, the Far East. That's why I poached Sam. He knows those markets. I didn't just hire him 'cause he was my mate."

"So he was good at what he did?"

"Very good."

"No problems you can remember?"

"None."

"He didn't run into any trouble with anyone?"

"What do you mean?"

"I'm looking for a reason he might have left. One of the possibilities is that he ran into problems here: lost a client money, got tied up in something he shouldn't have."

McGregor made an *oh* expression. "I doubt it."

"Why?"

"I run a tight ship. I like to keep an eye on what's happening out there. This is my baby. My investment. It's in my interests to keep the balance sheet close because I need to make sure we're not losing our clients money and pissing away the goodwill we've built up over the last five years. Most of my people out there, they're good, but they need a steady hand. Someone to step in and tell them what to do, and make sure they're not making bad decisions. Sam was different."

"He didn't need his hand held?"

"I'd pull him in here for a meeting now and again, but mostly I let him run riot. He was my biggest earner. I cut him some slack."

I got the sense that, in a weird way, McGregor was enjoying this: being the center of attention, being some kind of go-to man in the hunt for Sam. In fact, as I studied him—his eyes scanning the office like it was a palace—I realized whatever friendship had existed between the two of them had always been a firm second place to status in McGregor's eyes. His job, the money he made, wandering the office as the boss—that was what was important to him; not Sam, not the people out there working for him.

"Julia mentioned that things have been tough recently."

McGregor looked disappointed I'd brought it up. "Yeah. Things have been hard since the economy went down the shitter. But it's the same for everybody."

"You froze wages and cut bonuses, correct?"

His eyes narrowed. "Yeah."

"I'm just trying to find out why Sam left."

"Well, he didn't leave because his wages were frozen."

"What makes you say that?"

"I froze them in December 2010. He left in December 2011. If he had a serious problem with me trying to save his job by freezing his money, he wouldn't have spent a year thinking about it, then buggered off without saying anything."

His eyes flicked to the door behind me and the receptionist came in, a carafe of coffee in one hand, two mugs in the other. She laid it all down on the table and started to pour. She asked if I wanted milk, but I told her black was fine. She knew how McGregor took it without asking. After she was done, his eyes lingered on her as she left.

"So, you think he would have come to see you if there was a problem, either with the job, with a client or with the wage structure?"

"Definitely."

"Was he the kind of guy to speak his mind?"

He shrugged. "We were mates, but he knew who was in charge."

We'd returned to McGregor's favorite conversation topic: him as boss. Either he was paranoid about his staff challenging his position of authority, or being in charge was a drug he couldn't get enough of. Either way, it was starting to piss me off.

"Was Sam any different in the six months before he vanished? Maybe he wasn't as effective at his job, or he seemed distracted by something?"

"Not that I noticed. He was bringing in money and developing his client base, and that was . . ." He stopped himself. He was about to say, *and that was all I cared about*, but—even to his ears—it sounded like the wrong thing to admit out loud. McGregor would only have noticed something was up with Sam if it had impacted negatively on his bottom line. In an emotional sense, he had no opinion of his friend, if he was ever really that. This conversation was going nowhere.

"Was there anyone else Sam worked closely with here?"

He eyed me as if unsure of where I was going. "What do you mean?"

"I mean, was there anyone—"

And then his phone started ringing. He plucked the receiver from its cradle. "Ross McGregor." He listened for a couple of seconds. "No, I absolutely did *not* tell him that. I told him we would be selective about the type of opportunity we'd present him. There's a difference." More silence. "He hasn't got the first idea about nickel export. He probably wouldn't be able to tell you where Norilsk is on a map." He listened for a few seconds more. "Okay, I'll be round in a minute." He put the phone down. "I've got a mini emergency."

"I can wait here."

He looked toward the filing cabinets at the back. "No offense, but I can't leave you alone. Half the company secrets are in here."

"Can I have a look at Sam's workstation?"

"No. You'll need a warrant for that. There's too much sensitive information on there, and I can't have you poking around in our client database. We've cleared most of Sam's personal stuff out anyway, if that's what you were after."

"I'd like to ask around out there, then."

He glanced at his watch and made no effort to suppress a sigh. I didn't care that he was annoyed. He may have been his boss, he may have thought of himself as a friend, but he wasn't close to Sam, and that made McGregor a dead end. But there was still the possibility that someone at Investment International knew what was playing on Sam's mind in those last few months.

"Yeah, all right," he said finally. "But don't distract them too much."

18

McGregor took me out onto the floor and introduced me to everyone. I watched the faces of his employees as he told them I was trying to find Sam. Some reacted, some didn't. Then he pointed toward a small meeting room on the far side of the office, wedged in a space next to the kitchen. I set up in there and started inviting them in one by one.

The first couple of interviews produced nothing more than an idea of how the office was divided: on one side were the people—mostly in their twenties—who went out drinking together three or four times a week; on the other—overwhelmingly, men and women with kids—was a separate group who headed home as soon as work was done. Everyone got on during the day, they told me, but the ones who did the drinking spent their whole week with half an eye on Friday. Friday was the big night out.

Six interviews in, I met Abigail Camara, one of the prominent names on Sam's phone records. "He sat opposite me," she said, proper East End accent, "so we used to have a lot of banter during the week. We were both big football fans. He was a Gooner, I've got a West Ham season ticket. That's what we generally used to text each other about. Taking the piss and that."

"Did you notice any change in him before he disappeared?"

"Change?"

"Did he seem any different?"

She shrugged. "Not really. He was always a pleasant fella. He took his work seriously, but he always gave you the time of day. I liked him a lot."

A few others failed to add much to my picture of Sam, then another name from Julia's list, and Sam's phone records, came to see me: Dave Werr. Almost off the bat, he started telling me a story about how they'd once dragged Sam kicking and screaming into a strip club. "This was, like, a couple of years back," Werr said, smile on his face. "We'd been out on the razz on a Friday, just like normal, but it was friggin' freezing and the girls didn't want to leave the wine bar we were in. So we split, grabbed Sammy and got the Tube across town to a strip club one of the boys had complimentaries for." He broke off and laughed; a long, annoying noise like a hyena. "Sam looked like he was shitting himself."

"He didn't seem keen?"

"He didn't fancy it at all." He laughed again and then, when that had died down, gave a little shrug. "Sammy just wasn't that sort of boy. Wasn't a Jack-the-Lad type. He liked a few jars with us—liked a laugh— but he was all about his missus."

"All about her how?"

"Some Fridays, and a few week nights too, he'd tell us he had to get home to her. He'd get twitchy, y'know. Be looking at his watch. And then all of a sudden, he'd be up on his feet and telling us he was leaving. When we asked him why, he said it was 'cause he wanted to get back and spend the evening with her. The women thought it was sweet—but the blokes thought he was wet." Werr let out another blast of his laugh.

"Was he always like that?"

"Into his missus?" He paused; thought about it. "Probably more later on."

"When's later on?"

"The last seven or eight months, I guess."

It was totally at odds with how Julia had described that last half-year: she'd said he'd become distant and highly strung, that he was never home until she was in bed.

"Did he ever mention anyone called Ursula Gray to you?"

"Who?"

"Ursula Gray."

A blank look and then a shake of the head. "No."

As Werr headed back to his desk, I felt a pang of sadness for Julia Wren: she was paying me to find her husband with what little money she had left, unaware of the lies he'd told and the secrets he'd taken with him. I needed to find out who Ursula Gray was, because that was what Julia had—indirectly—asked me to do. And once I had the answer, I would be closer than ever to finding out why Sam left. But if he'd been having an affair, there would be no happy ending for Julia Wren.

19

"What is it you wanted to see me about, Healy?"

Healy looked across the desk at DCI Craw, and then out through a glass panel to the CID office beyond her. It was seven in the evening and no one had gone home. Detectives were at workstations, talking to each other or on the phone, solemn expressions on every face. Some were facing the map of London at the other end of the office, red pen marking out key areas and coming off in lines to photocopies and Post-it notes. At the very top, the photographs of the two missing men: Wilky and Evans.

"Healy?"

"I wanted to talk to you about my role here, ma'am."

She raised an eyebrow. "Really?"

"I wanted to see if I could be of more use to you."

"In what way?"

He glanced out into the CID office and then back to Craw. "I understand there are people who don't think I should be here," he said to her, and as she shifted in her seat, coming forward, he could smell a hint of citrus on her. "And I know, with the greatest of respect, ma'am, that you're probably one of them."

She frowned. "Don't second-guess me, Healy."

"I wasn't—"

"You don't know what my position is. I've never made that clear."

He nodded. "I just wanted to tell—"

"No, let me tell *you* a few things," she said, leaning on her desk and dragging a mug of tea across to her. "You're—what? Forty-seven?"

"Yes, ma'am."

"And you've been on the force how long?"

"Twenty-six years."

She leaned back in her seat again and pulled open the top drawer of her desk. A second later she dropped a file down in front of her. It was Healy's. "This," she said, pointing to the file, "is why a lot of people don't think you should be here." She let the pages of the file fall past her thumb, a waterfall of paper passing across her skin. "When you went looking for your daughter off the books, when you teamed up with a civilian, when you waved a gun in another officer's face, you took twenty-six years of your career and pissed it up against the wall."

She looked at him from under the ridge of her brow, as if waiting for a reaction. He wasn't going to give her one. Instead, he just focused on her face, on not breaking her gaze. He'd spent the last thirty-eight days batting off questions and taunts; trying to prove he could restrain himself, that he regretted his actions, that he was someone different now. But the truth was, he wasn't different.

And he didn't regret anything.

He didn't regret going after the piece of shit that took his girl, and he didn't regret going up against the cops who tried to stop him. He could play their games now, he could act how they wanted him to, but it would never change how he felt: he could never forgive cops like Davidson and Sallows for trying to get in the way of him finding Leanne. In their eyes, he was some sort of heretic: the traitor, the backstabber, the man who showed no contrition about the things he'd done. To him, they were even less than that. If they hated him, he hated them more.

"Are you too old to change, Colm?"

He looked at her. Her voice was softer now, and the change threw him for a moment. "No, ma'am," he said. "I don't believe I am."

"Are you going to make me look like an arsehole?"

"In what way, ma'am?"

"If I give you a little rope," she said, eyes fixed on him, same expression on her face, "if I give you a little rope, are you going to hang me with it?"

He studied her. She was quite attractive—slate-gray eyes, a face full of sharp angles—but she gave off the air of not being too particular about how she looked. Her hair was short, tucked behind her ears and swept across her forehead at the front. It was a haircut built for practicality, for the job, just like everything else: gray trouser suit, and no jewelery apart from a thin wedding band and an even thinner gold chain.

"Healy?"

He looked out to where Davidson was sitting at one of the computers. When Healy turned back to Craw, she'd swivelled in her seat, following his line of sight.

"If you give me a chance, ma'am, I will show you what I can do."

Craw's eyes were fixed on Davidson, who was up and moving around the office. "He outranks you now. How does that make you feel?"

"It doesn't make me feel anything, ma'am."

She smiled. "I'm new in this station but I know a little of your history, and I think we can safely say that your best days were a few years back." She reached forward to a picture frame on the desk—one facing away from Healy—and turned it so he could see. It contained a photo of her, with two teenage girls. "I don't condone what you did, but I get it. Someone takes something from you, you have to claim it back. Until you've had kids, you don't understand that." He tried not to show his surprise, but she must have seen a change in his face: she nodded once, as if to tell him he'd heard correctly, but then caution filled her eyes. "Like I said, though—I don't condone it. You were rash and you were stupid. You put people's lives at risk, as well as your own."

Silence settled across the office. She rocked gently back and forth in her seat, her eyes moving to a second window, which looked out over the station car park. In the darkness, snow was falling, passing under the fluorescent orange glow of the security lights. When the wind picked up, flakes were blown in against the glass, making a soft noise like fat crackling in a pan.

"What's your personal situation now?"

"Personal situation, ma'am?"

"Are you still with your wife?"

"I'm not sure I understand the relevance of—"

"Are you still with her?"

Healy paused. "No. We're separated."

Craw eyed him. "This isn't the speech the chief super wants me to make to you. It's probably not the speech most of them out there want me to make to you either. But I've watched you over the past month and a half, and—even before you came to me today—I'd been thinking about how we could better harness what skills you have. I needed to see that you were prepared to keep your head down. I needed to see that you were willing to show restraint." She paused; eyed him. "Truth is, we're short on numbers and we're in need of experience. So if I give you some rope, the fewer distractions you have, the less you have to go home to, the better it is for me."

"Yes, ma'am."

"But if you make me look like an arsehole, even once . . ."

"I won't."

A long silence and then she snapped his file shut. "What do you know about the Snatcher?"

He looked out into the office, to the cops working the case and then to the two faces on the wall above the corkboard. "Two victims so far. Steven Wilky and Marc Evans. He takes them from their houses at night. No bodies. No trace of the victims."

"What else?"

"There's never any sign of a break-in, which suggests he knows the victims, or has at least befriended them prior to taking them. They're both men, both about the same age—late twenties to early thirties— and they're both homosexual. There are text messages from the suspect on the victims' phones, but nothing we can use: he purchases a new SIM card and phone each time, in cash, giving a bogus home address, then he dumps the phone somewhere we can't find it. He never uses e-mail, social networking or picture messaging."

"Anything else about the victims?"

"They're both small men. I think I read one of them was only five-five."

"So?"

He studied her. She wasn't asking because she didn't know the answer. She was asking because she was testing him. "So, smaller men fit his fantasy."

"And?"

"And they provide less resistance. He's probably bigger than them, which is how he's able to overpower them."

"What else?"

"The hair."

"What about it?"

"He shaves their heads before he takes them and he leaves the hair in a pile at the end of their beds."

"Why do you think he does that?"

Healy paused. "Maybe he's trying to dehumanize them."

"In what way?"

"Perhaps he feels that, by removing their hair, he's removing their dignity. Forcing them further into a position of inferiority. That's how he would want them."

She started turning her mug, her mind ticking over. "You seem to know the case pretty well for someone who's been working burglaries for five weeks."

"I've just overheard things."

A smile drifted across her face. She didn't believe him. She'd seen right through the lie: with no one to go home to, he'd used the late nights to go through the Policy Logs and the HOLMES data. "Tonight, I want you to take copies of the victims' files home with you—officially. I want you to read them, and I want you to know them better than anyone else out there."

"Yes, ma'am."

"Because tomorrow morning I want you in at 6 a.m. on the dot. If you're even one minute late, you'll be back to working burglaries."

"I won't be."

She looked up at him. "You've got a lot to prove, Healy." He didn't respond, because he didn't agree with her, but he let her know he was willing to play ball. "I need you to be better than everyone else. You make one mistake and we're both in the shit. So bring your wits with you, and whatever it was that used to make you good. Because from tomorrow, you're working the Snatcher. And you're going to help nail him to the wall."

20

An hour later, there were only two members of I2 left to interview. The first, Iain Penny, was one of the dominant numbers on Sam's records, and Julia had listed him as one of Sam's best friends. He was in his late thirties, pale and tubby, but well groomed.

I reintroduced myself to him and told him what I did. It was basically an exercise in making him feel good: how, because of his relationship to Sam, he was my best hope of finding him, how the rest of the office had said he was the person to speak to. He wasn't much of a challenge to read: when he spoke it was without hesitancy, his eyes reflecting the words coming out of his mouth, all of which was a pretty good sign. I'd interviewed plenty of liars and eventually a secret started to weigh heavy, even for the good ones; Penny didn't look like he had much to hide.

"How long have you known Sam?"

"He joined I2 before me," Penny said, "but when I started, I was put on the desk next to him and Ross asked Sam to kind of take me under his wing. We pretty much hit it off from the start. Sam was like the unofficial boss on the floor, so we all looked up to him and respected him, but he would muck in and help us out, and he'd always be there for you. That's why we liked him."

"He was universally liked at I2?"

"Yeah, definitely."

No one had said otherwise in the interviews that morning. In fact, the standard response, pretty much from the beginning of the case, was that Sam was a lovely guy.

A lovely guy who lied to his wife.

"You were his best mate at I2?"

"That's how I saw it," he said. He shrugged. "But then he upped and left without saying anything to me. This is a guy I've known for four years, a guy I used to socialize with, talk to and text all the time. My girlfriend and I used to get together with Sam and Julia on weekends; be round there for barbecues or out on the town. We went away for weekends with them, helped them move house when they bought that place in Kensington, looked after it when they were away. I thought we were pretty close. It always felt that way. But, like I say, maybe he felt differently."

"So it was a surprise when he disappeared?"

"A complete shock."

"You never saw it coming?"

"No. Not at all." He paused, but I sensed there was more to come. "He did change a bit toward the end. Not massively. I'm sure most people at I2 didn't even notice. But I knew him better than most—and I could definitely see it."

"What do you mean by 'change'?"

He shrugged. "Just got quieter, you know? Sam always used to joke around, join in with the banter." He smiled. "He used to do a cracking impression of Ross, actually."

"And he wasn't like that at the end?"

"No. Definitely not."

"Did he ever confide in you as to why?"

"No. Like I say, maybe he just felt differently to me."

After Penny disappeared back to his desk, I watched the last of I2's employees come across the floor toward me. She was attractive: five-eight, slim, dressed in a tailored skirt suit, with shoulder-length black hair and dark eyes. She introduced herself as Esther Wilson, another name on the list, and when she said she was from Sydney, I put her at ease with some talk about the city's beaches.

After a few minutes I returned to Sam.

"I didn't know him that well," she said. "We used to go out—a big group of us—and I'd chat to him, like I'd chat to any of the guys on the floor. We texted a few times, mostly about work stuff. I knew him as a colleague, but I wouldn't be able to tell you anything about him as a person; any family stuff. Only what I've heard about him since."

"Which is what?"

"Obviously everyone talked about him a lot when he went missing. Everyone had a theory on where he might have gone, and why."

"What was your theory?"

"I didn't really have one. Like I said, I didn't know his personal circumstances, so I'd just be speculating."

"So what would you speculate?"

She shrugged. "I know Sam was pissed off when the pay freeze kicked in. We all were. It affected us all. But I think it got harder for Sam when his wife was made redundant." A pause. "Iain said she was laid off some time last year."

"Do you and Iain talk a lot?"

"We work together. We both do a lot of business in Russia, so it's not unusual for us to chat over coffee and after work. Him and Sam were good mates—I think he felt like he needed to offload on someone after Sam left. I was just around."

I made some notes. "What was Iain's theory, then?"

Movement passed across her face, and I could see the answer: that Iain had had a theory, but not one he'd shared with the other people on the floor. "You'd really be better off speaking to Iain," she said. "I don't like getting involved in stuff like this."

"Stuff like what?"

She shifted in her seat, her eyes flicking to me, then out through the window behind me. For the first time she looked uncomfortable. But then, a second later, she managed to completely change her expression, as if she'd raised a disguise. I wasn't sure whether she was hesitant because she genuinely didn't like office gossip, or because I'd strayed close to something and now she was trying to back away from it.

"Ever hear Sam talk about a woman called Ursula Gray?"

Her face remained impassive. "Ursula?"

"Gray."

Another shake of the head. "No, I haven't heard that name before."

Normally I could get a handle on people pretty quickly, but Esther Wilson was different. Phlegmatic. Cool. I thanked her and watched her go. When she got to her desk, she opened the top drawer, reached in and took out a packet of cigarettes. I scooped up my notes and walked to the door of the office just in time to hear her tell one of the others that she was heading out for a smoke.

21

Esther Wilson headed out of the big glass doors of One Canada Square. As soon as she was outside, she swung her bag across to her front and started to dig around inside, taking out her mobile. Then she crossed South Colonnade and headed toward Jubilee Park. I was eighty yards back, on the opposite side of the road, where the shade had formed in thin strips around the bases of the towers. Eventually, as she entered the park, the shade disappeared and I had to hang back and watch her cut across the grass and find a bench facing the Citigroup Center. She was talking to someone on her phone.

The call lasted about three minutes. After she was done, she remained where she was but kept looking back across her shoulder to Heron Quays. She seemed flustered. About five minutes after that, she glanced back again—around fifty feet to the right of where I was standing—and spotted someone, giving them a quick wave. The park and its approach was crowded, so it was difficult to zero in on who it was until another woman broke through, making a beeline for the bench. She looked about the same age as Esther and wasn't too dissimilar in looks: slim and attractive, a little taller, but not by much. She had blond hair, scraped back into a ponytail, a red skirt and a white blouse.

The woman perched herself on the bench and Esther immediately launched into conversation. No smile, no greeting. The blonde didn't seem perturbed, as if she expected it to be like that, which presumably meant she was the woman Esther had called. I moved a little closer, positioning myself against one of the park's snaking stone walls, and got a clearer view of the other woman. If she'd walked here—if Esther had phoned her out of the blue in the middle of the afternoon—then her work must have been somewhere close by. That was backed up by the fact that she hadn't brought anything out with her. No bag. No jacket. Esther thumbed open a packet of cigarettes and offered one to the woman.

The conversation went on for a couple of minutes, the other woman eventually taking part. But mostly it was Esther talking. Finally, the blonde reached out, put a hand on Esther's arm and spoke sternly and seriously to her. When she was done, she stubbed her cigarette out and then—looking at her watch—got up and left.

I followed her, leaving Esther on the bench, back across the park in the direction of the docks. She wasn't heading for the bridge across to the South Quay, so she had to be heading into one of the buildings running in an L-shape around Bank Street, right in front of us. The routes and grass verges of the park were busy so it became easy to merge with the crowds, but I kept a good distance just in case. On the other side of the park, she moved in a diagonal toward 40 Bank Street, a thirty-three-floor tower toward the corner of Heron Quays. I made up some of the distance between us and, as she entered the foyer, stepped through after her and followed her around, past the front desk, to the elevators. I didn't look much like I belonged in the world of investment banking, but no one paid me much attention as I waited, just behind the woman, for the lift to arrive. Twenty seconds later, the elevator doors slid open and we both stepped in.

I moved past her to the back. She didn't even look up. By now she had her phone out and was scrolling through her messages. A couple of others shuffled into the space. One older guy—in a dark, expensively tailored suit—looked me up and down like I'd just crawled out of the sewer, but by the time the doors closed, everyone was facing forward, there was silence, and the space had filled with the choking stench of male aftershave.

The woman was across from me, on the other side of the elevator, half turned, her hip against the side of the lift, her eyes fixed on her phone. Up close, she seemed older—early thirties—but she was still very attractive. There was a hint of Asian in her, in the shape of her eyes, in her nose and chin, but you could only see it if you looked hard.

The elevator pinged, she looked up and, when the doors opened, she moved left and out of sight. This time I let her go. On the wall in front of me was the name of her firm: Michaelhouse Credit.

Back out in the sun, I grabbed my phone, went to the browser and found Michaelhouse Credit on the Web. Halfway down, they had a "Meet the Team" page. The woman wasn't on there. It was just management. I scrolled further down and found a list of partners: other financial firms in Canary Wharf that the company worked alongside.

This'll have to be my route in.

I dialed the number for the company and waited for it to connect.

"Michaelhouse Credit."

"Oh, hi. My name's Alex Murphy and I'm calling from Credit Suisse.

I just had a meeting with one of your team but she didn't leave her name or contact details with me."

"Oh, I'm sorry, sir," the woman said. "Shall I put you through to the—"

"She had blond hair and was wearing a red skirt."

"Oh, that's Ursula."

"Ursula. *Right*."

"Ursula Gray."

22

Ursula Gray emerged from the elevator into the cool, air-conditioned lobby at 40 Bank Street just after 5:15. I was right across the foyer from her, leaning against the glass front. Three or four men followed her out and they were all looking at her. It wasn't hard to see why. Not only was she beautiful, but she was immaculately dressed. Her blond hair hung loose at her shoulders now, not in a ponytail like earlier. As soon as she was out of the lift, she took her phone from her handbag and started checking it.

"Ursula?"

When she heard her name, she glanced toward me, automatically closing in on herself. It was a natural defensive movement. She didn't think she knew me, and—even though the foyer of the building was thick with other office workers—she couldn't be sure what I wanted. I held up a hand to tell her everything was fine and, as I took another step toward her, there was a flicker of recognition in her eyes. We'd never met but Esther would have given her my name and it didn't take much work in Google to find details of my previous cases and pictures of how I looked.

"I'm David Raker."

She chose not to reply initially, but then she seemed to change her mind, as if her silence was some sort of indication of guilt. "Do I know you?"

"Yes," I said. "You do."

"I'm pretty sure I don—"

"You were with Esther Wilson in the park today."

A momentary pause. Nothing in her face. "I'm sorry?"

"I know who you are, Ursula. You know who I am. I don't care what you've done, all I care about is Sam Wren."

No response.

"I'm trying to find out where he went."

"What's that got to do with me?"

I didn't bother replying to that: she saw the answer in my face. "Why don't you let me buy you a drink?"

We found a bar on South Colonnade. On the walk over, Ursula didn't say much. Maybe she was working out a plan. That was the downside with cold-calling people who had something to hide: they automatically felt the need to suppress and create because they hadn't prepared and were scared about saying the wrong thing.

I ordered a beer and she asked for a glass of wine.

"Julia Wren has asked me to find out what happened to Sam."

She brushed some hair away from her eyes but didn't say anything.

"I think you can help me."

"How?"

I took a copy of Sam's phone records out of my pocket and unfolded it in front of her. "This shows that you two called each other 97 times between 7 January and 2 September last year, and you sent each other 186 texts."

A flutter of panic for the first time. "What are you talking about?"

"You know what I'm talking about," I said, and turned the phone records around so she could see her number, his number, the minutes they'd spent talking and the texts they'd sent. "I don't care what it was that you and Sam were doing. I don't. Really. But I've been paid to find out what happened to him—and that's what I'm going to do."

The bar was crowded now, music and laughter and mobile phone conversations in the background—but all I got from Ursula Gray was silence.

"Ursula?"

She shook her head. "I . . . I don't know where to . . ."

"Were you sleeping with Sam?"

She reached out for her wine glass and slid it toward her. No indication that she was or wasn't. No indication she'd even heard the question. But then she shivered—as if a long-dead memory had crawled its way out of the ground—and looked up. "Yes," she said quietly, taking a sip from her glass, her eyes fixed on a space off to my left. "I wanted to be with him."

"Did he want to be with you?"

"At the time I thought he did. But at the end . . ." She smiled momentarily, but it wasn't a smile with any warmth and, for the first time, her defenses were down.

"You started seeing him in January last year?"

"Yes."

"How did it begin?"

"Michaelhouse were doing some work with I2, and he was seconded across to my office. He trained me, I trained him, we sat next to one another and forged a good friendship. There was flirting too, I guess." Another smile, this time more genuine. "A *lot* of flirting. And then, one night just before Christmas, we all went to the same party—this event over at the North Quay site—that Esther had got us tickets for. I'd just split up from my boyfriend, Esther didn't know much about Sam's personal circumstances, and I didn't bother to ask. We flirted, we got drunk. That was how it began."

"Did you sleep together that night?"

She glanced at me, a mixture of embarrassment and incredulity. And then reality seemed to kick in and she realized that their secret wasn't a secret any more.

"No, we didn't sleep together that night."

"So, what happened?"

"We just kissed."

"You already knew Esther?"

She nodded. "I've known her for years. She's one of my best friends. We went to university together, did the same course, lived in the same house."

"Did she know about you and Sam?"

"No. Not during the time it was going on." She looked down into her wine glass. "I told her after Sam went missing, though. I hated not being able to tell anyone. Bottling it up only made it worse. So I told her, but made her promise to keep it to herself."

Which was why she'd lied to me: to protect her friend.

I backtracked. "How did Sam react the day after you kissed?"

"He was cold as ice," she said distantly, replaying the morning after in her head. "He didn't talk to me for a couple of weeks. That really hurt. But then, slowly, he started to come back round, and one day at lunch we got chatting about what had happened."

"What did he say?"

"He said he liked it."

"That was when the affair began?"

"Yes." She traced a finger through the condensation on the side of her wine glass. "That was when it began. He came back to my place after work one Friday evening."

"And after that?"

"After that . . ." Her eyes flicked to me and away: more embarrassment, but not about the affair, or the idea of it, but about having to reveal details of their sex life to a stranger. "Are you asking me how often we had sex?" she said finally, trying to paint me as some kind of voyeur.

"I want to understand why Sam left."

She sighed. "We would do it every day at work. We found an empty office on the forty-sixth floor in Sam's building and we'd go there."

"What about evenings?"

"Sometimes, if he convinced her he was working late."

"Weekends?"

"No. Never weekends."

That tallied with what the phone records showed: there were no conversations between Sam and Ursula on Saturdays and Sundays. "Why not weekends?"

"He wanted to be with her."

"It sounds like he was conflicted."

"He was. I think he always loved her, even when we were doing what we were doing. He told me a couple of times he wondered what life would be like with me, if we were a couple, but that was about as far as it went. I wanted him more than he wanted me. I . . ." A pause. "I felt something for him. I thought he felt something for me. But now I can see the relationship for what it was. I can see what he wanted from it."

"Which was what?"

"Sex," she said, as if the answer was obvious. "I was like a bloody schoolgirl; so wrapped up in it, I couldn't see the difference."

"Did he ever talk about his sex life with Julia?"

"A little."

"What did he say?"

"He said he didn't fancy her."

For a man, Sam didn't have much of a sex drive, Julia had said to me.

"Did he say why he didn't fancy her?"

"No." She brushed more hair away from her eyes. "He obviously loved her. I could see that after a while; can certainly see it now. But he used to say—when it came to sex—she didn't do it for him."

"In what way?"

"In any way."

I wrote that down. It seemed weird that he would feel like that about Julia—and yet still commit to getting married.

"Do you think he cheated on her before he met you?"

"No."

"How come?"

She looked out through the windows of the bar. "He was ballsy and confident in his work, single-minded, which was why I was attracted to him in the first place. But he wasn't like that at all in bed. Not to start with, anyway. He seemed almost . . . inexperienced."

"How?"

A frown cut across her face, but it was more a look of discomfort than anything else. "Maybe 'inexperienced' is the wrong word," she said, "because that suggests he didn't know what he was doing. He definitely knew what he was doing. But there was always . . ." She faded out, and then looked up. She wasn't going to finish. I didn't know if it was because she couldn't articulate what she meant—or she was hiding something. There seemed to be a hint of a half-truth in her eyes, a flicker, a shadow, but not enough for me to build an accusation on.

"There was always what?" I pressed.

"I think he was twisted up over what we were doing."

"He felt guilty about cheating on Julia?"

"Yes."

"Is that why you think he cooled things off toward the end?"

She seemed surprised I knew about the change in their relationship, but the phone records showed the calls and texts between the two of them had started to die out from 2 September. The relationship had been burning itself out. "In the last two or three months, he'd tell me he was busy over lunch, or pretend he had a meeting, or had to work late," she said, not exactly answering the question, and I decided not to jump in but come back to it later. "He just changed."

"Changed how?"

"Became different. Preoccupied."

"Did you ever talk about it?"

"I never got the chance. He became very quiet, really highly strung and stressed out. It was never like that before. He was easy-going and fun."

This was returning to the same place all conversations about Sam seemed to retreat to: he was a nice guy, he was easy-going, he didn't have any reason to leave, but he changed in those last few months. The minor details were different, but everyone was saying the same thing. His finances, his affair, how he felt about Julia, everyone had a theory, but no one had an answer.

"Nothing else sticks with you?" I asked.

She glanced at me, down to her wine, then back up. A frown formed on her face. "There was this one time . . ." She paused again, trying to recall the details; rubbed a hand across her forehead. "It was about two or three months after we started seeing each other. He came back to my place for a couple of hours and we . . ." She looked at me. *Had sex*. I nodded for her to continue. "Anyway, he started to ask about my previous relationships."

"What did he ask?"

"It was weird. He wanted to know the details. Like, *all* the details. He wanted to know how long I'd gone out with each of them, how many times I'd slept with them, what our sex life was like, that kind of thing." She paused, forefinger and thumb pinching the neck of her glass. "I only really thought about it after he disappeared, because it never struck me as odd at the time. We weren't married, we were just having sex. Him wanting to know what I'd done, what I liked, it was all a part of it; part of the affair. The excitement. When it's taboo, when it's risky, when people see it as wrong, you'll do anything. *Try* anything. Because it doesn't matter any more. All the stuff you've always wanted to do, you just . . ." She looked at me, shrugged. "You just do it."

"So why did it feel weird when he asked?"

"It was just strange coming from him."

"You pegged him for a straight arrow?"

She nodded. "Definitely."

I looped the conversation around to a point we'd left unfinished earlier. "How did you react when he started cooling things off?"

"React?"

"Did you just accept it?"

She shrugged. "I could see myself becoming a bunny boiler, the psycho bit on the side, but I couldn't help it. I couldn't bear the silence; going from all-in to all-out." She stopped; looked downcast. "So, no, I didn't just accept it."

"What did you do?"

She glanced at me, a reluctance in her face. "I started following him."

"When was this?"

"Things started to change in early September, and by the middle of October I wasn't getting anything from him: no calls, no texts. I found that very hard."

"So you started following him at the end of October?"

"End of October, beginning of November."

"How many times did you follow him?"

"Only twice. The second time I started feeling ridiculous. I was angry with him—jealous and hurt, I suppose—but I got a dose of clarity half-way through the evening the second time and that was when I left."

"Where did he go?"

"Both times, it was just down there, to the Hilton." She was pointing over my head, in the direction of South Quay. "He just sat there in the bar by himself."

"Doing what?"

"Nothing. Just drinking. Like he was deep in thought."

"That was it?"

"That was it."

Deep in thought. But about what?

"You never told Sam you followed him?"

"No. He would have flipped."

"And done what?"

"He wasn't violent, if that's you mean. We only ever had one fight in the time we were seeing each other. But he wouldn't have taken kindly to me following him."

"What was the fight about?"

"It was a Friday night," she said, remembering it instantly. "August, in the weeks before he started getting weird. He was in the shower and his phone went off. It was right there next to me on the bed, so—without even thinking, really—I glanced at the display to see who was calling. It was just an automatic reaction. I saw the name, it didn't mean anything to me, so I just assumed it was a client of his. When he came back out, I told him his phone had gone off and he was fine about it. Really relaxed. Then he checked to see who'd called, and it all changed."

"Changed how?"

"He went absolutely crazy. Started accusing me of snooping around in his phone, of going through his private things. It just came out of nowhere. I tried to tell him I hadn't done anything, that I hadn't looked at his messages, that I didn't even know who the guy was who'd called him, but he wouldn't believe me. I'd never seen him like that."

"Who was the caller?"

"Some guy called Adrian."

"No surname?"

"It just said Adrian."

I noted it down. He definitely wasn't on Julia's list, which meant she didn't know about him, and although I didn't remember seeing an Adrian in the phone records, it didn't mean he wasn't there. Spike had got me eighteen months of calls and texts from Sam's phone, and—in the first run-through—I'd concentrated on repeating numbers and the people who'd contacted Sam the most. Adrian was a reason to go back to it.

"Did you ever find out who this Adrian guy was?" I asked.

"No. Sam was too busy screaming in my face. I was determined not to sit there and take it, but I couldn't fight back. He just *blitzed* me; completely shouted me down."

"Did he apologize?"

"The next day, yeah. But a couple of weeks after that he started backing away. That was the end for us. That was the moment things really changed." She paused, one of her eyes blurring. "And then four months later he was gone."

23

By the time I got back to the car, I had a name: Adrian Wellis. There had been just one call in the entire year and a half I had records for: 5 August, just as Ursula had described. The call lasted eight seconds, which presumably meant he'd dialed in, got voicemail and then hung up. Sam never phoned back; Wellis never tried again. And yet, in order for Ursula to read his name on the display, Sam must have put Wellis into his address book. So why would Sam go to that kind of trouble for a person he was never going to ring?

As Spike had done with all the other numbers, he'd managed to source a street address off the back of the call. Tierston Road, Peckham. It was only five miles from Canary Wharf, which meant I could have been down there inside thirty minutes, barring traffic jams. But I knew heading down now meant heading in blind.

Liz had once said to me that the reason I did what I did, the reason I put my life at risk for the missing, was because I was trying to plug holes in the world that couldn't be filled; trying to prevent other people from feeling the way I had. She meant Derryn. She meant her death, and everything—all the grief and anger—that came after. I understood that, saw the truth in it, even told her—and maybe believed—that I could control that part of me and become a different person. Not detached exactly, but not so affected by the people I found either. When you became affected by them, by their stories, by the people they'd lost, you took risks: you stepped into the dark, not knowing what was there—and the only armor you took into battle was the debt you felt to the families.

I knew Liz was right and, for a time, I'd resisted the temptation to stray back into the shadows. I stayed rooted to the right side of the dividing line, taking the cases, working them and closing them off, then leaving them alone. But it couldn't be like that forever. Seeing through my commitment to the lost, to their families—however I did it and whatever it took—was who I was. It was woven into me. When Derryn died, a little part of me went too—and the space she left behind was never filled; only replaced, temporarily, by the people I returned to the light. I wanted to be with Liz, wanted to be in her life. But she'd never fully understood that part of me.

That was the fault line in our relationship.

And, ultimately, maybe the force that would tear us apart.

Adrian Wellis lived in a tatty two-story red-brick terrace house with a concrete garden and sheets for curtains. Behind it was a sink estate called The Firs: a monolithic series of concrete blocks, housing almost ten thousand people.

Outside it was still hot and airless: clouds didn't move in the sky, leaves didn't move in the trees, just the faint shimmer of a heat haze coming off the tarmac. All along the road, windows were open, but at Wellis's gate there was a strange, eerie kind of silence to the place. No music. No kids. Only the distant sound of cars on the Old Kent Road and the occasional squawk of a bird. The doorbell didn't work, so I knocked a couple of times.

No answer.

There were two mottled glass panels in the door. Inside was a hallway with three doors off it. Stairs off to the right. Close to the door was a lightbulb with no lampshade.

I knocked again and waited.

The front garden was a mess; only a garden in name. Everything had been paved over and left to decay. The slabs were uneven, weeds crawling through the gaps between them. Four big concrete blocks were in a pile at the end of the driveway. On top was a flowerpot, no flowers in it, just earth.

When there was no answer for a second time, I headed out, down to the end of the road, and around to the back of the houses. Every home had a six-foot-high fence marked with a number. Wellis's had been painted on, the paint running the full length of the gate and collecting in a pool on the step at the bottom. He'd never bothered cleaning it up. I tried the gate. It was locked.

Walking back around to the front, I knocked for a third time.

"Mr. Wellis?"

Again, nothing. No sound of movement from inside. I put my ear to the door, just to be sure, but the house was quiet. No voices. No television. For a brief second I thought about trying to pick the locks—then reality kicked in. In broad daylight, it was too risky.

All I could do now was wait.

24

It was just before 9 a.m. when Healy walked past the visitor center in the prison. Inside, a network of tables and chairs were bolted to the floor, populated by identically dressed prisoners and the people who had come to see them. Everything was under surveillance by CCTV, while guards circled the room, their eyes moving from table to table.

Beyond it, the corridor ahead looked sick: pale green linoleum, matching walls, empty noticeboards and reinforced windows into vacant, dark rooms. At the end was a counter, a window pulled across, with a guard on the other side at a computer. He had silver hair and milky eyes, half-moon glasses perched on the end of his nose. When he saw Healy approaching, he slid the window across.

"How you doing, Colm?"

"Pretty good, Clive. You?"

The guard nodded. He had a slow, considered style, which Healy had never been able to read in all the years he'd known him. It could have been age, or it could have been a natural distrust of people. "You're late today," the guard said.

"Yeah, I know."

"Well, you better get going."

Healy's eyes drifted up for a second to the sign on the wall above the window. Black letters on peeling white paint: HIGH SECURITY UNIT.

"Yeah," Healy said. "I better get going."

After passing through security, he moved along another corridor, doors on either side, the distant sound of voices audible. The prison cells were directly adjacent, though there were no windows until he got to the end of the corridor. He slowed up. Two rooms, both behind security doors, but with reinforced glass panels that Healy could see in through. He stepped up to the first.

Inside, seven men were seated on chairs in a semicircle. Different faces, different builds, but all dressed in prison uniforms. Healy got in even closer to the glass. As he angled his body, he saw her. The psychologist.

All the prisoners were watching her. She was perched on the edge of a chair opposite them, talking.

"There you are," Healy said quietly.

It was biting cold as he waited in his car outside. Snow was shovelled into piles all around him, the early morning still blanketed by a fuzzy kind of half-light. After a couple of minutes, the woman exited the prison and started to head out across the car park. Her scrawny frame was hidden beneath a sheepskin coat, her hair tied into a messy, uneven ponytail, her eyes fixed on her phone. Ever since his return to the Met, he'd been using the database to find out about her, looking into her life piece by piece, building a picture of who she was. But not within sight of Craw. Not within sight of anybody else.

Her name was Teresa Reed. Forty-eight. Divorced, no kids. She'd been coming to the prison on weekly visits for nineteen months. Same day every week, same purpose: to interview and talk to the prisoners. To Healy, none of that really mattered, other than the fact that she didn't have kids. That suited him fine. If she'd had kids, it would have made it harder to formulate his plan, and harder still to execute it. With kids, there was guilt, fuzzy thinking, emotion, a million reasons not to hurt her. Without them, she had no responsibility to anyone but herself, and no one to miss her.

He got out of his car and pretended to fiddle around in the pocket on the driver's door. He'd been watching her for almost six weeks, and today was the first day he was making any sort of contact with her. He glanced up to see her getting closer. Healy had parked here for a reason: it was right next to her Mini. She had to come across him, and step in next to him, to get to her car.

He heard her shoes in the slush about six feet away from him, closed the door of his car and then purposely bumped into her without looking.

"Oh, I'm sorry," he said, looking at her.

She glanced at him. "No problem."

They stood like that for a moment, across from one another, and he saw how old she looked close up. Weathered. *That's what happens when you spend your life making nice with scumbags.* Healy frowned. "Do I know you?" he said.

She returned the frown. "I don't think so, no."

"You're not Teresa, are you?"

Her face softened. "Yes," she said, and then paused, obviously embarrassed she didn't recognize him. "I'm so sorry . . . I can't quite place your, uh . . ."

He held up a hand, forced a smile. "It's fine. Colm Healy. I work at the Met. I think you came into my station after the riots last year."

Her mouth formed an *O*. Healy had checked all this. He didn't know her and had never met her, but he'd found her in the system when the station chief superintendent, Bartholomew, had had some ridiculous idea about getting psychologists involved in the interviewing of looters. There was no thought behind it other than getting him into his favorite place—the papers—but Teresa Reed had been one of the shrinks he'd brought in.

"Anyway," Healy said, locking the car. "Nice to meet you again."

"Yes," she said. "You too."

He left her, walking off toward the prison building. When he heard her Mini start up and drive off, he turned around and headed back to the car. Unlocked it. Slid in at the wheel. His heart was beating fast and his palms were slick with sweat, even in the cool of the morning. Slowly the windows of the car began to steam up and he wondered whether he was doing the right thing. But then he felt the burn of grief and anger in the center of his chest, and any doubts were washed away.

25

While I watched the house, I used my phone and went searching for Wellis online. Facebook was the world's greatest detective. Inside a minute you could get yourself a picture. And if there were holes in their privacy settings, seconds after that you had their whole life. It was even easier if you had an unusual surname. My Facebook account was a shell—no details, no photos, no posts—but it got me access to other people's, and although I couldn't see Wellis's wall, info or friends, I could see all his photos.

There were fifteen in all: Wellis at the beach, in woodland somewhere, standing on the edge of a lake with a hunting rifle. He was five-ten, stocky, about forty, with a shaved head. He had a tattoo of a crucifix on the side of his neck. In most of the photos he was on his own, but when he wasn't he was always with the same guy: taller, thinner, late thirties. They both had looks I didn't like, but Wellis—his eyes small, like an animal's—I'd have to watch the closest.

After a while light began to fade from the day, the sun burning out in the sky, the clouds bleeding red and orange. Inside twenty minutes it became a different world: shadows grew deep and long, like vast curtains being pulled across a stage, and although the temperature didn't drop much, a faint breeze picked up, whispering past the car and down toward the house.

Twenty minutes after that, I heard voices on the other side of the road.

Two men were approaching, silhouettes beneath the faint orange glow of a street light. I lowered myself into my seat, using the lack of light as a disguise, and turned the radio off. They drew level. They couldn't see in, but I could see out.

One of them was Adrian Wellis.

In real life, he looked a little shorter than five-ten, but in all other areas he was exactly the same as his photo: fierce, shaved head, dark eyes. He wore a red bomber jacket over a blue check shirt and dark blue trousers. All name brands. I thought about the reasons a man might live in a place like his if he was making enough money to buy £200 trainers, but then my eyes fell on the guy next to him. Taller. Thinner. Blotchy skin and graying hair, and without Wellis's sense of style. He was the other guy in the photos.

They got to the house, and Wellis started fiddling around in his pocket for his keys. But when he finally found them, he paused.

He looked along the row of houses.

It was like he'd sensed someone had been here. In the front garden. Up to the house. In the still of the night, it was possible to hear the other guy asking him what the matter was, but Wellis didn't reply. He just stared at the front of the house—and then up the road toward me.

Even though there was no possible way he could see me, no way he could know I was watching, it felt like he'd zeroed right in on me. He took a step away from the house, his trainers crunching against a crumbling piece of concrete, and then he stopped, one foot slightly in front of the other as if he was primed, ready to strike. There was something different about him now. He stood rigid, his body taut, his eyes oil-black circles in the shadows. He stayed in the same position—absolutely still—for a long time, hands out either side of him, fists balling and opening, over and over. And then eventually he said something to the other guy and let the two of them into the house.

A light went on in the hallway. The door closed.

And I waited some more.

Not long after, the front door opened again. The other guy stepped out, into the night air, and pulled the door shut. He stood there for a moment, lighting a cigarette, and then started making his way up the road in my direction. I sank back down into my seat and watched as he passed the car and headed up toward a fork in the road about thirty yards behind me. In between a pair of street lights, where it was more shadow than light, he perched himself on somebody's broken garden wall and waited.

The rhythmic glow of his cigarette.

The brief light from a mobile phone screen.

A couple of minutes later, headlights emerged from the darkness. The road was even quieter now, so the noise of the car traveled across the stillness: every tick of the engine, every stone spitting out from under its wheels. Just short of the man, it stopped and killed its headlights. It was a blue Toyota. The windscreen was just a rectangle of darkness. No shape inside. No idea who was driving. The man got up off the wall, flicked his cigarette out into the road and walked to the car. He bent down at the passenger window.

There was a short conversation, not lasting more than thirty seconds, and then the car's lights switched back on, the man stepped away, and the vehicle pulled a U-turn and headed back up the road. The man stood there, not moving, just watching the car all the way along the street until it melted away in the night. Once it was gone, only then did he move from his spot and head back toward the house.

As he passed, I noticed something in his hands.

Money.

At 4:40, dawn started to break and light edged its way across the sky, a faint, creamy glow the color of tracing paper. But in Adrian Wellis's house, the lights remained on. Throughout the night there'd been movement inside: a shadow passing, a silhouette forming, but never for very long. All I knew for sure was that they hadn't been to bed.

At 5 a.m. the front door opened and the other guy emerged, dressed in the same clothes, his hair a little ruffled, his clothes not on properly. *Why's he taking a walk at 5 a.m.?* He was carrying a black holdall. Halfway along the road he stopped, unzipped it, checked inside and then closed it again.

I got out of the car.

He clocked the movement, his eyes pinging toward me. I stepped around to the back of the BMW and flipped the boot. He carried on walking, his interest in me lost. In the boot, next to the spare wheel, was my escape plan; there in case it all went wrong. I removed the crowbar, slid it into the back of my trousers and made a beeline for him.

"Excuse me, mate."

He looked back. No reply.

"Excuse me," I said again, and this time he stopped.

"*What?*"

He glanced down at the holdall, as if I might be coming for that, and shifted it behind one of his legs to protect it.

"What d'ya want?" he said.

South London accent. So he's from around here somewhere.

"I'm looking for Adrian Wellis."

Another frown. His eyes moved from me to the car then back to me.

He shifted position slightly and glanced down the road to the house. Panic in his face.

When he turned back to me, he shrugged. "Never heard of him."

But even if I hadn't seen him come out of Wellis's house, I would have seen right through the lie. He couldn't play this game—he wasn't canny enough—and all of a sudden I saw him for what he was: Wellis's lapdog.

"What's your name?" I asked.

"What the fuck's it gotta do with you?"

"I'm just interested."

"Fuck off," he said, and started along the road again.

"You're going to help me find Sam Wren."

He stopped and looked back. "What did you say?"

"You heard what I said."

He turned fully toward me, bag swinging around to his front, and tried to make himself bigger and more aggressive. But it didn't work. A man who barely weighed ten stone wasn't going to be a match for me. He wasn't going to be much of a match for anyone. Inside a couple of seconds he knew his ruse had failed and seemed to shrink in his skin. I took a step in his direction, just to underline its failure.

"Let's go and see Adrian," I said.

"He doesn't like strangers inside his house."

"Yeah, that's what I figured."

"So he's not going to open the door to you."

"No. But he'll open it to you."

26

The man stopped outside the house and knocked a couple of times. We waited. Ten seconds later, a silhouette moved along the hallway, distorted in the mottled glass panel. I took a subtle step away from the door as the silhouette leaned in toward the peephole. Then the lock flipped and the door came away from the frame.

Adrian Wellis filled the gap.

He was dressed in his boxer shorts. Nothing else. I could see the crucifix tattoo at his neck, and more on his body: a snake's head on his left breast; the numbers 666 on his hip. "What the hell are you doing back?" he said to the man, and then, as he took a step closer, spotted me off to the side. His eyes flicked between the man and me, and he pulled the door back as far as it would go. He had a faintly amused expression on his face. "What the fuck is this?" he said. He was Welsh.

"He stopped me on the street and I—"

"Shut up," ordered Wellis. He turned to me. "Who are you?"

"I want to talk to you about Sam Wren."

Something registered in his eyes, like a flash of torchlight cutting through the dark. On. Then off. "Who?"

I didn't bother repeating myself.

His eyes narrowed. "What's your name?"

"Ben Richards."

"Who do you work for?"

"I don't work for anyone."

He frowned for a moment, then broke out into a smile. Perfect teeth. Expensive, just like his clothes. He pursed his lips. "I don't know who you're talking about, Ben."

"I think you do."

Beyond him the decor was probably the same as the day the house was built. Most of the wallpaper had either fallen from the walls or been torn off. The carpet was threadbare, from the front door to the kitchen at the back of the house. Three or four holes had been punched into the staircase and walls, about the size of a boot, and there were stains everywhere: on the walls, on the carpet, on the stairs. The house was filthy.

I looked back at Wellis. "So?"

He studied me a while longer, then looked at the man standing next to me. There was a mix of disgust and pity in his face. "You want me to invite you in, is that it?"

"Not necessarily. We can chat here."

"I don't do my chatting on the doorstep."

"Then it looks like I'm coming in."

He snorted. Didn't say anything. Didn't move.

"Or I can head back to the car, dial 999 and tell them you know where Sam Wren is. It's up to you, Adrian."

He stared at me, then stepped back and let the man through.

"No," I said. "Your friend stays outside."

"You dictating the terms now, is that it?"

"It's simple maths. Two of you, one of me."

The thin man stood there in the hallway, waiting for Wellis to tell me where to go—but Wellis ordered him to wait outside, and his face took on the look of a disappointed teenager. He dropped the holdall to the floor—making a clattering sound; metal against metal—and did as Wellis said. I stepped inside the house and pushed the door shut.

The house stank of sweat and fried food. In the living room the TV was on, but the screen was blue, as if a DVD had just been turned off. I shifted around, my back to the wall, so I had Wellis in front of me.

"What do you want?" he said, running his tongue around his mouth.

He didn't seem conscious of the fact he was semi-naked. Or if he did, it genuinely didn't seem to bother him. His body was squat; not fat, but hard and chunky, muscle in his chest, through the center of his stomach and up into his arms. He rolled his shoulders back and then brought his hands together in front of him.

"I want to know what happened to Sam Wren."

"Who?"

"You know who he is."

"Do I?"

"You're in his phone."

He shrugged, didn't seem worried. "I'm in a lot of people's phones."

"You called him in August last year."

"And?"

"And you put him on edge."

Wellis smirked. "And?"

"And I want to know why."

"What the fuck's it got to do with you?"

"I guess we'll see."

"Yeah?"

I nodded.

Wellis shook his head, like he couldn't believe what he was hearing. "Let me just remind you of something, dickhead. You're in *my* home."

"I can see that."

"So, what, you're RoboCop—is that it?"

"I'm not a cop."

"Then who the fuck are you?"

"I want to find out what happened to Sam Wren. So I can either get the answers from you, or I get them from Lassie out there, but I'm going to get them."

He took a step toward me, ready to attack.

Then, from above us, there was a noise. A bump. Like a big, dead weight being dropped. Wellis shot a look upstairs. I followed suit.

"What was tha—"

But before I could finish he was on me.

He came forward, his arm across the front of his face, using it as a battering ram. He went through me, almost lifting me off my feet, and slammed me against the wall.

"Eric!" he shouted and the front door burst open.

The other man headed past us and upstairs, taking two steps at a time, as if he knew exactly what he was being summoned for. Wellis shoved harder with his forearm, pressing it in against my neck, forcing my body against the wall and my head up. I tried to swing a punch, but he blocked it and arced a fist up into my guts.

It was like being hit by a train.

I shifted my weight left to right and the movement rocked him back on his heels. Only a fraction. But enough. I drove a fist into the side of his head and managed to connect with his ear. He stumbled back half a step and I jabbed a second punch—as hard as it would go—into the center of his throat. He made a sound like air escaping from a balloon, shrinking in on himself.

But Wellis was a fighter.

He channeled everything he had into a swing, connecting with the area around my heart. It was like he'd punched through me. I hit the wall so hard and so fast the whole house seemed to shake. The door rattled in its frame. The plasterboard rippled. As I was catching my breath, he moved quickly to the holdall, unzipping it.

A second later, he had a knife.

His fingers were laced through three holes in the rubberized grip. The blade was curved, about three and a half inches long. I stepped away from him and saw, inside the holdall, more knives, some rope, handcuffs—and a white vest and jeans, both belonging to a female, dotted with blood.

"You shouldn't have come here," he said, breathless. I didn't respond. "Now I'm gonna have to take care of you."

Upstairs, I could hear the other man moving around.

Quick footsteps.

Wellis edged toward me, knife out in front of him. He was forcing me back toward the kitchen, into a space where there was no exit.

"Ade!" the other man screamed from upstairs.

Wellis glanced behind him. An automatic reaction.

And I made my move.

From behind me I yanked out the crowbar I'd taken from the car. It was short, stubby, no more than a foot and a half long—but when it connected with the side of his head, Wellis went down like he'd been shot. His eyes rolled back; every muscle in his body turned to liquid. Then he was flat on his back on the carpet, lights out.

I turned him over on to his front.

"Ade!" the man shouted again from upstairs. "Quickly!"

Grabbing his arms, I dragged Wellis through to the kitchen and then went through the cabinets. In between a bottle of bleach and a tube of rat poison, I found a roll of duct tape. I bound Wellis's ankles and wrists and looped the tape around his head a few times, covering his mouth. By the time I was done, he was slowly starting to come round. Eyes flickering like butterfly wings; eyeballs rolling up into his head, as if trying to tune himself back in. I had about five minutes before he returned to something like full strength.

Moving back through the hallway, I padded up the stairs. No creaks. No sound. At the top, in one of the rooms, I could see a loft hatch was open. A ladder had been pulled down and propped against the carpet. The man was halfway up, body inside the loft, legs still on the steps. As I edged in closer, I spotted something else.

Right on the edge of the loft space.

Blood.

I moved quietly into the room and stopped at the bottom of the ladder; more blood was falling from the lip of the hatch. It hit a space about half a foot from where I was standing, forming a pool on the hard, matted fibers of the carpet. The man was just standing there, looking off into the darkness at whatever was up there. Not moving now. Just breathing in and out.

"Ade," he said again, but this time there was no purpose in his words, no urgency, and I realized something: he was crying. Soft sounds. Sniffs. "Ade," he said again.

I reached up, hands either side of his ankles.

"*Ade!*"

He looked down, and saw me. Shock in his face. Then fear. Then anger. I grabbed his ankles and pulled him off the ladder. He fell hard and fast, cracking his head against one of the steps, before landing awkwardly right on the ball of his foot. He yelled out and collapsed. I grabbed him by the collar, got him to his feet and drove him back, into the wall. The wind whistled out of him.

"What's your name?"

Tears and blood on his face.

"What's your *name*?"

"Eric."

"Eric what?"

"Eric Gaishe."

I glanced up, into the loft space. "What have you done, Eric?"

He sniffed. More tears in his eyes.

"I think I killed someone."

27

I pulled Gaishe, hobbling, to the bathroom, pushed him inside and told him to stay put. Then I returned to the spare room. Above me, the loft hatch was a big, black space. I only had a T-shirt on—nothing to cover my skin, nothing to prevent prints—so I grabbed a shirt from a nearby wardrobe, tore it in two and wrapped the material around both hands. I didn't know what awaited me in the darkness. Not exactly. But, given this house and the people who occupied it, it couldn't be anything good. As I started to climb, dread slithered through the pit of my stomach.

Halfway up, a moth escaped from the shadows and, at the lip of the hatch, I could see the full extent of the blood: running along the edges, soaking through into the insulation. Another rung, then another, and suddenly my head was inside the crawl space.

And I saw her.

Matted, unwashed hair. Skin stained with a mixture of grease and sweat. The woman was on her stomach, part of her face in a bed of insulation, skeletal arms out either side, legs spread. Her head was tilted toward me, one of her eyes looking up as if she'd been trying to claw her way back out of the loft. And there was blood everywhere: her face, her arms, her ribs, her legs. Thin, painful knife cuts had been used as a torture tactic, not enough to kill her, but enough to subdue her, and the rest was just bruising, everywhere, scattered all over her like spilled ink. There was a brick beside her, coated in her blood. A couple of strikes to the head from Gaishe, and then there would have been nothing but silence. No fight in her any more.

No life.

I looked at her: drawn and wan, she couldn't have been more than eighteen. There were older bruises on her arms and legs, around her collarbone, next to her eyes and hips. I felt anger force its way up, blooming in my chest.

And then she blinked.

It was so quick, so unexpected, I wasn't even sure if I'd seen it. I turned my head and put my ear to her mouth. And I felt it. Soft, warm breath.

Shit. She's alive.

I thought about what I was going to do. But not for long.

Ultimately, there wasn't a choice to make.

Using the house landline, I called for an ambulance, gave them the address and where she was in the house. "You'll need police here too," I told them, then hung up. She hadn't moved from her position in the attic by the time I returned to her, but her visible eye was more alert. It swivelled from left to right, as if she was trying to focus on me.

"It's okay. You're going to be all right. This will all be over soon." I couldn't touch her; didn't want to leave any more evidence than I had already. "I need to take care of something, okay? By the time I'm done, the ambulance will be here. You'll be all right."

A gurgle in her throat.

"I promise you'll be okay."

". . . *hmmmm hurrrrrr* . . ."

"You're safe now."

". . . *done lim hurd mm* . . ."

I started down the ladder—and then stopped.

Done lim hurd mm. Don't let him hurt me.

I looked at her. Her body, her face, painted with blood. "I won't let them hurt you," I said. "Not Adrian. Not Eric. Not any more."

But it seemed to give her no comfort, and then—slowly, inch by inch—she started shaking her head. ". . . *nnnnnnn a . . . is* . . ."

"Try not to move."

". . . *no . . . adrrri . . . nnnn . . . no . . . e* . . ."

And as she lay there with her life leaking out of her, something unspoken passed between us—and I realized what she was telling me.

Not Adrian. Not Eric.

She was talking about someone else.

I moved down the ladder, wiping each rung clean with the shirt. At the bottom I looked around: what had I touched? I had about seven or eight minutes before the ambulance arrived—maybe a little more if the traffic was bad.

Downstairs, Wellis was still on the kitchen floor, his eyes open, staring at the ceiling. He was woozy: when he tried to roll over on to his back, he couldn't. I left him and wiped down the door frames, door handles and walls.

Next, I headed back upstairs, one half of the shirt around my hand, one half tucked into the back of my trousers, and opened the bathroom door. Gaishe was inside, perched on the edge of the bath. As soon as I looked at him, I felt the burn in the center of my chest. "Come here, shit-head." I grabbed him hard by the arm. His face was still streaked with blood and tears and he looked terrified. A man out of his depth, led astray by someone much worse than him. Now he was as deep in as he could get.

I marched him downstairs and shoved him into the wall at the bottom. He stayed there, just staring off at Wellis, and I realized he was dazed as well as scared.

I can use that.

"Eric," I said. "Give me a hand with Adrian. We need to get him out of here before the police arrive." He thought he recognized something in my voice—something positive, something he could cling on to—and he came over immediately.

We hoisted Wellis on to his feet, I cut the duct tape at his ankles and wrists, and tore it away from his mouth. Then I told Gaishe to get me a long coat from Wellis's wardrobe. He did just as I asked. When he returned, we dressed Wellis in it. I buttoned it, and left Gaishe holding him while I did one last circuit of the house. At the bottom of the ladder I told the woman that she was going to be fine, and that the ambulance was on its way. And then, grabbing the crowbar and the duct tape, we all left.

Gaishe was on one side, I was on the other, Wellis was in the middle. Gaishe had blood on his face, I had a crowbar and a shirt tucked into the back of my trousers, Wellis had no shirt or shoes on—but it was still early, not even six, and there was no one around. "Are you going to help us?" Gaishe asked as we got to my car.

"Yes," I lied, and flipped the boot.

I glanced up and down the road. No one watching. No one around. I lined Wellis up, his eyes widening as he continually tried to focus, then I pressed his head down and forced him into the back. He folded easily; he still didn't have the power to fight me.

"What are you doing?" Gaishe said.

"What does it look like?"

"You're putting him in there?"

"Yeah," I said. "And you're going in too."

He frowned, and then I grabbed him by his neck and jammed him down into the space. He climbed in clumsily, hit his knee and his head, but then finally came to rest next to Wellis. They both looked up at me, one dazed, one scared. Rapists. Animals.

And then I shut them in.

28

They now had a third photograph to pin to the wall of the incident room. Steven Wilky, Marc Evans and the very latest: a twenty-four-year-old office cleaner called Joseph Symons. He'd been gone eight days by the time his father reported him missing, nine by the time the task force realized they had another victim and had descended on his place in Clerkenwell, a pokey fourth-floor flat in a tower block called Dunkirk House. Healy had given Craw a lift from the station.

Now they were the only ones left in the apartment.

The approach to the flat had been in near darkness—the lights in the hallways out, the ones at the entrance too; broken, vandalized—and Healy stood by himself in the bedroom looking at the bed. Forensics had taken the hair from the pillow, fibers from the sheets and trace evidence from the floor, and finally the flat had a strange kind of silence to it. The faint creaks and groans of the walls and floorboards, the drip of rain on the windowsill, but nothing else.

Healy stepped away from the bed, turned and took in the room. There was no sign of a break-in, which meant—just like Wilky and Evans before him—Symons knew who the Snatcher was. He'd invited him in, maybe innocently, maybe not so innocently, but he would have had no idea who he really was, and no sense of what was to come. From there, the case became guesswork. When did the Snatcher strike? How did he suppress his victims? How did he get them out without being seen? Where did he take them? What did he do with them? The press—ravenous, pumped-up and baying for blood—referred to him as a serial killer, but you were only a serial killer if you killed people. All the police had so far were three missing men, all tied together by a single piece of evidence: the hair from their heads, left on their pillows.

For a moment, sudden and uncontrolled panic hit Healy. *What if you can't find him? What if you haven't got it in you any more? What if this one breaks you like the one before?* He took another step back and reached out to the nearest wall, his mind turning over and over like a trawler being rolled across the waves.

He remembered Leanne, his daughter; the way she'd looked when he'd found her body, and the road he'd had to walk to get there. And then he remembered the case before that. The one that had ripped his life, and his marriage, apart: two eight-year-old girls killed down in New Cross, and he'd never been able to find the bastard who did it. It had consumed him, completely and utterly suffocated him, until one day it all came out: he discovered his wife was having an affair and he flipped. In a moment of weakness, a moment that was filled with so much shame and regret he could hardly bear the weight of it, he hit his wife.

Don't let them see you like this. Don't show any weakness.

He stepped away from the wall, breathed in and moved to the window in the bedroom. It looked down across the rain-soaked front entrance of the tower block. In a patch of darkness out toward the main road, he could see flashbulbs going off, and cones of light where TV reporters were broadcasting live. Off to the left, where a thin walkway connected this building with the next, people watched, gloved hands on the railing, breath forming above their heads like balls of gauze.

"You all right?"

He looked around. DCI Melanie Craw was standing in the doorway of the room, head tilted, eyes analysing him. She'd given him his chance, made an unpopular decision, and for that he owed her. But she still looked at him like all the others did: waiting for the moment he said something or did something stupid; the moment he screwed it all up. And sometimes her gaze was even more intense than that: sometimes it felt she was looking right into his head, reading his every thought, and he became worried that she'd figured out what he was doing at the prison.

"There's no sign of forced entry anywhere?" Healy asked.

Craw stepped into the bedroom. "No. Symons is just like Wilky and Evans. Our suspect is definitely invited in. Most likely he follows them, gets to know their routines, then initiates a meeting and gains their trust."

"And when he gets inside the flats, he drugs them."

"That seems the most likely course of action, yes."

"Because how else does he shave their heads, right?"

"Right."

"But what about once they're drugged?"

She looked at him, seeing that he had a theory. "He leaves with them."

"But there have been no witnesses at any of the scenes. So, how do you carry a grown man like Symons out of a fourth-floor flat without raising any suspicion?"

Craw shrugged. "You wait for the right moment."

"Or you don't knock them out."

She stepped closer, frowning. "What do you mean?"

"I agree that he drugs them," Healy replied. "It makes them much easier to control that way. There's no way they would allow him to shave their heads otherwise. But I don't think they're unconscious while he's doing it. In fact, I don't think they're unconscious at any point. Wilky, Evans, Symons: I think he gave them enough so they were malleable— and then I think he walked them right out the front door. And he'll do exactly the same to the next one."

Date Night

It had been a long time. As Jonathan Drake waited in his flat, perched on the arm of a sofa, the TV on in the background, he tried to remember how long. Maybe a year. Maybe more. You lost track after a while.

He didn't mind dating, he didn't mind meeting new people, but he hated the build-up. He hated the early stages, the moments where you initiated conversation in the hope they wouldn't automatically turn you down, and then the weeks after, where everything was about making an impression, about saying the right things at the right times. None of it came easily to him. He wasn't asocial—quite the opposite, in fact—but the process was never one he'd been 100 percent comfortable with, ever since he was a teenager. Chatting people up in nightclubs, at bars, at house parties, it all just felt so false. Because of that, for a long time he couldn't be bothered with it. He didn't want the embarrassment. He spent months actively avoiding dating and, after a time, became very comfortable with his decision. He even grew to quite like it. He could go out with friends, with the people he worked with, and not feel under any pressure. He watched everyone else ride the tidal wave of men and women, in clubs, in bars, and it gave him a great perspective on how empty and unsatisfying that lifestyle was. But eventually, everyone—even those for whom detachment becomes second nature—starts to feel the ache of loneliness. And a year later, he realized something: humans weren't meant to be alone. They needed company.

So here he was.

He'd met this one by chance, while walking home, and they'd continued chatting on their daily commute. Drake preferred it that way. When you met someone unexpectedly, you sidestepped the really inelegant moments, the uncomfortable "Do you come here often?"-style conversation, because you weren't expecting anything to happen. And then it was easier to move to the next stage: where both of you liked the look of each other, and you gradually started to develop some kind of bond. He was nervous, but he was excited too about what the evening had in store for them.

Getting to his feet, he padded back through to the bedroom and looked at himself in the mirror. He was five-eight, slight, not handsome exactly—he knew that much—but rugged and dark. He had tiny pockmarks in and around the slope of his nose, running in an arc at either cheekbone, but it was the only part of him he disliked.

He turned and looked around at his flat.

Thin, worn carpets, faded wallpaper, damp in the corners of the room. Off to the right, in the kitchen, he could see a watermark had stained the cream linoleum. There were no pictures anywhere. No plants. No decor of any kind apart from a bookshelf full of books, and a TV perched on top of a wheeled cabinet. He'd have liked a better flat, but he was pretty philosophical about it: the rent was cheap, and there was no one else to help pay it. Until he got a promotion at the store, or won the lottery, this would do fine.

A knock at the door.

Drake studied himself in the mirror again. "Come on, Jonny Boy," he said. "This could be the one. This could be the start of something good. Time to turn on the charm." He stood there for a moment more, brushing himself down and smiling at the fact he was giving his own reflection a pep talk, and then he headed across the flat to the door. Before opening up, he looked out through the peephole. His date looked a little different than he remembered: somehow slightly older, but cleaner cut and better-looking. It was difficult to make out too much more: a bunch of youths had been through the hallway a couple of days before and smashed all the lightbulbs for no other reason than they could.

He unlocked the door and pulled it open.

"Leon," Drake said.

"Hello," Leon Spane replied. "How are you doing, Jon?"

Drake held out his hand. "I'm good. You?"

"Really good, thanks," Spane said, smiling.

They shook. Spane had big hands, but they were cool and clammy, and in a weird kind of way, Drake was pleased. Maybe he's as nervous as me, he thought, and then he invited Spane in. Spane thanked him with another smile, and stepped past, into the flat.

"I like your bag," Drake said.

Spane brought the satchel he was carrying around to his front, as if he'd never thought to look before. "Oh. Thank you. I'm a bit of an eBay addict." He paused, as if he'd noticed the rest of what he was wearing. "I might need you to give me a few fashion tips, actually. I remember you said you worked in fashion."

"Well, I work in a clothes store."

"That's good enough." He smiled. "I'm always looking for new fashion ideas."

Drake looked Spane up and down: smart tan leather boots, name-brand jeans, a black shirt and a black thigh-length jacket. "I think you look pretty good," he said.

Spane laughed. "And I didn't even have to pay you to say that."

Drake grabbed his jacket from a peg and slipped it on. The two of them looked at each other for a moment, and then both broke out into smiles at the same time.

"You didn't have any trouble getting here, did you?" Drake asked.

"No. No, not at all. I know Hammersmith a little bit."

"That's good. Thanks for coming down here."

Spane patted his bag. "The Tube was why they invented books."

Drake nodded. A reader. That was a good start. "I booked us a table at a restaurant just down the road. An Italian. I hope that's okay with you."

"Absolutely. That sounds great." Spane looked around the flat and his eyes fell on the toilet on the other side of the living room. "Could I be rude and ask to use your loo? It's not usually the kind of first impression I like to make, but I came straight from work."

Drake laughed. "Of course you can. It's just over there."

Spane thanked him, slipped off the satchel and dumped it onto the sofa, then headed to the bathroom, pushing the door closed. Drake wandered through to the kitchen.

The flat was designed so that the kitchen was offset from the living room, the whole thing partially hidden behind an old-fashioned serving hatch, and you could enter the kitchen from either side. Drake flicked the lights on and looked in the fridge. He wanted to make sure that he had some wine chilled for later on. He already had a good feeling about tonight, but some alcohol might help loosen them both up a little bit more once they got back.

He closed the fridge and moved back into the living room. Spane was still in the bathroom. Maybe he's puking up, Drake thought, and the idea made him smile. He dropped into one of the chairs and checked his phone. A few e-mails from friends. If it didn't go well tonight, at least he could keep them entertained with the gory details. Before he'd gone into relationship exile, his tales of dating disasters had always amused his mates.

Suddenly Drake had a thought, got up and headed back into the kitchen. He didn't bother flicking on the lights this time; just opened the fridge and slid out the bottle of wine he'd been looking at a moment before. Sauvignon Blanc. What happens if he doesn't like white wine? He cursed himself silently. Should have got a bottle of red as well, just in case. Then, across the top of the fridge door, he noticed something.

The bathroom door was open.

He pushed the fridge door shut—an automatic reaction—and for a moment the flat was plunged into darkness. All the lights were off.

A second before, they'd all been on.

He felt his heart shift and he moved forward slowly in the dark, to the light switch in the kitchen. He flicked it on. Above him, a strip light hummed and then broke out into a stark white glow. Through the serving hatch, he could see out into the living room—but only about halfway. Around the edges of the room were thick blankets of shadow, like curtains pinned from ceiling to floor. He looked left, out to where the bathroom was, and then right, into the living room. The kitchen light made it even harder to see into the dark.

"Leon?" he said.

No reply.

He moved left, toward the bathroom. "Leon?"

This time his voice betrayed him, and a ripple passed through it. He cleared his throat, as quietly as he could, coming around the edge of the wall dividing the kitchen from the living room. He flicked a look into the empty bathroom, and then fixed his eyes back to the living room, trying to will them to see more. He knew where everything was placed in the flat—he knew the layout, he knew where the light switches were—and yet, as he moved further in, it was like being in a place he'd never been before. He was disorientated.

"Leon?" he said again, scanning the flat.

Nothing.

Gradually, though, his eyes were starting to adjust to the light, and in front of him shapes were forming. Furniture. The TV. The music system. His PC on an old stand his parents had given him. Spane wasn't there.

Which meant he was in the bedroom.

Then, something twinged in Drake's neck.

A short, sharp pain, there and gone again. He reached up and touched the area just below the curve of his jaw and, when he brought his fingers back, in the shadow of the room he could see something even darker on them. He rubbed them together. Blood.

What the hell . . .?

He felt a shiver pass through him. Quick and sharp. And a split second later he knew why: Spane was behind him.

He turned.

"Fuck!"

Drake stumbled back, tripping against one of the sofas and falling to the ground. Spane had been on his shoulder the whole time, his face contorted by shadows, his body twisted and wrapped in them. He seemed bigger in the darkness—taller, wider, more threatening—but as Drake desperately tried to get to his feet again, his legs gave way. Spane stepped forward, out of the dark, towering over Drake as he looked up from the floor. He was wearing pale latex gloves and, in his left hand, holding a syringe.

"Whatthefuckareyoudoin . . ." Drake said, but as the words came out of his mouth, they didn't sound quite right. And then he realized something else: he was starting to feel woozy. His muscles were relaxing. His head kept rolling left to right. When his vision cleared a little Spane leaned down, pulled him up, dropped him into one of the armchairs and turned on the lights.

"Whatsssssoingon?" he asked again, his speech slurred.

Spane didn't respond. He carefully placed the syringe he'd used into the satchel and then brought out a small leather pouch. Drake tried to haul himself up, but his arms had no strength. He couldn't support himself. Every muscle in his body had liquified. When he tried to use his legs, place them down flat to the floor and maneuver himself forward, nothing happened. The whole time Spane calmly unzipped the leather pouch.

"Whatssssssssssssoingon?" Drake asked again.

His speech was getting worse by the second.

Spane opened the leather pouch, holding it in the middle like a book. With his left hand he adjusted something, and then looked back at Drake. "I'm really glad we have this chance to be alone," he said, his voice so soft it was barely audible. He laid the leather pouch down on the sofa as carefully as if it were made from glass, and then parted Drake's legs. Drake couldn't do anything about it. He had no reaction. No fight.

Spane moved in closer, positioning himself level with the knees. "This is how it's going to be from now on," Spane continued, his voice gentle, almost affectionate. And then he looked up from beneath his brow, his eyes so big and dark they were just holes in his head. A whimper passed up through Drake's throat; a reflex, like a noise from a cornered animal.

Spane smiled, stood up and went back to his satchel. He rummaged around inside and brought out a wooden bowl about a foot in diameter. He moved back to Drake, pulled him forward so he was doubled over, his head between his legs, and placed the bowl on the floor at his feet. Drake tried to sit up, but nothing happened. He had no power. No muscle. No bone.

"Leon," Drake said, his words blunted and dulled. "Leon, pleeeeashe."

No response.

Then a buzz.

"My name's not Leon, you fucking queer."

Suddenly, Drake felt cold metal at the nape of his neck, traveling up through the center of his head to the crown. A second later, his hair cascaded past his ears and landed, feather-like, in the bowl.

"Whaaaaatareyoudooooin?" Drake slurred.

A pause.

"I'm shaving your hair, Daddy."

PART THREE

29

There were a series of empty warehouses three miles away that I'd once used as a place to meet sources. Since leaving the paper, I'd only been back once. That time, I'd brought the person here under cover of darkness. This time, I had two men in the boot of my car and the sun was carving down out of a clear blue sky.

The road leading in was built in a T-shape, the neck barely big enough for two cars to pass. At the end, it opened up: ten warehouses, all in a line, all facing back down the way I'd come. At one end was a disused railway bridge, arches carved into it like big, dark holes bored straight into the earth. As I swung the car around and backed it in against one of the buildings, a smell came in on the breeze. The arches were dumping grounds: metal shells, so rust-covered it was impossible to tell what they'd once been; kitchen appliances stripped to their bones; old cars and machinery reduced to debris.

I grabbed the crowbar from the front seat and then took them in one by one, Gaishe first. He was scared. Out of his depth. He didn't weigh anything, and he didn't fight me. I secured him inside, then came back for Wellis. Popping the boot, I stepped back, expecting him to kick out. But he didn't. The sunlight was strong, angling right into the BMW, and as he moved a hand to his face, shielding his eyes, I grabbed him by his arms and dragged him out, dumping him on the concrete.

He lay there on the floor, looking up.

"Get to your feet," I said, pushing the boot closed.

He didn't respond. Didn't even move. He just stared up at me, unable to find me at first. Then he pulled into focus and spotted me about two feet away.

"Get up, you piece of shit."

He clumsily got to his feet, saying nothing. But at the entrance, as I followed him in, he looked back over his shoulder, eyes feral and aggressive.

Inside was a space about one hundred and eighty feet long. The sun drifted in through the gaps in the windows and brickwork, glinting in the smashed glass scattered across the floor. It stank like a toilet. To my right was an old office area, looking out over the warehouse. There was still some furniture in it: a couple of heavy oak desks and four chairs, picked apart and broken, but still basically usable. Gaishe was tied to one of them with duct tape—wrists to the arms of the chair, ankles to the legs. He looked up as we approached, an odd mixture of fear and relief in his face: fear of what was coming, relief that Wellis was here with him, to share in whatever was planned.

Wellis got to one of the chairs and then looked back at me. "You don't know what the fuck you just stepped into here, Ben. You know that, right?"

I threw him the duct tape. "Tie your ankles to the legs of the chair."

"Did you hear me?"

"Tie your ankles to the chair."

The same expression as before: hostile, his rage barely contained. Then he turned, tiny fragments of glass crunching beneath his bare feet, and dropped into the seat. Once his ankles were secure, I got him to tape one of his wrists down, then I did the other.

"Let's start with Sam Wren."

I perched myself on the edge of one of the desks and put the crowbar down next to me. No response from either of them.

"Eric?"

Gaishe looked at me.

"Do you want to tell me about Sam Wren?"

He glanced at Wellis again, but Wellis hadn't moved an inch. He was just staring at me, the corners of his mouth turned up in the merest hint of a smile.

"What's so funny?"

Wellis shrugged.

"This is all a joke to you?"

He shrugged again. I stepped in closer to him and, as I did, he tried to come at me—teeth bared, fists clenched—forgetting he was tied down. The chair rocked from side to side, teetered on one leg for a second and then toppled over and hit the floor. His head smashed hard against the ground, chips of glass cutting into the dome of his skull, and the coat we'd dressed him in came open. Next to him, Gaishe gasped and pushed back and away, the wheels of the chair carrying him off for about five feet. I dropped to my haunches next to Wellis and looked at him. He was gazing up, blood on his face. I'd get nowhere with him. Threats, torture, none of it would work. A man who lived in the shadows already knew too much about its consequences.

I moved to Gaishe, grabbed his chair and pushed it across the room, away from Wellis. Glass crunched beneath the wheels as we moved. We hit the far wall of the room and I held him there, facing the bricks, unable to see Wellis. "What's going on?" Gaishe said, a tremor in his voice. I turned back to Wellis. He'd shifted position on the ground and was looking at us. He didn't have any real affection for Gaishe, nothing with any meaning, and probably didn't care what happened to him— except Gaishe knew things.

Important things.

I leaned in to Gaishe. "Here's how it's going to play out, Eric: you're going to tell me how you know Sam Wren, how he got involved with you two, what happened when he did and how it all ended. You're going to tell me all that. And when we're done with that, you're going to tell me about the girl. The girl you killed."

Panic in his face, and then a stark realization about what he'd done. After that, his smell hit me: sweat and dirt and cigarette smoke.

I glanced at Wellis.

There was a different expression on his face now. He couldn't hear what I was saying to Gaishe, couldn't see Gaishe's face either. He had no control any more. He couldn't order Gaishe around. He couldn't tell him what to say. He couldn't influence him, or threaten him, or manipulate him. He was helpless.

"How do you two know Sam Wren, Eric?"

Gaishe glanced at me, wide-eyed and terrified. He looked like he was about to say something, but his eyes strayed to Wellis and he stopped himself. "I . . . I can't . . ."

"You can't what?"

"Ade will . . ."

"Ade's tied up on the other side of the room," I said. "Ade's not in control here any more. I am."

Gaishe swallowed. "I, uh . . ."

"What do you want to know?"

A voice from behind me. I turned and looked back at Wellis. It was just how I'd imagined it going: by stepping in, he could control what information was revealed. Gaishe would give me everything he knew—but everything Gaishe knew wasn't everything Wellis knew. So it was a trade-off: Gaishe would be easier to pick apart, but Wellis was the man who'd give me Sam Wren.

"What do you want to know?" Wellis repeated.

I left Gaishe facing the wall.

"Start at the beginning."

"I went to see him."

"About what?"

He eyed me for a second, a natural defense mechanism kicking in. He never told his business to anyone. "I had some money—I thought the stock market might be a good place to start. So I went along and asked him to invest it for me."

I smiled. "You're an investor—that's what you're telling me?"

"It's true."

"Don't bullshit me, Wellis."

"The cops were sniffing around my business," he said, his voice even, "and if they ever kicked down my door, I needed to look legit. I needed a legitimate source of income. So I went to see Wren."

"Why him?"

"Someone I knew told me about him. This guy said Wren was in finance."

"Who was the guy?"

"Just a guy who I do some business with."

I looked at him.

He shrugged. "Believe what you want to believe."

"So what's your business?"

"Transportation."

"You mean trafficking?"

He shrugged again. "Call it whatever you like."

"Is that how that woman ended up in your loft? A little present to yourself?"

He didn't say anything.

"It doesn't bother you?" I asked him.

"What?"

"The lives you're ruining?"

"I don't lose a lot of sleep over it," he said, his face a blank. He wasn't even trying to coax a reaction out of me. It was just a statement of fact. "You can't call up an escort agency and ask for a thirteen-year-old.

There's not a number for that in the Yellow Pages. So I run a service for people."

"You're talking about paedophiles."

He could see the disgust in my face. "I make sure we vet them first, if that makes you feel any better. First time someone new gets in touch, we take a look at them, we get their name, just in case there's any blow-back." He glanced across to where Gaishe was still sitting, facing the wall. "The girl was for Eric, anyway. She got off the boat from Romania, or Bulgaria, or wherever the fuck she was from, and started earning straight away. She was a right goer. Tight little body. We had a few boys who liked her. Eric was one of them."

"You like them young too?"

"She was sixteen. That's legal where I come from."

"So you don't mind raping the legal ones?"

He didn't say anything.

I could hardly bear to look at him now. "What about Sam?"

"I told you. I had some money, I wanted the business to look kosher. We were earning a lot of cash and it was getting hard to hide it under the floorboards."

"You went to see him."

"Like I said."

"And what happened?"

"What do you think happened? I gave him some money and he invested it. Three weeks later, he'd made me a small profit. So I gave him more, and he invested it, and so on and so forth." He sniffed. Rolled his face against his shoulder, trying to dislodge a chip of glass stuck to his cheekbone. "What, you don't think I can carry that off? You got a good look at my house earlier, but you missed my wardrobes. In my ward-robes I've got expensive clothes. Good suits. Good shoes. That's where my money goes. Not on the house, or a car, or holidays in the Bahamas. In my business, none of that shit matters. It's all about appearances. If you look good, people will believe anything."

"And you had Sam fooled?"

A movement in his face. But no reply.

"Wellis?"

He glanced at me and then away. "He did due diligence on me and that was fine. I'd put everything into place in the months before I went to him, so I sailed through that. I've been doing this a long time, so I know what to hide, and what to keep on show." He pursed his lips. Dispassionate. Detached. "But Wren was a clever boy. He had this natural suspicion. I could see that from the start."

"He found out about you?"

"He found a hole in my story. A payment I'd made. He traced it forward to the recipient, and then he found out who the recipient was. And then it all fell apart."

"Who was the recipient?"

"One of the guys that brings people in for me."

"How did Sam know who he was?"

"He used a CRB check, I imagine."

"The guy had a record?"

"Correct."

A noise outside.

I got down off the desk and walked to the doors of the warehouse. At the far end, a homeless man was trying to get to his feet inside one of the tunnels. An oil drum had tipped over, spilling dirt and ash all over the floor. When I got back, Wellis hadn't moved, but Gaishe was looking over his shoulder toward us. I told him to turn around, then seated myself on the desk again.

"What are you gonna do with us, Ben?" Wellis said.

"Do?"

"You gonna kill us? You don't seem the murdering type to me."

I looked down at him, his eyes like mirrors, reflecting back all the pain and suffering he'd caused during his life. "You don't know what I am."

He smirked. "You're not a killer."

"I guess we'll see."

The expression fell from his face.

"So what happened after he found out about you?"

"I told him I'd gut him if he ever breathed a word to anyone, and I'd slice up his wife while I was at it." He shrugged. "Looking back now, maybe I should have done that. But at the time, Wren was useful to me. He legitimized my cashflow."

"So he just carried on?"

"Pretty much."

"How often did you speak?"

"Three or four times a week."

But there had only been one, eight-second call on Sam's phone in the entire time he'd been dealing with Wellis. "You used prepaid mobiles."

"Correct."

That was why the calls never appeared on the phone records. All except one. "So why did you call him that one time?"

"When?"

"There's a single entry on his phone records for your number."

He looked nonplussed. "It was a mistake. I had his real number, in case I needed him in an emergency and I couldn't get hold of him on the prepaids. That day, he was pissing me off: he wasn't answering his phone, I needed to speak to him, and the longer he was AWOL, the angrier I got. I did it without thinking."

One tiny mistake—but enough to lead me to him.

"Did you meet in person?"

"Once a week in a hotel close to his work. I always liked to look him in the eyes and make sure he wasn't screwing me."

The hotel was the Hilton on the South Quay that Ursula had described. *He just sat there in the bar by himself. Like he was deep in thought.*

"So how did he disappear?"

"How the fuck should I know?"

"You didn't have anything to do with it?"

Wellis grinned. "What do you think? The guy was making me a shit-load of cash—why would I vanish him into thin air then, when I could have done it months before when he first found out about me? If I wanted him dead, he would have been dead already."

"Did he take any of your money with him?"

"No."

"You've no idea where he went?"

"No."

I studied him. There was nothing in his face. No hint of a lie. I looked across the room at Gaishe. He was no liar—or at least not one who could lie with any competence. "What about you?" I asked, and he turned in his chair, eyes wide. "Do you know where he went?"

He shook his head.

I looked at my watch: 8 a.m. It was time to close this down. "What was the name of the girl?"

He frowned. "What girl?"

"What girl do you think? The girl in your loft."

"What do you care?"

"I want to find out what happened to her."

"What are you, her guardian angel?"

"Just tell me her name."

Wellis stared at me. "Don't know," he said finally, his tone flat and even. "Don't know what her real name is. Don't know what any of the men and women we get in are called. They're not here so I can get to know them. They're here to make me money. They're here for people like you and people like your boy."

"My boy?"

"Wren."

"What about him?"

He studied me for a moment, seeing if I was playing him. Then he broke out into a smile. He glanced toward Gaishe. "He doesn't know!" he shouted across the room.

"Don't know what?"

He shook his head. "What kind of a detective are you?"

"What are you talking about?"

"Wren. He used our service once. Must have been a month before he left. Asked me if I could set him up with someone. As long as he paid the going rate, I couldn't have given less of a shit. A customer's a customer, after all."

"Who did you set him up with?"

"Can't remember."

"What was her name?"

"Her?" Wellis smiled. "It wasn't a her, dickhead. It was a him."

30

Finally it made sense: Wellis was the reason Sam lost all the weight. He'd come into Sam's life, ruined it, turned it upside down and Sam was dragged under with him. He couldn't eat. He couldn't sleep. I knew as well why Sam never wanted to talk about his work to Julia, and why—even after the affair with Ursula Gray ended—he was working so late. Wellis was turning the screw, demanding more and more. And if Sam refused, he'd put his wife in danger.

I imagined that was also part of the reason for ending the affair. He couldn't carry on with Ursula while he knew Julia was in the firing line. Sam was many things—a liar, a cheat, an accomplice—but he wasn't cruel. He was never apathetic. He was conflicted, unable to articulate his feelings or admit to the world what he really was, but he loved his wife deeply. Maybe not as a wife—maybe only as a friend—but he loved her all the same.

Ursula was just an experiment; a bridge for him to go halfway. He'd spent an evening asking her for every detail of her previous relationships: the men she'd seen, who they were, what they did together. It seemed likely Sam was building up to something with Ursula; using her as a vessel, trying to pluck up the courage to invite another man into their bed. It was everything he could never ask Julia to do, and the reason Sam and Julia didn't have a sex life. He married her because he was still trying to deny what he felt. Maybe he thought he could push it down and bury it somewhere. But as the marriage went on, it became more difficult to control. Ursula was a route that got him some of the way. Wellis, despite the misery he wrought in Sam's life, could get him to the other side.

"I set him up with a nice little Albanian kid," Wellis said, enjoying the moment. He pushed his tongue in against his cheek in a blowjob gesture. "Fresh out of the fridge, this kid was. Nineteen, skinny, cute little tattoo on the back of his neck. Spoke pretty decent English, and was willing to suck cock for pennies. That's how you want them: young and willing and ready to bend over."

"What was the kid's name?"

"I *told* you: I don't know their fucking names."

"Where does he live?"

"Why, you gonna go round there and try to find him?"

"Where does he *live*?"

A pause. "The kid's dead."

Somehow another lost life didn't seem all that surprising. Wellis was like a black hole. He drew people in so deep and so fast, they couldn't find their way back out.

"You killed him?" I asked.

Wellis didn't reply.

"*Did* you?"

He shrugged. "I suppose, in a way, I did."

"What does that even mean?"

When I looked down at him, a gentle movement passed across his eyes, like he was on the verge of telling me something. But then he stopped himself.

"The kid was in the wrong place at the wrong time," he said quietly.

I stepped away from them both, trying to clear my head.

And then my phone went off.

Central London number, one I didn't recognize.

"Hello?"

"Mr. Raker?"

"Yeah."

"It's Rob Wren—Sam's brother."

Wellis was watching me, looking up from under his brow. Suddenly, there was something I didn't like in his face. I kept my eyes on him as I talked.

"Thanks for calling me back."

"No problem. Sorry it's taken me a couple of days. I've been out in San Francisco since the weekend and have only just checked my messages."

"I'd like to talk to you."

"Sure."

"Are you at home?"

"No, in the office."

"Where are you based?"

"Tower Bridge."

I got the address from him and told him I'd be there in thirty minutes, then I hung up. Wellis was still looking at me. "What the hell are you staring at?" I said to him.

A smirk, but no reply.

And then a flash of a memory: back to when I'd heard a noise outside earlier. I'd been out to investigate. It had turned out to be nothing.

But I'd left him alone.

Suddenly, Wellis was moving: wrists and ankles not bound to the chair any more, sliver of glass in his hand. He jabbed it toward my face, and as I stepped back to avoid it, he charged me. It was like being hit by a bullet. He put everything into it, forcing us both across the office and into the far wall. The whole room shook: glass breaking in the window frames, dust and debris raining from the ceiling. And then he disappeared past me and out through the main door.

I rocked forward, onto the front foot, and went after him—but those precious seconds had cost me. As I hit sunlight, he was already heading out toward Kennington Road. A second after that, he was gone from view. I stopped. Once people saw him, saw what he looked like, they'd be calling the police.

Which meant I had to leave.

"*Shit!*"

I slammed the flat of my hand down onto the front of the car and glanced in at Gaishe, who was looking over his shoulder at me. In his face, it was obvious he finally saw the reality of his situation: that Wellis didn't care about him and never had—and no one was coming back for him. I grabbed the duct tape and the crowbar, then used the tape to cover the car's registration plates, back and front.

At the wheel, I went over the next hour in my head: when the police turned up, Gaishe would be able to give them a pretty decent description of me—but he didn't have my real name. Witnesses out on Kennington Road would be able to identify the car that left minutes after Wellis—but they wouldn't have my plates. Wellis wouldn't be turning up at his local station any time soon, so I didn't have to worry about him for now. He'd be lying low. Keeping out of sight. But he'd come back for me eventually. He'd want revenge. He'd see me like I saw him: a loose end that, sooner or later, needed tying up.

But, for now, that didn't matter.

What mattered was Sam Wren.

And the lie that was his life.

31

Robert Wren worked for a PR agency on the banks of the Thames, with views out to Tower Bridge and HMS *Belfast*. The offices weren't hard to find: they were in a cube-shaped glass and steel building, with a massive digital clock set about halfway up and a replica of the Wright Brothers' Flyer hanging in the foyer. Inside, the foyer was huge and airy, and— about fifty feet above me—a mezzanine café looked out over the Thames. I walked up to reception and asked for Wren.

I'd promised him I'd be thirty minutes, but that was before Wellis screwed up my plans. I'd screwed up too, and that was what rubbed at me. Cases ate away at me the whole time I was on them—but rarely like this. The way Sam had vanished, his journey on the Tube that day, the way his life was just a hollow shell built on lies and half-truths, it all added up—and as it added up, the pressure built.

Robert Wren emerged from one of the elevators on the far side of the foyer. He was older than Sam—at a guess, thirty-five—and, with blue eyes and fair hair, he looked like an overweight version of his brother. He was dressed in an open-neck white shirt, a pair of dark blue denims and tan shoes so shiny they reflected back half the sunlight in the build-ing. He was every inch the PR man.

We shook hands. "How long have you been doing this?" he asked as we headed to an elevator and rode it up to the café. I was struck by how softly spoken he was. Julia said he was a partner at the firm and I could tell he'd got to the top through self-control and reliability, rather than by being some kind of maverick, coming up with unworkable plans and screaming at his staff until he backed them into a corner.

"Finding missing people or finding Sam?"

"Missing people."

"Almost four years."

"What did you do before?"

"I was a journalist—but don't hold that against me."

He laughed, but it all felt a little fake. I'd dealt with thousands of PRs during my years on the paper and very few were genuinely interested in you. Most were able to put on a pretty convincing show, though, and Robert Wren was definitely doing that. He got a couple of coffees and then brought them over to a table in the café, along with a selection of pastries.

"I didn't know if you were hungry, so I just grabbed everything," he said, and he broke out into that same laugh again. This time it sounded different; less like one from the PR manual, and more cautious somehow. After that, he started talking about his brother, initially in quiet, somber tones, and then—as he tracked back through their childhood and the period after their parents passed on—in a much warmer, more expansive way.

"Were you two close?" I asked.

"Yes. I mean, we fought—fought all the time growing up, and even when we were adults and supposed to know better—but, yeah, we were brothers. We always made time for each other. We used to meet up for lunch, and after work for a drink, because, as I'm sure Julia told you, I commute in from Reading, and I've got a couple of kids, so it was much harder for me to meet up with Sam on weekends without military-grade planning."

I got out my pad and set it down on the table. "What was your impression of Sam during the year before he went missing?"

"Impression?"

"Do you think he changed during that time?"

He frowned. "Not really."

"You never got that from him?"

He paused for a moment and looked off to the marina. "I remember when he came in here one lunchtime, spitting bullets because they'd cut his bonuses. He vented big time that day. I'm sure he did the same at Julia when he got home." He stopped for a second time and then started shaking his head. "After that, he became a bit disillusioned with the whole thing. I remember he talked a couple of times about finding another job, but what job are you going to find in the middle of a recession?"

"Julia said he was worried about the mortgage."

"Yes," Wren said, nodding. "It gave him some sleepless nights, particularly when Julia was made redundant. I told him not to stress about it. I told him, if it came to it, we'd help them out. But Sam . . ." He sighed and leaned back in his chair. "Sam was very independent. He was hard on himself; put pressure on himself. He was definitely cut out for investment banking. He was a lovely guy, don't get me wrong, but he had a tough streak; he could swim with the sharks. He also found it difficult to accept charity, particularly after so many years of making big bonuses."

So Sam definitely hadn't left that day because he was worried about paying the mortgage. An offer was on the table from his brother, one Sam had been too proud to communicate to Julia. Or maybe too preoccupied. She was still under the impression the bailiffs would be kicking down the door any second.

Wren looked at me, and for the first time there was a sadness in his face. A shimmer flashed in one of his eyes, then he flattened his lips, as if this was some kind of a defeat. "I wouldn't have put Sam down as the kind of guy to walk away. Not someone who abandons his family. But we all have a tipping point, I guess."

"So what was Sam's tipping point, do you think?"

Another flash of sadness, but something else too: the same thing I'd noticed when he'd laughed earlier. *Nerves.*

"Robert?"

He shook his head. "Nothing he ever spoke about. Nothing that would make him up and leave like he did."

"But something *did* make him leave."

Wren looked at me. "Right."

"So something was bothering him."

"Like I said, I think the financial side of things really got to him."

"But you'd offered to help him."

A moment of hesitation. "He felt boxed in by the fact that he couldn't earn what he was capable of earning. And he felt pressure to provide for Julia, especially after she was made redundant. I'm certain that's why he left."

"Did Sam tell you something?"

His eyes narrowed. "What do you mean?"

I leaned forward, into his space, and he reacted exactly how I wanted him to: he moved back, seeing confidence and certainty in me. "I think we both know that Sam left because something was eating at him," I said. "What I want to know is what you know."

He was frowning. "I don't understand."

"Here are the theories, Robert. Sam left because he couldn't face up to his financial responsibilities. I don't believe that, especially now. Sam left because Julia and he were fighting, and that drove him away. I don't believe that either, even if she does. What husband disappears at the first sign of a fight?" I paused, let him take it in. He was still frowning, but I could see a shift in his expression. Something giving. "Do you want to find him?"

His cheeks colored. I wasn't sure if it was anger or embarrassment, and at this point didn't really care. "Yes, of course I do," he said, his voice raised for the first time. I left it there to see where it took us—but it didn't take us anywhere. He peered down into his coffee cup, his thumb and forefinger turning it gently, and then looked up.

"I can't . . ."

"Can't what?"

His lips flattened again. "Who gets to hear this?"

"Gets to hear what?"

"This. This conversation we're having."

"Who *don't* you want to hear it?"

He leaned back in his seat and looked around the café. It was quiet now. The mid-morning meetings were over and lunch was yet to come. Behind Wren, the sun reflected in every panel, collecting in a pool on the floor of the foyer below us. The building was air conditioned but Robert Wren had small dots of perspiration all along his hairline.

His eyes came back to me. "About ten, maybe twelve years ago, Sam and I went on a cheapo package deal to Ibiza. Had a week there. We were both single, no ties, just went over to have a bit of fun. One night we were in this club and we'd had an absolute ton to drink, and we got separated. I'd seen him earlier in the night with this girl, really attractive, and they'd been getting on, so I left them to it. I hooked up with another girl, we had a good time . . ." He paused, twirled his finger: *and the rest of it*. "Anyway, she left and I went looking for Sam. About five minutes later, I found the girl he'd been chatting to—but she was with some other guy. I asked her where Sam was and she said he'd left in the middle of the evening and never come back. She was pissed off, understandably."

He looked around him again, but the nearest people to us were a couple of men on a table on the far side. "I looked all over the club but couldn't find him anywhere, so I went outside. Nothing out front, but around the back—in the car park—I found Sam talking to someone. I was drunk. Annoyed. I'd spent half the evening trying to find him and all the time he was in the bloody car park. So I started over toward him, ready to let him have it, but when I got closer he started kissing this woman, and I thought, 'Leave it until the morning. Let him have his fun for tonight.'" He brought his coffee toward him, eyes distant, replaying the moment over. "Except . . ."

"It wasn't a woman."

He looked at me, not sure how I'd put it together. "Right."

"It was a man."

He nodded. "How did you know?"

"Was that the first time?" I asked, sidestepping the question.

"Yes."

"Did you bring it up the next day?"

"Yes."

"And what did he say?"

"He called it a 'mistake.' Said he was drunk, didn't know what he was doing. But it wasn't much of a lie. We could both see through it. After that, he just . . . broke down."

"No one else knew?"

"No. He made me promise not to tell anyone. Not a soul. When he started dating Julia, I had to sit there saying nothing to her, nothing to Mum and Dad before they passed on. They died without even knowing who their son was. Mum would have understood. Dad was more old-fashioned, but he would have come round. I used to have screaming matches with Sam, telling him over and over it wasn't fair on Julia, on his family, that mostly it wasn't fair on *him*. But he was so conflicted. He just didn't know how to handle it."

"Did he ever do anything about it?"

"You mean talk about leaving Julia?"

"Or cheat on her."

I knew the answer—but I wanted to see if he did.

"He never talked about leaving her," he said after a while. "I know it sounds weird, but those two were really close. He loved her—maybe not in the way a husband should love his wife, but he still loved her. He was just so confused: he could pretend he was something he wasn't in front of her, so she didn't get hurt. But I was like the release valve. When we got together, he let it all come out. I felt so desperately sad for him."

"So did he cheat on her?"

They were close, Sam confided in his brother, so I expected Robert Wren to start talking about Ursula Gray. But instead—as he traced a finger across the table, collecting spilled sugar granules into a pile—he didn't mention her at all. Maybe he didn't even know.

"One time, I was over in Canary Wharf seeing a client, so I met him for lunch. This must have been, I don't know, late November—a few weeks before he disappeared. He seemed a bit quiet, but that was how he was sometimes. Not around Julia, but around me. I understood that. I knew what he was trying to process. At the end of the meal, he became quite emotional. Not crying exactly, but everything he said was very heartfelt. He said he loved Julia—just kept saying that over and over—and, as we talked some more, I started to realize it was all born out of guilt. He felt guilty about something. Not just keeping this secret from her, lying to her, but something else."

"What?"

He didn't reply, but I rode out the silence.

"Sam might have been a risk-taker at work, able to put on a front for them, but he wasn't like that outside. Not with this. He'd spent years—from before I even saw him at that club—pushing these feelings down . . . and, finally, he did something about it."

"You mean he'd met someone?"

"Yes."

"Who?"

"He didn't really give me many details, but I got the subtext."

"Which was what?"

Wren colored a little. "He'd paid for a prostitute."

I remembered Wellis's words from earlier: *He used our service once. Must have been a month before he left.* "How did he meet him?" I asked.

"He didn't say."

"Did he tell you the guy's name?"

"No."

"Where they met?"

"No."

"*When* they met?"

"Uh . . ." He massaged his brow. "I'm pretty sure it was 11 November. I remember I flew out to California for a conference the next day."

"Did Sam say *anything* about the guy he met?"

"Not really. I think he might have said the guy was foreign."

I set him up with a nice little Albanian kid. Fresh out of the fridge, this kid was. That's how you want them: young and willing and ready to bend over. I sighed, looking out to the boats, to the people on the edges of the docks. The first man Sam had slept with had been brought into the country in the back of a lorry, against his will. I doubted either of them imagined their lives turning out that way, even if there was a strange kind of symmetry to their meeting: both were prisoners, one of them chained to Adrian Wellis, the other shackled to his own guilt.

Wrong time, wrong place.

That was how Wellis described the eventual death of the Albanian kid.

I turned back to Robert Wren. "He definitely never mentioned the guy's name, or where the two of them met? I need you to think hard about that for me."

Wren looked off, to a space behind me, his mind ticking over. "He never named the guy or said where he lived, but I do remember him mentioning one thing."

"What was that?"

"It was just a . . ." His eyes finally came back to me. "It was weird. He said the prostitute lived in this place where there were no lights. He said he got to his door, on to the floor this guy was on, and all the bulbs were out. It was completely black. Sam had an iPhone, had some sort of torch app on there, so he got that out and used it to navigate his way along the corridor. And when he got to the flat he said it felt . . ." He stopped. "He said it felt like someone was there."

"In the corridor with him?"

"Yes."

"Did he have a look around?"

"Yes. He said he shone his torch around."

"And no one was there?"

"No."

"So there wasn't anyone with him?"

Wren looked at me and shrugged, and I could read the gesture as clearly as if he'd spoken the words. *I guess not. But then, that was who my brother was at the end.*

A tormented, confused man.

32

12 March | Three Months Earlier

Healy tabbed through the next page of search results. It was getting hard to concentrate now. He'd been at it for hours, trying to find any sort of opening. A pinprick, a puncture, however small. But the third victim, Joseph Symons, was just like the others: a man who left nothing of himself, or his kidnapper, as he was pulled away into the dark.

He leaned back in his seat and looked down to the board where the two faces had become three and the map had been widened further. They all lived in similar places—decaying, decrepit housing estates or tower blocks—and they were all men who weren't immediately reported missing: single, no ties, no reason for their disappearance to raise any alarms. But, after a while, even the lonely are missed. All three had some friends or some family that started to get concerned by the lack of contact, and all three had been gone between four days and two weeks by the time the pile of hair was found on their pillow. The first victim—Steven Wilky—barely registered as a blip on the radar, but when one of the tabloids got wind of the second, Marc Evans, it became uncontainable. Evans was the son of a respected politician, estranged from his father but not completely out of touch. Twelve hours after the police kicked down the door of his flat, the headline that would define the case ran on the front pages: "Invasion of the Body Snatcher."

Sleet blew in against the window of the office, sliding down in thin, sludgy trails. Healy watched it, then turned back to the HOLMES data. He tabbed through some more pages, his eyes scanning the locations from which the victims were taken, the approximate times, the lists of worthless trace evidence, fingerprint lifts and fibers. It led nowhere. It all led nowhere.

"Well, well, well."

Healy swivelled in his chair. Behind him, Kevin Sallows was perched on the edge of the next desk along eating a cheeseburger. The occupant, a cop called Carmichael, was gone for the day. An amused smile broke out on Sallows's face, and Healy got a glimpse of partly chewed meat and lettuce.

Sallows looked at his watch. "You clocking overtime, Healy?"

"Yeah," he said, turning back to the data. "Something like that."

"Ten o'clock at night—you should be heading home to your good lady wife about now, shouldn't you?" Healy felt himself tense, and Sallows picked up on the movement. "Oh, sorry. That was insensitive."

Healy turned in his seat, all the way around this time.

Sallows was still smiling. "Why are you wasting your time here?"

"Where?"

"Here," he said, gesturing to the computer with the half-eaten cheeseburger. "You think the rest of us didn't do our homework?"

"I'm playing catch-up."

"Fucking right you are. You remember why?"

Keep in control, he thought. *Just keep in control.*

"Hello?"

Healy ignored him.

"What, are you deaf now too?"

"No, I'm not deaf," Healy said. "I remember why I'm playing catch-up. I was off looking for the piece of shit who killed my daughter, while you were back here with your thumb up Davidson's arsehole."

Sallows's face dropped. "What did you say?"

"You heard what I said."

"Yeah, I heard," Sallows replied, and dropped the rest of the cheeseburger into the bin next to Carmichael's desk. He stood up. "You remember why your girl left?"

Keep in control.

"No? Well, let me remind you: she left because you punched her mum in the side of the head. You remember that, big man?"

"She didn't leave because of that."

Sallows snorted. "Is that a *joke*?"

"You've got no idea what you're talking about."

"Yeah?" Sallows leaned in, meat on his breath, food in his teeth. "Face it, Healy, you can't handle this. You can't handle the pressure. Those eight-year-old twins got to you so much you ended up putting your missus in a neck brace. You ended up driving your daughter away, into the arms of a fucking psychopath. Doesn't this"—he gestured to the incident room—"ring any bells for you? This is the same as those girls. Three victims, and we don't have *shit*. Nothing. What happens when

Craw turns to you and asks you to step up? What'll happen when you can't find the answers? You gonna crumble again?"

Healy felt his muscles harden. He pressed his teeth together, trying to force all the anger out.

Don't react. Don't slip.

Sallows leaned in to him. "Of course you're gonna crumble, Colm. It's who you are. It's what you do. You couldn't even save your own daughter."

In the blink of an eye, Healy was up off his seat, nose to nose with Sallows, pushing forward until Sallows hit the desk behind him. Anger erupted so hard and so fast, Healy's vision blurred, like a windscreen smeared with rain, and the noise around him became sounds from another room: dim and distant and undefined. "You mention her name again," he said slowly, his voice trembling, "and I will fucking end you."

Sallows stared at him.

And then broke out into a smile.

He maneuvered himself away from Healy, and made a point of brushing himself down, as if he'd somehow become contaminated. Then he winked and dropped his voice to a whisper, so no one else in the room could hear it. "That's the Colm we know and love," Sallows said gently. "And that's the side of you that's gonna help us finish you off for good."

2 *April*

Healy had been waiting five minutes by the time Teresa Reed finally emerged from the High Security Unit. As the pale blue door sucked shut behind her, she headed to a locker about twenty feet away, opened it up and started to fish her things out. She didn't spot him, didn't even look round, but even if she had it wouldn't have made a difference. He'd been watching her for over two months and she barely seemed to notice anything beyond what *she* had to do. Other people, other lives, they didn't matter until she ran into them head on.

As soon as she'd grabbed a canvas bag, tie-dyed and scruffy, a mobile phone and her car keys, she pushed the locker shut and headed out past him. He waited until she'd gone through the main doors and then followed. As he moved outside into the fresh spring air, he thought about what he was doing. *Of course you're gonna crumble, Colm. It's what you do.* He felt fire erupt in his belly and pushed it back down. Fuck Davidson and Sallows. They weren't important. He'd take care of them, just as he'd take care of Teresa Reed. He'd take care of all of them eventually. But everything needed to be done right.

He felt around in his coat pocket.

What he needed was still there.

Healy picked up speed, scanning the car park for any other signs of life. No one close. That suited him fine. Rain had fallen in the night, so he was careful not to place his feet anywhere they were going to make a sound. He didn't want her to hear him coming. Not yet.

Eight feet short of her, she started fiddling around in her handbag for her car keys. *They're in your pocket, you dozy bitch.* A few seconds later, she must have realized and felt around in her jacket for them. Her Mini was five cars down, on the right.

"Excuse me!" Healy called from behind her.

She looked back over her shoulder, initially unaware she was being spoken to, and then slowing as she saw Healy coming after her. She stopped. "Yes?"

"Teresa, right?"

Her eyes narrowed. She obviously didn't recognize him at first from their meeting five weeks before. Then it seemed to click. "Ah, yes. Uh . . . Colin?"

"Colm."

"*Colm.* Right. You're the policeman."

"That's right." He engineered a smile. "You recognized me today."

She flushed a little. "Yes. Sorry about the last time."

He held up a hand in a *don't worry* gesture. He reached into his pocket. "Here. You dropped this as you left." He handed her a small folding umbrella.

She reached out and took it, a frown on her face. "Oh. Right."

"Is something the matter?"

"Uh, no. I just . . ." Teresa Reed looked up. "It doesn't matter."

But he knew what she was thinking: *I didn't think I'd brought this with me.* And she hadn't. He'd been to her house and found it outside, in the front garden, next to one of the flowerpots. She must have placed it down there and forgotten to pick it back up.

"Anyway," Healy said. "Given the weather this week, I thought you might need it. It doesn't really suit me, to be honest, otherwise I would have kept it for myself."

She laughed. "Well, thank you."

"You're very welcome."

Healy rode out the silence, letting her make the next move.

"Well, uh, thanks again," she said. "Maybe I can buy you a coffee as a thank you or something?"

He looked enthusiastic. "Oh, that would be great."

She broke out into another smile, obviously thinking she saw something in Healy: excitement, or anticipation, or relief that she'd finally taken notice of him.

But it wasn't like that at all.

And soon she would find out why.

33

Outside Robert Wren's offices, the day was baking hot and tourists were everywhere. I returned to the car, parked under cover five minutes' walk away and, in the shade, realized I'd been awake for thirty hours. I could feel myself drift, the pull of sleep strong and comforting. And then, like an alarm clock going off, my phone burst into life. It was a central London number—but not one I recognized.

"David Raker."

"Mr. Raker, it's PC Brian Westerley here."

Westerley had promised to call me back today—Friday—and he'd followed through on that promise, despite any misgivings he may have had. That marked him out as a straight arrow; someone who was true to his word and wouldn't fall back on his commitments. He may not have been the greatest cop in the world—his sloppy work on Sam's case suggested as much—but if he had an old-fashioned attitude toward responsibility, he may still have some useful insight.

"PC Westerley—thanks for calling me back."

"Well, I didn't have much choice, did I?"

I let him have his moment. "Did you get a chance to pull the file?"

"Yes. I don't know what you expect to find, though."

"Maybe nothing," I said. "Or maybe you have some insight I hadn't considered or wasn't able to find." It was a crude tactic but the uniforms at the bottom of the food chain usually spent half their existence wiping boot prints off their faces.

"Okay," he said. There was already a change in his tone, suggesting my tactic had worked. "What do you want to know?"

We started talking about Sam, about the day he disappeared and about the file Westerley had opened on him. He said he'd initially spoken to Julia at the station on Earls Court Road, but had followed it up with a visit to the Wrens' home.

"Julia said you pulled the footage from the Tube as well."

"Yes."

"Were you able to locate Sam?"

I heard him leaf through a couple of pages. He was probably trying to get back up to speed on the fly. It didn't really matter, though. If he'd managed to locate Sam, spotted where he got off the train, Julia wouldn't have hired me to find him. "He got on the Tube," Westerley said eventually, sounding like he was reading directly from his own report, "and he didn't get off again."

Thanks for the info. "You didn't see him get off?" I asked.

"No."

"How far did you follow the footage?"

"All around the Circle line until it terminated at Hammersmith."

"It didn't bother you that you couldn't find him?"

He muttered something I couldn't make out, but it was obvious he didn't like this line of questioning. It made him look amateurish, and if he felt like this was a character assassination, he'd close up. I moved things on.

"What background did you do on Sam?"

"Background?"

"Relationships? Finances? Work?"

A pause. "I looked into it," he said, but it was an obvious lie. If he'd been twenty years younger, he might have seen it as a challenge. But not now. Now he prioritized his cases according to how difficult they were, and how much of it would blow back at him if it didn't get put to bed. There wouldn't be a lot of fallout from Sam Wren's disappearance because he didn't tick any of the boxes: he wasn't underage, he wasn't female, he didn't suffer from mental health problems and he wasn't a danger to the public.

"Did you recover any personal possessions?" I asked.

"Like?"

"Well, he had a briefcase with him the day he disappeared, for one."

"I put in a call to the Tube's lost property department to see if there was anything with Wren's name on it. But that was a dead end."

"But you took his toothbrush away, right?"

"Right. We always try to do that in missing persons. You never know when it may come in useful. We got some fingerprint lifts and a DNA sample from the brush."

"Did either of those lead anywhere?"

"Nowhere new."

That stopped me. "What do you mean, 'new'?"

"We obviously had his details on file from that incident twenty months back. He was never charged with anything, but it's just something we do."

"What incident?"

"That fight he was involved in."

"Fight?"

"Oh, I thought you'd know this."

I'd done a basic background check on Sam the day after Julia had first approached me to see if he had any kind of record. He didn't. Julia hadn't mentioned anything about a fight either, which meant one of two things: she'd lied to me, or at least chosen not to say anything—or, more likely, it was so minor, she hadn't thought to bring it up.

"What was the fight about?" I asked.

"Uh . . ." I heard Westerley turn a couple of pages. "Two men started at each other's throats at the entrance to Gloucester Road Tube station at about 7:45 a.m. on the morning of 14 October 2010. One of them, a Simon Mbebeni, claimed the other, Robert Stonehouse, racially abused him at the ticket machine. Stonehouse had a mate with him, James Quinn. Quinn's been done for public order offenses before and, in the subsequent interviews, admitted to having something of a problem with the UK's immigration policy, so who knows who really instigated it? Maybe Stonehouse, maybe Quinn, but Stonehouse admitted telling Mbebeni"—more pages being turned—"'You can't get away with that here, you fucking monkey' after Mbebeni appeared to jump the queue. He also admitted to throwing the first punch and breaking Mbebeni's nose in the process, but only after Mbebeni had pushed him into the ticket machine."

"So where does Sam come in?"

"He entered the station about ten seconds after it all kicked off, and tried to help Underground staff break it up. He had to contend with Quinn, Quinn got aggressive and attacked Mr. Wren. Mr. Wren fought back and punched Quinn in the throat, probably not intentionally, but Quinn blacked out and got rushed to hospital. It looked like Mr. Wren was going to be charged, but his solicitor eventually got the charges dropped."

"What did the others get?"

"Stonehouse got a year, Quinn six months and Mbebeni got a suspended sentence, a fine and two hundred hours' community service. One of the London Underground employees was also cautioned—CCTV footage showed him laying into Stonehouse big style."

"Who was the employee?"

"Uh, his name was . . ." A pause as he searched for it. "Duncan Pell."

The guy in the booth I'd talked to at Gloucester Road the day before. *Interesting.* He'd been weird when I'd tried to ask him questions: defensive, introverted, agitated. Something didn't sit right then, and it sat even less comfortably now. If he had the capacity to put his fist through someone's face, plainly he was no shrinking violet.

"Pell got a caution and a £500 fine," Westerley went on, "but his representative argued—successfully—that he was trying to protect the public from Stonehouse and Quinn, so Pell got to keep his job and didn't have to do community service. I have to say, it probably helped that Quinn was a massive racist, and that Stonehouse threw the first punch at Pell. It's much easier to get people on your side when you don't start the fight and when one of the men you're up against thinks Hitler was an okay kind of guy."

"What do we know about Pell?"

"Know about him?"

"What's his background?"

More pages being turned.

"Ex-army. He enlisted at sixteen, worked his way up to lieutenant, left at thirty-one after two years in Afghanistan. Prior to that, he'd been in Bosnia. So basically perfect preparation for working on London Underground." He chuckled to himself.

I thanked him and hung up. The clock was showing 11:49. My mind returned to the very start of the case; to Sam getting on the Tube.

I dialed Ewan Tasker's number.

"Raker."

"How you doing, Task?"

"Yeah, good. You?"

"Tired."

"What, you been up bumping and grinding with the missus all night?"

I smiled. "You've got a one-track mind."

"It's the only action I get at my age."

"Listen, I need another favor from you. Last one, I promise."

"That's what you always say."

"I need some more CCTV footage."

"From when?"

"Same day, 16 December, but I need everything—literally, everything—you can lay your hands on. Ticket halls, walkways, escalators, elevators, everything."

"Gloucester Road only?"

I thought about it. On the footage I had, Sam disappeared between Victoria and St. James's Park. "Gloucester Road through to, say, Westminster, just to be on the safe side."

"You got it."

"One other thing."

"Here we go."

"Same deal," I said. "But Gloucester Road on 14 October 2010."

"Just Gloucester Road?"

"Just Gloucester Road."

"October the . . .?"

"Fourteenth."

"That's nineteen, twenty months back."

"Right."

"What are you going back that far for?"

"I'm going to watch a fight."

34

Julia Wren was the manager of an Italian called Sal's on Bayswater Road. The plan had been to call her, to find out when she'd next be home and to tell her what I'd found out about Sam. It was going to be painful, but she deserved to hear it. Instead, when she picked up, she insisted I came to her work. She was on shift until midnight, and she wanted to hear where I'd got to. "It might not be the sort of thing you want to discuss at work," I said to her, but that only seemed to harden her resolve. So I headed for the restaurant.

Inside, it was half full and Julia was sitting at a table near the back, going through some receipts and cross-checking them against print-outs. She seemed a little brighter than the last time I'd seen her, perhaps because she thought I might be bringing some positive news. But by the end of this, she would probably wish I'd never arrived.

As one of her waiters got me a cup of coffee, we talked about the restaurant, and then finally she asked how things were going with the case.

"I need to tell you a couple of things about Sam."

An expectant look. "Okay."

"Some of it's going to be hard to hear."

Now a frown started to form. "Okay," she repeated.

"Maybe we should discuss this somewhere more private."

"Just . . ." She paused. "Just tell me."

"How well did you know the people he worked with?"

"I knew them well enough," she said, but she was uncertain of herself now.

"Who did he talk about?"

"Ross, obviously. Iain. Sam and I used to go out with Iain and his girlfriend from time to time. There were a couple of others too. Esther. Abi. I think a guy called Dave."

"Did he ever talk about his secondment to Michaelhouse?"

"Yes, of course."

"Ever mention an Ursula Gray?"

"Ursula?" A pause. "Yes, he mentioned her."

"Much?"

She stopped. Frowned. "Quite a bit, I guess."

"What did he used to say about her?"

"I can't really remember. Nothing that particularly sticks with me. He used to tell me what they'd been working on; clients they'd been to see."

"Did you ever meet her?"

"No." A hesitation. "Yes. Uh, I mean, not really."

A weird answer. I studied her for a moment. "Not really?"

"A couple of times. I never chatted to her much."

I paused, letting the silence prepare the way for what I was about to tell her, when I noticed a subtle change. Her eyes snapped to me, as if she was worried I might notice something, and I was reminded of that first night I'd met her, when she'd skipped around the fact that she and Sam had been fighting. Back then, it had been out of some misplaced belief that I would judge her. Now it felt different. Now it felt like deception.

"Are you okay?" I asked.

"Sure."

I watched her. "Julia?"

She flinched at the mention of her name, and when she looked up she had an expression etched into her face that didn't house one grain of truth: a smile that was as thin as paper, eyes that held no warmth, a mouth so small and tight it was like she'd tried to force it closed to prevent anything coming out.

And, in that moment, I suddenly understood.

She'd managed to convince me that the lie she told me that first night was about the two of them fighting; about the guilt she felt in continually pushing him for the truth about his work. But it wasn't that at all. Not even close to it.

It was the affair with Ursula.

"You knew about it," I said.

She didn't reply and, in the silence, I had to bite down hard to prevent myself reacting. I leaned back in my seat and drew my coffee toward me.

"I'm sorry," she said finally.

I didn't respond, trying to figure out what her reasons might be for telling me another lie.

"I found out late last August," she said quietly.

"Then why the *hell* didn't you tell me that?"

"I just . . ." She paused as the waiter passed, and then watched as he disappeared down to the front of the restaurant where a waitress was busy laying tablecloths and putting out cutlery. "When I read about you, when I was researching you, I read this article about your cases. And this one bit of it stuck with me. It said you never took on work like this. Affairs. Stuff to do with money. I thought, if I told you the truth, you'd never agree to help me."

"It was a newspaper report, Julia."

She looked at me, puzzled.

"It's *fiction*. No one's called me 'Mindhunter.' The tabloids just made it up like they make everything else up. Journalists don't decide what I do and do not take on. *I* decide it. You should have told me *everything*."

"I just didn't think you'd—"

"You should have told me."

"I didn't want to do anything to stop you from helping me."

I said nothing, and looked away.

"Look at me," she said, but was gesturing toward the restaurant. "I'm a manager of an Italian restaurant on £27,400 per year, have no husband, no brothers or sisters, both my parents are gone, and I've got a mortgage so big, some days it's all I can do not to cry at the thought of it. At least with Sam, whatever his flaws, I had a home. He had a good job, was on good money and—even if we had to become more frugal—it's easier to face up to those sacrifices if you're doing it with someone else."

"So not telling me about the fact he was having an affair for the best part of a year would do what exactly? Stop me from bringing him back so he can pay the mortgage?"

She frowned. Hurt. To her, it felt like she was bleeding out and all I was doing was picking and prizing at the wound. I realized I was just offloading on her now, letting the frustration out, but it was difficult not to. I was sick of the lies.

"You know Robert has offered to help you out?"

"He offered to help Sam out."

"He said you didn't have to worry about the mortgage."

"Did he?"

"You don't believe him?"

She smiled, but there was nothing in it but sadness and humiliation. "How exactly do you ask someone for £3,000 a month for an indefinite period?"

"He's family."

"He's *Sam's* family."

I didn't bother responding. If she didn't want to end up homeless, she was going to have to find a way of swallowing her pride.

"How did you find out?"

This time there was no movement in her face, no bunched muscles or lack of eye contact. No hidden half-truths. "He left his Facebook up one Saturday while he popped to the shops." She stopped. I'd checked Sam's Facebook on the first day and the messages hadn't been there. He'd deleted them all. "I saw she'd mailed him and my curiosity got the better of me. She was flirty and intelligent, and men like those things. Even Sam."

She meant, *Even Sam who never wanted sex*. Except he did want sex. He thought he wanted it with Ursula because he thought Ursula might be willing to experiment with him. But then even that wasn't enough.

"What did the messages say?"

A jealous twist to her face, and she tucked a strand of red hair behind her ear. "She didn't recount what they did, but the suggestion was there, barely even hidden."

"Any specifics?"

"In one of the e-mails she told him she couldn't stop thinking about him."

"Had he responded to her?"

"No."

"Not at all?"

"Not that I could find."

That made sense: Julia found out about Sam and Ursula in August. By then, Sam was already trying to kill off the relationship. By mid October it was all over.

"Did you confront him about it?"

"No."

"Why?"

She looked at me as if she'd spotted something unspoken in my question. "Do you think I haven't got any pride—is that it?"

"Don't turn this around."

"It would have been the easy thing to have forgotten about him. Easier than lying to you. But sometimes you've got to be realistic."

"Realistic?"

"I couldn't afford to be on my own, and Sam . . ."

"Sam what?"

She took a deep breath and made minute adjustments to the papers on the table in front of her. "I think Sam was doing something much worse."

"Like what?"

"I think he may have been involved with someone else."

"Other than Ursula Gray?"

"Yes."

I sat back in my chair, hands wrapped around the warmth of the coffee cup. "Who would he be involved with?" I asked, but then realized she wasn't talking about another affair. She was talking about Adrian Wellis.

She pursed her lips, as if this was the bit she liked least. "One Sunday, just before he disappeared, I got home early from having lunch with a couple of friends. I called out to him three or four times but he never heard me. Never heard me come up the stairs either. When I got to the top, the bedroom door was open and he was sitting on the edge of the bed with this big bag in his lap, talking to someone on the phone."

"Who was he talking to?"

"I don't know. But, whoever it was, Sam kept saying to them, 'I can't invest a bag full of dirty money. You need to transfer it *legitimately*.' He just kept repeating it, over and over, getting angrier and angrier. But eventually he seemed to get shouted down."

"The bag was full of money?"

She glanced at me. "Yes. Full of it."

It was Wellis's money. Sam had seen a hole in Wellis's finances, found out who he was, and—all the way up until the end—Wellis took revenge by turning the screw. Wellis had his boot on Sam's throat and wouldn't let go.

"Did you ask him where he got the money?"

"No. I just stood there and watched him."

"Why?"

She paused. "After the call ended, he started crying."

"So you never said anything to him?"

"No. I was scared. I suppose that was another reason I didn't say anything to you to start with; why I kept some of these things to myself. He was obviously involved in something bad. I was scared about what might happen if it got out that I knew. And . . ." She paused. "And the other thing was, I'd never seen him cry before; not once in all the time we were together. So I knew he was hurting." She stopped again, and I understood the subtext: a part of her *wanted* him to hurt, for all that he'd done to her. "To me, it didn't really matter if it was hurt over wherever the money had come from, or hurt over the affair, or both, because I realized as long as I didn't say anything, as long as I didn't tell him what I knew, that regret, that pain, it wouldn't go away."

"He'd have to live with it."

She nodded. "I don't hate him, I don't wish harm on him, but I think he got off a little easy. He *owes* me. That's why I want you to find him."

I pushed my coffee cup aside. There was no telling how much damage this had done. Her senseless lies—spun out from a mix of fear, financial doubt and a misguided desire for revenge—were as harmful as they were aimless. "What if he's dead?"

A movement in her eyes, like a flame dying out. She understood what I meant: *what if the time you've wasted has cost you?* "I hope he's not."

"But if he is?"

She had a look on her face now that I'd most often seen in the grieving: all grayness and distance, like there wasn't enough thread in the world to stitch her life back together. Her loss was incomplete. A circle that didn't join. Until there was a body, until there was a reason, there was no closure. It was the heart of missing persons.

"I want to know where he went," she said finally.

As I watched the faint trace of tears in her eyes, the grief, the anger, I decided not to tell her about who Sam really was. That time would come. But it wasn't now.

Eventually, she looked up. "Will you find him for me?"

"Let's be really clear on something first. You holding back all this information because you think it will somehow affect the way I do my job—it just means it takes longer to find him, and you have to pay me more money. It's *insane*. I get sick of people lying to me, but I accept it as part of my job. What I can't accept is being lied to by the one person I expect to tell me the truth. So, if you do it again, I walk."

She nodded.

I let the silence sit there between us, let her chew on my anger, and then I got out my notepad and flipped it open. "Did Sam ever tell you about a fight he was involved in?"

"A fight?"

"At Gloucester Road Tube station, back in October 2010."

Recognition sparked in her face. "Oh right, yes. He was interviewed by the police about that. The whole thing was ridiculous. He was trying to act as peacemaker."

"Did he ever mention a guy called Duncan Pell?"

"Was he the one who worked for London Underground?"

"Yeah. You remember him?"

"Of course. They met up one time."

That stopped me. "Who—Pell and Sam?"

"Yes."

"They *knew* each other?"

"Yes. Duncan was really grateful to Sam for helping him out because things got quite nasty in that fight. So he offered to buy Sam a drink. And Sam accepted."

35

The extra CCTV footage from Ewan Tasker turned up at 9 a.m. the next morning. It had been sent in a plain envelope, with no return address. Inside were two unmarked DVDs. Liz had left early to prep a case, even though it was a Saturday, so I set to work straight away, firing up my Mac and playing the first disc.

The footage from 14 October 2010.

The fight at Gloucester Road.

In the desktop folder, Task appeared to have got me the whole week, 11 October through to 17 October. Each subfolder contained a different day. Alongside the folders was a Word document, which turned out to be a note from him: "Had to get a week here—once you go back further than a year it's saved in seven-day blocks." I double-clicked on 14 October. Inside were two different video files: 5 a.m.–2 p.m.; 2 p.m.–12 a.m. I opened the 5 a.m.–2 p.m. footage and then dragged the slider forward to 7:30.

At 7:33 a.m., Duncan Pell drifted into view. He came from the left-hand side of the camera, up from the booth he'd been in when I'd talked to him at the station. He was focused on something: head still, eyes fixed, cutting through the crowds like a knife.

Then I realized what he was doing.

There were three doors into the ticket hall. At the left-hand one, propped against a sandy brick pillar, was a man holding a piece of cardboard. It was difficult to make him out at first, but as Pell arrived he shifted around and I saw him more clearly: not all that old—forty maybe—but disheveled, dirty, cloaked in a long winter coat and a thick roll-neck sweater, with dark trousers and dark boots. He had a beard, unruly, uncared for, and a black holdall on the floor next to him.

The slightly washed-out quality of the footage made it hard to see the writing on the cardboard, but I could make out one of the words right at the top. *Homeless.* I leaned in even closer as Pell started talking to him. After a minute, Pell was gesturing, pointing over the homeless man's shoulder, then—when the man didn't appear to get the message—he started jabbing a finger into the man's arm as if delivering a warning. After that, the man shrank a little, the resolve disappearing, and he bent down, picked up his holdall and moved off. Within a couple of seconds, he was gone from view.

Pell returned to his booth, out of sight.

Three minutes later, at 7:41, two men entered the station.

They were laughing at something. One of them was tall, skinny, dressed in jeans and a T-shirt, with a thin jacket—all despite the cold—the other smaller, but not by much, and dressed more practically: a thick coat over denims and white trainers. I didn't know what James Quinn and Robert Stonehouse looked like, but these two seemed a decent fit: they had small, combative faces, they were the only men I'd seen enter the station together in the fifteen minutes I'd been watching, and as I saw one of them take out an Oyster card and gesture toward the self-service machines, a well-dressed black guy arrowed in from the right of the picture and nipped into the queue in front of them.

Simon Mbebeni.

Over the phone, PC Brian Westerley said the official police report had Stonehouse as the instigator, and I watched as the taller of the two men—the one wearing a T-shirt and summer jacket—said something to his friend. Mbebeni turned around, frown on his face, and spoke to them. Stonehouse smiled at Mbebeni and shrugged. Mbebeni—six foot, around fifteen stone, plainly not about to be intimidated—took another step toward them. And then Stonehouse threw a punch.

It missed Mbebeni and he moved quickly to react: he pushed Stonehouse back into a ticket machine on the right, Quinn getting knocked aside on the way through. Stonehouse came back, fists swinging, and connected with Mbebeni's face. A second later, as the footage glitched a little, I could see blood all over Mbebeni's shirt.

Then, from the top of the picture, came Sam Wren.

At first he seemed oblivious to what was going on, checking his phone, but then he looked up and was pulled right into the eye of the storm. As Stonehouse and Mbebeni squared off again, Quinn stepped back into Sam. All around the ticket hall, people had stopped and backed away, some looking on in horror, others faintly amused. Quinn turned to see who he'd bumped into, Sam said something—an automatic reaction to being hit—and Quinn punched him. It was just like a lot of fights: created out of nothing. Sam clutched his face and took a couple of steps back.

Then he moved toward Quinn.

I paused the video. This was only the second time I'd seen Sam in motion. I'd looked at photographs of him over and over, and I'd watched footage of him disappearing into thin air. But now here he was, a different man at a different time. He looked bigger around the face, healthier, but he also looked more assertive, more forceful, and not only because he'd just been attacked. Maybe this was the Sam everyone talked about: the one who worked as an investment banker, who earned six-figure bonuses, who could swim with the sharks. At the end he was none of those things. At the end he was small, confused and forlorn. A man with none of the fight left in him.

I started the video again. Within a couple of seconds, Pell emerged from the same position as earlier, heading toward Stonehouse and Mbebeni, and then Sam was on Quinn—Quinn half turned away from him—and throwing a punch. It looked clumsy, but because of Quinn's position, it was devastating: it connected with Quinn's throat, and—in the blink of an eye—his legs gave way and he hit the floor. It was difficult to make out Sam's face after that: he was bent over, hands on his knees, blood dripping from his face to the floor, as more Tube staff emerged. One made for Quinn, the other for Stonehouse.

Except Pell already had Stonehouse.

Mbebeni was somewhere off to the side, leaning against a wall, looking dazed. Stonehouse was wrestling with Pell, the two of them locked together, arms on each other's shoulders, gritted teeth, fierce, unrelenting expressions like neither of them was about to give in. Finally, Pell got the better of Stonehouse: he swept his legs out from under him—a quick, efficient movement—and Stonehouse hit the deck hard. I remembered for a moment what Westerley had told me about Pell being an ex-soldier, and that immediately seemed obvious in how he moved, in how precise he was. But as the clock rolled on, as I expected Pell to suppress his opponent and keep him there until he had help, he instead went on the attack. When Stonehouse hit the floor, Pell clamped a hand around his throat and jabbed a fist into the side of Stonehouse's face. Once. Twice. Three times. Stonehouse was done already, limp and unresponsive, but Pell just continued punching, over and over, even as Stonehouse lay there unconscious, until finally, like a light switching off, he stopped, got up and looked down, a foot placed either side of the body.

About ten seconds later, a couple of cops rushed in through the doors at the front of the station, and Pell stepped away from the body for the first time, straightening out his jacket and looking around the hall. His eyes locked on to Sam, and he moved across and said something to him. Sam looked up at him, as if he didn't know who Pell was or what he wanted, then he seemed to process whatever it was that Pell had asked, and started nodding slowly. A few seconds later, Sam pointed to Quinn on the floor. He must have known by then that he'd done some serious damage to him. Quinn hadn't moved an inch.

But it was Pell I couldn't take my eyes off.

As Sam stood there, his hands still on his knees, in shock and worried about what he might have done, Pell was looking off toward Stonehouse with nothing in his face at all.

No emotion. No regret.

As if he didn't feel anything.

36

After seeing him in action, I figured the rest of the footage on the DVD would give an even better sense of who Duncan Pell was. For Sam, the pattern mostly remained the same: he'd come in through the three-arch entrance at Gloucester Road and head across the ticket hall toward the turnstiles. The only day that changed was the day after the fight. Sam didn't turn up at all. I assumed that was down to the events of the previous twenty-four hours: he'd been in a fight, he'd punched a man unconscious and the police had probably warned him it might be about to get worse. He would have been shaken up by what happened, which is why he must have taken the day off work.

But Duncan Pell was different.

He came to work the next day, and every morning—just as on the morning of the fight—he'd stick to the same routine: head for the front of the station where the homeless man had returned, and ask him to leave. Except he didn't just ask. Every day he became a little more aggressive: only pointing and gesturing initially; then actually planting a hand on the man and pushing him away from the entrance; then grabbing him off the floor and dragging him along the pavement until they both disappeared from sight. Finally, Pell resorted to another tactic: he dropped to his haunches, the man slumped at one of the entrances, and Pell leaned in to him and said something into his ear. The reaction was instant: the homeless man glanced at Pell like he couldn't believe what he'd heard, and Pell grabbed him by the arm, hauled him to his feet and threw him off, out of view. The man's black holdall remained in shot for a moment, before Pell kicked it off in the direction he'd thrown the man.

No other Tube employee got involved at any point. Only Pell. Some looked on, but none of them said anything. But then, on the final day of footage, something changed: the man didn't turn up. For the first time in a week, presumably the first time in a long time, he wasn't sitting at the entrance, knees to his chest, fingers clasping his cardboard sign.

He was gone.

I made some lunch for Liz and me, and then we sat out on the decking at the back of the house and had a couple of glasses of wine. It was a beautiful day: beyond the trees at the bottom of the garden, the mark-less sky was vast.

"You found your guy yet?" Liz asked after a while.

"No. Not yet."

A long pause. I looked at her.

"Do you think this is the one?" she said.

"What do you mean?"

She shifted forward in her seat. "The one you can't save."

There was no malice in the comment. No bitterness. Liz wasn't like that. And yet I saw where the words had come from. I could trace them all the way back to their origins; to an interview room in east London eight months before when she'd told me who I was: a man trying to fix holes in the world that couldn't be fixed. Sometimes I worried our relationship had become defined by that conversation.

"I don't give it a lot of thought," I said eventually, reaching over and taking her hand. But it wasn't much of a lie. We could both see through it to what lay beneath. All the doubts and fears about what we had—and whether it could go the distance.

37

Fifty minutes later, a car pulled up at the front gates. At first I thought it was Ewan Tasker, but then realized it wasn't a Porsche. A man in his fifties, gunmetal-gray hair and a mustache to match, got out of a Volvo and came up the drive. I moved to the front steps.

"Afternoon," he said.

"Can I help you?"

In his hands was a Manila file.

He stopped about six feet short of me, hitching a foot up on to the first step, and eyed the front of the house. "My name's Detective Sergeant Kevin Sallows."

I nodded. "What can I do for you?"

He didn't ask me who I was, which meant he already knew. "Sorry about intruding like this," he continued, even though he didn't seem sorry. "I've got a few questions I was hoping you might be able to answer. I know it's a Saturday, the sun's out and there's beer to be drunk. They won't take long."

I opened my hands. "Sure. If I can help, I will."

He tapped the file against his thigh and cleared his throat. "Yesterday we arrested someone called Eric Gaishe." My heart sank. He paused, looked at me, but couldn't see anything worth stopping for. "A real arsehole. No education, no job as far as we can tell, no home address. He hasn't said anything since we brought him in, other than one minor slip-up when he told us some guy called Ben Richards dumped him at a warehouse in Kennington."

So Gaishe hadn't mentioned Wellis, or his connection to the events at the house, even though Wellis had hung him out to dry. Maybe it was out of some skewed kind of loyalty. Or maybe Gaishe was scared about what Wellis might do to him if he talked.

"Thing is, guys like Gaishe are a waste of oxygen: record as long as my arm, nothing to contribute to society. If some bloke took it upon himself to go all Charles Bronson, then that's fine by me. It's just one less piece of shit for me to scoop up."

He paused, forefinger tapping out a rhythm on the file.

"But yesterday we found Gaishe's prints all over a house just off the

Old Kent Road, near The Firs. We also found some weapons in a hold-all. You know The Firs?"

"Not really, no."

"Where dreams go to die."

I shook my head again.

"House belongs to an Adrian Wellis."

I looked at him.

"You heard that name before?"

"No, I haven't."

"Not sure if he lived there, or if he just rented it to Gaishe. Difficult to tell when Gaishe is playing dumb. Wellis *seems* pretty kosher—no record, properties across the city—so I'll give him the benefit of the doubt for now. But you never know people—not really—do you, Mr. Raker?"

"I guess not."

"There was a girl inside that house," he went on, as if he hadn't heard me. "Gaishe kept her locked up in there. Raped her. Beat her. Almost killed her." *So she wasn't dead. I'd made the right decision.* "Someone called an ambulance for her from the phone in the house, and it wasn't Gaishe. So who could this mystery man have been?" He finally flipped open the front of the file and tapped a finger on the top sheet. "Says here you have a habit of stumbling across crime scenes, Mr. Raker."

It was my file.

"What are you talking about?"

"I'm sure I don't need to explain." He was referring to a case the October before. His eyes flicked up at me. "Says here that, on 23 October of last year, you turned up at a house up in north London and there were two dead bodies inside."

I gazed at him. "If that what it says, it must be true."

He didn't say anything else, just scanned the rest of the file. When he was done, he took a step back from the porch. "Most civilians go their whole lives without reporting a crime like your one." Sallows looked at me again, and I got the sense this was somehow personal for him, that he'd specifically asked to be here. *Have we crossed paths before?* "I mean, it's a hell of a thing, stumbling across a scene like the one you found, right?"

I shrugged. "It's the nature of my work, sadly."

"Missing persons?"

"People who are missing for a long time tend not to turn up alive."

"But you have to admit you're like a magnet for trouble."

"Why would I have to admit that?" I said to him. "If you're accusing me of something, then come out with it. Otherwise, I think we're done."

He nodded slowly. "You found that farm up in Scotland."

It had been eighteen months since I'd walked on to that farm and almost lost my life, and the scars on my body remained. Not as painful as they once were, because all pain died in time, but a reminder of what had been done to me, like a memory that would never fade.

"That case . . ." He stopped, shook his head, and his eyes flicked to me. "I read some of the paperwork. I read your interviews, the statement you made, what you said went on up there. I was interested because, at the time, I had this religious nut going round killing people and dumping their bodies in Brockwell Park, and I thought to myself, 'Maybe my case is related.'" He paused, studied me again. "It wasn't, by the way."

I remained silent.

"Here's the thing, though: I'm not sure how much of your statement I believed. I mean, we all know what they did to you up there . . ." His eyes moved to my body. "But there were gaps. Big gaps. There were bullet holes all over that place but no one to account for them. Not a single person. So who fired the guns? You said it wasn't you. You said it was them. But they were either dead or they'd vanished into thin air."

"So?"

"So ten months later—in October last year—suddenly you're back, and we're picking the bones out of the mess you made in those woods over in east London."

I frowned. "Have you got a point, Sergeant Sallows?"

"If you say that wasn't you at that house yesterday," he said, ignoring me, a smile—lacking any warmth—lost beneath his mustache, "then I guess I'll have to go with it. I mean, whoever it was wiped the place down, so it's not like we've got any evidence. But witnesses at the warehouse say they saw an unidentified man running full pelt away from the scene dressed in only a coat, and a gray BMW 3 series leaving shortly after." He turned and made a show of eyeing my BMW, parked on the drive next to him. And then he looked back at me. "Not dissimilar to this one, actually."

He let that sit there.

Again, I didn't respond.

Finally, he continued. "So if you say you weren't there at the house, and you weren't there driving that BMW, then I guess that's what we have to run with. But it doesn't mean I think you're telling the truth." He paused and flipped the file shut, eyeing me before speaking. "In fact, quite the opposite. I think you're a fucking liar."

38

At Ealing Common Tube station, I grabbed a Travelcard and headed down the steps to the eastbound District. I was on my way to see Duncan Pell for a second time.

It was two on a Saturday afternoon, so the platform wasn't empty, but it was still pretty quiet. I moved about three-quarters of the way along, to where the sun arrowed through a gap in the roof. It must have been in the high twenties now: heat haze shimmered off the track, shadows were deep and long and the building shifted and creaked around me. A couple of seconds later, my phone went off.

I grabbed it and looked at the display. *Terry Dooley.*

Dooley was part of my old life; a source I'd managed to get my hooks into as a journalist, and one who had been forced to come along for the ride ever since. He was a reluctant passenger. In a moment of madness, he and three of his detectives had visited a brothel in south London, where things turned drunk and nasty and one of the cops put a prostitute in a neck brace. The next morning the story landed on my desk. I'd called him and offered to keep it out of the papers if, in return, he got me information when I needed it. It was a better trade for him: he was married with two boys, and if there was one thing Dooley hated more than dealing with me, it was the idea of battling for custody of his kids. I hit Answer. "Carlton Lane." Carlton Lane was where the brothel had been.

"Funny," said a voice. "I was hoping you wouldn't answer."

"How you doing, Dools?"

"Yeah, great," he replied with zero enthusiasm. The line drifted. I heard footsteps and then a door closing. "You got five minutes, then I've got to get the boys to football."

I'd called him as soon as Sallows had left. Dooley hadn't answered, but I'd left a message on his voice-mail, asking him to call me back. Tasker and Dooley were the two sources I used most from my previous life: Tasker was more reliable, more discreet and less prone to putting obstacles in my way; but Dooley was like the oracle. He kept his ear to the ground, knew the comings and goings at the Met, and had his fingers in all sorts of pies. I couldn't work out why Sallows was trying to squeeze me. I'd made problems for myself by staking out the house, calling an ambulance for the girl and letting Wellis get the better of me, but there was still little for the cops to go on. A witness spotting a car a bit like mine wasn't going to lead to the Met turning up on my doorstep, not if they didn't even have my plates. So what had got Sallows interested in me?

"Did you listen to the whole of my message?" I asked.

"Nope."

"That's great, Dools."

"What do you want me to do?" He gave a little snort, as if by asking him to check his messages properly I was asking the impossible. I could see things his way: we went months without talking, and just as he started to believe he'd got rid of me from his life, he picked up the phone and there I was. "In case you hadn't noticed, I've got a real job here, not some Mickey Mouse operation like you."

I ignored him. "Does the name Kevin Sallows mean anything to you?"

"Sallows?"

"Yeah. You know him?"

"Don't know him personally, but I know *of* him."

"Who is he?"

"Career cop. Old school. He was part of the Snatcher team."

"But he's not any more?"

"I don't know exactly what went down."

"Which means what?"

"Which means I don't know exactly what went down. Not the gory details. That investigation is locked down tighter than a Jewish piggy bank."

"So what *do* you know?"

"Something blew up between a couple of the cops there—something really big—and then Sallows got kicked off the case and shipped off to south London somewhere. He's working the shitty cases they wouldn't even give to a half-cop like you."

"Why?"

"Like I said, I don't know the gory details."

"What about the edited highlights?"

"You might wanna put in a call to your one-time sparring partner. He'd probably know more about it than I do. You can relive the days when you and him sailed into the Dead Tracks like Laurel and Hardy."

"You mean Healy?"

"The very same."

"He's working the Snatcher?"

"Yeah. Don't you *ever* watch TV?"

"I haven't been following the case."

"He's maneuvered himself back into the big time. Don't ask me how he managed it. The shit you and him got up to last year, he should be getting bummed in the showers at Pentonville, and you should be there watching."

"What do you mean 'back into the big time'?"

"Way I hear it, he's pretty much playing second fiddle to the SIO."

"Who's the SIO?"

"Melanie Craw. The chief clown at the circus."

"You know her?"

"No. But people tell me she's a bitch with ice for blood. You probably need to be when you've got a deranged killer pissing all over your career. I give it one more dead homo before they pull the plug on her."

"So she fell out with Sallows?"

"Fell out, didn't rate him, didn't like the way he dressed—who knows?"

"Has Healy been playing ball?"

"Old Lazarus? Of course he has. He's a clever bastard. He's probably been on his best behavior since the start of the year; probably managed to keep himself in check even while the people there are chipping away at him. But you can bet your arse he's been spending the whole time plotting some sort of revenge mission."

"Against who?"

"Who'd you think? Against everyone."

39

9 April | Two Months Earlier

Craw swiveled gently in her seat, half turned away from the men in her office, her gaze on the incident room. She wore every hour of the investigation on her face: dark rings under her eyes that she'd tried to disguise with makeup; the pale, almost translucent skin that shadowed insomnia; the faraway look of someone who'd imagined many times over what it would be like to walk away. Forty days after the third victim, Joseph Symons, went missing, they still had nothing.

Next to Healy was Davidson. On the other side of Davidson was Sallows. On the left-hand side of the office were other, senior CID cops: Sampson, Frey, Richter and then Carmichael, who had a notepad in his hand and was tapping a pen against his thigh. He hadn't written anything down yet.

Finally, Craw looked back at the group. "I've got to do a press conference in two hours. I've got to go out there, in front of half the journalists in the country, and I've got to tell them what we've found and how we're going to catch this bastard." She reached down in front of her and picked up a piece of paper off the desk. It was blank. "This is what we've found. What's written on Carmichael's pad is what we've found. Six weeks after Symons gets whisked off into the night, and we're in the same place as we were when Wilky got taken. And he's been missing *eight fucking months*." She smashed the flat of her hand on the desk—papers gliding off, pens rattling, her keyboard leaping from its position—and turned and looked out at the incident room again.

Silence. Then the gentle squeak of her chair as it moved back and forth.

"So one of you give me *something*."

Healy waited for Davidson or Sallows to leap in; to try and build something from nothing, just so they could score points, but even they realized it was pointless. The case had already crossed that line. What it needed now was something to jump-start it.

"Ma'am," Healy said, and everyone in the office turned to him.

He glanced briefly at Davidson and Sallows, their eyes narrowing, a faint look of disgust on Davidson's face. Sallows made an obvious show of smacking his lips together like anything Healy said left a bad taste in his mouth.

"What is it, Healy?" Craw asked.

Healy turned his attention to her. "In October 2010 a man was found stabbed to death on Hampstead Heath. He—"

"We've already been down that road, Colm," Davidson said, a hint of amusement—unseen by Craw—on his lips. When he turned to Craw, he'd wiped his face clean: no amusement, no expression of any kind. "You'll remember, ma'am, that DS Sallows came to see you about this case a couple of days after our first victim, Steven Wilky, went missing back in August last year. HOLMES put it forward as a possible connection, given the circumstances of Wilky's disappearance."

Craw nodded, but her eyes didn't leave Healy. "I remember," she said. In her face Healy could see an invitation to continue, not just because she was desperate for a lead, but because she wanted to see whether her instincts about him had been correct.

"I know Sallows looked at this before," he said, and shifted forward in his seat. He hadn't made any notes on this; this was all from memory. A couple of days earlier, he'd come into work and found the drawers of his desk had been pulled out and tipped all over the floor. Later the same day, in a Snatcher briefing, when Craw had asked him something, he'd opened his notepad to find pages had been ripped out. He'd stumbled his way through her question, to the amusement of Davidson, Sallows and some of the other cops, but he'd looked disorganized and amateurish. Craw had shown nothing, but it must have put doubts in her head. Now he was going to redress the balance.

"So what have you got that's new?" she asked.

"Nothing, ma'am."

"Then we're done here."

"There are too many connections between the Snatcher victims and this case for us to bin it entirely," Healy continued. "Not without looking at it properly."

"We looked at it properly the first time, Healy," Davidson said.

"We need to look at it again."

Sallows smirked. "Are you saying I can't do my job?"

"No."

"You think I wasn't thorough enough the first time round?"

"No."

"Then what?"

But Healy wasn't looking at Sallows, he was looking at Craw. She held his gaze for a moment and then scanned the room. "Who's up to speed on the Hampstead Heath murder?" Sampson, Frey and Carmichael all shook their heads. They would have seen that it had been marked up as an early potential lead when they joined the investigation after the second victim—Marc Evans—was taken, but they wouldn't have gone into detail on it if it had already been relegated to a sideshow on Sallows's say-so.

"Okay," Craw said, looking at Healy, "you've got two minutes."

He nodded. Davidson glanced at Sallows and shook his head. Healy ignored them and looked at the other cops. "The victim's name was Leon Spane."

"Spane?" Sampson asked.

"Yeah. S-P-A-N-E. Spane was a twenty-eight-year-old from Tufnell Park. His naked body was found on the edge of Hampstead Heath, near Spaniards Road, on 19 October 2010. He'd been stabbed in the throat. The blade went so deep it perforated the skin on the back of his neck. His penis had also been removed—postmortem, with the same knife—and left in the grass next to him. Lividity suggested he'd been brought from wherever he'd been killed." Healy paused, letting them take it all in. All eyes were on him now, even those of Davidson and Sallows. "And whoever killed Spane had shaved him."

"Shaved him how?" Carmichael said, from the back of the room.

"Shaved his head," Healy replied. "Right before the body was dumped."

A tremor passed across the room, and a couple of the cops—Frey, who was the newest member of the team, and Sampson—both looked at Craw. Her eyes were still on Healy. "You understand why we dismissed it though, Healy—right?"

"Yes, ma'am."

"This is about as far from our guy's MO as you can get."

Healy nodded. "I agree, ma'am."

"Our man takes them, and he keeps them. *Or* he leaves their bodies concealed. *Or* he dumps them somewhere remote. He doesn't leave them on Hampstead Heath, in plain sight, in the middle of a city with seven million people in it."

Healy nodded again.

"The first victim, Wilky, has been missing since 11 August 2011," Craw went on, "and we still haven't found his body. The second, Evans, since 13 November. The newest, Symons, since 28 February. They don't come back."

"Yes, ma'am."

"He isn't aggressive either," Sallows said, stepping in, sensing an opportunity to kill Healy off. "At least not at the scene. There are no signs of a struggle at any of the victims' flats or houses, and no sign of a break-in. They all lived on their own, in their own places. Spane didn't. Plus there's the doubts over the hair: Healy says someone shaved Spane's hair for him, but forensics say the hair was shaved *before* he died, so it's just as likely—in fact, probably *more* likely—that Spane shaved it himself." Sallows paused, glancing at Craw, but she made no effort to stop him. "And what you can safely say about our guy, beyond all reasonable doubt, is that he isn't the type of killer who's going to dump a body and then spend the next minute messily chopping the victim's dick off. In fact, with no bodies to find, our guy might not be a killer at all."

"What does he do with the men if he doesn't kill them?" Healy asked.

Sallows glanced at Craw but didn't say anything. Craw leaned forward at her desk and laid both hands flat to the surface. "Is that it, Colm?"

"Don't you think it would be worth looking into?"

"Sallows looked into it."

He glanced at Sallows and then to Davidson; there was a hint of a smile on Davidson's face again, as if he sensed the whole room were now seeing Healy for who he was: a fraud of a cop. "I'll take this case," Healy said to her, "and I'll run with it. It won't impact upon my time, but I will report back as soon as I find anything. It'll be off the books."

"Just like normal," Davidson said quietly, but loud enough to be heard.

"Fuck you, Eddie."

"All right, calm down," Craw snapped, shooting them both a look. Davidson slid down into his chair, arms crossed on his belly, a satisfied smile on his face. Over his shoulder, like a parrot, Sallows was an exact replica. Craw turned to Healy. Everyone in the office was staring at him. Davidson winked, out of sight of Craw. Sallows had a look on his face that was so clear it was like Healy could see right into his head. *You're done*, he was saying. *You had your chance—and you crumbled.* But Healy wasn't about to crumble. Not now. Not in front of them.

"You missed something," he said, staring at Sallows.

The smile fell from his face like a stone dropping down a well. "What the hell are you talking about?" he said, incensed—but Healy could see the doubt in him now.

The minute you brought up my daughter, the minute you tried to use her as a way to get at me, you changed the game. Now I'm going to put you in the fucking ground.

Craw shifted forward. "Healy?"

He turned to Craw. "Sallows is responsible for checking the CCTV footage from each of the buildings the victims were taken from, is that right?"

"Yeah," Sallows interjected. "I checked them all and there's nothing to find."

"Not true."

"Get to the point, Healy," Craw said.

"There are consistencies at all of the scenes—the type of victim, their build, their sexuality, the type of location they live in, the hair on the pillow. There's something else too. At each of the crime scenes there's been no working internal lighting."

Craw's expression changed. "Explain."

He glanced at Davidson and Sallows: Davidson was watching him, eyes narrow, head tilted, trying to see where this was going; Sallows looked as white as a ghost.

"Every interior light leading up to the flat, including the hallway the flat is on, has been out. In the latest one, in Symons's building—at the front entrance, at the foyer—the whole floor was out. There were no working bulbs *at all*."

"These places are shitholes," Sallows said.

"It's not just that," Healy replied. "I went back and checked the CCTV footage from each of the scenes. It's difficult to make anything out on the night the victims were taken. You can see vague figures passing in and out of the building, but not much apart from that."

"*So?*" Sallows said.

"So I went back and requested the footage from the two weeks prior to each of the victims being taken—of the front of the building and the foyer; as much of the interior as I could get hold of—and I watched it back." He turned to Craw. "The lights were working at all of the crime scenes three days before the victims were taken."

Silence. No sound at all, from anyone.

But a few of them knew where this was going. Craw dropped back into her chair, thin fingers massaging her brow; Davidson shifted, looking anywhere but Healy.

Sallows just stared into space.

"Two nights before, a man walks up to each of the buildings and he systematically dismantles or breaks every single light at the entrances and inside the foyers of the tower blocks. We don't have CCTV for the individual hallways, but we can assume he kills the lights there too. It's the same man, wearing the same clothes, every time: black trousers, hooded top, no way to identify him. But we have him on film, we've always had him on film—and we know what he's wearing, his physicality, his build and how he's able to walk them out the front door without being seen." Healy kept his eyes on Craw, but in his peripheral vision he could see the rest of the room. Already Davidson had come forward on his seat, away from Sallows's space, like a snake moving for shade, leaving his friend, his fellow tormentor, isolated and alone at the back of the room. "The problem was," Healy continued, fixing his gaze on Sallows, "we were too lazy to check any further back than the night they were taken."

Silence.

Craw finally looked up at Healy, then across to Sallows, then out to the rest of the room. "Okay, back to work," she said. "Kevin, stay where you are."

They all filed out, Healy following Davidson.

Once they were out of sight of Craw, her office door slamming shut, he stopped and watched Davidson head off between the desks to his seat at the far end. A couple of minutes later, Healy looked up to see Davidson watching him.

He stared back.

One down, one to go.

40

At the steps to the ticket hall at Gloucester Road there was the stench of fried food and perfume. Groups of teenage boys, coated in their father's aftershave and clutching identical brown McDonald's bags, were standing beyond the gateline, laughing riotously as one of them—out of sight of the station staff—stealthily fed his fries into the credit card slot on the self-service machine. Adjacent to the group was the booth by which I'd introduced myself to Duncan Pell two days before.

But today he wasn't there.

I scanned the hall and spotted three Underground employees: one at the turnstiles, one by the entrance and one, the closest to me, sweating under the glass-domed interior, as the sun cut down through the roof. He was about five stone overweight, his hair was matted to his scalp like he'd had a bucket of water poured over him and there were huge sweat patches under his arms. He'd be a pool of water by the time his shift ended. I moved across to him.

"Is Duncan Pell around?"

He looked at me. Shook his head. "Nah, mate. Not 'ere today."

"Day off?"

"Who knows with Dunc."

"How do you mean?"

He studied me closer this time, and then shrugged. "S'posed to be 'ere at five," the guy said, "but then he called in sick."

"That a regular occurrence?"

He was watching a couple of kids at the turnstiles now. They were laughing about something, whispering to one another, only one of them holding a ticket. He took a step toward them, ready to give chase if they jumped the barriers, but if he made it as far as the entrance before he was out of breath, it probably would have been a personal best.

I tried again. "Is Duncan off sick a lot then?"

But the man wasn't really paying attention any more. "Look, mate, he's not 'ere, all right?" he said. "I dunno where he is." Then he shuffled off toward the boys.

I looked across the ticket hall toward the second guy, stationed at the main entrance, but then something else caught my attention: a staffroom door to his left, the station supervisor half in, half out, talking to someone inside. I made a beeline for it. By the time I was halfway across the ticket hall, the supervisor looked like he was about to leave. I slowed my approach, angling the direction I was coming in from so he wouldn't spot me in his peripheral vision, and as he stepped away and headed off beyond the gateline, I slid a foot in between the door and frame, and slipped inside.

It was small and clinical: a counter on the left with a microwave, kettle and toaster on it, three tables with chairs in the middle and a calendar on the right. No windows, just the faint hum of air conditioning. Right at the back was a vending machine and a bank of nine lockers. At the table nearest to me was a woman, back to me, reading a magazine while eating a sandwich. Facing me was a man, cross-legged, newspaper open in front of him, fiddling with something on his phone.

"Excuse me."

They both looked over.

"My name's James Braddock," I said, taking another step toward them. "I'm from the British Transport Police. I was just chatting to your SS and he said it would be okay to ask you both a couple of questions. Would that be all right with you?"

They glanced between them and mumbled agreements.

I asked for their names. The woman was Sandra Purnell; the man only offered his first name: Gideon. She was fully invested in what I was saying from minute one, but he seemed more reticent. "I'm looking for a colleague of yours," I said, and moved to the center of the room. "Duncan Pell."

They looked at each other, and the woman broke into a smile. Not one with any humor, but with some insight; as if there were a lot of people looking for Duncan Pell. It seemed like she was about to speak, but then she just cleared her throat.

"Your SS said he was ill," I lied.

"Yeah, that's right."

"And that he's ill a lot."

She paused. "I'm probably not best placed to answer this. I'm just part-time. Gid would know better than me."

I looked at him. "Gideon?"

He shrugged. "What do you want to know?"

"Is Duncan Pell off ill a lot?"

"Enough," he said.

I turned back to the woman. "So he isn't a well man?"

She studied me, teetering on the brink of committing. "Some people reckon he's got that—what's it called?—PT . . ."

"PTSD," said Gideon.

I flicked a look at him and then back to her. "Post-traumatic stress?" She nodded. "Right."

"Ever remember him acting strangely at work?"

"Personally, no."

"What about secondhand accounts?"

She paused again, as if gossip wasn't something she was comfortable with. "I've just heard stories about him, that's all."

"What are the stories?"

"That he's generally a bit rude to people. I just thought he was quiet, but one of the girls in the office told us all a story."

"About what?"

She colored a little, embarrassed at what she perceived to be telling tales. "About how he flipped out one lunchtime when the coffee machine stopped working." She looked across to the counter. There was no coffee percolator there now. "He just went crazy."

"And did what?"

"Punched a hole in the wall."

I looked around the staffroom and spotted an uneven piece of paneling on a wall to the right of the counter. "He had a temper on him?" I asked.

"That's just what I was told."

Gideon moved in his seat. "Do you mind if I ask why—"

"Thanks a lot to both of you," I said, cutting him off and heading for the door of the staffroom. And for the first time, on the back wall, I saw a corkboard, full of photos of the men and women that staffed the station. In the bottom row was Gideon, and his surname: Momodou. On one side of him was the ticket inspector I'd chatted to when I'd first been in and talked to Pell—early forties, half-moon glasses, built like a middleweight boxer; his name tag said he was Edwin Smart—on the other side was the overweight CSA I'd walked up to when I'd arrived today, looking as flustered in his official photo as he did out on the floor. Appropriately, given how little he'd wanted to help, his name was Darren Cant. But, right at the end, staring into the camera lens, no emotion in his face at all, was the only one I really cared about.

Duncan Pell.

So where are you, Duncan?

Behind me, a chair scraped against the tiled floor and I heard Momodou get up from his table. But before he got a chance to repeat his question, I opened the door of the staffroom and headed out, taking the stairs back down to the platform. As I waited for the next train to pull in, I watched him come up to the bridge and look down. I stepped behind a pillar, out of sight. About ten seconds later, I came out from behind my cover again and saw him returning to his lunch.

Then my phone started ringing.

I took it out and looked at the display. Withheld number.

"David Raker."

"Raker, it's me."

It took me a couple of seconds to place the voice. *"Healy?"*

"We need to talk."

41

We met in a coffee house opposite Shepherd's Bush Market. Healy was already inside, sitting at the window so he could watch me approach from the station. Two mugs were on the counter in front of him.

He looked different from when I'd last seen him. He'd lost a little weight, had had his red hair cut and styled, and wore a tailored suit. He appeared fresher, more professional, with none of the ferocity I'd spent so much time reining in the October before. And yet there was just the hint of *something*; a trace of the old Healy. As I moved inside the shop, shook hands with him and sat down, I wondered how long it would be before it came out.

"You still drink coffee, right?" he asked, pushing one toward me. "Black, no sugar."

"Well remembered."

"I'm clever like that."

He nodded and a moment of silence settled between us. It wasn't uncomfortable exactly, but it wasn't relaxed either. The old Healy was a hard guy to like. He did his best to piss you off and fight you on everything. The new one seemed more controlled, but no less intense. I could see his brain ticking over, trying to figure out what he needed to say to me and why. He hadn't told me a lot over the phone, which was fairly typical of him. In his search for Leanne, he'd spent so long bottling things up, working her case off the books and keeping it concealed, he'd eventually forgotten how to articulate himself.

"How have you been?" I asked.

"Fine. You?"

"I'm okay."

He nodded, but didn't probe any further.

"How are Gemma and the boys?"

A flicker of sadness in his face. "They're good."

I hadn't seen him for over seven months, but as I watched how he sat—his bulky frame perched on the edge of the stool; his hand wrapped around the mug, wedding band still on—it didn't feel like it.

"So I hear you're back in the big time."

He looked at me. "Who'd you hear that from?"

"Someone I know at the Met."

His eyes lingered on me—that trace of the old Healy—and then he broke out into a small, tight smile. It was a token effort; hardly even there. "That's right."

"How's it going?"

The smile dropped away. "That's what I need to talk to you about."

This time it was my turn to look suspicious. His face was turned away from me, half lit by the sun coming in from outside, half darkened by the shadows of the shop.

"What's going on?"

He took a long, drawn-out breath. "They don't know I'm here telling you this, and if they found out, I'd get my arse handed to me. So you need to keep this on the QT."

"I can't tell anyone anything if I don't know what it is we're talking about," I said to him and, almost immediately, he reached down to his side where a slip case was leaning against the legs of the chair. He brought it up and unzipped it. Inside were six files. Four were thick, rammed with paper, all contained within identical manila folders. A fifth was about half the size, in a green folder. The last was the thinnest—maybe only ten pages, in a charcoal-gray surround—and was the one he took out.

"I've just come from Julia Wren."

That stopped me dead. "*What?*"

"You're working for her, right?"

But I didn't hear him. My mind was already shifting forward: why would he have been to see Julia? Was this to do with Sam? Did I miss something? Overlook something? I reached into my coat pocket and took out my phone. On the display was one missed call, received while I was on the Tube. Julia. She'd been calling me about the police.

"Raker?"

I glanced at him. "Yeah."

"You're working for her?"

"Yeah, I'm working for her. So?"

"Have you found her husband?"

I shook my head. "No."

"Well, the Met are going to ask you to shut this down."

"What are you talking about?"

"They're going to turn up on your doorstep"—he looked at his watch—"in about an hour, and they're going to want you to stop look-ing for him."

"Why would I do that?"

He handed me the file. On the first page was a color picture of Sam. "Because they think Samuel Wren is the Snatcher."

42

It had been 108 days since the third victim, Joseph Symons, was taken. Some people in the Met, some cops who Healy didn't believe deserved to be cops, started talking about the end; whispers in the corridors at first, and then—like a wave of chatter—it filtered down through the hallways and into the meeting rooms. They believed a man who had taken three people and never been found could just stop; turn it off like a light. Or if they didn't believe that, they held on to the remote possibility he'd got caught up in something else: that he'd been forced off the radar; that he'd been charged with another crime or gone to prison on something unrelated. But Healy knew it hadn't happened like that, and so did Craw and the rest of the Snatcher team. And at 11:14 p.m. they got the call to prove it.

It was a tower block in Hammersmith, sitting in a patch of land between the flyover and the river. The call had come in from a neighbor who knew the occupant of Flat 312 and said she hadn't seen him for three days. Ordinarily they'd chat in the corridors of the third floor every day when he returned from his job as a shop assistant. But the last time she saw him was the Tuesday before. She'd heard him leave for work, had even watched from her window as he headed off toward Hammersmith Tube station— but that was the last time she saw him. She thought she might have heard him come home that night, perhaps the sound of his door opening and closing, perhaps even the faint sound of conversation in the hallway, but she couldn't say for sure. She definitely didn't see him or hear him on Wednesday, and she hadn't seen him since. It was now Friday night.

The tower block was perched on the edge of a grass bank that dropped down to a rusting fence and the train tracks beyond. It was one of five, all connected via walkways, all part of the same estate. If it hadn't have been for the media, camped out in a space to his far left, lightbulbs flashing, camera crews jostling for space, there might have been a strange kind of stillness to the place; a lack of light and sound, as if a pregnant hush were hanging in the air. In the walkways, in the alleyways, in the windows,

Healy could make out figures—their faces freeze-framed in the glow from the police lightbars—looking on as things played out. At any other time, this was one of the most dangerous housing estates in London. He'd stood over bodies in this place. He'd knocked on doors and told parents their kids weren't coming home. But now even the gangs and the dealers stood back and watched in silence as another came into this place.

One who was even worse than them.

After coming up the stairs—every light out, just like the others, bulbs smashed in the stairwell—he put on the forensic boiler suit, zipped it up and moved into the flat. Again, it was a carbon copy of the flats the other victims had lived in. Healy spotted Craw in the kitchen. There was a door off the living room, opening on to a bedroom. Chief Superintendent Ian Bartholomew stood in the doorway. Healy glanced at him but didn't greet him. Bartholomew had started to get involved personally about four weeks after Joseph Symons went missing. "Three is three too many," he kept saying in daily briefings, as if no one on the task force felt anything for the men. Craw hated it; maybe hated him too. She'd never said as much to Healy, but her feelings were barely concealed: there, just below the surface, bubbling and stewing until one day in the future she would either say something she regretted to Bartholomew's face, or she would walk into his office and hand in her resignation.

"Melanie," Bartholomew said to Craw as she arrived from the kitchen. "What the bloody hell am I supposed to tell the media?"

Most of this, Healy knew, was down to him. Bartholomew had been there when Healy had been trying to find Leanne; and there in the aftermath, desperate not to give him a second chance. The decision to pull him on to the Snatcher case was Craw's, and hers alone, and now she would be held accountable if it all went wrong: by Bartholomew, by Davidson, by anyone with a grudge against Healy. All Healy knew was that he owed it to her for giving him a chance—and he owed it to her not to make any mistakes.

Bartholomew backed out of the bedroom, letting Healy take in the crime scene, and stepped closer to Craw. "Melanie," he said again, using her first name to cushion the blow of what was coming next. "I think it's time I took over the media briefings. This needs to come from the top. They need to see that we're taking this seriously, and that we won't just sit back and accept what we've got here tonight."

"With all due respect, sir, I've never put an impression across to the media that we weren't taking these crimes seriously."

"Don't take it personally," he said, holding up a hand to her, as if he'd barely heard her. "I have full faith in you and your . . ." He paused, glancing at Healy. "*Team*."

"Is there anything else you want to lead directly, sir?"

He looked at her, trying to find the insubordination in her face, but Craw looked at him blankly. "No. You carry on as is. I trust you. I'll take the media hit."

Bartholomew left.

Healy glanced at Craw, who looked back. There was nothing in her face, nothing unspoken. No indication that she thought any less of Bartholomew, even though he'd just relegated her from the front line of the case. He was happy for her to work the hours and feel the pressure build, but he wasn't going to let her have her day in the sun if they ever caught the Snatcher. And yet she remained silent. Healy admired her even more for her poise.

He looked into the bedroom for a second time. The hair had been placed in a neat pile on the pillow. Just like Wilky. Just like Evans. Just like Symons.

"What was this one's name?" Healy asked, looking at Craw.

"Jonathan Drake," she said.

43

I shook my head as I flicked through Sam's file. The picture of him was from the day of the fight at Gloucester Road, taken in the station afterward when it looked like he was going to be charged. His face was puffy across the middle, where he'd been punched; traces of blood around his nose and a deep purple swelling on one cheekbone.

But there was nothing else in his record.

It was clean.

"I just don't see this," I said.

Healy nodded, as if he'd expected that reaction from me. "We turned up at his work and went through his computer. They assumed he wasn't coming back, so they'd cleared out much of what was on his PC. But they didn't clear out everything."

As Healy slid a hand into the slip case, taking out the four matching manila files, my mind rolled back to Investment International a couple of days before. I'd asked to go through his work PC myself, but McGregor, his boss, had wanted a warrant. I should have worked around it, should have got at his PC somehow—even though, at the time, I could never have imagined it would lead to this—and, as I silently cursed myself, Healy laid the files down in front of me. I knew what they were instantly.

The Snatcher victims.

He went to the second one down and opened it. A scrawny white man—no more than nineteen or twenty—looked out at me. It wasn't official police photography; it was a shot in a living room, brightly lit but overexposed. The man was smiling, a crooked expression weighted to one side of his face in a shy, almost coy fashion. He was thin and wiry, a red T-shirt hanging off him, a pair of denims pulled tight at the waist, and he was perched on the edge of a sofa that was either about to fall apart or deliberately retro.

"That's the second," he said. "Marc Evans."

Except, according to his file, he wasn't called Marc Evans at all. That was just an alias; presumably the name most people he met and worked with in London knew him by. His real name was Marc Erion—and he was Albanian. Suddenly, I knew exactly where this was going as my mind flashed to Adrian Wellis, cut and covered in glass, looking up at me from the floor of the warehouse in Kennington. *I set him up with a nice little Albanian kid. Fresh out of the fridge, this boy was. Nineteen, skinny, cute little tattoo on the back of his neck.* I glanced at Erion's personal details. Nineteen. Five-seven. Ten stone. A rose tattooed on to the back of his neck. Never registered at any port in the United Kingdom. Because he'd come into the country in the back of a lorry.

"We estimate Erion, aka Evans, came into the country between March and October last year," Healy said. "His father was a politician back in the motherland, but Erion wasn't what you'd call a chip off the old block. They didn't talk much, mostly because Erion Jr. was a Grade A fuck-up. Flunked college, flunked the job Daddy set him up with, got in with the wrong crowd and ended up stealing money from the family bank account to try and pay his way through his smack addiction. The old man booted him out and then Erion ended up getting in with an even *wronger* crowd, and some time last year he landed in the UK, most probably in the hands of the Albanian mafia."

Except he didn't. He ended up in the hands of Adrian Wellis.

And then a second realization hit me.

The kid's dead, Wellis had said.

You killed him?

I suppose, in a way, I did.

What does that even mean?

The kid was in the wrong place at the wrong time.

Originally, I thought he was admitting to killing Erion himself. But it wasn't that at all. He delivered him. He probably only realized afterward, as Erion's face was plastered across the front pages, but Wellis had unknowingly handed the Snatcher his next victim. He'd met the Snatcher too. He told me he always vetted the punters first time out, but Wellis would have been funneling so many men Erion's way, the vetting process would have been a shambles. And even if he *did* recall a face, even if—as unlikely as it seemed—the Snatcher had let his guard down and somehow made himself known to Wellis, Wellis couldn't have said anything. Go to the police, and he invited the Met into his life. His operation. His secrets. So he said nothing and accepted Erion as collateral damage. *Wrong place, wrong time.* He was right about that, at least.

Healy eyed me, as if he sensed my mind was on something else, and he wanted to know what. "Wren had Erion's number tucked away on his work PC, disguised as a business associate. Never called him, but the number was there."

"Wait a second. If he never called Erion, how did you pin this on Sam in the first place? If there was no phone call, there's no route from Erion back to Sam."

Healy didn't reply. Instead he placed a hand on top of the files. It was meant to look casual, a movement so slight I wouldn't even notice. But I did, and it immediately pissed me off. He wanted to remain in control, wanted to establish a hierarchy between us, and in doing so he'd forgotten his association with me, the things we'd done and the sacrifices I'd made for him. But there was something else in the gesture too. I saw it in his eyes, in his expression, a mix of suppression and guilt. He was keeping something back from me. But not just from me—from everyone.

"Do you know much about him?" Healy asked.

"Who?"

"The Snatcher."

"I want to know how you came to Sam Wren."

He could see he'd annoyed me. "This is all off the record, understand?"

"Don't talk to me like I'm an amateur."

"You're upset about your boy. I get it."

"He's not my boy—and it's got nothing to do with that."

"Don't be an arsehole, Raker."

"I'm not being an *arsehole*, Healy. But you call me out of the blue after seven months of silence, and then you treat me like I've never met you before. I know trust is hard for you, but believe me: if you can trust one person, that person is me."

I waited for the fireworks, but instead he just looked at me and I saw again how desperately he was trying to keep a lid on things. In a strange way, it made him easier to read. Everything he'd stopped himself from saying had built up in his eyes—all the smothered emotion, all the words he'd had to let go since returning to the Met—and I caught a glimpse of a man, perhaps only weeks from here, unable to bury it any more.

"You're gonna want some background."

I looked at him. "Fine. Just get on with it."

He eyed me for a moment and then leaned closer, and I could smell coffee and aftershave on him. "He takes them from their homes. First one went missing last year, on 11 August: Steven Wilky. On 13 November he takes Marc Erion aka Evans. On 28 February he grabs Joseph Symons, and this past week it was Jonathan Drake. Drake's neighbor called us yesterday evening, said she hadn't seen Drake around since Tuesday, and she saw him every day. Mother-hen type. Uniforms turned up there, then called us. The only thing this guy leaves behind is their hair. He shaves it all off and places it on their pillows."

"Why does he do that?"

Healy shrugged. "You tell me."

He meant, *You're the man who knows Wren.*

Except I obviously didn't know Sam Wren at all.

"It's a power thing," I said.

He looked at me and nodded: to exert power over them; to reduce the victims to less than they were. I tried to put that into context; tried to imagine why Sam might do that, what in his life might make him *want* to do that, but I couldn't ally the two. Nothing I'd discovered about Sam Wren, even as I trawled through the secrets and the lies, connected with the crimes of this man. Shaving their heads, trapping them, vanishing them into the night—none of that felt like Sam to me. Except, of course, there was one area that was definitely a fit: their sexual preferences. If the Snatcher was taking men, he was turned on by them, wanting power over them, even if ultimately he was trying to deny it.

And Sam had been in denial for years.

"The assumption is the Snatcher's gay?"

Healy shrugged. "Who knows now? That's what we always assumed, that's what profilers kept telling us. But Wren is married—and he's straight."

You're going to have to tell him.

"There's no semen at any of the scenes," he went on, "no sign of either consensual sex or sexual assault. This guy is careful. We've lifted prints from every scene, prints not belonging to the victim, but they don't lead anywhere. He doesn't touch their pillows when he puts the hair there, but we *have* found tiny pieces of wood, which probably means he shaves their heads into some kind of bowl and brings it across like that; touches the pillow with it while he's placing the hair there."

I glanced out of the window. "There's something you need to know."

"What?"

"About Sam."

His eyes narrowed. "What?"

"What Julia wouldn't have told you, because she doesn't know . . ." I turned back to him. "Sam *was* gay. Or maybe bisexual. Or maybe just curious. But he wasn't straight."

"Fuck me." He smiled briefly. "I think we've got our man."

"Now it's your turn. What led you to Sam's work?"

He moved his hand from the files and pulled the bottom one out of the pile. He handed it to me this time. It almost looked like a conciliatory gesture.

I flipped the front cover of the folder. Another man in his twenties. The same height and the same build as Erion, but better-looking; square-jawed and dark. He was smartly dressed and standing in bright sunlight, squinting a little but his features and face were very clear. I scanned his personal details. Jonathan Drake. Twenty-seven.

The Snatcher's fourth victim.

"You wanna know how we ended up at Wren's work?" Healy said, a finger tapping the Drake file. "We put in a request for phone and e-mail records as soon as Drake's disappearance came to light, and were still waiting on getting them back when a London Underground employee called us up this morning—after seeing Drake's name in the media—and said he'd found a phone on the platform at Westminster station during his patrol on Thursday night."

"It was Drake's?"

"Yeah. We sent a team down there to find out if there was anything else, but it was just the phone down there. No sign of Drake or anyone else."

"Was Sam's number on the phone?"

"Yes."

"Doesn't mean he had anything to do with this, even if he somehow knew Drake."

"Wrong," Healy said, shaking his head. "Wren left a voicemail."

44

Jonathan Drake's face looked up at me from the file. In among the paper-work was the transcript from the voicemail message: "Hi Jonathan, it's (*pause*) Leon Spane. Just wanted to let you know that I'm really looking forward to seeing you tonight." Aside from Sam not even using his own name, there was no explanation for what the mobile phone was doing just sitting there on the platform. Nothing for why a man who had been gone six months had suddenly made a telephone call. Before I could look any further into the paperwork, Healy disrupted my train of thought, shifting forward and picking the file up, and all I was left with was a flash of a memory.

"How do you even know it's Sam?"

"It's Wren. It's his voice."

"That's been verified by forensics?"

"Initial tests say yes. We'll know for sure tomorrow."

"So why did he call himself Leon Spane?"

"He's protecting his identity." He looked at me. "Plus it's a cute little touch."

"In what way?"

"Spane might be connected to the Snatcher." I waited for Healy to expand on that, but he didn't. "Anyway, that doesn't matter for now. What matters is that it's Wren."

I'd come back to Spane. But for now I returned to the voicemail mes-sage: the Met reckoned Sam had called Drake on the evening of 12 June. The mobile phone records that Spike had got for me only ran up until 1 June, and Sam had made zero calls from the time of his disappearance until then. So why suddenly use it on 12 June?

"I'm still having a hard time seeing this," I said.

The smile fell from Healy's face. I'd touched a nerve; unintentionally, but I'd done it all the same. He didn't want to hear this. He didn't want obstacles put in his path. He was able to control himself against men he hated, against those who had an agenda against him, because he was determined not to arm them with anything they could use. But against me, against a man who had no reason to come at him, no agenda, he didn't have to maintain the facade any more.

"You're having a hard time seeing this?" he said, grimacing. "We've got Erion's number on Wren's computer and his voice on Drake's mobile phone."

"What's Sam's connection to the other two Snatcher victims, though?"

"You struggling to understand my accent or something?"

I held up a hand, trying to cool him.

"Wren knows Erion and he knows Drake," Healy said. "He's been in contact with both of them. What's the next logical step? That he knows Wilky and Symons."

I didn't say anything.

"Give me a fucking break, Raker. You know what this means."

"It's an assumption."

"You'd make the same one."

I couldn't argue with that. If Sam knew two out of the four victims, if he'd been in touch with them, then it was only a very small step to Wilky and Symons.

"This just doesn't feel like Sam."

He snorted in derision. "This is a *murder* investigation, not some carnival sideshow. Cases aren't built on how you *feel*. This isn't the fucking magic circle."

"I wouldn't have pegged Sam for a killer."

"*Sam.*"

I frowned. "What's that supposed to mean?"

"Maybe you're getting too cozy with him," Healy said, and sank some of his coffee. "You ever thought of that? You need to separate out what you *think* is the truth—what you *want* to be the truth—from what is *actually* the truth."

"Is there anything else linking him to the crimes?"

"Anything else but his own *voice*? I don't know how you've found it in your vast experience of working murders, but generally they're not standing there with their dicks out holding the murder weapon when we arrive on the scene. This is as good as it gets." Healy glanced at me, his hackles rising again. "And here's another thing: the Snatcher's a planner. He watches these guys for weeks, he gets to know their routines, he doesn't leave room for error. He even takes out all the lights leading into and out of the building. Every single one. I couldn't get my head around why there was no lighting in the places he took them from. Then I realized every one was the same. He sweeps the building before the night he takes them, and then he walks them out in total darkness."

"What's your point?"

"What's my point?" He smirked. "My point is, I chatted to Julia Wren and she said your mate *Sam* was working late at work *all* the time. So what's the betting he wasn't *at* work? What's the betting he's out there getting a hard-on, picking himself a new victim?"

"Or he could really have been working late."

He shook his head. "You live in fantasy land, Raker. Your guy is the best lead we've had in almost a year of trying to track down this arsehole. We've got him all over two of the vics, he fits the profile like a glove and, all of a sudden, he's mysteriously disappeared and no one—not even *David Raker*—can find him. The only thing batting against all that is this whimsical shit you're spinning about some kind of gut feeling."

"He's been missing six months."

"So?"

"So he hasn't disappeared 'all of a sudden.' And why take two of them and then disappear yourself in order to take the next two—and *then* leave a voice message on the latest victim's phone *and* be careless enough to lose it on the Underground? The Snatcher's left no trace of himself until now. There's no sense in him suddenly deciding to leave his name and number on Drake's phone."

"Sense? What, you think this guy is *lucid*? You think he's logical? What's logical about shaving people's heads and killing them? He's a nutjob." He paused; regained his composure. "You get close to people on a case. I know that. I've done the same. Sometimes it's hard to accept what they've done when you get attached to them."

"I'm not attached to him."

"It sounds to me like you are."

I went to answer, went to fight my corner again, when I stopped. *Had I become too attached to Sam? Had I bought into his life too much,* failed to process the truth out there on the periphery of his life? He was a fraud. He'd lied to everyone important to him. And he'd been leading a double life—which was exactly what the Snatcher had been doing. I looked at Healy and saw the way he was studying me. I backtracked through our conversation and then back even further, to the people I'd spoken to, the lies I'd unearthed.

And then something emerged from the dark.

It was weird, Robert Wren had said to me when he'd told me about Sam going to see the prostitute I now knew to be Marc Erion. *He said the guy lived in this place where there were no lights. He said he got to his door, on to the floor this guy was on, and all the bulbs were out. It was completely black . . . And when he got to the flat,* Wren went on, *he said it felt like someone was there.* Sam meant there, in the corridor with him.

Had Sam told another lie? Or was there something more at play here?

"I'm not attached to him," I said again.

"Whatever."

"Do you even value my opinion, Healy?"

"You looking for an ego massage?"

"*Do you?*"

He just stared at me.

"Or is this simply about getting one over on the cops you hate?"

"It's not about that."

"Then what's it about?"

There was a sudden kind of sadness to him and, for the briefest of moments, I saw a flash in one of his eyes; the same one as earlier. He was definitely hiding something. He looked away, and when he turned back he'd composed himself and there was nothing in his face. No emotion. No expression. Just a blank.

"Healy?"

"It's about getting the guy respon—"

"Responsible for these crimes, blah blah blah. Look, if you value anything I did for you last year, if *any* of that meant *anything*, you owe it to me to—"

"I don't owe you shit."

I paused. This was how Healy's anger played out: indiscriminate and damaging. But even though I knew that, even though I'd dealt with this over and over the October before, it still stuck in my throat. It provoked me and irritated me, and—in my most uncontrolled moments, moments I tried to contain—it made me want to hurt him back.

"Why are you still here?"

He looked at me. "What?"

"You've got the evidence. You've obviously got all you need to know about Sam from his wife. She's told you how he disappeared, what her life was like at the end, how he started to change. You know all that already. Now I've just filled in the rest of the blanks for you. So why are you still here?"

His eyes turned to his coffee mug.

I leaned into him. "Don't bullshit me, Healy. I never thought this was a social call so I'm not upset you aren't asking me how I've been keeping, but don't try to pretend this is something it isn't. You called me because you want to know what I've got, so you can take it back to the station and pretend it's all your own work. You want to solve this case by yourself so you can prove them all wrong. But mostly you're using me because you've got some doubts about something. So what have you got doubts about?"

He didn't say anything.

"I'm not your enemy, Healy, remember that."

"So what are you?"

I shook my head. "I don't know. I don't know *what* we are."

We sat there for a while, both of us nursing identical mugs of coffee, both of us at the window, on identical stools, looking out at the same street. I studied our reflections in the glass and remembered a moment from the last time we were together, sitting at the window of a coffee shop just off East India Dock Road, Healy telling me about the case that had broken him, the case that had ended his marriage. Then, as now, I looked at him and thought, in another life, things could have been different. In so many ways we were the same. In so many ways we reflected one another, all the qualities and the faults, the lingering sense of loss. But Healy's control, over himself and over his emotions, would only ever be tenuous, because that was who he was—and *that* was what separated us. However far out of the hole he managed to claw himself, he'd always be slipping back in.

"The disappearance thing bugs me," he said finally. It was as close to an apology, an acknowledgment that I was right, as I was going to get, so I accepted it with a nod of the head and we moved on. "Like you say, why take Wilky and Erion, then disappear?" He paused. Looked at me. "And the phone is the other thing. Same as you. Why would Wren leave a message? He's been careful. He hasn't made any mistakes. Leaving a message is a mistake."

"This is what I know about Sam. His whole life was a lie, but it wasn't something that came easy to him. It weighed heavy. He was in complete denial about who he was. It took him ten years to pluck up the courage to sleep with another man and when he did . . ."

I stopped.

Should I tell him about Wellis? If I did, the police would corner him faster than I ever could on my own, and it would be one less loose end to worry about. But if they got to Wellis, that would invite questions about the girl at the house, about what happened at the warehouse, about Gaishe and about the anonymous call I'd made. Sallows, the cop who'd come to my home looking into the attack on the girl, would have even more ammunition to come at me with. But the flipside was obvious: if I didn't tell Healy, Wellis remained out there—and he remained a threat to me.

I studied Healy, saw the way he was trying to play it straight, trying to reboot his career at the Met without straying outside the lines, and, in a weird way, suddenly trusted him a little less for it. The old Healy was accountable only to himself, but that at least made him less invested in what I did, and how I worked the laws of the land. This new one had a responsibility to the people he worked with, a determination to promote his own career and show them how good he was, and that meant he had a rulebook. So I didn't tell him about Wellis. Not yet.

"'When he did' what?" Healy asked.

I looked at him. "Huh?"

"You said, 'It took him ten years to pluck up the courage to sleep with another man and when he did . . .' When he did what?"

"When he did sleep with another man, he chose Marc Erion."

"You knew about Erion?"

"I knew Sam slept with a prostitute. I didn't know who it was."

"How did the two of them even meet in the first place?"

"I don't know," I lied.

He studied me. "So you really think Wren didn't do this, despite everything I've just told you?"

This was why Healy had called me. This moment. This question. With me, he could do what he couldn't at the Met: put himself out there, expose his doubts. And off the back of that question, I suddenly felt a little sorry for him. Because basically, Healy was lonely.

"I don't think the Sam I've got to know is capable of that."

His eyes narrowed. "But?"

"But maybe this isn't the Sam I know."

45

Healy was heading back to Jonathan Drake's flat, near Hammersmith Bridge, so he offered me a lift down to Hammersmith Tube station so I wouldn't have change lines on the journey home. We didn't say much on the walk to his car—the same battered red Vauxhall estate that smelled of wet dog he'd had the previous year—but as he unlocked it, he looked across the roof at me like he knew what I was going to ask.

"What's the other file you've got?"

He paused for a moment, key in the door, the strap from the slip case slung over his shoulder. His eyes flicked to the slipcase, and there was a moment's hesitation when he probably saw himself endangering his career again. A part of him didn't trust me, like I didn't trust him—perhaps it would always be that way between us—but I sensed this file represented something personal to him. All cops had them: a case that they couldn't close and that no one else would back them on—or a case that proved them right.

"Get in the car," he said, and flipped the locks.

When both doors were closed, he laid the slip case on his lap, unzipped it and then took out the sixth file: the one in the green folder. Sam's had been the thinnest but this one wasn't far off. It must have only run to about twenty pages, which meant it was either simple and wrapped up quickly—or, more likely, it was unsolved. He handed it to me.

"Meet Leon Spane," he said.

I flipped the front cover and, as soon as I saw Spane's face, he felt familiar. I tried to claw at the memory, tried to drag it back into the light, but couldn't place him. The man was gray-white, bloodless, eyes open and staring off into space. It was a shot from his autopsy. He was older than the others—mid to late thirties—and, according to his physical description, slightly bigger too.

"Who is he?"

"He was found on Hampstead Heath."

"When?"

"Twenty months ago. October 2010."

"He's different from the others."

"He wasn't taken from his home." He flipped forward a couple of pages to the coroner's report. "Whoever killed him stabbed him in the throat and cut his dick off."

"Bloody hell."

"Yeah."

"So how do you think they're linked?"

"I always knew he was a part of this—*always*—but after Wren made the call to Drake and used Spane's name, I knew for sure." He pointed to Spane's photograph. "Plus, his head was shaved just before his body was dumped."

I nodded. "Was he also gay?"

"Impossible to tell."

"How come?"

"He had no family. We never had anyone claim him."

And then it hit me. I flicked back to the picture and, through the corner of my eye, I saw a frown form on Healy's face.

"Raker?"

I didn't reply, just looked down at Leon Spane: no beard, no hair, no holdall or cardboard sign. Shaved and lifeless, he looked so different from the CCTV footage.

But he was still the same man.

He was the homeless guy at Gloucester Road.

There was no way to prevent the police getting to Sam. If they believed he was the Snatcher, they were going to be unstoppable. It might have been different if I could push back with something but, four days after Julia Wren arrived in my life, there was no exit I could see, no physical route out for Sam, not even a hint of where he might have been until Healy turned up and told me about Jonathan Drake's phone.

As we said good-bye I'd thought, for a brief moment, about telling Healy what I already knew about Leon Spane: his connection to Duncan Pell and, in turn, Pell's connection to Sam. There were reasons for doing that; good reasons that might lead them to the Snatcher. But then I saw the next hour—the Met doorstepping me, dismantling the work I'd done, threatening to bring charges if I didn't drop the case—and all I felt was discomfort: about handing something over half finished; about failing to get Julia the answers she sought; but mostly about letting the police hunt Sam Wren when, deep down, I wasn't even sure he was the killer.

46

By the time I got home, an unmarked Volvo was already bumped up on the pavement outside the gates of my house. When I was about twenty feet away, both doors opened and two plainclothes officers got out. From the passenger side came a woman in her early forties: skinny in a black trouser suit, short blond hair tucked behind her ears, a sharp, angular face and eyes like puffs of ash. But it wasn't her I cared about, it was the man who got out from the driver's side. I slowed to a halt as Eddie Davidson pushed his door shut, looked at me, then leaned against the side of the car, a smirk on his face.

He'd been one of the cops wrapped up in what happened on my case the October before, and he'd disliked me pretty much from the first moment we met. He saw me as a hindrance, as Healy's crony and collaborator. Things had only got worse as the case went deeper. When I'd left Healy at Hammersmith, he'd warned me again that the Snatcher team would be coming to my house, and that they'd ask me to close down my search for Sam—and he'd told me Davidson would probably want to be a part of that. I'd never been much of a believer in destiny, but I wasn't surprised he was back. Life had a way of binding you to certain people, and when it did, it became hard to extricate yourself from them.

The woman approached me first.

I guessed this was Craw, the senior investigating officer. She wore a tired look, worn down by months of trying to chase the same man, but I got the impression straight off the bat that she knew nothing about me beyond what Davidson had told her. He wouldn't have painted me in my best light, which was why I assumed she'd taken on a fierce, stern expression, as if she expected me to create problems as soon as I opened my mouth.

"Mr. Raker, my name's DCI Craw." She got out her warrant card and held it up. I didn't bother checking it, just looked at Davidson. He was dressed pretty much the same as the last time I'd seen him: jeans and trainers, T-shirt and black leather jacket, his stomach like a planetary mass, his face oddly proportioned: small eyes, big nose, wide mouth. He winked briefly and then stepped away from the car. "I think you know DS Davidson."

"Unfortunately I do."

Craw didn't respond. "We're here to talk about Samuel Wren."

"Well, you'd better come inside then."

We sat in the living room, Craw stiff on the edge of the sofa, Davidson perched in a chair on the other side of me, so we were in a triangle with me as the apex. It was a classic move; an effort to cramp me in the place I should feel most comfortable.

"We understand you're doing some work for Julia Wren," Craw said.

I looked at her, then at Davidson. He was on his best behavior with the boss around, face unmoving, eyes fixed on me. "She asked me to look into Mr. Wren's disappearance. I'm in the preliminary stages of doing that. What is it you want to know about him?"

A little snort from Davidson.

Craw glanced at him, then back to me. "We don't need anything from you. We're here today to ask you to halt the search for her husband. I'm not at liberty to discuss the reasons why, but unfortunately this isn't a process that's up for negotiation."

"Has Mrs. Wren agreed to this?"

"Ultimately, it's not up to her."

I shrugged. "Fine."

Both of them looked at me.

"Fine what?" she said.

"Fine. Do what you have to do."

Davidson came forward on his seat. "That's *it?*" he asked, the first thing he'd said since they'd arrived. "You're just gonna sit there and let us take this away from you?"

"You're the police. What choice do I have?"

"Is this a joke or something?"

"DCI Craw just asked me to halt the investigation."

"That never stopped you last time."

I looked at him. "You're right. It never stopped me last time, because last time you'd fucked things up so badly I had no choice but to try and put them right."

Anger flushed in Davidson's face. "What did you say?"

"You heard what I said."

"You almost destroyed our case."

"I found you a killer."

"You're not even a fucking cop."

"Well, I guess that makes two of us."

Before Davidson could come at me again, Craw stepped in, hand up. "Okay, okay, that's enough of that crap." She glanced at Davidson, giving him a look that said, *Calm down*, and then shifted closer to me. "Mr. Raker, I want to be quite clear with you that if you cross us on this, we *will* have to take you down. You need to step back *completely*."

"Fair enough."

"You *will* be charged."

"I understand."

Davidson eyed me. "What aren't you telling us?"

"DCI Craw said she didn't want to hear what I had on Wren."

"No, I don't mean that," he said. "Whatever you've found out about Wren, we'll find it too, and we'll find more and do it better. We're *better* at this than you, Raker, just remember that. No, I'm talking about what else is going on in that head of yours."

"I don't know what you're talking about."

"Bollocks."

I shrugged. "I don't know what you want me to say."

"You're full of shit, Raker."

"Do you want me to say that you're better than me, is that it? You're not better than me. You're half a cop. You don't use the badge as a way to understand people, you use it as a way to intimidate and bully. That's why you could never find the guy who was taking those women last year—and that's why you'll never find the Snatcher."

Davidson erupted. "Who the fuck do you think you're talk—"

"How do you know that?" Craw interrupted, her voice even and calm, looking at me. Davidson glanced at her, aghast, cheeks flushed, beads of sweat dotted across his face.

"What?"

"That Davidson's working the Snatcher?"

"I must have read it in the papers."

"He heard it from Healy," Davidson said, almost trembling with rage.

"Last time I saw Healy, he was burying his girl in the ground," I said to Davidson. "Do you think he's calling me up to relive old times? We hardly even talked when we were working together, so a catch-up is pretty low on my list of priorities."

"Have you got anything you want to tell us?" Craw asked.

I frowned. "What do you mean?"

"You say you read the papers, so I guess you know who I am, you know who Davidson is and apparently what case he's working, and you know we're here about Sam Wren. So I'm going to credit you with enough intelligence to put two and two together."

"You think Wren is involved in the Snatcher case."

A gentle nod of the head.

"No, I haven't got anything to tell you," I said.

But her eyes lingered on me. Maybe she believed me, maybe she didn't, but she was smart and switched on—and I knew instantly that this was a different sort of cop from Davidson and Healy. She was in control of her emotions, able to sit back and analyze.

And that made her dangerous.

I was going to have to watch Melanie Craw.

I called Julia and listened to her tearfully describe how the police wouldn't tell her what was going on. I told her they'd been to see me too, had asked me to step back from the case, and that I'd agreed. It would have been easier to tell her the truth—that I was still going after Sam, but now through Duncan Pell—but then she'd have that burden to carry, that lie to tell, and the police would eventually pick up the scent. I needed to stay ahead of them.

As I waited on Spike to call me back with an address for Pell, I thought of something Liz had said to me once. *You don't have that mechanism that tells you when enough is enough. You don't know when to stop.* I didn't know how to respond to that at the time and I didn't know how to respond to it now. But without Pell, without using him to try and find Sam, without getting Julia the answers she needed, I had nothing. No missing person to bring back into the light, no hole to fill. Nothing to define my life.

Duncan Pell lived about a quarter of a mile from Highgate Tube station, in a tiny house on the edge of Queen's Wood. The road was nice but Pell's house wasn't. It looked like a late addition to the street; out of place among the big, red-brick fronts and gleaming bay windows that surrounded it. It was tucked away, half hidden behind a copse of trees, and the driveway slanted downwards, so you were forced to approach at a jog. It was just a box—completely square with no external features and nothing to distinguish it—and, as I approached it, passing the manicured lawns and spotless fascia boards of the other houses, I wondered what Pell's neighbors made of him. I also wondered how he could afford to live in an area like this. Either London Underground were paying more than I'd imagined, or he'd been left the house by a relative.

The lawn hadn't been mowed in weeks. Big, overgrown trees cast shadows across the house, and there were weeds everywhere: the grass was infested with them, but they were crawling through the driveway as well, fingering their way out of the cracks and up the side of the house. There was a red ceramic pot in the corner, with nothing growing in it, and a tap with a hose attached.

The front of the house had two windows, the curtains drawn both sides. I rang the doorbell and waited, watching for any sign of movement behind a small glass panel, high up on the door—but none came. I pressed my finger to the buzzer a second time, leaving it there, listening to the sound reverberate around inside the house but, ten seconds later, I got the same lack of response.

No approaching footsteps.

No sound inside at all.

I moved back up the driveway and headed down to the end of the road. From right on the corner, between a couple of monolithic fir trees, the gardens of the houses in Pell's row were visible. Beyond was Queen's Wood, its trees housed inside metal fencing, its endless canopy a patchwork of leaves. Pell's back garden was pretty much a mirror image of the front, all grass and weeds and neglect, but it was built on two levels: a stone staircase connected them, the bottom one leading down to a rear gate. It was the easiest and quickest way to get onto the property, because there was no padlock—just a slide bolt—but it was far too exposed: all the neighbors' windows looked down across it, and it backed right on to the edge of the woods and one of the approaches to Highgate Tube station. It was too risky.

I headed back up the road and returned to the front door, trying the bell for a third time. "Duncan?" I said, keeping my voice low so the neighbors wouldn't hear. But still I got no response. I turned and looked back at the street. The house was hidden so well behind all the natural growth, it was like a homing beacon for burglars. I took out my wallet, flipped it open and slid out a couple of thin hairpins.

Now I was the burglar.

I'd learned to pick locks in South Africa during my second spell there, from an ex-member of the National Intelligence Service. He was an arrogant, pigheaded racist who I'd interviewed on six separate occasions as part of a feature I was writing on the country, postapartheid. His views were abhorrent, and his refusal to apologize for the things he'd done even worse, but he seemed to believe we shared some kind of kinship, however misguided, perhaps because I was the only person who'd ever spent any sort of time listening to him. I'd rarely picked locks as a journalist. As an investigator, outside of the rule of law, I did it often.

I hated it.

The difficulty. The precision. The frustration.

Working the kinks out of the hairpins, I took a look back out at the street and dropped down at the door. It was a cylinder lock—the same kind I'd learned with—so I had a small advantage. But the one true thing the South African had said in all the time I spent interviewing him was that lock-picking wasn't like the films. The next ten minutes of failure proved him right—until, finally, the door popped gently away from its frame.

I paused, waiting for an alarm to start beeping and, when nothing came, entered the house and pushed the door shut behind me. Straight away it was clear Pell must have inherited the house. It was like stepping into a 1970s sitcom: an awful beige carpet, worn thin by traffic and scattered with stains, and wallpaper, thick and dirty, bleached yellow with smoke. In the kitchen, dishes were piled up in the sink; burger cartons and chip paper; food dried to a hard crust on the plates and worktops. The house was hot and stuffy from having been closed up, but there was a musty, decrepit smell as well, as if every inch of the house—even the foundations it had been built on—had reached the end of its life.

I headed upstairs. At the top were two bedrooms and a bathroom. The first bedroom was where he slept: a bed had been pushed in among built-in wardrobes and a mattress dumped on top. No sheets. No duvet. Just a sleeping bag. A side table was next to that with an ashtray on it. The room smelled strongly of smoke. To my left was a separate stand-alone wardrobe. I opened it up. There was hardly anything inside: two or three suits, three London Underground uniforms, a pair of jeans and a couple of shirts. At the bottom, lined up, were his boots: all steel—toe capped, all black with red stitching—the same as he'd had on the day I'd first met him at the station—and all polished until they shone.

I headed for the second bedroom. It was the hottest room in the house, sun beating down through the window, forming a square on the carpet. Dust was caught in the light, drifting from one side of the room to the other, and there was a strange smell. Sweet, like air freshener. In the far corner was a wardrobe. It looked old: dark wood, ornate design around its edges, chips dotted along its side and base. I opened it up. There were more clothes inside—more suits—and some cheap rip-off Magic Trees that smelled vaguely of aftershave, which I guessed he was using to combat the musty smell of the old wood.

At the bottom was a bag.

I dragged it out and dumped it on the floor, then unzipped it. On top was a coat, big and puffy and covered with dirt. It looked like he'd been gardening in it. I pulled it out. The sleeves were ripped and chewed at the ends, stained all the way up to the elbows in grease, and the back was filthy: black and torn, like it had been rubbed down with coal. I checked the pockets. One side was empty but the other had a folded piece of paper in it: a flyer. At the top was a black-and-white photocopied picture of a doorway, with a man standing outside it, smiling. He was holding a cup of something. Underneath, all the print had been smudged, as if the flyer had been inside the pocket for a long time. I looked at the coat again and a memory stirred in me. Had I seen it before somewhere? It had a strange smell. Not just dirt and grease and body odour, but something else. A dusty, oily kind of scent. *Like the smell of the Tube.* Pell had been wearing the standard uniform when I'd talked to him at Gloucester Road, but I started to wonder whether I'd seen the jacket in the booth behind him at some point. Glimpsed it and not even realized. I turned it on to its front and flipped it open. Inside, the insulation was coming through in a couple of places and then I spotted something else. Another stain.

Blood.

Not much, but enough: soaked into the collar of the coat.

I set the coat aside and returned to the bag. It had three other things inside: some cardboard packaging, a leather pouch, and a series of printouts rolled up into a tube and secured with an elastic band. I took out the card first and saw it wasn't packaging at all—or, at least, not any more—but one side of a brown cardboard box, messily cut out with a blunt pair of scissors. There was nothing on one side but more dirt.

I flipped it over.

More grime. More dirt. And more blood. But the blood wasn't what caught my attention this time. It was what was written across the middle of the board in black.

Homeless. Please help.

I glanced at the flyer—realizing it was for a shelter—and then at the coat next to it. Now I knew why I recognized it.

It had been Leon Spane's.

Reaching down into the bag, I took out the leather pouch and then the roll of printed pages. The pouch was soft leather, closed at either end and bound in its center with a tie. I pulled at the tie and the pouch fell open, like a bird spreading its wings.

Knives, one after the other.

Different lengths, different blades, different edges, different grips. But all of them had one thing in common: blood on them, congealed and dried, sticking to the leather and to each other. I placed them down on the floor next to the coat, next to the flyer, next to the cardboard sign— and I opened up the printouts.

They were maps.

I laid them side by side, but quickly realized it was the same map, reprinted over and over again, just at different magnifications. I brought the one with the closest view of the area toward me. It was Highgate. I could make out Pell's house. I could see Queen's Wood, and Highgate Cemetery to the south. And then a trail, running parallel to the Northern line and branching off right. Some kind of footpath. It cut between housing estates as it carved east, and halfway along, as nature became more dense, Pell had marked it with red pen.

And then I realized it wasn't a footpath.

It was a disused railway line.

48

They called it Fell Wood. I found it about half a mile south of Highgate Tube station, on the other side of a row of trees shielding the path from the road. I entered through a metal gate that squeaked on its hinges, and passed under a thick covering of oak trees, expecting woodland to unravel around me. Instead, after thirty yards, the trees thinned out and the railway line emerged, graveled in patches but mostly just overrun by grass.

The tracks and the sleepers had long since been ripped up, but there was still a raised station house ahead of me, its legs straddling the old platforms on the left and right of the path, its old ticket office perched directly above the line. It was derelict. The ground-floor entrance, the windows and the doors were all bricked up; the windows on the second floor were all broken. Either side of me, trees and grass reached up into the clear blue sky. But when the breeze came, foliage shifted and grass swayed, and I saw modern houses beyond the treeline, kids running around in the gardens, dads standing over barbecues. I passed under the station house, its old bones creaking and moaning in the sun, and carried on.

Pell had circled a spot about a mile from the station I'd just passed. As I walked, the trees got thicker on both sides, and after about ten minutes a railway tunnel emerged from behind a weave of oak and ash trees. All around the entrance was graffiti, up to about the eight-foot mark, but mostly it was vines, seas of the stuff, the crumbling facade clawed at by twisted branches and covered in a layer of green moss.

Inside the tunnel, sound faded, like a dial being turned down, and as I stood there, facing into a circle of light at the end of fifty yards of complete darkness, I suddenly felt a strange sensation, as if someone was standing right on my shoulder.

I swiveled. Behind me, the station house was just a blur in the distance, distorted by heat haze and half disguised by trees. Its second-floor windows were like black holes carved into the bricks, and some of the rear of the building had fallen away: about three-quarters of the way up, the roof had caved in and part of the wall was destroyed. In the roof space, I thought I could see movement, a flash of white—like a face—but after a while a bird emerged, flapping its wings, and took flight up and across the treeline.

I turned back and headed into the tunnel.

Halfway along, all noise died. No birds. No wind. No cars. I was struck again by the strange acoustics of the old line, the way volume ebbed and flowed, and when I got to the end, it changed again: gravel and grass became just grass, the distant sounds of the city returned— and two hundred yards ahead of me was the mark on Pell's map.

Another station.

It was smaller than the first one but perched on a raised island of concrete, which bisected the line. Either side were where the westbound and eastbound tracks had once run, both now reclaimed by nature. Further down, on the left-hand side of the station, was another building, this one in behind the treeline. It was bigger, more modern, a small chimney-like structure rising out of its roof, its walls mostly hidden behind thick foliage. As I moved up on to the island, I got a better view and could see a series of ventilation shafts adjacent to the chimney.

I turned my attention back to the station. Every window and door was bricked up, but a blanket of glass, gravel and debris still crunched under my shoes as I passed along the eastbound platform. Once I was halfway along, I dropped down on to the line and crossed toward the second building. The closer I got, the more of it I could make out beyond the trees. Seconds later, I spotted a space on its wall where a sign had once hung, age and weather rinsing the color off and on to the brickwork.

It was the red and blue symbol of the Tube.

Suddenly it made sense: this was a two-part station. The island platform and station house fed the overground line, a track that had once run between Highgate and Finsbury Park. Below ground had been a deep-level station—accessed via the second building—cleaving its way through the belly of the city, now disconnected from the network. A ghost station, shut down, bricked up and forgotten.

But not by Duncan Pell.

The Tube station was surrounded—almost swamped—by trees and foliage, but a path still remained, cutting through the overgrowth to the entrance. I headed in. It was uneven, the concrete broken, but it led all the way through to a narrow passageway and a staircase down. At the bottom, a rusting metal grille should have been pulled shut and padlocked to stop people from entering.

Except the grille wasn't all the way across.

And the padlock was on the floor.

49

Fifteen feet away, in the gnarled bark of an old ash, I found a fallen branch. I picked it up, broke it in two and gripped it like a baseball bat, the thicker end facing up.

Then I headed down.

When I got to the grille, I stopped. Shapes formed in the dark on the other side and, as I maneuvered myself into the gap, my eyes adjusted to the light and I could make out an old ticket office. Off to the right, barely visible in the darkness, was a lift: its doors were open, but another grille was pulled across. This one was still padlocked.

I got out my mobile, and used a light app to illuminate the area beyond the lift. It was a corridor, about thirty feet long, old-fashioned wooden phone booths on the left and then a door at the far end. Another sign, more difficult to read, was screwed to the wall above. STAIRS. They must have led down to the platform. Except there was no way to get down there now: the lift was padlocked and the door was bricked over.

A noise behind me.

I turned quickly and looked back across the ticket hall. My phone only reached so far into the darkness. Six feet. Maybe less. Something shifted in the shadows above my eyeline, right up in the corner of the room. I lifted the mobile higher. At the very limit of its glow, gray-blue in the light, I could see what it was. Bats. There were eight of them, hanging from a support beam in the roof. One of them was moving, its wings twitching.

I took a couple of steps back toward the office and, as I did, felt a faint draft at ankle level. Not much, but enough. When I stopped again I could hear it moving past me: a whisper, soft and unrefined, like a child's voice. Eventually it faded out, as if sensing I was listening, and then I realized something else: it was freezing cold. The whole place—the whole building— was like a refrigerator. Turning the phone in the direction of the draft, I felt goosebumps scatter up my arms.

And then I found two further doors.

One was bricked up.

The other was ajar.

The darkness seemed to close in as I moved toward the open door.

In front of me, there was no break in the shadows. No sliver of daylight. In the silence, all that came back was the thump of my heart in my chest, over and over, pounding in my ears.

Two feet short of the door, I smelled something.

Beyond was more darkness, thick and impervious, and when I raised the phone I saw it was another staircase down, this time bending around and out of sight. On either side were black wrought-iron handrails. Glazed tiles were on the walls, some broken and on the steps. The same smell drifted past me and out into the room I was in. A stench of decay.

I started the descent.

Before the bend in the staircase, there was a moment where I felt the same breeze as before, felt it pass my face and cling to me, thick and gluey, as if trying to warn me not to go any further. But I carried on. At the bottom was an old staffroom. It was about forty feet long but narrow. There were no windows. On one side, attached to the wall, was a counter. It was a big slab of wood, topped with small white tiles, but the tiles were mostly broken or on the floor in front. On top were a couple of animal traps, big and rusting, a series of knives and some rope. There was no other furniture. The smell was horrendous; a stench of death and suffering that stuck to the back of my throat.

Yet the room was empty.

Further into the darkness were more tools: a saw propped against the counter, a knife, rolls of duct tape. And something else: specks of blood on the white tiles, dotted all along the counter top like a trail on a map.

Then, in front of me, something shifted.

The phone's glow didn't reach the far wall, but something in me— some small voice—said not to go any further. I stood there for a moment, heart thumping in my chest, the smell, almost unbearable now, clawing its way into my nose and mouth and staying there like dust. Then— finally—I stepped forward and, on the edge of the glow, two blobs of light came back. At first I couldn't see what they were. Then, too late, I realized.

Boots. Black, with steel toe caps and red stitching.

Just like Duncan Pell's.

He's in the room with me.

50

He launched himself out of the darkness, hood up, leading with his fists. I was barely ready for him, almost side on, but instead of trying to cut me down, he went past me. My body had been prepared for the impact, ready to absorb the blow. Instead, I felt the dead air move, an arm brush mine, and then he was already on the stairs, heading up into the ticket hall above us.

A second later, I followed.

As I came out of the bend on the stairs, I saw him exit through the metal grille and head up the stairs to the line. I tried to close the gap but he was fast. *Ex-army. Fit.* At the stairs I slowed. Up ahead, it was a blind turn back on to the line, so I came up on the left-hand side to avoid being hit or surprised. But there was no one waiting.

The line was silent.

I took a couple of steps through the trees to where the old eastbound line met the station house. Nothing now. No sound. No movement. The ground was hard, dried and compact. I moved along it, the platform about five feet above me on the island, glass and dust and brick scattered all over it. Halfway down, I placed both hands on the island and hauled myself up. Next to me, the station creaked in the hot sun. I didn't move. Just stood there and listened. No sound but the station house, baking in the heat.

Crack.

A sound from the other side.

Glass beneath boots.

I moved quickly around the front, watching where my feet fell, and stopped at the edge of the building. Then I peered around the corner, along the westbound side.

No one on the platform.

No one on the line.

I came out from behind the station house. About two hundred feet further along, the island became a ramp and dropped down to meet the path. Fifty feet beyond that, the trees began to close in, swallowing the old line whole. There was nothing now. No breeze at all. The only thing that came back were my footsteps, moving across the thin layer of glass and dust. As the island dropped down, the two lines merging into a single path, I saw a flash of movement up ahead.

I carried on, my feet returning to the grass of the line, weeds crawling through the cracks in the baked earth, masonry kicked off on to the old track from the island. There was so much of it—chunks of brick, shards of roofing, clumps of tile. One wrongly placed foot and my ankle would snap.

As the trees grew thicker and the shadows longer, there was a subtle change in the atmosphere: the foliage seemed to drop, as if reaching out, and another tunnel emerged, almost from nowhere, like it was part of the trees and grass; all but carved from them. It was as gun-barrel-straight as the last one, but it was even longer, the daylight at its end just a pinprick against a slate-black wall. I walked right up to it, stopping short of its entrance, but the closer I got, the more I started to sense something. Something defective and amiss. Places were shaped and molded by their history, by the events that had taken place in them, but mostly they were shaped by the people who had passed through them.

I stepped inside and felt wet mud beneath my feet. The further in I got, the more the temperature seemed to drop. For a moment I felt adrift. My eyes hadn't adjusted. The ground was uneven and shifting under my boots. I slowed slightly and, as I did, I heard something ahead of me, like footsteps softening, getting further away from me. Then there was no noise at all.

I stopped.

"Duncan?"

My voice echoed along the tunnel and then vanished, as if absorbed by the dark. The daylight at the other end was about the size of a dinner plate, but it was below my eyeline, like I was heading down into the earth, rather than over it. I glanced back over my shoulder to where I'd come in: the entrance was about forty yards back, a circle full of trees, and hazy in the distance was the island and station house. I thought briefly about backtracking, about returning to the sunlight—because even after being inside the tunnel for thirty seconds, I could barely see anything; maybe ten feet in either direction.

Then another sound from in front of me.

I slowly stepped back, placing my foot as carefully as I could, and felt the heel of my boot disappear into soft mud. There was a gentle sucking sound, barely any noise at all, and yet—in the silence—it was like a scream. Suddenly, there was movement in front of me. As I stepped back again, caught mid-stride, he came out of the darkness, almost ripped from it, and—before I had a chance to react—I was being slammed against the ground, wind fizzing from my body, white spots flashing in front of my eyes.

A moment of confusion.

I started to get up, hand flat to the mud path.

And then a boot swung out of the dark, not even there until it was inches in front of my face, and as I tried desperately to avoid it, the steel toe cap connected with the bridge of my nose—and I thumped back violently against the ground for a second time.

And this time I blacked out.

When I came round again, I was still in the same place. My head felt like it was on fire, pain in the bridge of my nose, in my forehead, around my eyes. I touched a finger to my face. My nose wasn't broken, but I could feel wet blood all down my lips and over my chin.

Getting on to all fours and then slowly, unsteadily, to my feet, I headed back the way I'd come in, eventually hitting the light. It was starting to cool off now, or maybe I was just so coated in cold mud that it only felt that way. As I stood there, wiping the blood and the dirt from my skin, dizziness hit me and a wave of nausea swept through my system. I put a hand to my mouth, trying to push it down, and as I did I realized the smell of the staffroom was still clinging to the inside of my throat, to my mouth and nose.

A second wave hit me—and this time I was sick.

When I was done, I wiped my mouth and looked back into the darkness of the tunnel. *Pell.* If he'd been using the staffroom, he'd been using it for something bad. The room may have been empty, but the smell of death remained, and so did the evidence of suffering. He knew the line. He knew how to navigate it, how to keep its secrets from people, how to use it against me. And he'd be long gone by now.

But even as I realized that, even as I saw the logic in it, a weird feeling passed over me.

Like someone was still watching.

Pell hadn't returned to his house, although I hadn't expected him to. I walked down his driveway to the tap and turned it on, washing my face with the lukewarm water. I rinsed off the mud, leaving great big wet patches on my jeans, and then I took off my T-shirt and turned it inside out. It masked some of the bloodstains; enough, at least, not to turn heads on the train ride home. Then, finally, I scrubbed down my boots. When I was done, I turned the tap off and stood there, watching the water run into the gaps between the patio slabs. But even washed down, I could still smell the room on me.

The blood and the death.

In my clothes, in the thread and the stitching.

In my skin.

51

For the first time in months, I dreamed. I was hiding behind a door in the bedroom, only able to see two ways: right, through the gap between door and frame; and left to Derryn's old dresser, where the mirror reflected back the door and the hallway beyond.

In the darkness of the hallway I could see shapes: figures, one queued behind the other, waiting to enter the bedroom. At first a feeling passed over me—the kind of sixth sense you only gain in dreams—and I told myself, *They're the people you've found; the men, the women, the kids, all of them tracked down, brought home and returned to the light.*

But then one of the shapes moved away from the group.

And I realized they weren't those people at all.

When I woke, my whole body was slick with sweat, the sheets beneath me wet, the duvet twisted around my legs and my stomach like a cocoon. I kicked it off, sat up and then remained there, perched on the edge of the bed, my elbows on my knees, my head in my hands. Behind me, I felt Liz stir. She made a soft sound, a gentle exhalation, and then her fingers were brushing the small of my back. "Are you okay, baby?" she said quietly.

I nodded and looked at the clock: 1:21 a.m.

Her fingers moved across my skin. "You're soaking. Were you dreaming?"

I turned and looked at her in the darkness of the bedroom. Behind her, the curtains weren't fully drawn and moonlight poured through the gap in a thin sliver the shape of a knife blade. It fell against her skin, her body and part of her face. She was so different from Derryn, our relationship so different, and yet for a moment they were both the same: the person I shared my life with—but not the things I'd seen, or the things I'd done.

"Yes," I said, taking her hand. I shifted back into the darkness, where she couldn't see my bruises. The less she saw of them, the longer we went without having to discuss my work, and why I did what I did.

"What was the dream about?"

"Just a . . ." I stopped myself and looked at her again. *How do I tell you everything I've done?* I brought her into me and we sat there in silence, and then, after a while, I felt her breath on my neck, her face turned to me,

still waiting for an answer. "I dreamed about some of my cases," I said
finally. "About the men I've hunted."

She looked at me, eyes narrowing slightly, as if she was searching for
the lie. I'd told them to her before, out of nothing more than a need to
protect her from the truth—from discovering a man she knew nothing
about—and she'd seen right through them. But I must have been convincing enough this time because she dropped her head back against my
chest and squeezed me. I felt my heart swell up with guilt, but let it go.
She couldn't know what I'd really dreamed of, because if I told her the
truth, she'd realize I'd deceived her. She'd defended me as a solicitor, and
supported me as her partner, but I'd only ever told her enough to get me
off. She didn't know every detail about the killers I'd tracked.

And nothing of the bodies I'd put in the ground.

The people in the hallway had been those killers, and they'd been those
bodies, waiting in line to enter the bedroom. The hiding spot I'd used in
the dream had been the same spot I'd used once, back at the start, when
one of them had come to my home in the middle of the night to kill me.
I understood why I'd returned to that hiding place in the dream and I
understood why those men—the ones now in prison, and the ones who
were nothing more than bones and earth—had come to me. They were
my memories. The men who'd tried to walk me to my grave. The men
who'd attacked me, shot at me and tortured me.

And right at the back, behind the devils and executioners, had been
someone else. A deep unease had slithered through my stomach as I
watched him—an ominous feeling, spreading fast like an oil spill—and
even though I told myself it was a dream, felt the unreality of it, I couldn't
pull myself out. It was like I was drowning. I just gasped for air, desperately trying to reach for the surface, and became frightened in a way I
hadn't been for a long time. And all the time, the man just stood there,
looking into the room at me.

Hood up. No face.

Just darkness.

PART FOUR

52

When I woke the next morning, the sun was gone. Through the gap in the curtains, all I could see was swollen gray cloud and rain spitting against the windows, breaking into lines and running the length of the glass. I returned to Pell's place in Highgate, found a parking space just up from the entrance, and sat there and waited. It was harder to be inconspicuous on a Sunday: even though it was raining, the clouds a granite gray, the gutters swirling with dead leaves and water, people passed the car frequently, on walks, with dogs on leashes, heading to the park or down the road to the Tube station. I tried my best to make it look like I was busy: I opened and closed the glovebox when people walked past, polished the dashboard with an old rag, got out to open the boot and look through it. But eventually, as lunch came and went and Pell still hadn't returned, I gave up and just sat there. The house remained the same as it had been the day before: fewer shadows because there was no sun, but its windows no less dark.

At just gone two, hungry and impatient, I scooped my phone up off the passenger seat and dialed Gloucester Road to see if Pell had turned up for work today. It seemed unlikely. The house had the lifeless feel of a building that had gone days without being occupied. When I finally got through, the lady I spoke to said he'd called in sick for the second day running, and before she could ask me anything in return I hung up. Pell wasn't ill; at least not in the way they believed he was. If he was strong enough to put his boot through my face, he was strong enough to make it into work. The question wasn't whether he was lying about being sick.

It was why.

An hour later, I glanced in my rearview mirror and noticed something.

I'd walked past it without even taking it in the day before, but now a memory flared, like a brief spark of light. Two cars behind me, on the other side of the road, a vehicle sat awkwardly between a Range Rover and a black Lexus. It was an old Toyota; an early 1990s Corolla, its blue paint damaged and chipped down the doors. But it wasn't just that the car looked out of place.

It was that I'd seen it before.

Three nights earlier, outside Wellis's home, I'd watched Eric Gaishe walk up to the corner of his street and wait for someone. Someone driving a blue Toyota.

This blue Toyota.

It had come down the road to Gaishe, he had leaned in through the passenger window and then—after the car left again—Gaishe had suddenly been holding money. A business transaction. At the time I hadn't thought about it, but now it seemed obvious. *You can't call up an escort agency and ask for a thirteen-year-old,* Wellis had said to me. *There's not a number for that in the Yellow Pages. So I run a service for people.* And the night I'd seen the Toyota, he'd been running that service.

And Duncan Pell had been the punter.

Wellis knew both of them, Pell *and* Sam, but it wasn't a coincidence. I could see that now. When Wellis had been telling me about using Sam to legitimize his business, he'd said, *Someone I knew told me about him. This guy said Wren was in finance.*

Who was the guy? I'd asked him.

Just a guy who I do some business with.

Pell. He went out for a drink with Sam after the fight at the Tube station. And some time after that—maybe right at the start when he was being vetted by Wellis, and maybe only in passing—Pell must have mentioned that he'd met this guy who was in finance. I looked back at his house, and something disquieting took flight inside me: Leon Spane was dead and dumped on Hampstead Heath, his holdall and coat in Pell's home; then there was the pouch full of knives, coated in blood; and finally, there was Pell's taste for underage prostitutes.

The task force thought Sam Wren had killed Marc Erion. They had evidence that was difficult to dispute, a killer every profiler in the land would tell you was gay, and victims who were homosexual. Sam looked good for this.

But Duncan Pell had a link to Wellis's prostitutes too.

And if I had doubts about Sam, I didn't have doubts about Pell.

Not a single one.

53

The inside of Pell's house was cooler than the day before. Outside, the temperature had dropped to the mid-teens and the rain had brought some relief from the heat. Inside, the stuffy, enclosed smell had been replaced by the stench of damp; deep in the walls, in the floor, in the ceiling. I made my way upstairs, into his bedroom, and went through his cupboards again. I'd been pretty thorough the first time, but I checked everything again anyway: every shelf, every drawer, under the bed, on top of the wardrobes. I moved across the hall to the second bedroom and did the same. The holdall was still in there, returned—along with the contents—to the way I'd first found it. Magic Trees swung gently as I searched the wardrobe, pushing clothes aside and sliding out shoe-boxes. Jewelery was in one of them: some chains, a couple of rings, and the two stars of an army lieutenant, loose among the rest of the clutter. In the others were receipts and old bills. I'd been through it all already.

I stacked them back inside and then closed the wardrobe door. It rocked slightly, the legs unsteady, and on top—on the other side of the ornate, carved front panel—I heard something shift. I reached over, feeling around. I'd done the same the day before and not found any-thing, but now my fingers brushed the hard edges of another shoebox. I teased it toward me until I could get a proper grip, then brought it down and flipped it open.

Inside were a stack of blank DVDs, numbered one through to ten.

I headed downstairs into the living room, opened the disc tray on the DVD player and pulled the TV toward me. It was sitting on an old-fashioned stool, in the same dark wood as the wardrobe upstairs. I dropped the first disc in, closed the tray and hit Play. The television kicked into life.

A black screen.

And then a picture: video footage of the inside of a flat. I didn't rec-ognize it. It looked small and pokey, half lit, a couple of worn red sofas and a kitchen behind that, most of it in shadow. Two other doors, one left, one right. In the right-hand one, the light was on and I could see the edge of a bed and a dresser with a mirror on it. In the left one the light was off.

The camera moved around constantly, as if the operator was getting comfortable, but then, after a while, something clicked and the picture was still. Now it was on a tripod. From behind the camera came Duncan Pell. He was naked. He walked across the flat and stood in the center, facing the room with the light on. He didn't say anything; just watched the bedroom, his right hand opening and closing beside him. On his middle finger was the silver ring with the rune on it, the one I'd seen him wearing at the station. As his fingers moved, it caught the light rhythmically, like a bulb switching off and on.

A minute later, a woman emerged, dressed in her bra and panties, stockings on, but only half pulled up. At first it was difficult to make her out. As soon as she appeared, Pell shuffled across to his left, obscuring her, and started playing with himself. But then he used his other hand to beckon her over—like an order—and she stepped toward him.

And I realized who it was.

The girl I'd found in Adrian Wellis's loft space.

My heart sank as I watched her edge closer, reluctance in every step. Everything she felt in that moment, all the fear and the panic, was written in her face.

Wellis reckoned she was sixteen, but she wasn't even close.

Pell pulled her to the sofas, dragged the tripod to one end of it and made her face the camera as he moved around behind her. Then he started having sex with her. Halfway through, as he got more and more aggressive, he slapped her back and buttocks—and after a while, the slaps became fists and tears started rolling down her face. I could barely bring myself to watch it after that. I reached forward to turn it off just as he pressed her face down into the leather of the sofa, her expression becoming almost contorted: all pain and suffering, eyes wet, mouth pushed to one side, the skin at her cheeks stretched to breaking point.

"Fucking hell," I said quietly, and hit Stop.

My eyes turned to disc two and I wondered, for a moment, whether I even had the capacity to watch any more. I'd seen the darkness in men, the things they were prepared to do to one another, but with kids it was harder to become detached. Where adults could disguise the pain and corruption that had been visited upon them, children wore it like a mark, branded by their suffering. All that would be left of this girl, whatever her name was and wherever she was from, would be a husk; a shadow of herself.

Finally, reluctantly, I put disc two in and pressed Play.

The same girl. The same flat.

As I watched, I remembered again what she'd said in the loft: *Don't let him hurt me.* She hadn't been talking about Adrian Wellis or Eric Gaishe. She'd been talking about Duncan Pell.

And then I noticed something else.

I shifted closer to the TV. At the far side of the shot was the edge of a long mirror, its reflection casting back the rest of the room. The doors into the bedroom and the bathroom. The sofas. Pell with the camera in his hand this time, and the girl on all fours in front of him.

But they weren't alone.

A ripple of unease passed through me as I leaned in even closer. To the side of the sofa, about seven feet from Pell and half out of shot, I could see a pair of legs, exactly parallel to one another.

Someone was watching them.

54

Across London, in a quiet residential street close to Wimbledon Common, Healy sat in his Vauxhall watching a mid-terrace, cream-colored house. It had a small concrete yard, well maintained. Two potted firs either side of a red door with a black knocker. Metallic blinds at the downstairs window, wooden blinds at the two top-floor ones. A kitchen and two bedrooms. Healy knew that, even though he couldn't see into any of them from where he was. He knew it because he'd walked this street up and down, countless times.

This was where the psychologist lived.

Teresa Reed.

He'd followed her back from the supermarket; watched her park her Mini and let herself in. She was alone. She was always alone. He knew her routine back to front now, and she had no one to warm her bed and little in the way of a social life. A couple of times he'd been here on a Saturday night, or a week night, and he'd seen friends of hers call in. But it was a rarity, and over the five long months he'd been keeping track of her, he'd used that. He'd bumped into her on purpose that first time at Belmarsh, and engaged her in conversation, for a reason.

And this was the reason.

Healy reached into his pocket and got out the photo of Leanne. It was a bleached, slightly blurred shot of the two of them, arms around each other, about two years before he found her. A different time. A different life. He felt one of his eyes tear up, but he didn't bother wiping it away. He let it break, let it trace the edge of his cheekbone and the corner of his mouth. Then, when he finally started to compose himself again, he looked up and saw Reed emerge from her front door, carrying a watering can.

There you are. Like clockwork.

He reached across to the glovebox, and pulled it open. Her routine was always the same on a Sunday. Half an hour after she got home from the supermarket, she started tending to her plants. She was a keen gardener; spent hours clipping them and cutting them back. This would be the best time for him to do it: when she was bent over one of the potted firs, her back to him, distracted by what she was doing. He looked down at the glovebox for a second time.

There was a gun inside.

Suddenly, his phone started going.

It buzzed across the passenger seat beside him, display facing up. Craw. *Shit.* He wiped his eyes and cleared his throat, then scooped up the phone. *Get yourself together.*

"Healy."

"Healy, it's Craw. Where are you?"

He cleared his throat a second time. "I'm at Drake's building."

Four words without any weight at all. They carried off into the space between the two of them and it took everything Healy had not to tell Craw what he was really doing. She didn't believe him, not a word of it, but she didn't ask again, and because of that he felt even more compelled to say something: part of him knew he owed her for giving him a route back in; the other part, even more hidden, just wanted to talk to someone about it.

But he couldn't talk to Craw.

He couldn't talk to anyone at the Met.

And the only person he *could* talk to—of his doubts about the case, and of his reasons for being here—was the one person who would get in the way of his attempt to rebuild his career.

Raker.

Twenty-five minutes later, Teresa Reed was finished and back inside. The glovebox was closed and the gun no longer visible. Healy knew he should have left for the station the minute Craw had hung up. Bartholomew had scheduled a meeting for two and wanted everyone in to hear his next revolutionary plan for catching the Snatcher.

But Healy hadn't left.

He'd stayed to watch Teresa Reed.

Any change in her routine, any sidestep away from it, and the whole thing went down the toilet. But, five months in, she was still doing the same things, in the same order on the same days. He knew her life; knew where she'd be and when she'd be there.

He could take her whenever he wanted.

Scooping up his phone, he scrolled through his address book. When he found the number he wanted, he hit Dial.

"Hello?"

A female voice.

"Teresa? It's Colm."

"Colm!" she said excitedly. "Are we still on for tonight?"

"Yes," he said. "I've booked us a table. I'll pick you up at seven."

55

Each of the discs was the same: the flat, the girl, Pell filming it all, and the terrible suffering that came after. I never saw the other person again. It was a man—you could tell from the shape of the legs; from the trousers and the shoes—but he was never glimpsed in the reflection of the mirror, never caught in shot. Yet, given everything I knew, the connection between Sam and Pell, and both their connections to Wellis, it wasn't hard to see where the police might go with this.

Sam was the man watching.

And somehow the two of them were working together.

The evening drew in fast as rain continued falling. I turned one of the chairs around and sat at the living-room windows, watching the light fade. At 8:30, I heard Liz come in through the front door and approach me in the darkness.

Don't mention the bruises, Liz.

Not now. Not today.

"Are you saving electricity?" she said, and perched herself on the edge of the sofa. I slid an arm around her and squeezed gently. She took my head in the crook of her elbow and started running her hands through my hair. "Guess that's the end of the summer."

"Are you pleased now?" I said to her, squeezing her a second time.

"Yes," she said. "I much prefer this."

"You all done with work?"

"Just about. Got a big day in court tomorrow, so need to make sure I don't show myself up for the massive fraud that I am." She was smiling. "How was your Sunday?"

"It was fine," I lied.

But she leaned away from me, as if immediately sensing something in my voice, and—even in the half-light of the room—I knew her eyes were falling on the bruises.

"What happened?"

"Nothing. I just ran into some trouble."

I studied the disappointment in her eyes, the distrust, the rejection she felt for all the promises I'd made to her about not putting myself on the line, and she shifted away from me, and then slowly got to her feet.

"I'm fine, Liz. Honestly."

"You're fine today," she said, looking down at me. "But don't you remember anything we talked about? Any of the things you said to me?"

I sucked down my anger. "It was nothing."

"Don't lie to me."

"He took me by surprise."

"They always do."

I got to my feet and stood there in front of her, the living room getting darker every second, only the faint blue glow of the DVD readout adding color to our faces. "This is what I do," I said to her gently. "This is my job. This is my life."

She looked at me for a long time, eyes not moving.

"I know it's your life," she said. "You've told me that over and over. This is who you are. This is what you do. I get it. But remember something: this is my life now too."

I didn't go after her. Instead, I switched on the computer and tried to concentrate on something else, watching back the footage Tasker had sent me of the day Sam went missing. It felt like I'd seen it a thousand times now, like I knew every second of it intimately: the way Sam moved, his path in, the crowds around him, the platform. But now, thanks to Task, I had the walkways, escalators and ticket halls too. Except Sam never used any of them. Because he never even used the platform.

Once he was on the train, he never got off.

I returned to the footage of the carriage itself, letting it run from Gloucester Road. When the train got to Westminster, it was like looking at a family photo; a snapshot of a scene I knew every inch of. The people coming off the train and those left on it: the clumps of protesters; the woman with her headphones on, oblivious to what was happening; the two men, one—in a suit—seated and reading, the other—a demonstrator in a red shirt with checked sleeves—picking up a sign and shuffling toward the doors. As I inched it on further, watching the same people take the same routes out, my phone started going. I flipped it over and hit Speakerphone. "David Raker."

"It's me," came a whisper.

"Healy?"

"You ever heard Wren talk?" he said, bypassing a greeting, the line absolutely silent, as if he'd locked himself away somewhere. "I mean, actually *talk*."

"You mean like on video or something?"

"Right."

"No, I haven't."

"Yeah, well, I have. I spent an hour watching a home movie of him at the station."

"And?"

"And the message he left on Drake's mobile . . ."

I looked down at the phone. "What, it's not him?"

"No, it's definitely him," he said, and then stopped. He sounded hesitant, unsure of himself. "Look, I haven't forgotten what you did for me last year."

He took me so much by surprise it was a couple of seconds before I caught up: he was talking about what I'd said earlier. *I know trust is hard for you, but believe me: if you can trust one person, that person is me.*

"I know what you did for Leanne."

"Are you okay, Healy?"

"I'm trying to rebuild my career," he went on, "I'm trying to do it right. I know you didn't give me everything you had earlier on, and that's fine. You're being careful. You don't know which side of the line I'm on now. I'd be exactly the same if I was in your position."

Another pause, and then a sigh crackled down the line. He sounded so different: sad, beaten and ground down. No anger. No fight. No resentment. Just an acceptance, as if he'd looked in the mirror and didn't like what came back.

"Are you okay?" I asked again.

"Yeah."

"Do you want to talk about something?"

"I haven't got anyone else," he said.

"What are you talking about?"

"I haven't got anyone I can turn to in the Met. If I show any weakness to Craw, she will start watching me, doubting me, seeing every tiny mistake I make as some kind of slippery slope. If I show it to Davidson, to the rest of them, they will tear me apart."

Another pause. I didn't interrupt.

"So I only have you, Raker. And now I need your help."

56

Healy was waiting in the shadows near Westminster Bridge, the glow of a cigarette between his lips. The October before, he'd been an ex-smoker, three months on from his last cigarette, but the whole time you could see him craving them. He nodded as I approached along the riverside. Next to him on the wall were two takeaway coffees.

"Thanks for coming," he said quietly, handing me one.

"Are you all right?"

He nodded, his eyes falling on my bruises. "You been in the wars?"

"Yeah, something like that."

"What happened?"

"I'll tell you later." I looked at my watch: 11:30. "What's going on?"

Healy stepped away from the station entrance and we shifted back further into the darkness. "It's Wren who left the voicemail message on Drake's mobile," Healy said.

"Definitely?"

"Confirmed now. Forensics did their thing. Got hold of some conversations he'd had with clients at work. The boss there has all telephone calls recorded, and keeps a year's worth on file, in case the FSA come calling."

He handed me a printout of a forensic report. Everyone had a different voice, a "voiceprint," determined by the unique anatomy of their oral and nasal cavities, vocal cords, facial muscles, lips, palate, jaw, even teeth. Forensic techs had used "articulators"—the individual way muscles are manipulated in speech—as a way to match the work calls that Sam had made to the voicemail message he'd left on Drake's phone. As I scanned the rest of the report, I saw clearly how the Met had mobilized the troops now: forensics were working Sundays, the rest of the task force had been working all weekend, everyone focused on the evidence in front of them, and the man at the center of it all: Sam Wren. Except maybe he wasn't doing this on his own. Maybe he had company.

"So why are we here?" I asked.

"You remember what we talked about before?"

"On the phone?"

"Yesterday, in the coffee shop."

I studied him. "We talked about a lot of things."

"About the things that didn't add up about this. Why a man who'd been so careful until now decided to leave a voice-mail message on his victim's phone."

"It says there in black and white that it's Sam's voice."

"It's Wren," Healy said. "I'm not disputing that."

"So what's this about?"

"After dinner tonight, I went back into the station and watched a home movie of Wren we'd been given by his missus. It's definitely him on the phone. I don't need forensics to tell me that. I can hear it. But . . ." He glanced at me and away again. "I don't know."

"What?"

"He sounds different."

"Different how?"

He studied me. "I don't know," he said again.

"Different how, Healy?"

He dropped his cigarette to the floor and crushed it under the toe of his boot. "I don't know," he said again. "It wasn't that he sounded stressed. Forensics would have picked up on any stress, that's what they look for. It didn't sound like he was being coerced or manipulated. It was more . . ." He paused. "It was more that there was no emotion in his voice at all. Nothing. Just empty words."

He paused for a moment, the cigarette packet in his hands. He started turning it between his fingers and then looked at me. "You want to find him, right?"

I nodded.

"I want to find him too. We want to find him for our own reasons." He paused, studying me. We both understood what his reasons were— he wanted to prove people wrong, people he hated—but I got the sense he was trying to work out what mine might be. "I know it's his voice on the phone," he continued, "I know he was the last person to call Drake, I know Erion's number is on his work PC . . . but something still bothers me. I don't know what it is. Maybe it's just the things you were filling my head with, but it's something. Thing is, I can't tell anyone about it because it's based on nothing. The evidence is there in plain sight—it's *there*—and all I'm left with is this vague . . ."

"Gut feeling."

He looked at me. *This is a murder investigation, not some carnival sideshow.*

Cases aren't built on how you feel. This isn't the fucking magic circle. He'd been hitting out at me as a defense mechanism. He didn't want me bringing problems to the table because then he had to deal with them. Then he had to take them back to an SIO who was constantly watching him, and a group of men and women who were waiting for him to make a mistake. But the whole time he'd taken what I'd said and filed it away.

My mind turned back to Fell Wood, to the old line, to the staffroom. And then more images flashed inside my head: Pell with the prostitute, beating her and raping her, and the man—momentarily caught in the mirror's reflection—sitting there calmly, legs exactly parallel, watching it all play out.

"You want the truth?" I asked.

He studied me. Didn't reply.

"I don't honestly know what I think about Sam."

It was the first time I'd admitted it out loud, the first time I'd even really admitted it to myself. I'd never seen Sam as a killer, and still struggled to see him as one now. Nothing I'd pulled out of the earth, in any part of his life, pushed me in that direction. But I'd seen men—good men—shackled to forces much darker than them; and then I'd seen the things those men were prepared to do, either because they wanted to, or because they were forced to. And in Sam's life there was Adrian Wellis and Duncan Pell. Both of them out there, somewhere. One a trafficker. One a hunter and a rapist.

"He might be working with someone," I said.

Healy frowned. "What?"

"I don't know how exactly. I don't even know if I really believe it. I'm putting all this together as I go along, but . . ." I stopped and looked at him. A part of me still didn't trust him not to take what I had and run back to Craw with it. He was trying to reboot his career, after all. But as I stood there, I noticed the look in his face, the loneliness and frustration, and realized the biggest part of him was still out there on his own—and, ultimately, that was the part of him I had to take a chance on.

"Your unsolved . . ."

A change in his face. "Spane?"

"Yeah, Leon Spane. I think I know who *really* killed him."

I told him about Duncan Pell, about Leon Spane, about the CCTV footage I'd studied and the DVDs I'd had to sit through. I told him about the girl and her connections to Adrian Wellis, about what I'd found out at the old line, and then about the man watching Pell and the girl in the videos. I didn't offer any theories, because Healy could see where this was headed, and, afterward, I started to wonder if I'd given him too much. But as he lit a second cigarette, I realized it was too late anyway. It was out there, in the space between us, and whatever he chose to do with it wasn't going to make much of a difference to me.

I was finding Sam Wren either way.

I looked out to the river, black and swollen, a wall of rainwater cascading down from Victoria Embankment. "What sort of person is comfortable doing that?" I asked.

"What?"

"Sitting there, watching Pell rape that girl."

Healy shrugged. "Someone who was just like Pell."

I nodded.

"Is that person Wren?" he asked.

"I don't know. I don't know why he'd sit there and watch a woman get beaten and raped. I don't know why he'd choose not to intervene. I don't know how he'd get into that situation in the first place. If—just for a minute—we're assuming he's the one taking these men, then this woman isn't even his fantasy. This is Pell's."

"So they're working together."

"I don't know. Maybe."

"You're still not certain that Wren's involved?"

"I didn't say that. I said I've never seen him as a killer."

"What about if Pell's doing the killing for him?"

"It's a stretch."

"Is it?"

He meant the CCTV footage of Pell beating Robert Stonehouse to a pulp on the floor of Gloucester Road station; harassing and bullying Spane, pushing him and kicking him; and he meant the station on the old line. Its smell. Its unseen history. Me being attacked in the tunnel.

"Pell's a soldier," Healy said. "He knows how to kill."

"I know."

"He could be taking the men for Wren."

"But Pell's into women."

"So maybe he's taking women too."

"But that's my point: who *are* these women? The Snatcher's left behind a trail, however slight. There's no trail leading to any missing women. And what about the girl on the DVD? She's alive. She's in hospital, but she's alive. If Pell wanted her dead, if this was part of the plan and some kind of reciprocal arrangement—if Sam's helping Pell and Pell's helping Sam—why let her live? Why rape her repeatedly, expose your identity on film and then hand her back to Adrian Wellis?"

Healy took a drag on the cigarette.

"I don't know," he said quietly.

"We need to go and see the girl."

"But first we need to do something else." He took a last drag on the cigarette and then flicked it out into the night. It fizzled out instantly. "We need to go in here."

"To the station?"

He nodded.

"Why?"

"To talk to the patrolman who found Drake's phone."

"Why?"

"Because he got spooked."

"About what?"

"Says he found it, just sitting there on the platform, at one in the morning."

"So?"

"So, why did no one spot it while the station was open?"

I looked at him—and he nodded once when he saw I'd made the connection.

"Because someone put it there after the station closed."

57

The patrolman was a guy called Stevie O'Keefe, and his Irish heritage appeared to begin and end at his name. He had dark, Mediterranean skin, even darker eyes and a jet-black Elvis quiff. At a guess I would have put him in his late forties or early fifties.

Healy had arranged with the Jubilee line's general manager for O'Keefe to take us down after hours. It was an irregular request, one Transport for London would probably have been keen to avoid given the security precautions they'd put into place since 7/7, but Healy had used the badge as a way in, and then peppered what came after with regular mentions of the Snatcher. I remembered the worst bits of Healy well, all the anger, the aggression and the fight, but he could play the game with the best of them. If he needed to turn down the volume, adjust his tone, come in softly, he could do that too.

We moved through Westminster station in silence. None of the escalators were switched on at night, so we used them like staircases, and then emerged into the turbine hall, a vast cathedral of stone and stainless steel, full of criss-crossing pillars. Westminster was the Tube's deepest ever excavation, and the journey to the Jubilee line saw you drop one hundred feet in a matter of seconds. Even then you weren't done: the Jubilee platforms were built one on top of the other, the westbound the deeper, and by the time you got to the bottom, you were more than thirty meters under the earth. *Down with the devil,* I thought, recalling something an old colleague on the paper had once said. Back when they'd first carved the Tube out of the earth in the 1860s, people were scared it might wake Satan himself.

It was a weird feeling heading through the building's spaces and not passing anyone, but more unsettling was the complete lack of sound: I'd read about people like O'Keefe, how they spent their lives walking through darkness and quiet, but I'd never appreciated silence, never fully understood it, until we got down to the line.

At the platform, O'Keefe hesitated briefly. Transparent screens had been erected all the way along, which—during the day—would slide back once the train was in the station. They were closed now and, beyond them, it was hard to make out the line without the help of a torch. "I found it there," he said quietly, pointing to the last of the screens.

"On the platform, at the end?" I asked.

O'Keefe just nodded.

"Are you okay?"

He glanced at me. "Sure."

His eyes flicked across my shoulder, along the platform toward the other end. I followed his gaze. The night lights were on but they barely seemed to make a difference. I turned back to O'Keefe, his eyes on the opposite tunnel. At the surface, when he'd first been introduced to us, he mentioned that he'd been a patrolman for twenty years, that he'd walked deep-level stations on the Northern and Central lines, and yet—as we stood on the platform—it was like this was his first time down here.

"Stevie?"

He glanced at me.

"You sure you're okay?"

His eyes came to rest on the right-hand tunnel, close to where he'd found Drake's phone. "I'm fine," he said, his voice more even now.

I glanced at Healy and gestured for him not to say anything. "Stevie, I need to know what's going on."

He ripped his eyes away from the tunnel. "Huh?"

"Is something bothering you?"

"No."

"What happened when you found the phone?"

He looked between us, then back to the tunnel. Healy rolled his eyes at me, out of sight of O'Keefe.

"It was just . . ."

"What?"

He glanced at me again. "Normally there's work going on in most of the stations," he said, the torch at his side. "'Engineering hours' and all that; when the trains aren't in service. Between one and five in the morning, there's staff all along the line, all through the night, people repairing, cleaning, making sure everything's okay. They were down here all last week when I came through, but when I found that phone on Thursday night, there was no one. There was no scheduled work." He paused and looked at me, his face half lit by the lamps above us on the platform. "It was just so quiet, and kind of . . ."

He trailed off and turned back to face the tunnel.

"Kind of what?" I asked.

"I've been doing this twenty years," O'Keefe said, his fingers tapping out a nervy rhythm on the flashlight, "but that night I found the phone, it felt different."

"Different?"

Healy's eyes narrowed. Suddenly he was interested again.

"We get tons of lost property down here," O'Keefe said. "People drop all sorts of things and don't realize. But that phone . . . it was like it had been *placed* there."

"Like someone had put it there deliberately?"

He didn't reply.

"Stevie?"

"Yeah, like someone had put it there."

"Where was it exactly?"

We moved toward the end of the platform, level with the last plastic screen on our left. On our right, attached to the wall, was a white bench. "It was on there," he said, pointing to the bench. "Just placed on top."

"Could have fallen out of someone's pocket."

"Could have," O'Keefe said, but he didn't sound convinced, and I could see why: the benches, dotted from one end of the platform to the other, were almost oval-shaped, built for leaning against. If a phone dropped out of someone's pocket by accident, the angle of the bench wouldn't stop its fall. It would bounce right off and hit the floor.

"Did you see anyone else in here that night?"

He shook his head. "No."

I turned to Healy. "Are the Met checking CCTV?"

"We've put in a request for the footage," he said, and then stepped toward O'Keefe. "Can we get down on to the line?"

O'Keefe jolted, like he'd suddenly been pulled from a dream, and brought a set of keys away from his belt. He selected the one he wanted, manually unlocked one of the screens and backed away. *As if he doesn't want to go first.* Both of us noted it, Healy glancing at me, before we dropped through the space and down on to the line. O'Keefe followed, more hesitancy in his stride, and as soon as his feet landed on the blackened concrete of the line, he stood there frozen, just staring into the tunnel. Something in him had been knocked out of kilter. He was a brassy, confident kind of guy—I could read that in him, right from the off—but he was showing none of that now.

"So what felt different about Thursday night?" I asked again.

O'Keefe paused, as if unsure how to articulate himself. The only sound, the only movement, was his fingers on the torch. After a while he looked at me, his face framed by the light from the platform. "It was like you could feel something bad down here."

58

The tunnel was about thirty feet across and about the same high, or maybe it just looked that way. It was hard to tell for sure. There were no lights on anywhere in front of us, except for a faint glow on one of the walls further down—perhaps a quarter of a mile on—which I assumed was from the platform at Waterloo, out of sight beyond the curve of the tunnel. Every so often we'd pass a red light on the left-hand side, a marker next to it, but the lights weren't built to illuminate, just to be seen. Once we'd passed them, they returned to the dark, as if swallowed whole by it.

After about five hundred feet, against the continual silence, I started to hear the very faint sound of dripping water. We were passing right under the Thames, and through some small space, some crack somewhere, a trace of it had found its way down.

O'Keefe swept his torch along the wall closest to us, picking out endless brickwork and thick electrical cabling, braided together like lengths of hair. Healy shone his torch off in the other direction, to the fixings and markers, and as our lights framed the wall, I saw a space, about six feet across, with a metal grille pulled across it. It looked like it led through to an adjacent tunnel. I stepped closer and as I did O'Keefe directed his flashlight at it.

"The Last Walk," he said.

"What?"

"That's what they call it."

"Where does it go?"

"Runs all the way under the river."

Healy moved in alongside me.

"People still use it?" I asked.

"No. It hasn't been used for years. They closed it off when they put the deep-level line in here. Before that, it was used as a transportation tunnel, bringing things in under the river and over to the other side." He paused, eyes fixed on the grille. "And before that, *right* back at the start, it was used to take bodies to the morgue at St. Thomas' Hospital."

"The Last Walk," Healy said quietly.

O'Keefe looked at me. "A lot of people reckon the old stations in east

London are the ones with the ghosts. But this place . . ." He stopped again. There was no humor in his face, not a hint of amusement or self-deprecation. "It's got a feel."

Healy smirked, reacting in the same way I would have done if I hadn't have seen O'Keefe's face. But once O'Keefe turned to look at him, Healy's smile dissolved and we all stood there, those last words echoing along the blackness of the tunnel.

"Can I borrow your torch?" I said to O'Keefe. He handed it to me and, as I moved across the tracks, stepping over the lines, I shone the flashlight through the grille to the space on the other side. The mix of light and shadows created patterns in the darkness of the foot tunnel, drifting across its walls, but it was only when I was standing right on top of the grille, looking through it, that I could see it was ajar.

I called Healy over and, as he approached, I pushed at the metal grille. It shifted slightly—juddering like a door stuck in its frame—and then squeaked backward.

"Is this supposed to be open?" I said to O'Keefe.

"No," he said, barely audible, from behind me. There was alarm in his voice and, when I remembered what he'd told us earlier, I realized why: every step we'd taken into the tunnel, every noise we'd heard, every entrance that was supposed to be closed, had further confirmed his uneasiness. *It was like you could feel something bad down here.*

Healy moved in beside me, and as I shone the flashlight into the foot tunnel, I could hear the drip of water again, and a very faint sound, rhythmic and soft. Above us, somewhere out of sight, people were working on the subsurface lines, cleaning the Circle and District. I passed through the grille, ducking under the frame and into the foot tunnel, and immediately the temperature dropped. On my right the tunnel ran parallel to the line, heading back in the direction of Westminster. On my left, it curved under the river, tracing the Jubilee. There was little definition to anything. Up close I could see brickwork and on the ground—uneven; scored and gouged by age—the floor was still marked by the wheels that had once passed along it.

Healy ducked into the tunnel, and then O'Keefe followed gingerly, pausing half in, half out of the entrance. I could see clearly what was going through his head. When I glanced at Healy I saw he looked disconcerted too, and, as I was about to try and put into words the sinking feeling I was starting to get in my guts, something made a noise.

I stood, eyes fixed on the darkness.

"What?" Healy said.

I held the flashlight up above my head and pointed it along the tunnel, back in the direction of Westminster. "Stevie," I said quietly, keeping my eyes on the beam as it carved off into the depths of the tunnel. "We're just going to have a look down here."

"I'm not supposed to leave you," he said.

"It's fine. We're just going to walk a little way along."

"What am I supposed to do?" he asked, and we both turned to look at him. What he really meant was, *I don't want to stay here.* I glanced at Healy again and then back to O'Keefe, and it was clear that we both saw the same thing: a man who had spent his life walking the line, reduced to this—panicked and edgy, maybe even borderline paranoid.

"Why don't you head back up?"

He studied me, then Healy, then asked for one of the torches. Healy gave him the weaker one. "It's fine," I said again, and this time he nodded, seemed almost relieved, and backed out from the grille. Seconds later, he'd returned to the tracks on the Jubilee line.

Seconds after that, he was gone from view.

59

The foot tunnel was dead straight, no deviation, no change of direction, the same uniform brickwork unfurling either side of us, the same stone floor beneath our feet. I thought, for a moment, about all the bodies that must have traveled this route, about the horse-drawn carts that must have come this way, their flatbeds home to the dead; and, as I did, a faint breeze picked up. It passed across us, almost *through* us, but—even after it was gone—a trace of it remained, like a murmur. O'Keefe had talked of ghosts, but it wasn't ghosts. It was something real, as if the place had absorbed its past. Every act. Every drop of blood.

We moved on.

After about two minutes, the flashlight picked out something further down, and I realized it was a staircase, knocked into an alcove on the left side of the tunnel. It wound upward in a steep spiral, a blistered handrail coiling around the steps. I got under it and shone the beam up through the middle. Sixty feet up, at the top of the steps, I could see a red door with EXIT printed on it. Healy walked on, using his phone for light, and, about thirty feet further down, stopped. Beyond him was a wall, painted white. The tunnel had been bricked up.

I started up the stairs. They were relatively new, but the metal was still stained and discolored, and the paint on the handrail flaked against my fingers. In the quiet, our footsteps echoed against them, the noise carrying off into the space below as the walls closed around us. Suddenly it was like being inside a crawl space. At the top, the alcove widened into a platform, about ten feet across, and there was the red exit door.

I tried the handle.

The door popped away from its frame, revealing a narrow room, dark on either side, and a second door directly opposite, partially lit by an emergency exit sign. On both sides were a series of cardboard boxes, stacked on top of each other. It reminded me of the famous deep-level facilities on the Northern and Central lines: former air-raid shelters, turned into storage units after the Second World War. There was no break in the boxes. No gaps. I stepped further in, past the edge of the door frame.

There was a musty smell, like old paper. Healy came in behind me and I heard him sniff the air. He removed a handkerchief from his pocket and wrapped it around his hand, leading the way across the room toward the second door. When we got there, he placed his fingers around the handle and looked back at me. "If you haven't got anything to cover your hands with, keep them in your pockets."

The best I had were the sleeves of my jacket, and although his tone pricked at my anger, I knew where the words had come from: he was off reservation, working from nothing but a gut feeling; I was the guy he'd invited along, the non-cop, the man who had looked his boss in the face and lied about Sam Wren. He was minimizing risk.

No prints. No trail.

He pressed the handle of the door down and pushed it open.

In front of us was another tunnel, partitioned from top to bottom. On one side was a second set of stairs, which, I imagined, would take us back up to the subsurface stations. On the other was a doorway. No door frame. No door. Just the space for one.

We inched forward, and as we did the storage room clicked shut and it was like the smell of paper, of age, disappeared instantly. In its place came something tangy and awful, like overripe fruit. I directed the torch through the doorway ahead. It was an old bathroom. Even from where we were standing I could see the cubicles, two of them, both stripped of everything, leaving only the toilets, shapeless and broken. Big basins were attached to the wall next to them, a splashguard above that. As we got level with the entrance and shifted the torch around inside, I could see another set of cubicles. I put a hand to my mouth and nose and zeroed in on the one furthest away from us, the only one with a door still attached.

There was blood on the floor inside.

Healy, still ahead of me, made for the cubicle. When he got there, he pressed his fingers to the door, ready to push it open. But then he seemed to hesitate. He glanced at me. There was no fear in him, no dread, no sense that he couldn't handle this moment as a professional. This wasn't about that. This was about a circle closing; about one part of his life joining up with the next. This was about spending nearly eight months away from the bodies—and about the last one being Leanne.

He swallowed, and then pushed the cubicle door open.

It squeaked on its hinges, and in the darkness—lit only by the beam of a torch—it felt like something shifted around us. Like the whole room turned a degree, awoken from its slumber. The smell was horrendous. Dense and gummy, filling the spaces around us so quickly it was like being suffocated. I moved in behind him, and against the silence could suddenly hear flies, above our heads, inside the cubicle, at our feet.

The body was in the toilet, feet in the dry bowl, legs and arms folded into itself, so—at first—it just looked like a ball of clothes. It was obvious why it had been placed like that: so no one could see it from outside. As I moved the torch over it, I could see it was a man, and his head was forward, chin against his chest, tucked in against himself in the same way as his arms and legs. Above him, a thick pipe connected the toilet to the raised black cistern. The man had been tied to the pipe to hold him in place, rope looping around his midriff and again around his neck and legs, keeping him in a ball, keeping him positioned exactly where he was. I traced the torch along his body, trying to see how he'd died.

"There," Healy said, realizing what I was doing.

He was pointing to a tear in the man's clothes, close to his ribcage. It was a deep knife wound, dried black with blood and squirming with insects. And as I moved the torch again, I saw more stab wounds, two in each leg, bigger and even deeper than the other one, there to stop him from getting up and walking away. He'd been put down, but not killed. His death had come over the next few hours. I wondered if he'd cried out for help, and if he had why no one had heard him. But then I caught sight of the edge of his face, and spotted duct tape. It was covering his mouth. He'd died in complete silence.

"Body's a day old at least," Healy said.

I took a step left, trying to get a clearer look at his face. I thought back to O'Keefe telling us there was something bad down here, and then noticed the man's skin: there were tiny grazes all over it, like he'd been sliced with a blade.

Or with shards of glass.

"I know him," I said.

It was Adrian Wellis.

60

As I'd expected, the stairs on the other side of the partition took me back up to the Circle and District lines. Healy said he would give me ten minutes before calling it in to Craw. I moved through the empty tunnels and up to the ticket hall, where Stevie O'Keefe was waiting with the station supervisor. Neither of them said much, but I got the feeling O'Keefe had been read the riot act for leaving us unattended on the line, and I also got the feeling he didn't particularly care. As I sidestepped a series of questions from the supervisor, I looked across at O'Keefe and saw a strange kind of acquiescence in him: an acknowledgment that he'd done the wrong thing, but that he couldn't bring himself to be down there. He offered to walk me out, and the supervisor—barely communicative by the end—just shrugged and watched us go.

As we walked, I thought about Wellis. He'd died the way he'd lived. He'd died a death he deserved. But even if I loathed everything he stood for, without pause, and knew that the world would be better off without him, it was hard not to look at a man in the aftermath of such a death and not feel troubled by it.

"I have an old friend," O'Keefe said, as I tuned back in. "Gerry. He does the same job as me on the Circle. We meet down on the Jubilee platform sometimes. Just a little routine we have. For some company, you know? Normally Tuesdays and Thursdays."

I nodded and smiled, but my thoughts were already moving on to where Healy and I went next.

"I just chatted to him," O'Keefe went on. "We were supposed to meet in our usual spot on Thursday, down on the platform, but Gerry never turned up."

O'Keefe stopped walking. I stopped too out of politeness.

"Thing is, he said he *did* turn up there."

"Where?"

"On the Jubilee platform—where we were tonight."

I frowned. "I'm not sure I follow."

"Gerry got there before me on Thursday, to the Jubilee line. Normally we just have a coffee and a chinwag. He brings the flask, I bring the conversation. It can get lonely down on the tracks all by yourself."

O'Keefe stopped and looked at me. "But when Gerry got down to the line, he said he kept hearing this noise, like a beeping. And when he followed it, he realized it was the phone."

"Wait, he found the phone *before* you?"

"Must have done."

"So why didn't he pick it up himself?"

"He said it was on the actual track itself."

"Beyond the screens?"

"Yeah. He said he opened up the screens and got down on to the line, but when he got down there he started feeling . . ." Another pause. "Started feeling strange."

"Ill?"

"No," he said. "Not ill."

He meant Gerry was like him. He meant they'd both felt something had been off that night in the dark of the station and its tunnels. Gerry didn't even have it in him to reach down and pick up the phone. He'd just backed up and walked away. Minutes later, O'Keefe had arrived and picked up the phone himself. But he didn't seem to realize what else he'd said, the bigger revelation: that when Gerry had found the phone, it was on the track itself. When O'Keefe had found it, it was on a bench, *on* the platform, in plain sight. As if it had been placed on the track originally to make it look like an accident, to make it look like just another piece of lost property. But then, when Gerry had failed to pick it up, it had been deliberately moved again, to ensure it was found the second time.

And there was only one reason to do that: to make absolutely certain the police were pushed in Sam Wren's direction.

I knew then that the Met wouldn't find anything on CCTV, because the cameras went off as soon as the station shut up for the night. Whoever had left the phone on the track had definitely been inside the station after hours. Whoever it was had to have felt comfortable here, had to have known the Tube, its lines, its tunnels. And, to me, there wasn't much doubt about who that person was.

Duncan Pell.

61

The next morning I woke to the sound of my phone buzzing on the bedside table. I pulled myself out of sleep and grabbed it. The number was withheld.

"David Raker."

"Raker, it's me."

Healy. I could hear the soft sound of cars in the background, and the occasional voice passing. He was in a public phone box. "You all right?"

"I'm eating shit for last night."

"What do you mean?"

"Craw. She's so far up my arse, she's practically in my fucking throat. I can't go for a piss without her giving me the eye." He paused, a sigh crackling down the line.

I looked at my watch. Five past nine. "What did she say?"

"About what?"

"About Wellis."

A pause. "I didn't call it in."

Somehow I wasn't surprised.

"If I call in Wellis, it turns into a shitstorm on a hundred different fronts," he went on. "I have to explain what I was doing down there, I'd have to pretend I don't know who Wellis is, would have to dream up some story for Craw about no one else being with me, despite O'Keefe and that station supervisor seeing you come in and go out."

"And if it gets out that Wellis is dead—"

"Eric Gaishe isn't gonna be scared about talking any more."

The only reason Gaishe remained silent was because he was terrified of Wellis's reach. With Wellis out the way, and if he had any sense, Gaishe would start angling for a deal, because he knew the clients just as much as Wellis. And that would eventually lead the Met to Duncan Pell.

"Then we're no longer ahead of the curve," I said quietly. "So if Craw doesn't know, why's she on to you?"

"She knows *something's* going on," he replied, and I remembered how she'd been when she'd come to the house. She was smart—even Healy's lies were struggling to protect him.

"You need to give her something."

"If I give her something, she'll know I've been withholding."

"I know. But it'll take out some of the heat."

I could hear a sharp intake of breath, as if his teeth were gritted. "*Fucking* Davidson. He's the reason she's like this. He's just there, putting ideas in her head."

"About what?"

"About you and me."

"There's nothing you can do about that. We did what we did last year, and there's no going back. But we did it for the right reasons, remember that." I paused, letting that settle with him. His daughter, the man who had taken her, those were the right reasons. "You could take a bullet for Davidson right now and it wouldn't make any difference."

Silence.

"There's something going on with him," he said finally.

"With Davidson?"

"Yeah. He doesn't say anything to me now."

"As opposed to?"

"As opposed to baiting me every bloody day. If they'd left me alone, I wouldn't have tried to shut them down. But since Sallows got the boot, Davidson's hardly said anything to me. Not directly. It's like I don't exist any more."

"You exist. He must have some other plan."

"Like what?"

I was about to say I didn't know, but then I recalled something in Healy's face the day before, a hint of sadness, of suppression. I thought at the time that it might be a secret he was keeping, unrelated to the case.

"You got any chinks in your armor?" I asked.

"What do you mean by that?"

He's not going to play ball. "I mean, have they got anything they can come at you through? Davidson's not going to outsmart you on police work, but he's not stupid. I've met Craw. She's clever. Watchful. She's not going to have her head turned by a guy like him. She doesn't care about the crap he's spinning for her. Maybe she's watching you more closely, maybe she isn't, but if she is it's not because of him, it's because you've set off alarm bells in her head about something. Spun a lie she doesn't believe."

"She thinks you and me are working together."

"Do you think that's all it is?"

Another small pause.

"Healy?"

"I don't know," he said eventually, and as I looked down at the phone I felt a bubble of anxiety. Not for me. I could handle it if the police turned up on my doorstep, if they found out I'd completely disregarded their wishes and continued to search for Sam Wren. It was Healy I felt uneasy for. He was lying to me, the only person he could trust, and if he was lying to me, it meant he had something he was willing to protect. And in my experience of him, that meant he was planning on doing something stupid.

"Be careful, Healy."

"About what?"

"About whatever you're protecting."

He didn't respond. The line drifted a little, and I could hear more cars. A horn. He was calling me on a public phone so there was no trace of contact between us. It had been the same every time: every call to me had been from a random central London number. It was so typically Healy: on the one hand, he had the clarity of purpose not to leave a trace of himself; on the other, it was likely he was harboring some rash and foolish plan.

"You still want to find your man?" he said after a while.

"Of course I do."

"Then meet me at King's College Hospital at twelve."

"Why?"

"Because that's where the girl on the DVDs is."

62

King's College Hospital was sandwiched between Coldharbour Lane and Denmark Hill, about two and a half miles south of the river, and it was a building I didn't have a single good memory of. In my days as a journalist, one of my sources had bled out in A&E after being stabbed in the chest. Then, four years later, Derryn and I had sat together in the oncology department, waiting for a second opinion we hoped would change the course of our lives. It didn't. The second opinion was the same as the first, except delivered with none of the tact, and when we left, we left the hospital system for good and she died six months later. I hoped my third time would be better, hoped it would bring some small glimmer of light—but given what I'd seen on the DVDs of Pell, and how the girl had looked when I'd found her in Adrian Wellis's loft space, I wasn't holding out much hope.

Healy was waiting in the car park at the rear of the campus. As I swung the BMW into a space, I killed the engine and watched him in the rearview mirror for a moment. He was scanning his surroundings, eyes everywhere, trying to see if anyone had followed him here. He probably had good reason to be suspicious, but there was a look on his face, a mixture of anguish and paranoia, which he'd have to lose if we were going to get anywhere with the girl.

We walked across the car park, light rain drifting from right to left, and headed inside. The corridors were cool and smelled faintly of boiled food and industrial-strength cleaner, even though every window and door was open for as far as the eye could see. The intensive-care unit was on the other side of the campus, so we followed the signposts through the bowels of the hospital, neither of us talking, just moving silently from one end to the other. About twenty feet short of the ICU front desk, Healy took me aside and brought me up to date.

"She opened her eyes for the first time yesterday," he said, "but she's still pretty screwed up. Cheekbones and nose were smashed in, and one of her ears has been torn. Plus she has all the cuts and bruises you'd expect a woman to have after being kept in a loft and raped repeatedly by a couple of fucking animals."

"What's her name?"

"Marika."

I nodded, and let Healy lead the way.

Marika Leseretscu was at the end of a long ward, the smell of food and cleaning products giving way to the oppressive tang of sickness. Outside her door stood a young, uniformed officer, an empty seat next to him with his hat perched on it and his jacket over the back.

"Morning," Healy said to the officer.

"Morning."

He got out his warrant card. "I'm DC Healy."

The officer nodded, and his eyes fell on me.

"This is . . ." Healy paused, just for a second, and I realized he'd tried to think of a cop who might have accompanied him here, who might have wanted to partner with him, and he couldn't think of anybody. Not one person. "This is James Grant, our psychologist."

I nodded at the officer.

He was young, which worked in our favor. "Yes, sir."

"We'd like a few minutes alone with the girl," Healy said, and moved us toward the room. The officer stood aside and we headed in and closed the door.

The room was tiny: twenty feet across, with one partially open window, a faded painting on the wall above her bed, and a cream-colored bedside cabinet. She was propped up on some puffy white pillows, but asleep. Next to her an ECG beeped, and a metal stand held an IV drip. She was wearing a nightdress stamped with the hospital's logo, and her face was almost entirely covered in bandaging. I could see her eyes, both of them closed; and, through the clear plastic of the ventilator helping her breathe, her mouth showed. Nothing else. A spot of blood had soaked through at her right ear.

I stepped in closer to the bed, and then noticed Healy. In the depressed light of the room, it looked like he had tears in his eyes. Sometimes I struggled to read or understand a single thing about him, but in that moment, as he looked down at the girl beaten and broken in front of us, I thought I understood where his head was at: Leanne.

"Healy," I said gently, and he looked at me. There was nothing in his face. "I need you to tell me what else is going on."

"What do you mean?"

"I don't want you doing anything stupid."

He didn't answer.

"Has it got something to do with Leanne?"

His body shifted, some of the rigidity leaving it as if a part of him had deflated—as if he'd been found out—but as he went to answer, as I readied myself for what was to come, the girl moved on the bed between us, the sheets tightening around her legs.

And she opened her eyes.

63

She looked between us, her brain trying to make the connections. Earlier, she'd gone to sleep surrounded by nurses. Now she was waking up to find two men she didn't know standing next to her bed. She immediately moved, trying to protect herself, turning on to her side and bringing her legs up into the foetal position. I felt a pang of sadness for her, felt the burn of anger too, but as I looked across at Healy, expecting to see the same, I instead saw a strange kind of stillness in him, as he retreated back eight months.

"Marika," I said gently, holding up a hand. Her eyes continued moving between us and, after a couple of seconds, I saw Healy snap out of the fug, like he'd stepped right out of a bad dream, and he glanced at me, ceding control of the conversation. "Marika, my name is David," I continued, keeping my voice soft. "You aren't in danger any more. We are here to protect you. But I need to know you understand me."

Her eyes finally stopped moving and fell on me.

"Do you speak English, Marika?"

No movement. She didn't seem to remember me from the loft.

I let the silence hang there. Healy eyed me—his way of passing judgment on my tactics—but this wasn't rocket science. She'd been pushed and pulled around, dragged, bruised and beaten the entire time she'd been in the country. If there was ever a time she remembered being able to trust someone, it was so far back it probably didn't even exist as a memory any more. There was nothing as heartbreaking as seeing a childhood destroyed; a succession of men had taken hers from her, and it was never coming back. Silence was the least we could offer her.

She blinked. Tears in her eyes.

"It's okay," I said quietly, and without moving any closer to the bed, I dropped to my haunches, down to her eye level. It was like rubbing away the dust and the grime on a windowpane and looking through to the other side: suddenly, despite the bandaging, I could see how young she was. In her eyes. In the movement of her mouth. In the small shape of her body, and the way her fingers clawed the bed sheets, like a comforter. In the videos she'd looked fourteen or fifteen. Now she looked even younger, barely into her teens at all, and my head filled with images of Pell—and what I was going to do to him.

I waited again. She was facing me, her back to Healy, and I could see him getting impatient behind her, shifting on the spot, glancing back out the door and into the corridor, as if he expected the cavalry to arrive any minute.

Then, finally, a spark of recognition in her eyes.

"You . . ." she said.

She'd spoken through the plastic mask over her mouth, her voice quieter and less refined. I nodded, and then sat back, on the floor. "I hope they clean in here," I said, smiling. She didn't react, but that was fine. Even if her trust could never be rebuilt, it was at least important that she knew we carried no threat. "Do you remember me, Marika?"

She just looked at me.

"Do you remember when I found you?"

"Yes," she said.

She studied me for a moment, the bandages tight against her skin, disguising the tiny movements that experts in kinesics, in the language of the body, would have called illustrators, adaptors and emblems. Without the whole of her face, it was possible to miss some of its subtlety—but I still felt a slight shift in her, as if her defenses had come down enough to allow me a little closer. "You save me," she said.

I smiled. "The doctors saved you."

She didn't reply, but I could see her face soften.

"Where did you learn to speak English?" I asked.

She removed the mask. "TV."

"You learned everything from TV?"

"Yes."

"What do you like to watch?"

"The men take me . . ." She paused. I didn't say anything, but I let her know I knew she meant Wellis and Gaishe, and all the other worthless pond life that had had a part in bringing her here. "They watch football. Most of time just football."

I nodded. "Do you like football?"

"Yes. I play for the, uh . . ."

"A girls' team?"

"Yes. In Cluj."

"You're from Romania?"

She nodded. A flicker of sadness. "Yes."

"Were you as good as Gheorghe Hagi?"

The sadness disappeared and in her face, for the first time, was a hint of a smile. "No," she said. "No one better than Hagi."

I smiled back.

Slowly, her legs slid away from her body, like part of a defensive barrier coming down, although she kept the sheets and blanket in close as a protective shield.

"Marika," I said after a while, keeping my eyes on her and not on Healy, who was half turned toward the door again. "Would you mind if I asked you a few questions?"

She didn't move. Didn't react.

I nodded again, letting her know I understood her reluctance. I shuffled across the floor, so I was about four feet away, still at her eyeline. "Let me tell you about the men who kept you," I said, "about the ones who hurt you. They will *never* hurt you again, do you understand? The two men that kept you, they're gone and they're not coming back. Now I need to find the others. But to do that, I will need your help, okay?"

She glanced at Healy, then back to me.

"I know it's hard."

Tears blurred in her eyes.

Then she nodded.

"Thank you." I reached into my pocket, removed my pad and placed it down on to the floor next to me. The girl followed every movement, a habit born out of having to predict the next development, the next attack, the next assault. "Do you feel ready?"

"Yes."

I asked her how she ended up in the UK, and from there she told us—in staccato, broken English—about her journey. She was one of four sisters, with an absent father and a chronically depressed mother. Tears continued filling her eyes as she told us how she was grabbed one day on the way back from school and thrown into the back of a van, and then the next time she was conscious, she woke up in a room full of men—four, maybe five of them—and they raped her repeatedly. She told me she was eleven at the time. It was all I could do to keep it together, to remain emotionless as the pain tremored through her voice, and I had to look down at my pad to prevent her seeing my anger and thinking it was directed at her. I wrote meaningless notes while she told me how she'd been pulled out of the room and into a lorry, then another van, except this time she was in a new country, and they didn't even speak her language.

"When did you first get here?" I asked.

"In UK?"

"Yes."

"December," she said.

"December last year?"

"Yes."

"So you've been here six, seven months?"

"Yes. That was when I meet Adrian."

The people who'd kidnapped her handed her over to Wellis, and from there she became a prisoner. As she talked, I realized she wasn't scared of Wellis—or, at least, not like she had been at the beginning—but the way he'd used her and treated her had left her with a look of inevitability, as if being dragged from one punter to the next was all she should expect from life. She had no money. No one to run to. Nowhere to go. It was a heartbreaking moment; one of those times when it felt like you were watching someone drifting out to sea, knowing the fate that awaited them, and all you could do was watch from the shore.

"He had friend," she said.

"Adrian?"

She nodded. She'd referred to him as "Adrian" throughout. She didn't know his surname and had probably only learned his first name from listening to their conversations. "He had friend called Eric. He always . . ." A pause. "He always look at me. Never say nothing. Just look. I didn't like way he look at me."

But eventually Eric Gaishe did more than look. I remembered Pell turning up the night I'd been watching their house, seeing him talk to Gaishe before driving off again. Gaishe must have told him Marika was unavailable, or Pell would have surely asked for her. Either way, it wasn't much of a shift: one violent rapist to another.

"Eric was one who hit head. I can't remember nothing after. Just remember you. You save me."

"Do you remember any of the other men who came to see you?"

Her eyes blinked, surrounded by the bandaging. Somehow I could see the answer without her saying a word: *After a while I stopped paying attention.*

"Do you remember a guy called Duncan?"

A blank.

"He used to film you?"

Now she remembered. From behind her, Healy couldn't see her reaction but when I glanced at him he could see exactly what I was telling him: *She remembers Pell.*

"He never told me name," she said, and her voice was so quiet it was barely even audible beyond the ECG and the murmur of conversations in the corridor outside. I didn't interrupt, though, just shifted in, across the floor, a little closer. "He was . . . strange man."

"Why?"

"He never say nothing. No words."

"Ever?"

"No words," she repeated.

"He hurt you?"

"Yes. Hurt me."

I remembered finding her in the loft, and remembered the words she'd managed to get out, through all the bruising and the blood and the damage: *Don't let him hurt me.*

"He was the one you were talking about?"

She frowned.

"When I found you in the loft, you said to me, 'Don't let him hurt me.' Was that man—Duncan, the one who filmed you—was he was the one you were talking about?"

"Yes," she said.

There was something in her face.

"Marika?"

"Yes. Him."

But as she looked at me, a lie passed between us, and fear bloomed in her face. It wasn't Pell she was talking about, just as it had never been Wellis. None of the DVDs Pell had of them were timecoded or dated, but if she'd landed in December, it meant the majority of them were filmed after Sam Wren's disappearance.

"Was it the man who watched you and Duncan that scared you?"

She glanced at me, trying to figure out how I knew.

"Was it him, Marika?"

It seemed to take her a long time to process the question, and when she finally did her legs came back up to her chest, and she resumed the foetal position. "Yes," she said.

"It was the man who watched you?"

"Yes."

"Did he only watch?"

Tears in her eyes now. "Yes."

"So why were you scared of him?"

"I don't know how to . . ." She paused. "Don't know words."

"Can you try?"

The tear escaped and she automatically went to wipe it away, but all she felt at her fingertips were bandages. She sniffed. "He never show face. I just hear him behind me."

"You never saw him enter or leave?"

"Never see him. Ever."

"Then how did you know he was there?"

"I hear door."

"You heard him come in?"

"Yes."

"That's it? You only heard him?"

"I see his . . ." She waved a hand. "In mirror."

"His reflection?"

"Yes."

"What did he look like?"

She shook her head. "Face was in dark."

"Shadow?"

"Shadow, yes. Mostly."

"You never saw any of his face?"

"Only once. A small . . ."

"A small bit of his face?"

"Yes."

"Did he ever say anything?"

She was staring off now, beyond me, into the middle distance. She might have been able to darken the memories she had of the other men, but she couldn't darken this one. Even faceless, she knew there was something up with him. Something bad.

"Did he ever say anything?" I asked again.

"He say words to . . ."

"Duncan?"

"To Duncan. He say words to him."

"Like what?"

She blinked. "He call me 'it.'"

"How do you mean?"

"He say, 'Fuck it. Hit it. Hurt it.'"

"He was telling Duncan what to do?"

"Yes," she said, her voice breaking a little now.

I took out a photograph of Sam. "Could it have been this man watching you?"

She studied the picture for a long time, saying nothing, her eyes wide beneath the bandaging, shimmering a little in the light of the room.

Then, finally, she ripped them away and looked at me.

"Yes," she said, a tear breaking free. "That could be him."

The minute we were outside the hospital, Healy lit himself a cigarette and we stood there in the car park watching the rain come down. Neither of us said anything, Healy trying to figure out where to go next, me trying to process what I'd just found out. Marika thought the watcher might have been Sam, which meant there was also a chance it might not have been. But it was certainly getting harder to back Sam, to deny he was involved, and that was eating away at me. I didn't call things wrong. I didn't read people wrong.

Except maybe, this time, I'd done both.

As if on cue, Healy started shaking his head, and when I glanced at him, a caustic, self-satisfied expression formed in his face. My hackles rose instantly. "So you still *somehow* think he's not involved then?" he said, blowing a flute of smoke out.

I looked at him. We were standing beneath an overhang, rain running off the roof and exploding against the ground next to us.

He glanced at me and saw my reaction. "What?"

"That's all you can say?"

"What are you talking about?"

"That's the first thing that comes into your head?"

He frowned. "What the hell do you mean?"

"I get her to talk in there because there was no way she was going to talk to you when you're bouncing around like you're waiting for your fucking dealer. Last night, I meet you at the Tube because you can't trust anyone and literally *all* you care about is bringing this home and stuffing it down everyone's throat. I do that for you, I look past your flaws, your anger, your capacity to create an argument out of nothing—and, having seen what just happened in there, that's the first thing that comes into your head?"

He just stared at me.

"Do you even realize how alone you are, Healy?"

"I don't know what—"

"That's just your problem, Healy. You *don't* know."

And I walked away.

64

Five minutes later, Healy finished his cigarette and flicked it out into the bushes running along the back of the hospital. He immediately felt like another. He was angry. Pissed off. He'd allowed himself to be manipulated, persuaded that Wren wasn't a part of this, and had then spent two days chasing his tail. Not any more. *Fuck Raker. Fuck them all.* He was going to take what the girl had told them—and he was going to put this to bed.

He moved off into the rain, pulling his jacket up over his head and making a break for it. But then, in his peripheral vision, he saw someone approaching and getting closer.

He slowed down. Looked around.

And his heart sank.

Sallows.

"Well, well, well," Sallows said, thirty feet to Healy's right, under a Metropolitan Police umbrella. In his left hand was a set of car keys. In his right was a digital camera.

Healy didn't say anything, his eyes flicking to the camera.

"Didn't think this was your part of the world, Colm."

Healy was about to form a lie, about to pretend he was visiting a relative, when he stopped himself. *See how much he knows first.* "It's not," he replied.

"So what are you doing here?"

"Following up a lead."

Sallows smirked. "Did someone steal a chocolate bar from the gift shop?" he said and then stepped closer, eyes fixed on Healy, watching for any shift of expression.

"That's more your area, Kevin."

"Is it?"

"You don't play with the big boys any more, remember."

But Sallows didn't react at all. No change in his face. No change in his stance. A fizz of panic stirred in Healy's guts: the only reason Sallows wouldn't take the bait was if he had something better. Healy glanced at the camera. *Something like photos.*

"You're a clever bastard, Healy." Sallows smiled, humorless and knowing. "Only you could pull off all that shit last year and *still* be standing here in front of me eight months later working the biggest case going." He made a soft sound, like he was still having a hard time believing it. "But here you are. Mr. Squeaky Clean. Except, of course, we both know it's all another lie."

Healy didn't respond. Sallows just looked at him.

"Well," Healy said finally, "as nice as this has been, I'd better be going."

Sallows suddenly made a move forward, right up close to Healy so they were only feet apart. Rain slapped against the umbrella, like a drumbeat, running off into the space between them. Sallows was completely dry. Healy was soaked through to the bone. "When you got me kicked off the Snatcher, you fucked with the wrong guy," he said, his voice suddenly laced with venom. "*Colm Healy* dropping *me* in the shit? Even *you* must see how fucked up that is? Everything about you, your situation, your lying and your backstabbing, it boils my piss. I mean, you're the guy who thinks it's okay to wave guns in the faces of the people you work with. You're the guy who worms his way back into the big time, who puts on this show for people—this fucking *show* that no one else is capable of seeing through—and you're *still* here working it off the books."

"You don't know what you're talking about, Kevin."

"No?"

"No."

"I saw you with Raker this morning. I've been watching this hospital every day since they brought that girl in here, because I *know* Raker was the one who made that call the day she was found and I *know* he was the one who dumped Gaishe at that warehouse."

"What Raker does has nothing to do with me."

"There you are again, Colm. *Lying.*"

"It's not a lie."

"It's a fucking barefaced lie, just like everything else in your shitty little life. You and Raker have cosied up again, doing whatever the fuck it is you two do together. I saw it coming a mile off, so when the girl was found, it was just a matter of being patient. It was just a matter of waiting here for you. And I thought to myself, 'What's the best way of making sure that everyone knows just what a lying sack of shit Colm Healy is?'" Sallows held up the camera. "Your time is up, Healy. You're done."

Healy tried not to show emotion.

But it didn't work.

Sallows broke out into a smile. "I'm realistic. I don't expect Craw to take me back and, to be honest, I wouldn't want to go back. I can't work for a malicious little bitch like that. But I'm going to enjoy hearing about the moment she asks you to clear your desk."

"What do you want, Sallows?"

"What do I *want*?"

"There must be something you want."

Sallows was still smiling. "I'd forgotten about your legendary sense of humor, Colm. What I *want* is for you to get what you deserve. And then, once I've done you, I'm doing Raker as well. You're both going to get what's coming."

Healy imagined going for the camera, imagined grabbing Sallows by the throat and ripping him to pieces. He realized he was opening and closing his fists, all the anger and frustration and desperation channelled through his fingers. If he didn't get the camera, everything was over. He was done. His life, his career, whatever semblance of normality he'd managed to claw back. But then Sallows glanced down, as if he knew what was going through Healy's head, as if he could read the movement of his hands like words being spoken aloud, and he handed Healy the camera.

Except it wasn't the camera.

It was just the case.

"The camera's in the car," Sallows said, watching the rain run down Healy's face, hair matted to his head, clothes stuck to him. "I don't know what concern that girl is of yours, I don't know what you're even doing here, or what you and that other prick have got planned. And to be honest, I don't really care. Honestly, I don't. What I care about is seeing you go down in flames—and if you take Raker with you, all the better."

Healy scanned the car park, desperately looking for Sallows's car.

"A guy who waves guns in people's faces can't be trusted," Sallows said, reading the situation again. "So while the camera's in the car, and the photos are still on it, I also took the trouble of e-mailing myself the pictures. Just to make sure they're nice and safe."

"Look, Kevin, we can work—"

"You're done."

"There must be—"

"You're *done*, Healy," he said again, and as the gentle sound of rain settled in the silence, Sallows headed back to his car, leaving Healy alone.

65

At Battersea Bridge, I pulled the car over. My head was so full of noise, I had to find a side street, bump up on to the pavement and write it all down. An hour later I was done. Twenty pages of my notepad full, everything I'd ever learned about Samuel Wren. In the silence of the car, I went through it all again, trying to see where things didn't join, trying to look for any kind of hairline fracture I could get into and prize open. But there was nothing new. Nothing I didn't already know. All that looked up at me was what had looked up at me before: a deeply confused man, blackmailed by a people trafficker and at the mercy of a reality he could never accept.

Where's the killer in you, Sam?

The rain got harder, popping against the windscreen like pebbles being thrown at the glass. I studied the picture I'd taken of the watcher from Pell's DVD. There was an obvious question that I'd never got the chance to discuss with Healy: if Sam was taking these men, if we were assuming he was the Snatcher and had brokered some sort of partnership with Pell, why would he engineer his own disappearance but Pell not do the same? Why vanish at all? If he'd managed to take his first two victims—Steven Wilky and Marc Erion—without leaving a trace of himself, if Leon Spane had been dumped on Hampstead Heath and not led back to either him or Pell, why go to all the effort of disappearing? They'd already got away with it. Whatever this was, whatever they were doing together, however it worked, they were already below the radar when Sam went missing. And the only reason you'd then go on to plan your disappearance was if something had started to go wrong.

Or if you weren't the killer at all.

"You were the victim," I said quietly.

On the way home, as I came off Battersea Bridge, I decided to stop at Gloucester Road station again. I seriously doubted Pell would be there, but the people inside worked with him, got to see him daily, and Pell still represented my best shot at finding out where Sam went.

As I entered from the street, I kept my eyes on the faces of the staff, moving between them as I walked inside. I was conscious of the lies I'd

told the last time I'd been in, and I remembered the guy in the staffroom—
the man called Gideon—and the way he'd reacted to my being there
about Sam and Pell. But, as I walked around the ticket hall, I realized I'd
caught a lucky break. I hardly recognized any of the faces, which meant
most wouldn't recognize me. I bought a ticket and headed through the
gateline, down to the platform and then back up again. I hadn't expected
to find Pell and I wasn't disappointed, but I did a sweep of the station just
to be sure.

At the booth, the overweight guy who'd been standing underneath
the glass dome two days before, bathed in a pool of his own sweat, was
perched on a stool, looking on disinterestedly. At one point, as I stood
there watching the crowds coming in, turning things over in my head,
he looked right at me but he didn't seem to remember me.

About ten minutes later, as I was thinking about leaving, I saw the
staffroom open—the same one I'd been inside before—and in the doorway appeared two faces I recognized: the woman, Sandra Purnell, who
I'd chatted to last time out; and a man, one whose name I was struggling
to recall, but who'd been here the first time I'd been in and talked to Pell.
He'd been a ticket inspector. *Eric. Edgar. Edward. Something beginning with
E.* I remembered seeing his photo and his name badge in the staffroom,
and I remembered the conversation I'd had with him that first time.
He'd been polite and helpful. In his staffroom photo he'd been immaculately turned out too—crisp uniform, styled hair, looking out through
expensive half-moon glasses—and he had dressed with the same care
today. I'd take that now: if he was detailed in the way he dressed, he
might be detailed in his thinking too. Any hint, however small, of where
Pell was, could get me a lead.

I headed over.

As I did, the woman unexpectedly reached out to the man and hugged
him. I stopped and watched. He suddenly seemed quite emotional. Not
tearful exactly, but lacking some color, lips flattened, eyes downcast.
When she was done, she rubbed his arm, they said good-bye to one
another and she headed off toward the station entrance. He just stood
there, a ticket machine slung over one shoulder, a backpack over the other.
Out of the backpack spilled some clothes—a running top decorated with
a square motif, a pair of well-used trainers—as well as some old, rolled-up
magazines. It looked like he might have been on the way to the gym, or
maybe he'd just taken the opportunity to clear out his locker.

"Excuse me."

He looked up. "Yes, sir?" he said quietly.

"I'm not sure if you remember me," I said, and I could immediately see he didn't. "I came in on Thursday last week and spoke to you about this guy."

I reached into my pocket and got out a picture of Sam. Just as I remembered him doing the first time, the man patted the breast pockets of his jacket, more out of habit than because he genuinely didn't know where his glasses were, then took the photo from me and held it up in front of him. Although only in his early forties, he had an old way about him: he raised the photo high up into the light coming through the glass dome and perched his half-moon glasses on the end of his nose.

"His name is Sam Wren," I said.

"Oh right, yes—I remember."

"You definitely don't know him?"

His eyes remained on the picture, but I could tell his mind had shifted elsewhere. Whatever he and the woman had been talking about had really got to him.

"Is this a bad time?"

"No, no," he replied, but I could tell he was being polite. He removed his glasses and slid them back into his top pocket. "Have you asked the other guys here? They'd know better than me. I don't actually work out of the station."

"Because you're a ticket inspector."

"We're called RCIs these days," he said, a small smile on his face. "Much posher."

I nodded, smiled back. "Mind if I quickly ask you something else?"

He shrugged. "Sure."

"When I came in last time, I spoke to you and another guy, Duncan Pell. Do you remember that?"

"Yeah, I think so."

"Any idea where I might find Duncan?"

"Is he in trouble?"

"No. I'd just like to speak to him again."

"They tell me Duncan's not been very well."

"Yeah, so I hear. Do you know where he might be?"

His eyes moved left, over my shoulder. When I followed his line of sight I could see the overweight guy from the booth had noticed us talking, and was coming over.

"Everything all right, Ed?" the big guy asked.

And then his name came back to me: Edwin. I turned around and the other guy was right on my shoulder.

"Fine, yes. This gentleman was just asking about Duncan."

Mr. Big eyed me with suspicion. "Were you in the other day?"

"I just want to ask him a couple of questions."

"You a copper or something?"

"More like 'or something,'" I said.

It went completely over his head, but when I looked back at the ticket inspector the corners of his mouth were raised in a smile. I took a business card out of my pocket. "My name's David Raker," I said to him. "If you think of anything, maybe you'd be kind enough to give me a shout. Any time of the day or night."

He took the card. "Okay."

"I didn't catch your name," I lied.

"Edwin Smart. Ed."

"Thanks for your help, Ed."

As I left the station and headed back to the car, my mind returned to the CCTV footage of the day Sam went missing. I'd been over it countless times, trying to find the join. But even though every viewing I'd had of it had been more meticulous than the last, they'd all ended up the same way: no Sam.

And yet as I walked, I felt a tiny shift in my thoughts, like I'd suddenly glimpsed the outline of a memory. Although I tried to pin down what it was, the harder I looked for it, the more of a blur it became. But as indistinct as the thought had been, something of it remained. A residual feeling. A certainty.

That the answers were still in the footage.

And they always had been.

When Healy finally got back to the station, he walked into the incident room to find a meeting taking place. At the front, Craw was addressing the Snatcher task force, Davidson sitting almost at her side, pad on his lap, pen in his hand. Both of them clocked the movement, Craw glancing across to Healy and then returning her gaze to the detectives in front of her; Davidson looking over, a half-smile forming on his face.

Healy moved to the back of the group and perched himself on one of the desks but he could barely hear anything Craw was saying. All he could hear was his own voice: had Sallows already sent the pictures? Did Craw already know about the hospital, about how he'd got together with Raker? And what lie could he spin to help minimize the impact?

There are no more lies worth telling if she knows.

The thought sent a bubble of bile up from the pit of his stomach, but he managed to pull himself forward, further toward the group. Davidson was swinging gently from side to side on his chair as he made notes. At the back of the group, one of the other cops looked around, saw Healy and nodded, but Healy was so distracted he didn't even remember the guy's name. All he could see were the decisions he'd made over the past few days, and—with absolute clarity now—how he'd become consumed by revenge. He'd wanted to show them. He'd wanted to shove their taunts and their jokes and the looks he got in the office so far down their throats they'd be choking on them. They'd used Leanne against him, they'd tried to grind him down and spit him out, and he'd become so focused on that, he hadn't been able to see where the road was leading. Raker was the only person he could trust—even after the hospital, even after the way things had been left, that still held true in Healy's head—but Healy knew he should never have sought Raker's help. Not now. Not this soon.

"Healy?"

He looked up. Craw was addressing him. "Yes, ma'am?"

"Did you get all that?"

"Most of it, ma'am."

There were a couple of sniggers, though he couldn't see where from, and as Craw stepped forward, in front of Davidson, Healy watched a smile form on Davidson's face.

You're done, he mouthed.

"Good," Craw said. "Because you're riding with me."

Craw told him to head toward Highgate. She didn't say much else. Healy drove, eyes on the road, hands on the wheel, and stared ahead, going over everything that had happened and everything that might be about to come. After about ten minutes they hit traffic in Holloway. For a while there was silence, just the sound of rain falling against the roof. Then, finally, Craw turned to him. "Where were you this morning?"

"I'm sorry I was late—"

"I'm not looking for apologies, Healy. Where were you?"

"I called you and left a message on your—"

"I got the message. You said you were going via Julia Wren's."

"Yes, ma'am."

"Why?"

"I wanted to ask her a couple of questions."

She pursed her lips, her eyes still fixed on him. She'd seen right through it. "Do you know where we're going, Healy?"

"Ma'am?"

"Do you know where we're going?"

"Now?"

She nodded. "Now."

"You said it was an address in Highgate."

"I know what I said. But do *you* know where we're going?"

He frowned. "I'm not sure I understand, ma'am."

"Let me paint you a picture, okay?" She paused, looking at him. "I invited you back on to this task force because I thought I saw something in you. A hunger. Some sort of contrition. I saw the hint of *something* worthwhile, so I wrote off all the politics and bullshit, I put up with having my arse handed to me by Bartholomew in weekly meetings, and having him make me look like an idiot in the press, because I thought to myself, 'If Healy does *one* good thing, if he gives me *one* worthwhile lead, the risk will have paid off.' Because, let's face it, this case, beginning to end, has been one giant clusterfuck."

He continued staring ahead, barely able to look at her.

"But, you know, I look at you, Healy, and all I see are secrets. And if I don't know what those secrets are, if I don't know what makes you tick and you won't *tell* me what makes you tick, how am I supposed to work with you? How am I supposed to defend you in front of Bartholomew? In front of everyone else? *Everyone* is against you, Healy—you know that, right? And your only friend, throughout all of this, has been me."

He looked at her. "I appreciate that, ma'am."

"Do you?"

"I do."

"Then tell me where we're going today."

He studied her. They were headed to Highgate. That had been where Raker had said Duncan Pell lived. Except he couldn't tell her about Raker, couldn't tell her about knowing Pell, until he figured out how much she knew and whether she had the photos.

"I don't know, ma'am," he said finally.

"Are you sure?"

He looked at her. "One hundred percent."

She nodded and then turned away from him, looking out into the rain as it drifted across the windscreen. "Early yesterday morning a man reported seeing something suspicious up in Highgate, close to Fell Wood. It's an old railway line."

"Suspicious?"

"Said he thought someone was trying to break into a house there."

"Whose house?"

"It belongs to a Duncan Pell." She glanced at him but he didn't react. "Ever heard of him?"

"No, ma'am."

She eyed him for a second and there was a fleeting hint of disappointment in her face. Then she moved on. "Couple of uniforms go and have a look and they find the front door open. No one's inside, but they call it in. Anyway, the investigating team enter Pell into the system and find he's already in there, along with our friend Samuel Wren. Both of them seem to have been involved in the same altercation at Gloucester Road Tube station in October 2010. So there's a link, however small. Both were originally arrested, but neither of them were charged. There was no indication they knew each other, but something's up with Pell."

They found the knives. They found Spane's jacket.

"He's got a set of knives in there with blood all over them. Bartholomew barks some orders and we get them rushed through forensics last night, and when you walked in on us I was reading out the results. The DNA from the blood on the knives matches up with DNA taken from the flats of every single Snatcher victim. Wilky. Erion. Symons. Drake. All four of them. Their DNA is all over the knives. And you know what else?"

Healy looked at her. *No. But I can guess.*

"Leon Spane's blood was on the blades too." She glanced at him. "We all knew he was one of the Snatcher's victims the minute Wren used his name for the message he left on Drake's mobile. But you saw it before that. Way before that. You believed Spane was a victim, even when everyone else doubted." She nodded once: an acknowledgment she should have listened to Healy. "Pell even had Spane's jacket and his holdall."

"Who made the anonymous call about the break-in?"

"Didn't leave a name."

"Where did he call from?"

"A payphone on Muswell Hill."

Which meant it was basically untraceable unless Craw signed off on CCTV footage being requisitioned from the street. Even then, there were no guarantees it would get them a face. *First Wellis, now Pell. It was Wren. Had to be. He's trying to close down anyone who he had any sort of contact with as the Snatcher because he's knows we're on to him. He's trying to insulate himself. This is the end game.*

"So what about Wren?"

"What about him?"

"Was his DNA on the knives?"

"His prints were on the knife grips."

"Shit. So Wren looks good for this?"

"I don't know," she said. "You tell me."

"Ma'am?"

"You were at his house this morning, right?"

He nodded. "Right. Yes, I was."

"So what did you find out?"

He couldn't think of a single thing to say. *There are no lies left to tell.* He glanced at her. "I didn't manage to find out anything new."

But even to his ears it was weak.

She shrugged. "Then I guess we head to Pell's house."

The conversation died away and they sat in silence for a while as the traffic eased, Healy inching the car forward, rain getting heavier and spitting up off the road as mist.

"I don't think I've ever been so disappointed," Craw said finally.

"Disappointed, ma'am?"

She shifted in her seat, all the way around, and just stared at him. He looked ahead, not turning himself, trying to act normally even as a slow wave of dread washed through his system. Then eventually, as the silence became unbearable, he turned and looked at her.

"You were right about Spane. You have good instincts, Healy. I knew it, right from the off. That's why I tried to get you involved. But the trouble is, you don't know how to curb them, you don't know how to control your instincts." She paused; seemed to deflate. "Davidson handed me some photos this morning of you and David Raker. I don't know what you were doing with him, and frankly I don't care. What I care about is that you looked me in the eye when I sat there and handed you a second chance, and you told me—you promised me—you wouldn't make me look like an arsehole. You *promised* me."

"Ma'am, I can explain."

"It's too late for explanations, Healy," she said, steely but quiet. She was angry but mostly she was defeated and, in a way, that was worse. "*No one* wanted you here, you do get that, don't you? Not one single person. Even cops who you go back years with, they can't afford to get too close to you, because you drag people down. This . . ." She waved a hand, her voice gradually starting to rise. "This agenda you've got. This is the one time you had to suck it up, you had to swallow your pride and you had to keep your head down. But you couldn't even do that."

"I didn't feel I could—"

"I don't want to hear any more," she said, and turned away from him, looking out through the windscreen. "When we get back to the station, you're going to walk into my office and you're going to hand in your resignation. You're going to tell me you can't handle the pressure any more, or you feel it's time to go, or whatever the hell excuse you want to make up. You're good at lying, Healy, so I'm sure you can come up with something inventive." She paused, glancing at him. "I like you, Colm. I've always liked you. But I can't trust you. And if I can't trust you to protect your own career, I can't trust you to protect mine. So now it's time to fall on your sword. And once you've done that, you walk away from the police and you never come back again."

67

Once I was back home, I returned to the footage. The last time Sam Wren was visible to anyone was the partial glimpse of his legs inside the carriage at Victoria. So that meant he definitely went as far as St. James's Park. Once the train entered the station I hit Pause and spent forty minutes going over the footage, rewinding it, tabbing it on, rewinding it, tabbing it on. By the end of it, as the train left St. James's Park and headed off toward Westminster, I was pretty confident he hadn't disembarked. I'd been pretty confident all the other times I'd looked, but this time I felt a real certainty, a belief I couldn't explain. I wondered whether writing out Sam's life, every moment I'd discovered or had explained to me, had cemented my view of him. I accepted all the evidence against him, because it was compelling and real and difficult to dispute. But when I looked at Sam Wren I didn't see a killer.

And I'd never seen one.

At Westminster, I paused the footage as the carriage doors opened. Everything I already knew about that day, everything I'd replayed over and over again in the footage, appeared on screen again. Two exits, one marked for those who'd landed at Westminster to take part in the protests; the other marked for those who worked close by, or were here to see the sights. The platform was already jammed, people everywhere, some bunched into pockets, some a little more spread out, but once commuters and protesters piled out of the train, it became a mass of bodies, some barely even identifiable as men or women.

About five seconds after the carriage doors parted, the fight broke out, further up the platform. As it did, the crowd seemed to get sucked toward it, like a black hole drawing them in, and a small amount of space was created at the near end of the station, closest to the camera and furthest away from where the confrontation was taking place. By that time, the Tube staff had already made their move, six of them descending on the fight and breaking it up almost immediately, two more coming in from positions off camera, at the bottom of the frame. One of them, a ginger-haired man I'd spotted on the other run-throughs of the video, was gesturing for people to continue moving toward the exits. The second was a stocky woman, stood at the doors on the end carriage, urging people out of the

train—particularly anyone in a red protest T-shirt—before feeding them
into the traffic flow created by her male colleague.

A red protest T-shirt.

Something flared, the vaguest tail of a memory, and as I fished for it,
my eyes settled on the inside of the second carriage. The one Sam Wren
had been in. I scanned from left to right, to every person I'd already
seen. The woman with her headphones on, oblivious to what was happening. The guy in the suit, sitting down, head in a book but momentarily distracted by the fight on the platform.

And then the second man.

The one in the red T-shirt.

The same memory flared again, unrefined and cloudy. Was there
something about him I hadn't noticed before? He was bending down to
pick up a protest sign, and positioned in a space behind a throng of dem-
onstrators looking to disembark. I couldn't see his face properly through
the glass, had never at any stage got a clear view of his features inside the
carriage—I'd just always known he wasn't Sam. He was too big, too tall,
had a different physicality, even different colored hair. There was nothing remarkable about him, nothing unique or unusual to make him
stand out. He was just a protester. He picked up his sign, he moved to
the doors, he left the train. I knew his movements, just like I knew
everyone else's by now.

But I didn't know his face.

I moved the footage on a couple of frames, and for the first time
concentrated solely on him. What he was doing. Where he was headed.
And as he leaned over to get the sign, I noticed a fractional movement
close to his body, so slight it was virtually invisible. I had to rewind the
footage just to make sure I'd seen it: *he already had the sign under his arm.* I
could see the very edge of it—a triangle of white plastic—slowly slide
out from under his elbow while the rest of the sign remained obscured
at ground level.

Which meant he'd never been picking up the sign.

He'd been picking up something else.

Next was the moment where he actually *did* bring up the sign. As the
video rolled on, it played out exactly the same way it always had: he
straightened, stepped toward the doors, turning his back to the glass,
and then there was a brief pause. Except now I saw something else I'd
never been looking for before: a weird shift to his right, like a jolt. *Like*

he was pulling on something. Seconds later, he turned around again, facing the glass, but the sign was fully up in front of him.

As if in a deliberate move to disguise himself.

Before long, he was back in shot: he was standing behind the protesters at the door, the lower half of his body visible, the red protest T-shirt over a pale blue fleece. But it wasn't an official protest T-shirt. As I'd noted the very first time I'd watched the footage, it had red and white checks on the sleeves.

Checks.

I paused the video.

Is it the checks?

I wanted to get a clear view of his face, but all I could see were his legs, part of an arm, and his hand holding the sign. There were other protesters either side of him, trying to squeeze their way out of the train, everyone jostling for space. But, even in among them all, even though I couldn't see his face, something about the man was suddenly familiar to me.

Do I know you?

I tabbed forward, quicker this time, punching at the cursor with my fingers as the footage rolled on. Moments later, he was finally at the doors and the crowds in front of him were fanning out onto the platform. Except for one person.

One person stayed close to him.

Which was when everything changed.

68

The man at the doors of the train paused and then joined the other groups being funneled toward the platform exit. I hadn't been looking for him. I'd been looking for Sam. I'd been looking for Sam *on his own*. I'd been looking for him in a suit, or in a protest T-shirt that had been pulled *over* a suit, *or*—at the very least—over a shirt and tie. If he'd removed his coat and jacket in order to put on the T-shirt, it made sense that he would have been carrying them, or they would have been inside his briefcase.

But Sam wasn't carrying a coat or jacket.

He wasn't even holding a briefcase.

And he wasn't leaving the train on his own.

The man with the sign had his arm around Sam Wren's waist, though if you weren't specifically looking, you could barely even tell. I'd never noticed before. It looked like the two of them had just been pushed together by the crowds. Sam was in an official red protest T-shirt, pulled over his work shirt, but he had nothing else with him. I'd always figured the briefcase had gone with him, because if he'd left it behind, it would have been shipped off to lost property and ultimately traced back to him. But it had never surfaced. So either it had contained nothing that could lead back to Sam—or any kind of link to him had been taken out of the case before it was left in the train.

He looked woozy, unsteady on his feet, but the man was keeping him close. This was the perfect morning to drug someone: there were so many people, so many protesters dressed the same, that no one batted an eyelid. Sam still seemed capable of walking, still seemed capable of being manipulated, but he had no fight in him, no way of preventing what was happening. That was enough to make him pass unnoticed. And the man knew *exactly* where the CCTV cameras were in order to save drawing attention to the two of them. There were only the checked sleeves of his red shirt, and the sign. No clear view of his face. He made sure the same was true of Sam too: inside a second of hitting the platform, he raised the protest sign above their heads, shifting it across so nothing of Sam's upper half was visible any more.

Inside eight seconds, they were both gone.

I rewound the footage.

Something squirmed through my stomach as I watched it all unfold again. This was the drug he must have used on Wilky, on Erion, on Symons and on Drake. This was how he was able to walk them out of their front doors. I couldn't see him drug Sam—maybe because he'd done it between stations—and, in fact, couldn't see Sam inside the carriage at any point once it arrived at Westminster. But when the man was bending down, presumably dealing with the briefcase, Sam's clothes and Sam himself—that had to have been moments after Sam had been jabbed with a syringe. From there, the man had been incredibly adept: he kept Sam on the floor, out of sight of any cameras—and the moment he turned his back and jolted to the right was the moment he yanked Sam to his feet again. Unseen by CCTV. Unseen by me.

I imagined what came next: if anyone had paid any sort of attention— and most people hadn't because most people were disembarking protesters, half watching a fight at the other end of the platform—he'd claim Sam had fainted. He'd have taken his jacket off, pretending that he was trying to get him some air. Then, as the drug kicked in, he would have made Sam put the T-shirt on, helped it on to him, knowing he was pliant. Putting a protest T-shirt on him, even as he lay there semi-conscious, would have looked odd, but it wouldn't have looked odd *enough*. People might have wondered what the man was doing—why he was putting the T-shirt on now, of all times—but once he was off and out of sight of the carriage, most of them would barely even recall it as a footnote. This was London, after all. A city where a body had once lain dead for five days in plain sight before anyone paid it any attention. A city where a jewelery shop's windows were smashed in by an armed gang and people just wandered past. He didn't have to worry about people remembering. He just had to get Sam off the train without being seen by the cameras. And but for a second—maybe even less—as they stepped out on to the platform, he'd managed it. I knew the footage better than anyone, had watched it more times than anyone, but it had taken me countless viewings—endless repetition, rewinding and inching through, frame by frame—before I'd seen him walk Sam out.

The Snatcher.

It had to be him.

But why take Sam? Why deviate from the plan? I let the questions go for the time being, moving the slider back to the moment they stepped off the train. And in the second they were both visible—Sam, drugged, looking down at the floor, the man next to him turning away and trying to protect his identity—I finally saw the face of a killer. I saw the man who had taken Sam Wren. I saw the man who had taken Steven Wilky from a flat half a mile from Paddington; Marc Erion from an apartment in King's Cross; Joseph Symons from his home north of Farringdon station; and Jonathan Drake from his flat in Hammersmith.

All homes close to the Tube stations.

All stops on the Circle line.

He was using it as his hunting ground, watching the men, following them, getting to know their routines and then moving in for them. He knew the Underground stations.

Because he worked them.

I'd looked right at him so many times in the footage as he'd moved around inside the carriage, his face a blur behind the glass. I'd watched so many times as he'd stepped out onto the platform, the sign shielding him and his victim from the cameras—and not once had I put it together.

But I knew why I had today.

His clothes were different from the uniform he should have been wearing on a Friday morning, and maybe he'd thought that was what would make him blend in. But, ultimately, it was the change of clothes that had given him away. Because now I saw why this time, of all times, I'd been drawn to him: a red T-shirt with checked sleeves. The same top I'd seen in his gym bag earlier in the day.

The Snatcher knew the Circle line because he worked it.

The Snatcher was Edwin Smart.

69

As I drove, I jammed my phone into the hands-free and dialed Healy's number. It rang and rang, with no answer. Finally, after half a minute, it clicked and went to voicemail.

"This is Healy, leave a message."

"Shit." I waited for the beep. "Healy, it's me. Everything's changed. It's not Sam or Pell you should be looking for, it's a guy called Edwin Smart. He's a ticket inspector on the Circle line. He took Sam. He took all of them. You need to tell Craw right now."

I killed the call, my mind turning over.

Craw.

I dialed the station that the Snatcher task force were working out of, then asked to be connected to Craw. "She's out in the field at the moment, sir, and I'm afraid I can't—"

"Wherever she is, she's at the wrong place."

"Well, sir, I can't—"

"No, *listen* to me: you need to connect me unless you want her to get back and find out *you* are the reason she couldn't stop a killer disappearing for good."

A pause. Then the line connected.

It rang ten times with no answer and then went silent. A click. And then it started to ring again. She was redirecting my call. On the third ring, someone picked up.

"Davidson."

Shit. Anyone but Davidson.

"Davidson, it's David Raker."

A snort. "What the fuck do you want?"

"Sam Wren isn't the Snatcher."

"*What?* I thought we made it clear to you—"

"Just listen to me—"

"No, you listen to me, you weasely piece of shit. You and that fucking sideshow Healy are *done.* You get it? He's cooked, and when he's done I'm gonna find the hole in your story and I'm gonna hang you out to dry. You think you're some sort of vigilante, is that it? You're nothing. Zero. And you're gonna be even less than that when I'm done."

"Do what you have to do, but you need to hear this."

"I *need* to hear this?"

"Sam Wren isn't the guy you need to be looking for, it's a—"

"No," he said. "We're done."

And then he hung up.

I smashed my fists against the steering wheel and looked out into the rain. *Healy's cooked.* Had they found out about him working the case off the books? A fleeting thought passed through my head—a moment where I wondered how he would react to that, and how he might endanger himself and the people around him—and then my mind switched back to Smart. I dialed Directory Enquiries and got them to put me through to Gloucester Road station. After three rings, a woman picked up.

"How can I help you?" she asked.

"I'm looking for a revenue control inspector."

"You'd be better off calling the depot at Hammersmith."

"His name's Edwin Smart."

He could have been at any station on the line, not just Gloucester Road. But I'd found him twice there and he seemed to know the people who worked in and around it. They liked him, he liked them—or, at least, he pretended to. But he could put on a show, and he could manipulate those around him, starting with Sam Wren and Duncan Pell.

"Do you know him at all?" I pressed.

"Edwin Smart?"

"Yes."

She paused. "What did you say your name was, sir?"

"Detective Sergeant Davidson."

I could sense a change, without any words even being spoken. Most people, even people who knew they had a duty to protect people's privacy, started to get nervous when the police came calling. "Uh . . ." She stopped again. "Uh, I'm not really, uh . . ."

I recognized the voice then: Sandra Purnell. The woman I'd spoken to in the staffroom, and the woman who had hugged Smart as I'd been about to approach him.

Something had been up with Smart.

"He's not in any trouble," I said. "I just need to speak to him."

She cleared her throat. "He's out for the rest of the day."

"Out on the line?"

"No. He's doing a half-day."

"He's on holiday?"

"Well, it's 18 June."

"What's the significance of that?"

"He always takes 18 June off. It's the anniversary."

"Of what?"

A pause. "Of his dad dying."

I was heading along Uxbridge Road, waiting for Spike to call me back with an address for Smart. He was ex-directory, with no trail on the internet. No Facebook page. No Twitter feed. No LinkedIn profile. No stories about him in local newspapers. None of the usual ways people left footprints. But as the woman at Gloucester Road told me about his father, something shifted into focus and, as it formed in my head, I pulled a turn into a side road and bumped up onto the pavement in order to let it come together.

I leaned into the phone. "What did his dad die of?"

"What?"

"Do you know what his dad died of?"

"Uh . . . cancer."

I killed the call and sat back in my seat.

Whatever he was doing with the men after he took them, he was doing because of what his dad had done to him. You didn't need to be a profiler to work that out. Killers were made, not born; the cycles of abuse rippled through from one generation to the next. But I imagined that when, in Edwin Smart's childhood, the abuse—in whatever form it got dished out—finally stopped, it was because his father got cancer. And when his father got cancer, he was left with no hair.

Just like the Snatcher victims.

He shaved their heads to make them like his father.

Daddy

Jonathan Drake woke with a jolt. Darkness all around him, everywhere, in every corner of whatever space he was being kept in. He'd been moved again. Every time he slept, he was shifted around the room. Most times he was conscious of it happening, but he didn't do anything about it. He was too scared. He just lay there, limp, as the man slid fingers under his naked body, as hands pinched his skin—the feel of them sending goosebumps scattering across Drake's body—and he pretended he was asleep. It was safer not to fight. Sometimes, though, he wouldn't know he'd been moved until he woke up. He imagined those times the man had drugged him. Then, when Drake felt in the darkness for the things around him he'd become familiar with, and instead realized there was nothing he could seek comfort in, panic would spread through his body.

He was face down on the floor this time, stomach in a patch of something wet, ankle bound to the wall behind him. He just lay there, looking off into the dark, trying to force his eyes to form shapes in front of him. But there was nothing, just like every other time. He closed his eyes and listened. He could hear something faintly, but whatever it was it wasn't coming from outside. The only noises that drifted around the room were those from inside it: the soft sound of electricity, and water dripping rhythmically somewhere close by. Sometimes he listened to the sound and used it to focus his mind, wondering how long he'd been kept here, and what was to come.

"I never got the chance to start on you."

Drake moved instantly, up off the floor, scampering back toward the wall on all fours. And then he sat there, knees up at his chest, scanning the darkness. He couldn't see the man anywhere, but he was there. The voice had sounded like it was right on top of him.

"Jonathan Drake."

Drake looked from left to right, desperately trying to seek the man out, his heart clubbing against his chest so hard it felt like it might bruise. Then, on his right, light suddenly erupted about twenty feet away from him. Drake automatically pushed back, reacting to the sudden change, but he was already tight to the wall, unable to go any further. He looped his arms around his knees and squeezed even harder, trying to form a protective barrier.

Then Drake saw the man.

There was no light directly on him, just a weak glow, but Drake could make out a head, a shoulder, part of a body, and a big hand sitting across the torch, turning it gently back and forth so that an arrow of light swung across the floor of the room, side to side.

"Jonathan is such a lovely name," the man said, and Drake—just for a moment—thought how ordinary he sounded. No accent. No twang. A softness to his voice that was almost as frightening as if he'd been screaming. "My father was also called Jonathan."

Drake swallowed. "Please. Please don't—"

"They used to call me 'Ed Case' at school." A snort of laughter. "I was always in trouble. Fighting, causing problems, answering back. I remember getting caned fourteen times once, right across the knuckles, because I told a teacher to fuck off. I guess that's what happens when you grow up without a mother. She died when I was one, so the old man brought me up. I sometimes wonder if life would have turned out differently if she'd lived. Maybe it would. Or maybe she would also have locked me in the cellar, beaten me senseless, climbed into my bed and made me touch her, like he did." The man stopped rolling the torch. "Do you know what I don't understand, Jonathan?"

"Look, whatever you want—"

"Shut your fucking mouth."

Nothing in the man's voice. No emotion. No volume. But there was something about him, about his stillness, that sent a chill fingering up Drake's spine.

"Do you know what I don't understand?" he repeated.

Silence. Drake didn't answer this time.

"When I had to take him into hospital for his treatment, when I had to do his shopping, change the TV channel for him, read to him and put him to bed, I looked at him and felt devastated by the thought that he might not be around any more. And yet, when I wasn't with him, this deep, burning hatred was just eating me up inside."

Drake looked around him. The glow from the torch had turned the light up just a notch, but it was still hard to make anything out. When he turned back to the man, he was staring at Drake, eyes black, face cast in strips of shadow.

"It was a different time back then."

Drake pressed himself against the wall again.

"No one spoke about those things. I never told anyone what he did to me. What he made me into." He started rolling the torch back and forth. "A fucking queer."

And then he stopped.

For the first time, Drake noticed the man was gripping something in his other hand, fingers around it, surface shining dully in the muted light. Oh shit. He had a knife. Drake tried to move away, tried to shift sideways, but the shackles tightened, and all he could do was look at the man, his skin crawling, his throat closing up, his eyes fixed on the object in his hand.

Then he realized it wasn't a knife.

It was a set of hair clippers.

The man reached into the darkness for something else and came back with a wooden bowl. The same one he'd used on Drake the night he'd taken him. He put it down, in between his legs, and leaned forward, so he was over the bowl, looking down at it. And then he placed the clippers against his head, right at the top of his skull where his hair was the thickest, and switched them on. Slowly he moved the shaver through his black hair, eyes on Drake the whole time, creating naked lines on his scalp like rows of plowed corn. There was no emotion in his face at all. No movement in his body other than his arm passing back and forth across his head. No sound but the mechanical whine of the clippers, a constant buzz that went on for what seemed like hours, hair falling gently into the bowl. Then, finally, when most of the hair was gone, he switched them off.

Eyes still on Drake.

He placed the clippers down on the floor beside him and started to unbutton his shirt. He had a taut body, toned, shadows forming in the muscles, a scar running from his right collarbone across his chest in a diagonal. He touched a couple of fingers to it, thick and pink like a worm, as if it bothered him somehow, then he started to undo the belt on his trousers, loosening the buckle and drawing it through the loops, one by one, until the belt was out. He tossed it across the room. He watched Drake the whole time.

Drake swallowed, hardly able to breathe now.

Tears formed in his eyes.

This was the end.

He wiped them away as the man sat there, muscles hard and defined in his arms, hands big and powerful, his gaze never leaving Drake even once. Drake knew instantly he wouldn't stand a chance. The man was too strong.

"Please," he begged softly. "Please don't hurt me."

But the man said nothing, his skin a tepid yellow in the torchlight. He scooped his clothes up and rolled them into a ball, hurling them across the other side of the room. Then he just sat there, his dark eyes on Drake's face.

"Please," Drake said again, barely able to form the words. A tear broke free and ran down his face. He let it run until it fell away. "Please. Please. Don't hurt me."

Finally, the man moved, raising a straightened finger to his lips and holding it there in a sssshhhhh gesture.

And then the torch went out.

Edwin Smart's house was about half a mile from Duncan Pell's and backed on to the old line at Fell Wood. It was almost on top of it, just beyond the line of trees I'd passed on my way to the Tube station. I'd walked past his house two days before without even knowing. Again, I tried to put it all together in my head: how Pell had first entered the equation, how he and Smart had begun working together, which parts were Pell and which were Smart. But there was nothing but noise around me now as I headed north toward Highgate. Rain hammered against the windows of the BMW. Horns blared. Tires squealed. Lorries rumbled past. I couldn't get silence, I couldn't get the time I needed to piece it together. And then my phone started ringing.

I reached across and answered it. "David Raker."

No reply. Then finally: "I got your message."

"Healy?"

No answer again. But it was him.

"Are you okay?"

He cleared his throat. "You were right, then."

"About what?"

"About Wren."

"It's not about being right or wrong."

"It's *always* about being right or wrong," he replied, his voice so small I could barely even hear it. He sniffed. I tried to make out any sounds in the background but there was nothing but silence. I turned up the volume on the speakerphone as high as it would go, trying to offset the noise of the rain, of the traffic, of a Monday in the middle of the city. "So how do you know this Smart guy took Wren?" Healy asked, but there was nothing in his voice. He didn't sound invested in the answers, just curious.

"I saw him."

"On CCTV?"

"Yeah."

"How did you miss him before?"

"He had a handle on everything. Every second of it. He knew where the cameras were, how to disguise himself, how to get Sam out. It was blind luck that I found him." *Or maybe fate,* I thought. If I'd left Gloucester

Road five minutes before I did, I'd never have seen Smart again, never talked to him, never seen the T-shirt in his gym bag or made the connection with his father.

"Raker?"

I filled in the rest of the details for Healy and then pushed the conversation on. "He lives in Highgate, close to Pell. I tried to call Craw, but all I got was Davidson. I need you to call her and let her—"

"They're all over Pell."

"What?"

"Tip-off. Caller said they saw someone snooping around Pell's place."

"Who was the caller?"

"It was anonymous."

"Could have been Smart."

"Could have been. If he's going to make a break for it, he probably thought the phone call would be enough to buy him a couple of days. You think that's what he's going to do—make a break for it?"

I thought of Smart's dad, of the anniversary. "Not today."

More silence. A sniff. "So what's Pell to him?"

"To Smart?"

"Yeah."

"He must be just an insurance policy. A scapegoat. Someone who would look good for all the terrible things Smart had done. Pell's angry and violent, and Smart would have seen that part of him early on. He probably saw it before anyone else, because a killer recognizes his reflection. When Pell started to go for Leon Spane, started pushing him around and making his life a misery, Smart saw an opportunity. I doubt whether Smart would have killed anyone by that stage, but he would have been thinking about it the whole time, it would have been consuming him, and Spane fitted the bill. He didn't have a home, didn't have a family, didn't have anyone who would miss him. And best of all, if people like me dug deep enough and found that CCTV footage of Pell being violent toward Spane—"

"You'd automatically suspect Pell, not Smart."

"Right."

I stopped, wondering whether to take it any further with Healy, whether it was even worth the effort, and then I realized it was worth the effort for me: I needed to get everything clear in my head, in some sort of order, and thinking aloud was the best way.

"Except Smart's first kill was a mess," I continued. "Everything about Spane was a mess. Nothing went to plan. There was none of the control or the finesse Smart showed with the other victims. He must have panicked after killing Spane, which was why he dumped him."

"Why'd he chop his dick off?"

I thought about it. "Maybe he was working out his frustration and his anger on Spane; he probably blamed him for it all going wrong. Or maybe it was more symbolic than that. In a lot of ways, I imagine Smart is like Sam: he's in denial about who he really is, and when he cut off the penis, he was taking away what made Spane a man."

"But then he went back to the drawing board."

"Right. After that, he planned it all out. He was meticulous, patient, determined not to make the same mistakes. He probably spent weeks following the men around after spotting them on the Circle line. He'd initiate conversation by pretending to check their tickets and, from there, I assume he'd start watching them, seeing who they were, their lifestyles, their routes, and then slowly begin to reappear around them. They'd have believed it was all by accident. But he wasn't bumping into them by accident: he was getting them to warm to him."

"How did he even know if they were gay or not?"

"He didn't. Couldn't. He just showed incredible patience. There must have been countless failures, men who caught his eye and turned out *not* to be homosexual, or proved too difficult to get at. But once he zeroed in on the viable ones—Wilky, Erion, Symons and Drake—he worked his way into their lives and then dragged them off into the night. And he didn't dump them this time. He kept them. Or, at the very least, he hid them somewhere deep."

"What about Erion?"

"What about him?"

"He was as risky as Wren."

"You mean because he worked for Adrian Wellis?" He didn't reply, but I knew that's where he was headed. I could sense a reticence in him to get involved, but at the same time he'd worked hard for these answers, and now he wanted to know how it all fitted together just like I did. "Wellis operated a policy of meeting potential clients face to face the first time," I said, letting it unfold. "He liked to know who he was dealing with so he knew where to drop the shitstorm if something went wrong. That was a major problem for Smart, so as soon as Smart chose Erion, he knew he'd have to deal with Wellis at some point because Wellis had seen his face, however fleetingly."

In front of me, traffic slowed to a crawl. It was all coming together now.

"When Smart saw me the first time I went to Gloucester Road, he probably worked out the worst-case scenario there and then: that I'd get to Wellis through Sam, which I did, and I'd eventually get to the man who'd taken Erion. As long as Wellis was alive, Smart was compromised, so he put a plan into place: he somehow got to Wellis in the days after he slipped from my grasp at the warehouse, and he lured him down to the line at Westminster. Persuaded him it was a safe haven, a place he could hide. Then he killed him and dumped his body there, somewhere no one would go or even think to look."

I expected some kind of reaction from Healy. But I got nothing.

"Are you okay, Healy?"

"And Wren?" came the response. "Smart set him up too."

"The message on the phone only came much later. By then he knew I was looking into Sam, and he'd started to panic again. The wheels had already been set in motion with Pell—he worked with him, had begun to move himself into Pell's line of sight, had seen the potential for violence in Pell—so Smart kept at it, placing Spane's coat and a set of knives at Pell's house; and then the DVDs of Pell with the girl. Smart must have realized that Pell's connection to the girl, and to the other prostitutes he'd used, would eventually lead back to Wellis, which was just another way for Smart to insulate himself. But Sam remained a problem. That was why the phone was so clumsy, why it never felt right. Smart recorded the message in desperation, hoping it would lead away from him."

"So I was wrong," Healy said, in a soft, stilled way I'd never heard before. I'd never heard him admit to a mistake in all the time I'd known him.

"Wrong about what?"

"I said the message wasn't recorded under duress."

"It wasn't, at least in the traditional sense. Smart didn't put a gun to Sam's head. All he had to do was pump Sam full of drugs and get him to read from a cue card. If he could walk them out against their will, Smart could also get them to say what he wanted. You remember what you said to me about that message on Drake's phone?"

"No emotion in his voice. Just empty words." I heard a deep intake of breath and then a sigh crackled down the phone line. "But why take Wren from the train? Smart had a foolproof MO. Why change it?"

I didn't have an answer, just another theory. "Maybe he became consumed by Sam for some reason."

"Consumed?"

"Obsessed." I shrugged. "Thing is, though, if Smart first saw Sam on the Circle line like he did with the others, then he would have followed him and found out—as soon as Sam got home—that he was married. Smart's thing, the thing that gets him off, is gay men. He wouldn't have known Sam was gay, not from his daily . . ." I trailed off, a memory stirring.

"What?" Healy said.

My mind moved back three days to my meeting with Robert Wren and then to the conversation Healy and I had in the coffee shop at Shepherd's Bush. Healy had accused me of being too invested in Sam as a person, of not being able to see the killer in him. But there had never been a killer in him. The lies he told were the lies I knew about. And he hadn't been lying when he'd talked to his brother about the night he met Marc Erion. *He said the guy lived in this place where there were no lights,* Robert Wren had told me. *He said he got to his door, on to the floor this guy was on, and all the bulbs were out.* We knew why the lights were out. Smart had been through the building a couple of nights before taking Erion, creating cover for himself. *And when he got to the flat,* Robert Wren had told me, *Sam said it felt like someone was there in the corridor with him.*

"The first time Smart saw Sam was at Erion's flat."

"How d'you figure that?"

"Something Robert Wren said to me." I paused, trying to line everything up. "Robert Wren said Sam went to see Erion on 11 November. Erion was taken on 13 November. Two days later. By then, Smart had already taken the lights out in Erion's building, and he was doing the last of his recon. When he saw Sam come up to the door of the flat, he liked the look of him immediately. Perhaps, given the risks he took to get him, liked the look of him more than any of the others. And because Sam had come to see a male prostitute, Smart assumed he was gay. So Sam wasn't part of the plan. But as soon as Smart saw him, he *made* him a part of it.

"He was different from the others: he lived with someone, he didn't live in the anonymity of a tower block, there was no way Smart could knock out lights in Sam's street and then walk him out without anyone seeing. So he had to come up with another idea. He would have known about the protests on 16 December, he would have foreseen the risks, but what risk there was in taking Sam from the train was reduced by the chaos of the protests. He must have got on at Gloucester Road, stayed close to Sam and then used the first opportunity that came his way. With or without the fight on the platform, he would have done it. But the fight just made it all much simpler."

"Yeah, but why not just take Wren outside on the street? That time of year, it's dark early, lots of shadow and cover. Much easier than from the inside of a carriage."

"But Smart knew the Circle line intimately."

"So?"

"So maybe, to him, the train *was* less risky than outside on the street. Or maybe he was just watching Sam that day, with no actual plan to take him, and then the fight kicked off and he saw his chance. Or maybe . . . I don't know, maybe it was symbolic."

"How do you mean?"

"Something to do with his father. Some connection to the trains."

The conversation died away and I hit traffic lights at the top of Heath Street, as it forked into Hampstead High Street. Rain chattered away against the roof of the car. The wipers whined back and forth across the glass. People passed along the pavements under umbrellas. And in that time, all I got from Healy was silence.

"I'm almost here."

No reply.

"Are you going to meet me at Smart's?" I asked him, and realized how prophetic this moment was. The October before, we'd ended up hunting the same man together. Now we were doing it again, as if we were bound to one another somehow. Two sides of the same coin. At the beginning, I'd always thought I was on the other side to Healy. Now I was starting to wonder if we weren't the same: built for the same reason, to hunt the same monsters. I glanced at the phone again as nothing came back but silence. "Healy? Are you going to meet me?"

"I can't do that," he said.

"Fine. Then you need to call Craw and tell her—"

"I'm not calling Craw."

"You need to tell her what's happening, Healy."

"It's too late for that."

"What are you talking about?"

He sniffed. Cleared his throat. *Is he crying?*

"Healy?"

"She fired me this morning," he said, and there was so much pain in his voice, it was like an electrical current traveling down the line. "They found out what I was doing."

"Oh, shit."

"So she fired me."

"I'm so sorry, Healy."

Silence.

"Where are you now?" I asked. Faintly, in the background of wherever he was, I could hear rain and the distant sound of people's voices getting louder and then fading.

"It doesn't matter."

"Where are you, Healy?"

"It doesn't matter any more."

"Don't go and do anything stupid."

A pause. "It's too late for that now."

And then he hung up.

71

Healy killed the call to Raker, flipped shut his phone and dumped it on to the passenger seat of the car. It was raining. A couple walked by, umbrella up, arms locked together, and then his eyes moved across the street to Teresa Reed's house. It was time. There was nothing to stop him any more. No future. Nothing to get up for, nothing to come home to. He had no job, a wife who hated him and sons who never answered his calls. He reached into the pocket of his jacket and took out the photo of Leanne, tracing the lines of her face, his finger moving across the creases and bumps of the picture. "He won't get away with it, baby," he said quietly, a deep, guttural sadness welling in the pit of his stomach.

I've got nothing else now.

Just you, Leanne.

When Teresa Reed answered the door, she broke out into a smile, came forward and kissed him. "How are you today, hun?" she said, touching her hand to his. "I didn't expect to see you so early." She looked at her watch. "I thought you were going to call."

"Something came up at work."

She eyed him. "Is everything okay?"

"Fine."

"Well, I've just put some coffee on."

He followed her into the house, through a hallway full of ornaments and ornate junk. He hated her taste. In the kitchen, she stood at the counter and finished putting some of the dishes away, talking about what she'd done on her day off. He barely even listened. All he could think about was what he was going to do next. About Leanne. About how he was going to avenge her death.

And about the gun tucked into the back of his trousers.

"You remember what I asked you?" he said to her, still standing in the doorway of the kitchen, rain running off his jacket. "About coming with you to the prison one day?"

She looked at him. "You mean watching me talk to the prisoners?"

"Yeah."

"I spoke to my boss about it after you asked," she said, taking two cups out of the cupboard, "but he wasn't massively keen on the idea. Sorry, hun."

"Why?"

"I think he's just worried it might aggravate the men." She smiled. "I've only been seeing them seven months. That's no time at all. I don't want to upset the equilibrium because, slowly, I'm starting to gain their trust. But there's also the problem that some of them see prison guards and cops—people like you—as the reason they're inside in the first place."

"That *is* the reason they're inside."

"I know. But it might promote negative feelings in them."

"They're rapists and murderers."

Teresa Reed paused, as if she'd glimpsed something in Healy that she hadn't seen before. "I know what they are."

"Are you sure?"

She frowned. "What's that supposed to mean?"

"What about Broadmoor?"

"What about it?"

"You talk to the prisoners there as well."

"So?"

"So, I'd like to go with you there."

She shook her head, her defenses up. "No way. It's a high-security hospital, Colm. We're talking about deeply disturbed patients. I can maybe talk to my boss again about letting you come along to Belmarsh with me, if that's what you really want. I know you say you just want to watch me at work, but if we concoct some story about you using it as a research trip for the Met, Belmarsh might sign off the—"

"I don't want to go to Belmarsh any more."

"Sorry?"

"I can get inside Belmarsh any time I want. I've been doing it five months already. I've been watching you talk to those men since January. I don't need to see their faces up close. They're not what I want."

"What do you mean, 'watching me since January'?"

"Belmarsh isn't what I want. Broadmoor is."

"What are you talking about?"

He studied her, the silence in the kitchen deafening. "Belmarsh was just a stepping stone. The thing to make you trust me. If you'd watched me go in there, take notes, look interested as you laughed and smiled and batted your eyelids at the rapists and the killers and the worthless fucking scumbags you call patients, I knew I could get you to take me to Broadmoor too. I didn't care how long it took, but at some point I thought you'd trust me enough to arrange it." He stopped. "But then I got fired today."

Her face dropped. Confusion. Fear. "I don't, uh . . ."

"So now nothing matters any more."

"Colm, I—"

He sighed, taking a step into the kitchen. He could feel the gun at the back of his trousers, shifting against the belt. "Do you know who you talk to up at Broadmoor?"

She backed up against the counter. "Talk to?"

"Your 'patients.'"

"I, uh . . . I talk to a lot of—"

"I'm only interested in one of them. The one who killed my daughter." A shiver of emotion passed through him. "And I don't care how you get it done, but you're the one that's going to take me to him."

PART FIVE

72

Rain swept in as I parked about fifty yards down from Smart's house, puddles forming in the gutters, leaves and crisp packets washing along the street. I grabbed my phone and got put through to Craw again, and while it just rang and rang the same as before, this time it went to voicemail. "DCI Craw, it's David Raker." I looked at Smart's house. It was a narrow two-story terrace, half-painted, half-brick, with a terra-cotta tile roof and white window frames. "Forget Sam Wren and Duncan Pell. The guy you're looking for is called Edwin Smart." I gave her the address. "I'm up here now, on my own, because you fired Healy and Davidson didn't want to hear what I had to say. I hope it hasn't cost you."

As soon as I hung up, I went through the same names again. Davidson. Healy. Craw for a second time. None answered. So I opted for the last resort: I dialed 999, gave them the details and told them to get Craw's team to come urgently. After I was done, I sat in the silence of the car, eyes glued to the house.

Minutes passed.

You're wasting time.

I glanced at myself in the rearview mirror. If I went in alone, I went in blind. I didn't know what it was like in there. I didn't know anything about Smart, beyond what I'd been able to pick up at the station. But that information was worthless now.

It was a lie, and he was a mystery.

So are you going in alone?

I flicked a look at the clock in the car. Another two minutes had passed. Soon it would be three minutes, then four, then five. Then it would be ten, and fifteen, and twenty—and every one of those minutes was a head start he shouldn't have had.

It's suicide going in blind.

But then I suddenly thought of Liz, of everything she'd said to me the day before. *This is who you are. This is what you do. I get it. But remember something: this is my life now too.* She was right. She'd always been right. If I was a different man, if I was a little better, perhaps I would have listened. Perhaps I would have been able to stop myself.

But I wasn't that man.

And Sam Wren was the only thing that mattered.

Water poured down my face, through my hair and ran off my jacket as I stepped up to the door. I didn't ring the bell. I didn't knock either. As much as possible, I wanted to avoid letting him know I was here. But when I grabbed the door handle, it bumped away from the frame, opening on to a small, tidy hallway. I immediately felt a prickle of unease. *Why would he leave his front door open?* I stopped, halfway in, halfway out, wondering if this was the right thing, after all. But I had no choice. I'd rung the police and they'd failed to act.

The hallway was carpeted in an old-fashioned maroon, but the walls were cream, hung with pictures of meadows and black-and-white photographs of old steam trains. On the left was a staircase, on the right a door into a living room. Same maroon carpet, same cream walls. A TV, two sofas, more paintings, more photos of trains. As I stepped further in, the carpet like a sponge beneath my wet boots, I saw brass-framed pictures of a young Smart looking drawn and emotionless: one in front of a Tube roundel, another outside the entrance of a station, the picture scorched by bright summer sun. Next to that was a picture of his father in the uniform of the London Underground, a ten- or eleven-year-old Smart at his leg. The photos were lined up on the coffee table, one after the other, all of them black and white, all of them the same theme, except the last one, which was in color.

This one was on its own.

It sat away from the others, on the edge of the table, and in front of it was a wooden bowl, placed there like an offering. It was full of hair. I took another step closer. In the photo, Smart was sitting on a chair beside a hospital bed, his father—mask over his face, mobile oxygen tank at his feet—beside him. The old man, stick-thin and shaven-headed, looked like he had hours left. But it wasn't that that drew my attention. It was what his father was wearing: a red T-shirt, with checked sleeves.

The shirt had belonged to him.

That's why it had been so important to Smart, why he'd had it with him today. And it must have been why he'd worn it the day he took Sam. Not only because it was red and he would merge with the other protesters, although that would have been in his thinking, but because it was another part of his routine, like the shaved head. A connection to his father. And the hair in the bowl—presumably Smart's hair—was the other. He hadn't been shaved at the station earlier, so this was fresh. The second part of the routine. The way he remembered his father—became like him, channeled him—on the anniversary of his death.

Behind me the front door was still open, rain slapping against the driveway and running off the porch roof. I left it like that, realizing the sound would disguise my movement inside the house, even if it immediately let him know I was here. I moved up the stairs. At the top was a small landing area with three doors: two bedrooms, one bathroom. Everything was neat and tidy, but old-fashioned—like a time capsule—and I wondered whether this had been his father's place.

I paused. Listened.

All I could hear was the rain hammering against the glass at the upstairs windows and hitting the steps at the front of the house. But as I moved around, checking hiding places, making sure he wasn't upstairs, I heard a voice.

I stopped in the center of Smart's bedroom and felt the silence settle around me. Beyond the rain there was nothing now: the faint sound of a car somewhere, a beep of a horn. I must have heard one of his neighbors. Except, as I moved back downstairs, the house creaking around me, as if shifting and changing shape, I started to feel a nagging sense that it wasn't one of his neighbors I'd heard, but someone much closer.

Pausing in the hallway, I looked back out through the front door at the deserted street, then into the living room, then on to the kitchen ahead of me. I primed myself, feeling my muscles tense, and edged forward. The kitchen was empty. I looked to the front door again, and turned back to the kitchen. A small, pokey L-shaped unit, wood painted white, with pale green worktops like beds in a hospital ward. A toaster. A pot of utensils. Some spices in metal jars. *Where the hell is he?* Directly to my left, two steps led down to a sunken office, empty except for a cheap-looking computer desk, a PC connected to a modem and a blue chair with four wheels.

Beyond that, on the far side, was the back door.

I took in the kitchen again. Over the sink was a window, looking out over a small garden. I moved across to it, the wet soles of my boots making a faint squeak on the lino. The garden was narrow but long. At the other end were a row of high trees, thick growth—weeds and long grass—clawing at their trunks. On the other side of the trees, partially visible through holes in the canopy, was the old line at Fell Wood. As rain and wind passed through, branches moved and opened up spaces in the leaves, and—on the other side—I saw a tall, cream-colored structure I recognized.

The ventilation shaft on top of the Tube station.

I stepped away and, as I did, a smell drifted toward me, a mix of metal and old dishcloths. The kitchen seemed pretty clean, the worktops wiped down, no food out, no crumbs even, but the longer I stood there, the stronger the odor got. I started opening up the kitchen cupboards one by one, trying to locate the smell, but despite all the things Smart was, all the terrible suffering he'd wrought, he'd managed to build a convincing lie. Everything spoke of normality. In the corner was the fridge, humming gently. And then my eyes happened to fall on the slim gap between the fridge and the wall.

There was a key, taped to the wall.

I reached in and ripped it off. It was a small brass Yale key, marked with a single red dot. I flipped it over, hoping to find some clue as to what it was for, when the smell came again. Less metal, more rot: maybe not wet dishcloths. Or maybe not *only* that.

Pocketing the key, I headed down into the office and across to the back door. I tried the key, but it didn't fit. Then I realized it didn't matter anyway: like the front door, the back was unlocked. My nerves were immediately put on edge. I swiveled, facing back across the office, but no one was there. No sound from the house. And as the wind rushed past me, drawn along the hallway from one door to the next, I noticed a tiny stain on the carpet, an irregular drip pattern running from the steps, across toward the back door. Not much of it, but enough.

Dried blood.

He'd tried to wash it out of the carpet, but had either given up or failed to see it all. I looked out through the door, seeing if there was any more, but if it had once carried on, out to the patio and across the lawn, it had been washed away by the rain. Yet the blood on the carpet seemed to be leading *out* of the empty house.

In the direction of the station.

73

There was a small gap in the trees, leading from Smart's garden to the line. As I emerged on to the path, about forty yards from the overground platform and the Tube station adjacent to it, the sound seemed to drop away. The patter of rain against leaves. A faint wind, whispering past me. Nothing else. As I stood there, a strange feeling of loneliness formed in me, as if I was miles from anywhere safe.

Moving to the platform, I reached up and dragged a piece of glass toward me. It was jagged but sharpened to a point, its surface creamy and coated with dirt. Removing a tissue from my pocket, I wrapped it around the end to avoid cutting myself, and headed for the path to the Tube station entrance.

At the top of the concrete steps, I paused.

I was drenched, water running off my face, soaking into my clothes, but I could hardly even see it on myself the light was fading so fast. I reached into my pocket and activated the torch function on my phone—then used it to illuminate the path down.

I could feel dirt and masonry crunch beneath my boots as I took the steps two at a time, light dancing off the walls, rain fading behind me as I entered the building. Once I was inside, the relentlessness of the dark made me pause, almost surprised me, even though I'd walked this same route two days before. I stepped further in and as I did it was as if something woke. A sound, like a voice, seemed to pass from one side of the ticket hall to the other, and all that remained was a chill; a coolness which sent goosebumps scattering up my arms and across my body. I swung the phone around the room, letting it settle on the space next to the ticket office.

The stairs down to the staffroom.

I shifted the shard of glass in my hand, holding it like a blade, realizing that I'd allowed myself to be drawn into this situation too quickly. *I should have gone through Smart's knife drawer, not grabbed some makeshift piece of window.* But it was too late now. I was here. I'd been quiet on my approach, had made hardly any sound at all, but if Smart was clever enough to avoid detection for a year and a half, he was clever enough to take advantage of any uncertainty. When I got to the door, I wrapped my fingers around the old, wrought-iron handle and stopped, just for a second, to prepare myself.

Then I opened it.

The smell was worse than I remembered, a deep, awful stench of decay that came up the stairs toward me and forced me back. I put a hand to my mouth and looked down into the dark, and it took everything I had not to turn around and walk out. *Except you can't leave. You can't leave before bringing them back into the light.* I felt air pass me at ankle level, icy cold, and as my mind started turning over, and I started to imagine what might be waiting, I realized it wasn't completely silent: there was a soft noise, like a buzz. It sounded vaguely like electricity being pumped through the walls of the station.

Except it wasn't electricity.

It was flies.

I started the descent. Halfway down, short of the curve in the stairwell, I felt an insect bump against my face, dozy in the airless room below. Another passed across the light of the phone, drifting in and out of its blue glow, and—as I got to the turn in the stairs—I could see more on the walls and ceiling. The smell was unbearable now, even with my hands at my face; a thick, tangy stink. And as the stairs came to an end and I stepped down on to the floor of the room, I saw why.

As I swung the torch around to my left, to where the counter had once stood, there was a slumped figure beneath it.

He was facing me, sitting up, his back against the wall, his head—though angled to one side—almost touching the counter. His feet were straight out in front of him. Above his mouth, in the space where his nose and one of his eyes should have been, was what remained. Mostly it was just a mess of blood and skin, the shotgun that had done the damage wedged between his thighs, one of his hands half caught in the trigger. The other side of his face was intact: an ear, a cheek, half a jaw, some of his freshly shaved head. On the floor next to him were a series of photographs: a Tube train pulling into an overground station; a boy eating on a platform; the same boy, much younger than before, with an ice cream; and an old man, his father, captured in black and white. Then, finally, clutched in his other hand, his fingers balled around it, was the red T-shirt with checked sleeves.

Edwin Smart.

74

I crouched down and glanced at Smart; at what was left of his head. It was featureless, the skin that was left like wallpaper falling away, the rest just a mess of blood and brain. Spatter fanned out in a semicircle above him, suggesting he'd put both barrels against the roof of his mouth. Stepping away, I moved to the stairs. In front of me, without the light from the phone, there was nothing but dark. I turned the display in my hand and started moving up. As I entered the ticket hall, I could see a square of light on the far side—the entrance—but either side of it, all around it, there was nothing but black.

A brief feeling passed through me, a strange, cognizant shiver, as if some part of me was sending out a warning, and I swung the light, left to right. When I did it a second time, I realized something: as I looked across to my right where the lift remained padlocked, the metal grate pulled across it, I saw a mark—a red dot—on the padlock, facing out toward me. I felt around in my pockets for the key I'd taken from Smart's kitchen.

A matching red dot.

Is the lift shaft where he dumped the bodies?

I thought for a minute about opening up, because if this was where he'd put them, somehow it felt wrong to leave the bodies there, in the darkness, for any longer—but then I realized it probably dropped eighty feet, and if it was dark in the ticket hall, it was going to be even darker in the well of the lift. The police needed to handle it.

So I headed out.

Halfway up the concrete steps, I stopped again.

Footprints.

Mine were in the middle, right through the center of the steps. These were off to the side, in a rough diagonal, from left to right. I hadn't noticed them on the way down, but, when I got to the top of the stairs, I could see them clearly: wet prints, size eleven or twelve, a mix of mud from the line, and dust from inside the station. They were fresh. I could see a route in, and—just adjacent to that—I could see the person's route out. I quickly moved through the undergrowth and on to the line.

No more footprints.

Heading back to the house, through the treeline, and into Smart's garden, I saw the back door was still open, swinging gently in the breeze. Inside I stopped, edging across the office and looking in through the kitchen. Even without seeing it, I could hear that the front door was still open, wind passing through the house. I headed along the hallway. There was nothing out of place, no sign anyone had been inside, so I pushed the front door shut, softly bedding it in its frame, then returned to the rear of the house and did the same to the back door. The noise of rain faded instantly, restricted only to the windows, where it swirled in against the glass.

Suddenly the silence shattered as my phone started ringing.

I killed it instantly.

Waited.

I backed up against the kitchen counter, trying to give myself the best view of both the office and the hallway, and then a text came through. I looked down at the display. I didn't recognize the number, but I knew instantly who it was from. Craw. *Got your message. On our way. DON'T do anything stupid.*

I dropped the phone back into my pocket. *Too late for that.* I padded through to the stairs, taking them two at a time all the way up. Paused on the landing. The rooms were empty, but I double-checked to be sure, then headed back down into the kitchen. Smart was dead. Sam and the others were probably at the bottom of a lift shaft. Which meant there was only one person unaccounted for.

Duncan Pell.

Then it came again. That same smell as earlier.

What is *that?*

I dropped to my haunches and started going through the cupboards again, seeing if there was anything collecting mold, any spilled liquids or rotting food. But Smart had kept his home in decent condition. I couldn't put a finger on the odour, couldn't quite define it in my head, but the closest I could get was the same as before: old dishcloths. That smell you got when they were screwed up into a ball and left, still stained with food and soaked with water, never quite drying, the odour just getting stronger. It wasn't unbearable, just unpleasant.

I closed the door beneath the sink, got up and walked around the kitchen, running a hand along the edge of the worktop as I moved from one side to the other.

And then I felt something beneath my boot.

I looked down. A slight indentation in the floor, the size of a beer mat, about two feet in from the skirting boards. I prodded it with the toe of my boot. There was something in the middle of it: a bump. I leaned down, running a hand across it, and then—in my peripheral vision— noticed something else: the lino in the corner of the room hadn't been set properly. It was curling up, as if it hadn't been stuck down.

Or it had been placed back in a hurry.

I went through Smart's knife drawer and picked out an old-fashioned potato peeler. Using the V-shaped end, I forced it down into the corner of the room, where the lino met the skirting board, and prized the lino away. It came out easily. I grabbed a handful of it and then pulled it back with me, edging across the kitchen. It unfurled like a layer of skin, peeling slowly away, revealing wooden floorboards underneath. The smell was stronger now, and I realized why: the floorboards had been wiped down, cleaned of whatever had spilled across them, but when the lino had been placed back on top, the floorboards hadn't been dry. Despite that, despite the swipes left on their surface by the cloth, they were still in immaculate condition, oak panels laid perfectly from one side of the room to the other. Except for one square the size of a beer mat.

In that space was a flip-up handle.

Under the lino was a trapdoor.

75

The only thing that gave the game away was the handle itself, cut into a space about two inches deep, and then a thin line running in a square—about two feet across by the same long—which marked out the edges of the trapdoor. The trapdoor was finished in the same oak boards as the rest of the room. I dropped down, gripping the handle as tightly as I could, and opened it.

The door locked at ninety degrees, on a hinge. Inside I could see a concrete staircase dropping down into the dark. Once the shadows sucked up the uneven steps and the crumbling stone walls, there was nothing else.

Just black.

I got up and looked around the kitchen for a torch, figuring he'd need one if this was where he'd been keeping them, and—after some searching—found one right at the back of the cupboard under the sink. It was black and rubberized, its casing marked with dust. I flicked it on and directed it down into the darkness. Further down, I could see part of the wall at the bottom of the stairs. It was covered in what looked like black egg cartons.

Soundproofing.

I felt a stir of disquiet, the cone of torchlight unable to illuminate anything else in the room below. Then I started down.

After five steps, my head level with the kitchen floor, I felt a subtle change in temperature, as if I was stepping into a freezer. There was a faint draft coming in from somewhere, and the distant sound of dripping, but nothing else. Once I was completely immersed, the kitchen just a square of light above me, I stopped and directed the torch down, into the spaces in front of me. It was a basement. Concrete floors, completely unfurnished. It was difficult to tell how big in the dark, but it must have been the length and width of the house. Every so often there were brick pillars—thick columns holding the building up—and attached to one of them I saw a metal plate flecked with rust, and a chain coming off to a pair of shackles. The shackles had a red dot on them. The same as the key from the kitchen. The key had never been for the lift shaft, just as the bodies had never been dumped there. It had all been a lie; an attempt to confuse.

I carried on down, pausing at the bottom.

Now I could smell something. Something worse than damp. I placed a foot on to the basement floor and slowly moved the torch from right to left. The beam glided past the mid-section of the room and—a split second later—something registered with me.

I moved it back.

In the darkness, barely illuminated by the torch, I saw something shift. I edged further in, keeping the beam high and my eyes fixed on the shadows. I passed one pillar, and then another. The second had started crumbling around its middle and, when I stopped for a moment, I could see why: it also had a metal plate and a chain attached to it—as well as another red dot on the shackles—just like the one close to the staircase. But this one had become almost detached from the wall.

As if someone had been pulling at it.

I felt a shiver pass through my chest, my body sounding an alarm, and then I refocused the torch on the shape.

It was a man.

He was on his side, ankle chained to a metal plate on the back wall, facing me but with his head tucked into the bend of his elbow. He was shivering. There were no marks on him, or at least none I could see. I dropped to my haunches and directed the torchlight away from him, off to the side where it wouldn't be directly on him.

And I saw someone else.

Another man.

This one was also chained to the back wall, about seven feet further on. He wasn't moving. I got to my feet, took a sideways step, and picked him out properly. There were bruises all over him, and it looked like his wrist might be broken. His arm was out in front of him, his hand a deep purple, angled away unnaturally. When my torch passed across his face, there was nothing in his eyes. No reaction. No color. I recognized him instantly from the files Healy had shown me: Joseph Symons, the third Snatcher victim. He wasn't dead, but he didn't have long: I could see the soft rise and fall of his stomach, bones showing through his broken skin, and there was dried blood all over his groin.

Like Leon Spane, Smart had removed his penis.

I covered my mouth, nausea rising in my throat, and swung the torch back around to the man in front of me, trying to concentrate on anything but Symons. The man moved slightly, out of the crook of his elbow, his head propped on the upper part of his arm.

It was Jonathan Drake.

He gazed right at me, eyes distant, as if the fight had been beaten out of him. But he didn't move, even though—for all he knew—I could have been Smart. I inched closer, using the torch to paint him in a soft yellow glow. On his back there were bruises everywhere, most either side of his spine.

"Jonathan?"

Something sparked in his eyes.

"My name's David Raker. I'm here to get you out, okay?"

He blinked. Whimpered.

"He's not going to hurt you again."

Drake shifted on the floor, coming toward me, but the chain locked into place at his ankle. I held out a hand, moving closer, and gently touched him on the shoulder. He flinched. He wasn't in as bad a state as Symons—physically at least—but then Symons had been missing since 28 February. Almost four months. Drake had been missing six days. He'd suffered, but not like Symons.

"It's okay. No one's going to . . ."

And then I saw the rest.

They were off to my left, in the opposite direction, chained to metal plates lined up on the outer wall. Some at the ankles, some at the wrists. There was about ten feet between each of them, and—when I could bear to look—I realized Smart had taken something from each of their bodies, just like he'd done with Symons. The one closest to me I knew straight away from the photo of him I'd seen in his file: Steven Wilky. When my torch caught his face, nothing came back; just a glazed stillness, his body curled up in the foetal position, his skin almost translucent, veins showing through like a road map.

Beyond him it got worse: the tiny figure of a man—a boy, really—head shaved, both hands locked together like he was praying. As I left Drake and inched through the darkness, past Wilky and on to the boy, I knew—even before I got to him—that it was Marc Erion. He was tiny and incredibly thin. Just bones. No fat at all.

I swallowed hard, and directed the torchlight beyond Erion to the other two bodies. Both were naked and shaved. Nearest to me, a man was half sitting up at the wall, arm attached to a metal plate above him. His breathing was soft and moist, like there might be blood in his lungs, and there were deep cuts all across his chest, his face beaten to a pulp.

But I knew who it was. On the middle finger of his right hand was a silver ring with a rune on it.

Pell.

They'd never been working together. Pell had been nothing more to Smart than another victim. Another piece of misdirection. I'd been chasing Pell, thinking he was the Snatcher, while the real killer had him locked up in his basement with five other men.

I took another step forward.

Beyond Pell was the last of them. Like the others, he was naked, every inch of him shaved, but there was no blood on him. No bruising. He was thin, drawn, but while he was chained at the ankle, Smart had made an effort to keep him pristine, as if he saw him as something better. Something special. Something worth taking a risk over.

I'd found Samuel Wren.

Five minutes later the house was crawling with police and forensics. Craw made me give my account of what happened, of all the events leading up to the point at which we found ourselves, and then asked me to wait in the semi-darkness of the living room, surrounded by photographs of Smart's father, and Smart as a boy. After an hour—after she'd been to the old Underground station, and down into the basement of the house—she came in, sat down and said nothing. We could both hear Davidson in the kitchen, telling someone to be careful with evidence, and when I looked at Craw I saw a kind of resignation in her, as if she was sick of this case, and maybe sick of her job. Men like Smart were a reset button: you thought you'd seen everything that people were capable of doing to one another, and then someone like him came along and you realized there was always someone worse.

I traced Smart's face in one of the nearest photographs. There was nothing unique about him. He was just a man. No distinguishing features. Nothing to make your eyes linger on him as he passed you. And that was what had made him so effective.

"Do you think he was trying to misdirect us?" she asked.

"With what?"

"With the padlock on the lift shaft. Marking it with a red dot like that."

I looked at her. "Are you asking for my input now?"

She smiled, and nodded to herself as if she understood my position. "You know, you and your friend Healy are very well suited, even if you don't see it."

"He's not my friend."

"And yet you like him."

I shrugged. "I like some parts of him, but mostly he just wears me out."

"Yes." She smiled again, a small movement. "He does have that ability."

"Is he definitely gone?"

She eyed me, but didn't seem surprised I knew Healy had been fired. "Yes," she said, "he's definitely gone. He went against protocol, broke the law and left me to clean up the mess. He's a liar, and I can't trust him."

I didn't say anything.

"You don't know all the details, Mr. Raker."

"David's fine."

"You don't know all the details, David."

"I don't expect I do."

"He deserved to go."

I met her gaze. "Then why are we still talking about him?"

She just nodded.

After a long silence, I said, "This isn't how it normally goes for you."

"How do you mean?"

"You understand people, what makes them tick, what makes them do the things they do. But you didn't get Smart, and you don't get Healy."

"And you do?"

"No. I never saw Smart coming, and Healy . . ." I paused. Shrugged. "I think I know him and then he does something stupid and I realize I don't know him at all."

"Then I guess we can agree on something."

"I guess we can."

Craw looked at the photos of Smart. "What is it with you?" she said.

"With me?"

"Come on, David, don't be coy. You know what I mean. How is it you always end up in these places, chasing down these men? How is it you always get here before us?"

I frowned. "Are you accusing me of something?"

"No. But you have a knack."

You don't know when to stop. Maybe it was as simple as that. Or maybe it really was something more. Some kind of twisted destiny.

"I don't know," I said finally.

She nodded, as if she wasn't all that surprised by the answer. Then she reached to the breast pocket of her jacket and took out a notebook. "Just wait there a second, would you?" She didn't wait for my response, just got up and headed out of the living room. A couple of minutes passed. A murmur of conversation in the kitchen. Then she returned, this time flanked by Davidson and another cop, one I didn't recognize.

"David, you know DS Davidson," she said, gesturing to him. Davidson looked at me, sober, unreadable. "This is DC Richter. He's going to take some notes for me."

"Notes?"

"We want to ask you a few questions."

"I'll call my solicitor then."

"We're not arresting you for anything," she continued, sitting down opposite me. Davidson pulled a chair out from the table and dragged it all the way across the living room so he was facing me on my left. Richter sat down at the table. "We just want to fill in the blanks. You know Samuel Wren, you know Duncan Pell, you probably know more than we do about Edwin Smart. We're not too proud to engage the help of an expert."

"So you *are* asking for my input?"

"I'm not asking," she said.

She'd let her guard down when we'd been alone in the living room. Now she was playing up to the crowd. Or maybe this was just her natural state, and the person I'd been with moments before—softer and more transparent—was all part of the act.

I shrugged, an indication she could start.

"Given the level of your relationship with Colm Healy over the past eight months, and the fact that you were knee-deep in bodies when we turned up here, I'm going to assume you're up to speed on the Snatcher case."

"What *is* the level of my relationship with Healy?"

"I think we both know—"

"No, we don't," I said, making a point of looking at Davidson. "Don't put words in my mouth or lay actions at my feet when you don't have the first idea what you're talking about." I let that settle, silence in the room now, then turned to Craw: "The trouble with your task force, is that it's manned by people who have no interest in its aims."

She frowned. "What the hell do you mean by that?"

"You know what I mean," I said, and in the moments that followed I saw her flick a look toward Davidson. "I called Davidson an hour before I got to Smart's house, spoke to him on the phone, tried to tell him what was happening, and he hung up on me."

"That's bullshit," he said from beside me.

"Is it?"

"Of course it is. You're a fucking fantasist, Raker."

I looked at Craw. "I called him to tell him to come to the house and he didn't want to hear it. If you'd got here after I called him, you might have been able to swoop on Smart before he showered the walls of the station with his brains."

There was no comeback to that. Off to my right, Richter was watching me, pen hovering above the notebook. Craw looked across to him. "You actually going to write anything down?" The irritation was obvious in her voice. I wasn't sure whether it was with me or with Davidson. "What was Smart using that station for?"

"I don't know."

"Really?"

I shrugged. "Look at the photos in this room. He had an attachment to the Tube, and to the railways in general, so the building would have meant something to him. But it was practical too. He kept hunting equipment in there."

"So?"

"So maybe he started off killing animals before he moved on to killing men. A place like that, abandoned and locked up, no one's going to come calling."

"And Pell? Where does he fit in?"

"The best person to ask is Pell."

"Yeah, well, he's in an ambulance."

I shrugged. "I don't even really know him."

Davidson snorted, and looked from me to Craw. "This is a waste of time, ma'am. The guy doesn't know what's the truth and what's a lie any more."

I kept my eyes on Craw. "I told you everything I knew earlier."

"*Was* that everything?" she asked.

"Of course it wasn't," Davidson said, before I had a chance to respond. "If you read the file about what him and Healy got up to last year at those woods—"

"I don't care about last year, I care about now."

Davidson stared at her, obvious disgust in his face, and then started to shake his head, sinking back into his chair. Momentarily, Craw's emotions played out in her eyes. I didn't bother getting involved, but I got the sense that after this was all over, Davidson's future was going to be high on the agenda for her. Even Healy would have seen the irony in that: Davidson following him out the door, or following Sallows into semi-retirement on the south London beat, after they'd teamed up to get Healy kicked off the force.

"Mr. Raker?"

We were back to Mr. Raker now. Not David.

"Like I said, I don't know Pell that well. I know what he does for a living, know he's ex-army, realized pretty early on he had a violent streak a mile wide; and even if he wasn't the same type of killer as Smart, he'd killed on the battlefield and could do it again back home. Smart would have encouraged that side of him. He would have been manipulating Pell the whole time, working him up into a frenzy in order to position him exactly where he wanted."

"You sound like you admire him," Davidson muttered.

"I don't admire him. I think he's a piece of shit."

Now the only sound was Richter frantically making notes.

"What about Adrian Wellis?" Craw said.

"What about him?"

"His buddy's locked up and won't talk to us. That Romanian girl was found in his house. When you gave us a rundown earlier, you said Marc Erion worked for him, Pell used to get his women from him, and this squeaky-clean facade Wellis built for himself is a lie. So where is he?"

I looked at her, blank-faced.

"Mr. Raker?"

If I told her where Wellis was, where his body was dumped, I let her know that Healy had taken me down there with him and broken another rule, and maybe this time she would bring him back in and maybe this time he'd get charged. There were other dangers too. Any conversation about Wellis would eventually lead to his house, to when I'd found the girl and made the anonymous call to police, to when I'd tossed Wellis and Gaishe into the back of the BMW and driven them to the warehouse.

Healy was already gone from the Met, his reputation in the gutter, so the first problem didn't really matter much. But I wanted to insulate myself and perhaps, on some deeper level, wanted Craw to hurt too. The minute Davidson entered the room, Craw started putting her trust in cops who'd lost sight of their calling; who came into work to seek revenge, to play with lives, and ultimately to misunderstand the people they worked with. She could see Davidson's flaws a mile off, but she'd brought him here for one reason and one reason only: to get at me. Healy was flawed too, perhaps irredeemably so, but everything he'd done, all the mistakes he'd made, were at least for the right reason: for his daughter, for the child he lost. Somehow I felt Craw recognized that side of him, despite her officiousness, because she was probably a parent herself and could imagine what a parent is prepared to do. But men like Davidson and Sallows didn't, and that made her guilty by association.

"I don't know where Adrian Wellis is," I said.

Davidson sighed. "Do me a fucking favor."

"Why would I know where he is?"

"Are we really going to believe this shit?" he said to Craw.

"Why would I know?"

"Because you know everything about him and you made that call from Wel—" He stopped himself. Eyes flicked to Craw. *From Wellis's house.* Except Davidson was so caught up in deceit, in his and Sallows's mission to get to Healy, and to get to me, that he'd forgotten what he could talk about, and what he couldn't.

By bringing in my unauthorized help on an open case like the Snatcher, Healy had broken every rule in the book, and it had made an easy win for them; easy to present to Craw and impossible for her to defend. Davidson gave her the photos of Healy and me at the hospital, and Healy got the push. But whatever Davidson and Sallows were cooking up for me was also off the books. It was an investigation that hadn't been approved by Craw, involving one cop already discredited by her, and another she was increasingly having doubts about. The irony was they were like Healy: putting something together—and trying to bring someone down— outside of the rules they had to abide by.

"I made that call from where?" I said.

He looked at Craw again. "We can't trust him. We can't trust anything he says. Everything that comes out of his mouth is a fucking lie."

Craw said nothing, just stared across the room at him.

Finally she got up from her seat. "Let me show you something," she said to me, and gestured for me to follow her.

We moved along the route put in place by the scene-of-crime officer, through the kitchen and down to the office. A forensic tech was at the computer. Next to that, inside an evidence bag on the desk, was a letter, written on lined A4 paper. It was from Smart.

"Simon," Craw said to the tech, "would you give us a moment, please?"

The tech did as Craw asked, got up and disappeared.

She pointed to the evidence bag. "This was left in the drawer of the desk. Why don't you have a read?"

I moved in front of her and studied the letter. It was headed with yesterday's date, the writing untidy and spidery. The last outpourings of a dead man.

My name is Edwin Smart, he wrote. *I am the man who the media have labeled "the Snatcher." I feel like the walls are closing in now. I could stay ahead of the police, just about, but now I've got this other investigator to contend with, this Raker, and I think they're working together, and the more I try to cover up what I'm doing, the more I'm losing control.*

I heard Davidson enter the room behind us.

It's strange. Sometimes I don't feel much like a killer. Sometimes I just feel like Edwin Smart. Ed. That guy is the guy everyone likes, the one they tell stories to and share jokes with. Some days I look in the mirror and I see that guy looking back, and I forget—just for a moment—who I am. Other days, all I can feel inside me is this ache, this need, and I remember who I truly am. A man who takes other men. A man who wants to touch them and feel them. Hurt them. A man who tortures and rapes them while they're begging me to stop. What my father would call a queer. He hated them, but it was all an act. He used to come into my bedroom at night and touch me, used to make me take his dick out when I was barely even old enough to know what it was. He hated himself, just the same as I did—but it was him who made me this way.

The letter covered all of one side and a quarter of the other.

I turned it over.

I hate who I am, but I can't stop. I hate my father, but I still love him. I know I need to run, to get away from here, but I can't. Tomorrow, his anniversary, is too special.

I placed the letter back down again.

Smart was a vicious, sadistic killer but one who was, at his most clear-headed, completely self-aware. In many ways, it was as sad as it was frightening.

"A fucking screw-up, just like his dad," Davidson muttered from behind me. He moved in level with us. I glanced at Craw, but her eyes were fixed on the letter, as if she was determined not to give her feelings away. Davidson looked me up and down, as if I had no place being here. "You must be loving this," he said, loud enough so everybody could hear. "You can be a real cop for a day."

A ripple of laughter from somewhere in the kitchen.

He snorted. "You're a fucking amateur."

I looked him up and down. Unmoved.

He leaned in to me, ready to go again, when Craw turned to him. "DS Davidson, why don't you carry on with whatever you were doing?"

He stood there, the two of them facing off.

"Are you having trouble hearing me, Eddie?"

He glanced at me, then at her. "No, ma'am."

He disappeared back into the kitchen, and then she turned to me, nothing in her face—no sense as to whether Davidson had pissed her off or not—and she handed me a business card. "We're going to need a full statement from you in the next couple of days but, in the meantime, that's my direct number on there."

I took it from her. She looked at me, silence between us, and it was obvious the tough decisions of the next few days were already weighing heavy on her.

"I'll see you soon, Mr. Raker."

77

All six men—Steven Wilky, Marc Erion, Joseph Symons, Jonathan Drake, Sam Wren and Duncan Pell—made it as far as hospital alive. Symons and Erion were in the worst condition and, as doctors tried to rehydrate them and repair some of the damage left on their bodies, Symons slipped into cardiac arrest, as if the only thing that had kept him alive in Edwin Smart's basement was the lack of movement. He lasted another fifteen minutes, two of those a desperate attempt to revive him after he flatlined. But at just gone midnight, as I lay in bed across the city, unable to sleep, there was no more fight left in Joseph Symons and doctors pronounced him dead. The others clung on.

Doctors talked of the complications of the men's injuries, of amputations and skin grafts and transplants, and the long road to recovery. Drake was relatively unharmed, on the surface at least. In the days that followed, though, he recounted how he'd been raped, how Smart had taunted him in the dark, how he woke up some nights and could feel him there, in the basement, but never see him. He revealed a little of the last conversation he'd had with Smart—the *only* conversation of any note—where Smart had talked of his father, also called Jonathan, and what his father had turned him into.

"In that last conversation we had, before you found me, he started telling me about his upbringing," Drake told the police in his statement. "He said they used to call him 'Ed Case' at school because he was always in trouble. He said he got caned fourteen times once, because he told a teacher to fuck off." Drake had paused at that point. The detective taking his statement thought it was because it was becoming too emotional for him. But it wasn't that at all. It was that, just like I had after reading Smart's suicide note, Drake felt a strange kind of sorrow for Smart, a sorrow he was desperately trying to fight because of everything Smart had done to him. "He said he grew up without a mother; that she died when he was one, so his father brought him up. He said he sometimes wondered whether life might have turned out differently if his mother had lived."

Duncan Pell—never a victim like the others but, in a different way, manipulated by Smart as well—had been semi-conscious as they'd brought him out. When he got to hospital, Craw posted an officer outside his room. Pell and the police had a lot to talk about too, not just in terms of his involvement with Smart, but about who Smart was as a person. In order to close the case, the police would have to use Pell to fill in the blanks, and then—beyond that—they would start looking into the terrible things he'd done too.

Sam was in the best shape of all, although the term barely seemed appropriate to describe a man who'd been brutally assaulted, over and over, for the entire time he was missing. I headed down to the hospital after finishing at the Smart house, and saw Julia Wren briefly. I told her we'd catch up when the time was right. She thanked me but in her face I could see her mind was elsewhere, and I didn't blame her for that. Her husband had returned, six months after disappearing into thin air. All she had for him were questions, one on top of the other, but—given everything I'd found out about him; all the secrets he'd kept from her and from himself—I doubted whether his answers would ever bring her the comfort she sought.

A couple of nights later, with Sam still in hospital, she called me at home and we talked for a while. "He keeps saying sorry to me," she said, but I couldn't tell over the phone whether that made it better or worse for her.

"Where do you think you guys will go from here?" I asked.

"I don't know. I guess it's just one step at a time."

"I guess it is."

"I know he regrets what he's done. I just . . ." She paused. I thought I might know where the conversation was about to go, but I didn't jump in. "It just doesn't feel like I thought it would feel, having him back. Does that sound strange?"

"No," I told her. "That doesn't sound strange at all."

The question that would probably never be answered completely was why Smart had treated Sam differently from the others, and why he felt he was worth taking such a risk over. With Smart dead, there could only be more theories and more guesswork. But as I'd sat there in his living room after finding the basement, waiting for Craw to come through, I'd looked at the photographs Smart had left behind and seen something in them. In the way his father stood. In his blue eyes and fair hair. In his thin frame and the far-away look in his eyes, troubled and isolated. It was a picture that recalled the very first photograph Julia had ever shown me of Sam, standing there in front of a window, drained and ground down, a week before he disappeared. No one could know for sure, but maybe, in Sam, Smart saw the man he loved and hated like no other. And maybe, by taking a man who looked like his father, in a place he'd once worked, dressed in the T-shirt his father had worn at the end, Smart thought he could get closer to him than at any point since he'd died.

By the time I got home after leaving Craw and the Snatcher team working their way through Smart's house, it was almost 10:30 and, next door, Liz's house was dark. I checked my phone for messages, knowing that there wasn't one from her, then went through my e-mail as well, knowing the same was true there. Once I'd showered and changed, I sat at the counter in the kitchen and thought about texting her, but couldn't find the right words—and, in some part of me, I wasn't sure if I'd mean them anyway.

An hour later I went to bed, and I lay awake most of the night.

78

The next morning the doorbell woke me. I stirred on the edge of sleep, unsure whether I'd even heard it, and then it came again, longer and louder. The clock said it was 8:58.

I sat up in bed and looked out through the curtains. The sun was shining again, the skies clear. I grabbed a T-shirt and a pair of tracksuit trousers and wriggled them on, then moved through the house to the front door. I'd been expecting, maybe hoping, for Liz.

Instead I got Healy.

He looked terrible, like he hadn't slept all night: his hair was a mess, not combed through or styled, his face etched with dark lines, his eyes bloodshot. His clothes were disheveled, one half of his shirt tail hanging out, his tie loosened, his trousers creased.

I pulled the door open.

"Healy."

He didn't say anything, just looked at me, and behind him—out on the street—I could see his Vauxhall, bumped up on to the pavement outside the gates. Behind that was another car, a gray Volvo. In the driver's seat, Melanie Craw was leaning over the steering wheel, watching us. When I invited Healy in, she nodded at me, started up the engine and pulled away. I watched her head off down the street and then turned to Healy.

"What the hell's going on?"

He stood there in the silence of the house, looking at me.

"Healy?"

"Have you got any coffee?"

I looked at him. "Sure."

We moved through to the kitchen and he sat at the counter while I brewed some coffee. Once it was on the go, I leaned against the sink, watching him, and for a moment he just stared at the floor, eyes dull and chipped, no light in them at all. After a while he seemed to become aware of the quiet and, with a long, drawn-out breath, looked up at me.

"Craw found me," he said quietly.

"Found you where?"

A pause. Eyes on the floor again. "Parked on the road outside the prison."

"Which prison?"

"Belmarsh."

"What were you doing down there?"

He glanced at me and shrugged. "Sleeping in my car."

"Why?"

He smiled. Sad and tight. "Why not?"

"Is that where you were yesterday when I called?"

He shook his head. "No."

"What's at the prison?"

He didn't reply.

I paused; let him have a moment.

He placed a hand flat to the counter top and looked down at his fingers, stained, blistered and cut. Then he sighed, deep and long, as if there weren't enough words to put it all together. "At the beginning of January, I found something out," he said quietly.

"What?"

"Something I guess I probably shouldn't have."

I pulled a stool out and sat down across from him.

"A guy I've known for years, an old drinking buddy of mine, works down at Belmarsh, in the high-security unit there." He sniffed. "About a week before I started back at the Met, I went out for a few with him and we got pretty pissed. Pretty emotional, I guess. He knew Leanne, knew the boys . . . I mean, our kids had grown up together."

He brought his fingers into a fist.

"He said there was this psychologist who came in every Monday to talk to the lifers down at Belmarsh. You know, the really worthless arseholes. The no-hopers."

I was trying to work out where this was going.

"Anyway, we were there, just the two of us, too many beers, too much emotion—I mean, this was only, like, eight weeks after I buried Leanne—and he let slip she did the counseling for a lot of these pricks. All over the place. The rapists and the killers; the paedos and the sacks of shit who don't deserve to see the light of day . . . and she . . ."

"What?"

"This guy, my pal, he said she did exactly the same thing over at Broadmoor."

My heart sank. "Oh shit, what have you done?"

He looked up, a shimmer in one of his eyes. Broadmoor was where Leanne's killer had been shipped off to.

"Healy?"

He shook his head but didn't say anything.

"*Healy?*"

"That fucking prick took my girl."

"What did you do?"

His face colored. "Are you listening to what I'm *saying?*"

"What did you do?"

"You were there. You saw it. He took my girl from me."

"Healy, what did you—"

"*He took my fucking girl from me!*"

His voice crashed around the kitchen, a noise so loud it seemed to rattle the glass in the window frames. And then when silence settled around us again, all I could hear was the coffee percolator and Healy, looking down into his lap, sniffing gently.

He was crying.

"Healy, look, why don't—"

Out of his jacket pocket he brought a gun, laying it on the counter top. The barrel was pointing toward me, but he immediately turned it around so it was facing off the other way. When he eventually looked up, tears streaming down his face, he pushed the gun across the surface toward me. "Take it," he said.

"What the hell are you doing with this?"

He shook his head. "I don't know any more."

"Were you actually going to *use* it?"

"I . . ." His eyes turned to the gun. "I don't know. Maybe. If I used her to get me inside Broadmoor . . ." He flicked a look at me. Shrugged. "I don't know."

"Did you *really* think you could walk into a prison with a *gun?*"

"I know."

"You wouldn't even get through the front gates."

"I know."

"So what was the plan?"

He looked at me. "I've been dating her since April."

"*What?*"

"She thought it was real."

I rubbed a hand to my brow. "This is insane."

"I know. I didn't . . ." He stopped. "I'm not sure I was ever going to use that thing, but she kept refusing to take me inside. She wouldn't even take me inside Belmarsh, and I'd been getting inside there myself, just watching her, for six months. I was already *inside* Belmarsh. What I wanted was to be inside Broadmoor. But while I had a job, while it was going all right at the Met, I was prepared to wait. Do it the right way. I could chip away at her until she gave in and started letting me tag along. I'd tell her it was field research, and eventually she'd take me right into the lion's den. And then I'd get in the same room as him, and I'd stick a fucking knife in his throat."

"This isn't you, Healy."

"No?"

"You're talking about killing a man."

"He took my girl."

"But you're not him. You're not a killer."

"Killing him would have made me feel something," he said. "It wouldn't bring Leanne back, but it would give me *something*. What else have I got?"

I looked at him. "You're not a killer," I said again.

"No job, no family," he replied, as if he hadn't heard me.

I didn't know what to say to that, so said nothing.

He wiped his eyes a couple of times and looked across me to the percolator. "How about that coffee?"

I got up and poured us both a cup.

"How did Craw find out about the prison?"

"She called me."

"This morning?"

"Yeah."

"Why?"

"Said she wanted to chat about what happened yesterday. Said I wasn't getting my job back but she wanted to talk. So I told her where I was."

"Why were you even at the prison in the first place?"

"I don't know really." He paused. "Just seemed right. I'd been watching Teresa—this psychologist—come and go out of that prison since January. Since the time I got my job back. And by the time I was done yesterday, my job was gone, and so was she."

"What do you mean 'gone'?"

"Oh, she's fine," he said. "I had a moment of clarity about five minutes after I got to hers. A flash of déjà vu. All the anger I felt for her, just building and building in me, was all the anger I felt for Gemma when she told me she was having an affair."

Gemma was his ex-wife.

"I hit Gemma," he went on, "but I wasn't about to do it again to Teresa. I didn't feel anything for her, but I was able to stop myself. And when I stopped myself last night, it was like I stepped *out* of myself, and I could see that part of me, plain as day."

"And this Teresa? Did she call the police?"

He shook his head. "No. She's a psychologist. Doesn't mean she didn't tell me I was a fucking bastard and she never wanted to see me again, but I think maybe, in some part of her, she knew why I'd done it. It might have been different if I'd actually pulled the gun, but I didn't, so she just kicked me out and told me she never wanted to see me again."

We sat in silence for a moment, both of us taking it in.

"Did Craw know what was going on?"

"I think she sensed that I was up to something from fairly early on. She can read people." He looked up at me. "She's a bit like you."

"Craw said she couldn't trust you."

He nodded, turning his cup. "It was hard to lie, especially after what she'd done for me, but early on I didn't really know what I wanted to do, how far I was prepared to go to get to him, so there didn't seem much point talking to her about it. I'd just use my contact to get into Belmarsh and watch this psychologist talk to the scumbags there. It ate me up inside seeing this woman talking to those shitheads, all nice and polite, like they were just regular guys—but knowing that was how she must have been speaking to him in Broadmoor too, that was what really got to me. While it was going well at the Met, I found it easier to keep a lid on it, and easier to maintain control. Suck it down, don't give them anything, keep the psychologist onside. That's all I kept thinking."

He took a couple of mouthfuls of coffee.

"But after I got the boot I thought, 'What does it matter any more?' I can carry on pretending I'm interested in her, or I can do what I've been thinking about for six months: put the gun to her head, and tell her I'll kill her if she doesn't find a way of getting me close to him. If I did that, if I did what I had to do to avenge Leanne and put that sack of shit in the ground, if I went to prison for killing him in the middle of his therapy session, who would care? I don't have a job. My boys don't speak to me. My wife hates my fucking guts."

"She doesn't hate your guts."

"She hasn't come back to me."

"You must understand the reasons for that."

He knew what I meant. The twin girls down in New Cross—the case, way before Leanne went missing, that had broken him—and then the aftermath: a moment he could never take back, a moment like a cut that would never heal, where he hit his wife.

"I understand the reasons," he said after a while, pain in his voice.

Neither of us spoke for a time, both of us looking down into half-finished coffee cups. Then I saw him look up and study me for a second, as if he was deciding whether to ask something or not.

"You remember what you said to me once?"

I smiled. "I said a lot of things."

"You said, 'There's no shame in hanging on. There's no shame in believing they might walk through the door at any moment.'"

I nodded.

"Do you still believe that?"

I looked at him, then across his shoulder to where a picture still hung of Derryn and me, backpacks on, halfway up a tor in Dartmoor. It had been taken the week before Derryn found the lump on her breast. The last week before the end began.

My eyes fell on Healy again.

"Yeah," I said. "I still believe it."

Derryn was buried in Hayden Cemetery, a sliver of parkland in north London, just off Holloway Road, between Highbury and Canonbury. As I pulled up in the car park, I felt a pang of guilt, as if I were somehow betraying Liz by being here. Maybe, in a weird way, I was. The first sign of trouble, the first sign of doubt, and I returned to my old life and to the woman who had shaped it. I rarely came back to the cemetery any more, but when I did it was always because I didn't know where else to go; how else to get past the way I was feeling. It was quiet, undisturbed, and after the search for Sam Wren, after everything Healy had said to me that morning, all the pain I recognized in him, the cemetery brought a strange kind of comfort, even if my memories of it were sad.

The entrance itself was a huge black iron arch, the name Hayden woven into the top, and as I passed through I could see the split path ahead of me: one branch headed down to where hundreds of graves unfurled in perfect lines on a huge bank of grass; the other bent up and around, partially covered by tall fir trees, into the western fringes of the cemetery, where Derryn's grave—in a tiny walled garden called "The Rest"—was situated. Adjacent to The Rest was the older, Victorian part of the cemetery, all mausoleums and tombs, winding paths and walled gardens. One of the reasons Derryn chose this spot, when she'd decided against more chemo, was for its sense of peace. Once you were inside the walls of The Rest, no wind came through; you were protected on one side by a bank of fir trees, and on the other by the huge Gothic structures of the old cemetery.

I moved through the gate of The Rest, the sun piercing a film of thin white cloud, and across to her grave. The last flowers I'd brought, months before, were nothing but a memory now; if they hadn't already been dead, they would have been baked by the sun and then washed away by the rain in the past week. I could see a trace of a petal on her gravestone but nothing more. Grass grew long at the base, up toward the date of her death, so I reached forward and tore some of it up, throwing it away and clearing a space.

Then something moved to my left.

I turned. Immediately beyond the wall was a huge tomb, its door facing out at me, flanked by two arched windows. On top was a stone angel, carrying a water bowl. I got to my feet and stepped away from the grave, opening up my view beyond it. A path led to its left, along a narrow trail, tombs on either side, simpler graves in between. Grass swayed gently along the trail, moved by the wind, but I couldn't hear it. All I could hear was birdsong and, distantly beyond that, the sound of an engine idling in the car park.

Behind me, I glimpsed a couple in their sixties, the woman holding a bunch of flowers, emerging on the other side of the fir trees and heading down toward the field of graves. And then, in the direction I'd seen movement, a bird swooped out from one of the trees, glided along the trail and soared up on to the triangular roof of a tomb further along.

I rubbed an eye; ran a hand through my hair. I was tired.

I knelt down again at the grave, brushing some of the dirt away with my fingers. Soil had got into the lettering, kicked up as people passed too closely. When it was clean, I looked around the rest of the garden and saw other families had been here more recently than me: the graves were decorated with flowers and vases, a handwritten letter on one, held down at the base of the headstone with a series of smooth pebbles.

Sorry I didn't bring a vase, I thought to myself, and then I smiled at how Derryn would have reacted, probably telling me that I'd have to bring the flowers before I got to apologize about a vase. I studied the polished marble of the headstone, her name engraved in gold, and then I touched the letters beneath it, the marble cold against my skin: *Beloved wife of David.* It seemed such a long time ago in many ways, and yet the two and a half years had gone in the blink of an eye. One minute I was watching her being buried, the next I was lying alongside another woman. Perhaps now I had neither.

Crack.

A noise to my left, like twigs snapping beneath feet.

Same direction as the movement.

This time I got to my feet and stepped fully away from the grave, eyes on the trail leading between the tombs. It ran for about a hundred yards and then started a slow turn to the right where I could see a stone entranceway, vines cascading down from above, huge pillars on either side like the gates to heaven itself. I'd walked it once before. It led back around the other side of the bank of fir trees and joined up with the field of graves. On the other side of the entranceway, out of sight, were the biggest structures of them all: massive mausoleums, standing like houses.

I moved out through the gate of The Rest and along the path. The tombs ran in a roughly symmetrical pattern, facing each other on either side of the trail, smaller, plainer graves in between. In this part of the cemetery, the front of the tombs and the graves, as well as the trail itself, had been kept clear, but everywhere else nature had run wild. It was thick and relentless, the occasional gap showing through to the car park at the bottom, but otherwise a twisted mess of branches and leaves.

Halfway along the trail, something rustled in the undergrowth. I stopped, looked down and saw a small animal—a mouse, or maybe a vole—disappear into a thick tangle of grass and nettles. Then, through the corner of my eye, something else moved. Just a flicker of a shadow. I looked up, replaying what I thought I'd seen—the movement from left to right, one side of the trail to the other—and headed toward it, quicker now, eyes fixed on a tomb about three-quarters of the way along. It was half turned away from the trail, the door facing me, pillars either side, a coat of arms under the roof. But when I finally got level with the tomb and looked into the area behind it, there was nothing. Just swathes of thick, green brush and the shadow of the entranceway, about twenty feet away now.

What the hell is the matter with you?

Wind whistled through the entranceway, as if drawn into it, vines hanging down from its top, swaying in the breeze. I stood there, feeling slightly disorientated, looking through as the trail continued on to the mausoleums on the other side. All around me were trees and graves. Nothing else. For a moment it was like being in a cramped space, one that was gradually closing in, and as I stood there trying to figure out what I'd seen, and why I *thought* I might have seen it, I felt my phone start to vibrate in my pocket.

I took it out. It was Craw's number.

"David Raker."

Interference. The line drifted.

"Hello?"

"It's Craw."

I could barely even hear her, and when I took the phone away from my ear I could see I only had a single bar. I moved back along the trail. "Can you hear me now?"

"Just about. Where are you?"

"Out and about. The reception's bad here."

"I need . . . you . . . thing . . ."

"I missed that. What?"

And then the line cut out. I stopped and looked down at the display again. Still only one bar, and now the wind was picking up. I glanced around me, trying to find a sheltered spot, but then the phone started to vibrate in my hands for a second time.

"Craw?"

The wind whipped past me, disguising any sort of reply, so I stepped into the doorway of one of the tombs, set back from the trail and protected under the overhang of a roof. The wind died down a little, replaced by birdsong and a faint drip.

"Can you hear me now?" I asked.

"Where the hell are you?"

"Right on top of a hill."

"Have you got five minutes?"

"Yeah, sure."

I looked back along the trail, to the edges of The Rest, and then the other way, to the entrance. In between, everything was suddenly still. No wind. No movement.

"Pell's made a run for it," she said.

"From the hospital?"

"Yeah. Got up in the middle of the night and disappeared. They didn't discover he was gone until this morning, which means he left between 2 a.m. and 7 a.m."

"Didn't you have someone watching his room?"

"Pell knocked him out, dragged him back into his room and switched clothes, then dumped the officer in the bed. After that, he just walked right out."

"And no one saw him?"

"He waited until the nurses were doing their rounds."

"He must know he's in deep shit."

"I've got teams out looking for him. He's got bruising all over his face, so it's not like he's going to be difficult to identify." A pause. "But there's a couple of things."

"What?"

"Smart's autopsy is this afternoon, so I guess we'll find out more then.

But his medical records list him as forty-one years of age, about fifteen stone, and somewhere around six-two, six-three. That sound about right to you?"

"Yeah. He was tall. Pretty well built."

"That's how he was able to control them."

"Right." I sensed something was troubling her. "Is everything okay?"

"It's . . . impossible . . . Pell . . ."

I frowned. "What about Pell?"

The line started drifting again.

"Craw?"

". . . hear me?"

"You're starting to go again."

"Thing . . . completely . . . height . . ."

"What? Can you repeat that?"

". . . height."

"What about his height?"

Then the line died. I tried instantly to return the call, but this time it failed to even connect. I dropped it into my pocket and stepped away from the tomb.

A blur of movement immediately to my right.

And then a short, sharp pain in my neck.

80

I opened my eyes. I was on my back, a canopy of leaves and branches above me. When I turned my head to the right, I could see the trail—maybe forty feet away, maybe more—and the tomb I'd been standing in front of. I felt my eyes start to roll, as if I were being pulled back into sleep, and when I fought against it, my head started to swim, and above me the greens of the foliage mixed with the blue of the sky and I felt a spike of nausea.

I closed my eyes again.

Images and sounds filled my head.

The entranceway through a tunnel of leaves to my left . . . the sound of birds in the trees and a faint wind, cool against my face and hands . . . my hands . . . my hands being pulled across the forest floor . . . my whole body being pulled . . . being dragged off into the woods by my feet, blocks of sun cutting through the canopy above me . . . he's going to kill me . . . hesgoingtokillme . . . hesgoingtokillme . . .

I ripped myself from the darkness.

Blinked.

Once. Twice.

Then I forced my upper body into action, moving left, back toward the trail, my legs barely even moving, crawling through the mud and the fallen leaves. I made it about two feet before I was exhausted. Turned over. Collapsed on to my back.

And that was when I saw him.

He was sitting with his back to me about ten feet to my right, perched on a fallen tree trunk. Black anorak. Hood up. He was looking through a break in the trees, down the slope to the car park about fifty feet below. I couldn't see his face, couldn't see anything of him except his hands, but as I looked across at him an image flashed in my head of the dream I'd had three nights before: a man in a coat, hood up, nothing but darkness inside.

Standing at the door to my bedroom.

Coming for me.

My body shivered, as if the ghosts of that dream were passing through me, and my eyes drifted to the tree trunk he was on: next to him was a hunting knife. Eight inches long, four-inch blade, charcoal-gray grip.

His hand was flat to the grip, almost hovering over it, like he was threatening to pick it up. I noticed some cuts on his hand; blood dotted along the fold of skin between his thumb and forefinger.

Suddenly, my phone started ringing. I watched him shift, looking off toward the trail and the tombs around it. The tip of his nose came into view, but nothing else. I followed the sound myself, trying to see where it was, and then I spotted it—in the middle of the trail—just a black dot from this distance. It vibrated across the scorched, flattened grass. Four rings. Five rings. Then it stopped. I wondered who it could have been. Healy. Craw.

Liz.

The man turned back to face the trees in front of him. From where I was lying, the cars were just about visible in the car park below. Two. Maybe a third, although it could easily have been an edge of a building. One of the cars I could see was mine. That meant, in the whole cemetery, there was a maximum of two other people. I didn't know if one of the cars was his but, either way, I couldn't rely on anybody coming past and finding me.

The cemetery was massive, the number of people here minuscule.

It was why he wasn't bothered about my phone.

"Duncan?" I said, trying to make the natural connections between events. Pell was on the run. It had to be him. "Duncan?" I said again, and this time he jolted, reacting to the sound of my voice. His hand, still hovering over the knife, lowered on to it, around the grip. Then his fist closed around the handle, and all I could see was his hand and the blade coming out of it.

I tried to pull myself to my feet, using the nearest tree, but my legs buckled under me, giving way like there was no bone, no muscle, nothing inside them. They were like liquid. Whatever he'd injected me with hadn't paralyzed me, but it had slowed me down. I could feel it working its way out of me, feel my system fighting back all the time, but when I finally had the strength to walk out of here, it was going to be too late. He was already moving off the tree trunk and coming toward me.

Get the hell out of here.

I dug my fingers into the cracks in the earth, the palm of my hands cutting on thorns, skin brushing nettles, and tried to drag myself forward. Behind me I could hear his feet on the forest floor, branches cracking, dried leaves crunching, as he came around the tree trunk toward me.

I got another three feet when a boot slammed against the ground to my right and he grabbed a handful of hair at the back of my head. I heard him grunt, felt his hand brush the skin at the nape of my neck, and then he forced his knee into the center of my spine. It was like being in a vice. I couldn't move. I looked out to the trail, left, right, praying someone was coming. But there was no one. We were alone. Even if I shouted out, forced up every sound I had, it would only be a second before he put a hand to my mouth.

My eyes flicked right, to the boot on the floor next to me. They were plain black. No pattern in them. No labels. Nothing distinctive. *No red stitching.* I couldn't see much else. Gray combat trousers, the ends of the leg frayed. The boots must have been a size twelve. *Bigger than Pell's feet.* As I tried to process what I was seeing, tried to formulate a plan—*any plan*—he released his hand from the back of my head and, inside a second, thumped me in the back of the skull. My face hit the floor. White spots flashed in front of my eyes. A ringing sound echoed from ear to ear. And then I drifted into darkness again and, by the time I returned, into the light, I was back where I started and he was on the log. Except this time he was facing me. And it wasn't Duncan Pell. It never had been.

It was Edwin Smart.

81

Smart shifted the knife across the tree trunk toward him and then faced me, hood still up. The swelling had gone down, but the cuts and bruises remained bad, one of his eyes half shut and puffy, a huge cut running from the right side of his head all across his face. The gash was traced by a thick purple bruise. But I recognized him now, even with all the injuries. I could see his bent nose, recognized the stiffness in his gait even as he sat, saw the dark eyes—one of them bloodshot—and knew they were his.

"Smart," I said, my voice cracked and soft.

Nothing in his face. No reaction.

I glanced at my phone, out on the trail, and remembered Craw's call. *His medical records list him as forty-one years of age, about fifteen stone, and somewhere around six-two, six-three.* But that didn't match the body they recovered from the staffroom in Fell Wood station and the autopsy was going to prove as much. Because that wasn't Smart, it was Pell. Smart had blown Pell's head off to prevent identification, or at least to delay it, and then he'd replaced Pell in the basement of his house and done the same: cut himself, smashed his face against a wall, let it bleed and watched the bruises form. All to give himself some time.

A chance of escape.

Except he wasn't escaping. He was here.

"Why aren't you running?" I said.

He looked down at the knife. "I intend to," he replied, his voice quiet, articulate. "I stayed ahead of the police for eighteen months, so I'm sure I can do it again, with or without this detour." He glanced at me. There was nothing mischievous in him, nothing playful. He spoke matter of factly; almost exactly the same as he had at Gloucester Road. "I don't have much time, but I had to take the opportunity to show you exactly what you did."

I glanced back at the trail.

"No one's coming for you," he said.

I looked at him. The hood was still up, his eyes dark under the ridge of his brow, glimpses of his shaved head visible when light escaped inside the coat.

Keep him talking.

"I saw your footprints at the station," I said. He just stared at me. I wasn't sure if he'd even heard me. "You wanted to make sure I found Pell down in the staffroom, which is why you followed me there. Once you saw I'd found him, you shut yourself in with all the others and you waited." He didn't respond, just studied the knife again. "When did you kill Pell?"

"I asked him around Friday evening," he said quietly. "That's why he never turned up for work. I knocked him out and kept him tied up in the basement. Then, when I saw you out at Fell Wood on Saturday, I knew you'd followed the clues I left at Duncan's house. I watched you in the station, snooping around. You weren't supposed to see me, but it didn't really matter. I had Duncan's boots on, so you still thought it was him. But even while you were chasing your tail with Duncan, I knew I wasn't safe."

"So you used him."

"On Sunday, I transferred him from my house to the station."

That's where the blood on Smart's carpet had come from: shifting Pell down to the staffroom. He probably walked him right out of the back door and across his garden like he'd walked the others out of their flats.

"I knew you were getting closer all the time," he said. "After you spoke to me that first time at Gloucester Road, I started following you, and I knew you were clever. I could see that." He paused. "To be honest, I foresaw yesterday approaching fast, so that was why I decided to move the plan to its final stage. When you turned up at Gloucester Road yesterday, I had to take a detour on the way to see my father."

"You went to Fell Wood and killed Pell."

"I killed him, and then I went to the cemetery for the last time. After that, I came home and started cutting myself." He shrugged. "Forensic tests would have picked up that I'd drugged Duncan. I had to make him malleable; to make it look like a suicide. But I'm sure the police would have picked up that it wasn't a suicide too, soon enough. It was only ever meant to be a diversion. I wasn't sure if the police were as close to finding me as you, but I decided against making a break for it either way. If I ran, the police would pull out all the stops to get to me, and I would only have had a couple of hours' head start yesterday afternoon. If I got to the hospital as Duncan Pell and I ran, I had a minimum of a day, maybe more, they had no real idea where I was headed, and they didn't even know I was Edwin Smart."

"So when you tried to misdirect police with the red dots—"

"It was just another distraction. The more questions without logical answers, the more difficult it is for them to find their way through them." He glanced at me. "I learned that early on when I was carrying out my work as the so-called Snatcher, even if—in recent days—I've been less accomplished. I'm afraid you panicked me, which is why I ended up making some stupid decisions."

"You mean leaving the phone on the line?"

"Leaving the phone on the line wasn't the mistake. If it had been found there, you and the police would have assumed Jonathan Drake had either dropped it from the platform, or dropped it through the window of the carriage while the train was moving through the station. It happens all the time. But I was watching that first patrolman and when he didn't pick it up, I got nervous and I placed it on the bench so it would definitely be found. That was stupid. I should have known it would be noted, sooner or later."

"So why didn't you kill me when you had the chance?"

He shrugged again, thinking back to the same moment as me: the darkness of the staffroom and then the tunnel on the old line where he'd put a boot through my face. "Again, a stupid decision. I suppose a part of me still thought it might play out how I wanted it to as long as I kept you focused on Duncan and Samuel. If you were alive, you could carry on down that route, but I should have figured out that you wouldn't. Like I said, you're clever."

I tried to think of where to go next.

But then he got up from the tree trunk, the knife in his hand, handle hidden in the cup of his palm, blade facing off behind him into the trees. "Anyway, as I said, I want to make use of the time available to me, so I need to make you understand what you did."

"What I did?"

He looked at me—blood in his eye, more bruises than skin, streaks of mauve reaching down like fingers toward his throat—and came over, dropping to his haunches beside me. And for the first time I understood what Sam, Drake and the others had seen. Not the ticket inspector, not Edwin Smart. The man inside Smart. Within a couple of seconds he was a completely different man, a monster, without even having to speak.

I glanced between his face and his hand, the knife gripped so tightly his knuckles had blanched, and, briefly, I thought about making a break for it. But I didn't know how much of the drug he'd given me, how much had left my body or how much of my body was even functioning. So I turned back to him, trying to face him down, and I saw something flicker in his eyes. A second later, I realized what it was.

A warning.

He drove the knife into my stomach, coming in toward me, teeth gritted, face contorted, and every atom of my body seemed to freeze. A piercing pain, cold and hard, drove into the spaces inside me, nerve endings firing, sending agonizing waves, like an alarm, shooting into my fingers, my toes and my head. Everything blurred: my sight, my hearing, the balance between dark and light, and the next time I was aware what was going on, he'd pushed me to the floor and was standing over me, knife in his hand, my blood dripping from it. I watched him bend over me, face coming down toward mine.

"That's what I never understood about you," he said, his voice still normal; soft and coherent. "You of all people should have seen what you were doing."

I felt blood running free of my stomach.

My shirt sticking to my skin.

"Your wife died of cancer too. You buried her here, just like I buried my father in Highgate. You must understand the importance of memories, of being able to reach out to them after they're gone. You must get that. So why did you take it away from me?"

He came in even closer to me, his breath on my face.

"My father was a violent, abusive, drunken prick, but he was my father. *My* father. It wasn't your choice to make. You forced me out into the open, you fucked with me, and you fucked with the only day that ever really mattered to me. My father is buried in this city, and I can never come back here, never come back to his grave, never be here for him because you and that prick I keep reading about in the papers—that cop, Bartholomew—have got in my way." He swiped the knife across my face, the air shifting around me. "So now I'm going to kill you."

But I could hardly hear him now. When I tried to breathe, it felt like air was being sucked into the wound, more going into my stomach than my mouth. He shifted position above me, and this time I couldn't even hear his feet on the floor of the forest. There wasn't just a depression in the sound, there was *no* sound. Only a faint ringing, deep inside my head somewhere, like a fire alarm going off in another room.

I watched him reestablish his grip on the knife.

This is it. This is the end.

And then he looked off toward the trail.

I was fading, my vision smeared, but I managed to roll my head in the direction he was studying, and make out two vague shapes coming up the path toward us. Smart glanced down at me, then back at the trail, and as the shapes came closer, my vision cleared momentarily and I recognized the people I'd seen earlier. The couple in their sixties. The woman was still holding the flowers, and they were still holding hands.

Smart glanced at me again.

Uncertainty now.

Turned the knife. Fingers tight around the grip.

Looked at the couple for a second time.

And then he ran.

He headed off, breaking on to the trail and left, out of sight of the couple, and made for the darkness of the entranceway. The couple were too far back to notice him, except maybe to see a blur of movement. I called out to them, screamed help as loud and as long as I could manage, but they didn't seem to react. When they got closer, I shouted it again, straining every sinew, every fiber of strength I had left. Yet when I was done, they didn't look over, didn't change course, didn't even seem to have heard me.

And then they walked on by.

I realized then I hadn't made a single sound. Nothing. Not one word. The voice I was hearing I could only hear inside my head. My capacity to speak, my capacity to hear myself, everything I'd ever taken for granted, was shutting down. My vision flickered—gray to white to gray, like an old TV signal—and then I completely blacked out for a moment. When I emerged into the light again, when objects formed in front of me—trees and branches and leaves—I was back in the forest, thirty feet from the trail, dying alone.

Get to your phone.

Get to your fucking phone.

I grabbed some grass and pulled myself forward, pain coursing down the front of my chest. There was blood everywhere, but mostly it was pain. I got about five feet and had to stop, my lungs barely filling now, my heart seeming to slow. I thought of Liz, of the last conversation we'd ever had—a fight about what I did, and who I was—and then I thought of

Derryn, of the moment I'd buried her here, in among these graves and tombs and memories. And then I reached around me for something else to grab on to, clamped my hand on a tree root and pulled again. And I kept on pulling, dragging myself forward.

Minutes passed.

Minutes that felt like hours.

But I got there, and when I got there I felt death moving in, as if my body had been prepared to hold out until I got to the trail, but no more. My vision blinked in and out, my hearing pretty much gone. I grabbed the phone, half hidden in grass at the edge of the track. My muscles were failing too now, but I held on to the mobile with everything I had and pushed Call. I didn't know who it would get through to. I didn't know whether it would even make any difference. I was dying. But I brought it to my ear and I waited for an answer.

"Raker?"

It was Healy. I tried to say his name.

"Raker?" he said again.

"Hea . . . ly . . ."

"Raker—are you all right?"

I swallowed. Coughed. "Hea . . . ly . . . I'm . . ."

"Where are you?"

"I'm . . . dyin . . ."

I dropped the phone.

And, finally, there was only darkness.

82

7 July

There was only one space left in the car park, right outside the entrance. Healy swung the Vauxhall into it and killed the engine. The sun was shining, coming in over the roof of the building and in through the windscreen, and as he sat there in his shirt and tie, sleeves rolled up, jacket across the backseat, he watched the people gathered to his left.

On the radio, playing softly despite the engine being off, they were talking about how police had finally found Edwin Smart. He'd been on the run for eighteen days and had been discovered living rough in scrubland east of Glasgow. Everyone soon figured out why. After everything that had happened at Hayden Cemetery, Healy had been back to Raker's place and been through his notes on Smart, and he saw that Smart's father had been born in East Kilbride. If he could no longer visit the old man's grave, maybe Smart figured the next best thing was his birthplace. The truth was, the relationship between father and son was, at points, too difficult to grasp. The father was a violent drunk, an abuser, a paedophile. The son was a killer in denial about himself, a kidnapper and torturer of men; he both loved and hated who he was, in the same way he loved and hated the man who had made him that way. In the days and weeks ahead, police and psychologists would begin to break the surface, but Healy wondered whether they'd ever be able to get at the answers within. By the time they did, *if* they even did, the public that was once so fascinated by the Snatcher, and the men and women at the Met who had tried to find him, would have moved on to something else.

Some other tragedy.

He turned off the radio, reached over to the backseat and grabbed his jacket, then got out of the car. Some people looked over, faces he recognized but didn't want to talk to. He shrugged on his jacket and then stood there in the sun, enjoying the warmth for a moment and forgetting—just briefly—what he was here for. Then he noticed some of the crowd were looking past him, out toward the gates of the church, to the street beyond.

He thought of Leanne then, of how Raker had helped him find her, and a flutter of sadness took flight, like a bird escaping from its cage. And then the hearse finally pulled into view, the coffin inside it, and Healy headed into the coolness of the church.

Acknowledgments

Once again, at every stage of *Vanished*'s development, I've been backed by an amazing team of people. When the going got tough, my editor, Stef Bierwerth, and agent, Camilla Wray, calmed my nerves, providing razor-sharp editorial insight and welcome words of encouragement. A special thank-you to everyone at Penguin HQ as well who have worked so hard on my behalf in the run-up to publication, as have the ladies of Darley Anderson (with an extra shout-out for the crack foreign rights team of Clare Wallace and Mary Darby). Huge thanks as well to my U.S. editor, Chris Russell, for being such an amazing advocate for the series, and to the team at Viking and Penguin who have worked so hard on this book and on the others.

Thanks to Alistair Montgomery for taking the time to answer my (almost certainly tedious) questions about the Tube's history, its ghosts and his life on the lines; and to Mike Hedges, whose fascinating insight into the police continues to make my life easier. *Vanished* wasn't always the easiest of writes, but my family offered unconditional love and support. Thanks to Mum and Dad, who never complained (and fed and watered me) when I decamped for days at a time; Lucy, for her support and part-time PR; Rich, for traveling the country with posters in his car; and, finally, to the Adamses, Ryders and Linscotts, for spreading the word, turning up and supporting me, laying on events, and everything in between. And, finally, to my two ladies: Erin, who keeps asking when she can read the books (and who promises not to repeat any of the swear words); and Sharlé, who never complains, never doubts, and—without whose incredible patience—the book could never have been written.

COMING SOON

The David Raker Mystery Series

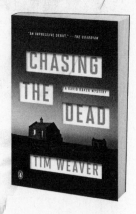

Chasing the Dead

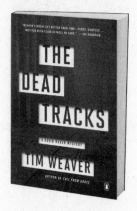

The Dead Tracks

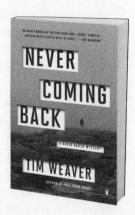

Never Coming Back

Fall from Grace

VIKING

PENGUIN BOOKS